Journeys Through a Fading Empire

Journeys Through a Fading Empire

J. Leslie Evenden

Media, Pennsylvania, May 2021

ISBN 978-0-578-94262-9

FICTION/Historical/Ancient
Keywords: Britannia, Gaul, Roman Empire, Dark
Ages

Published by WiltonLogic LLC
Media, Pennsylvania, USA

forma papillarum quam fuit apta premi!
quam castigato planus sub pectore venter!
quantum et quale latus! quam iuvenale femur!
singula quid referam? nil non laudabile vidi,
et nudam pressi corpus ad usque meum.
cetera quis nescit? lassi requievimus ambo.
proveniant medii sic mihi saepe dies.

Ovid, *Amores* 1.5, lines 20–26

Map of Important Places

The locations and names in this map are based on the map "La Gaule administrative au Vᵉ siècle" in *La France avant la France* by Geneviève Bührer-Thierry and Charles Mériaux (Belin, 2014), p. 23. The borders of fifth-century Gaul did not correspond exactly with those of modern France.

The exception is the town of Agininum, which I have placed in the location of Aginnum (Agen in modern France), but which has been fictionalised to facilitate the telling of the story. Little appears to be known about the layout of Roman Aginnum.

ℭ Chapter 1 ℰ
Verulamium, Britannia, 412 CE

One of the first warm days of summer was coming to an end. The evening breeze filtered into the dining room, the air and the setting sun softened by the light curtains draped across the open windows. Ophelia sighed to herself. The voices of the men, her husband Cornelius and their neighbour Junius, passed in through one ear and out of the other. Politics again, day after day, year after year; politics and anxiety. And now, to make matters worse, an uninvited guest who could not be refused a place at dinner.

"Visiting from Londinium, Drusus?" said Cornelius, a note of uncertainty in his voice, when Drusus Astrebanus entered the room.

"My brother could not come himself, unfortunately," said Drusus, "or should I say, fortunately. He is in the process of negotiating his marriage." Drusus threw a quick glance at Ophelia. For years, since childhood, it had been assumed that Vitellus Astrebanus would marry her younger sister, Hypatia, and with that marriage unite two of the most powerful families in Britannia Prima.

"To my cousin, or is she a second cousin?" said Cornelius hastily, to cover any embarrassment. "Milesia Cornelia."

Junius smiled.

"Vitellus is a lucky man. A tidy fortune comes with her, no doubt. She's an only child?"

Then the marriage plans had fallen through. Ophelia was unsure why. She had already been married off herself and had left the family home when the crisis unfolded. Neither of her parents had cared to put the details in a letter. Perhaps the hope of a fortune had something to do with it after all, Ophelia reflected.

"With our family lands, and Mistress Milesia's property in Londinium and Durovernum, my brother will be one of the leading chiefs in the south, if not the leading chief." Drusus gave another hasty glance at Ophelia to see if his remarks were hitting home.

My father would take exception to that claim, thought Ophelia.

Publius Julius Ursinus was the governor of Britannia Prima, the west of Britannia. No one had been sent by Rome to fill the post in living memory. It had become her family's by right. Publius Julius considered himself the leading chief amongst the Britons, being a Roman citizen of consular rank, little though that might mean these days.

"I hope your brother'll be able to do something about these pirates." The city vice-magistrate and his wife made up the party. "One of my farms beyond Camulodunum was burned last month. That's the second this year."

"I've come straight from Camulodunum," said Drusus. "I've been speaking at the tribunal."

"The tribunal?" queried Junius. "I thought they'd all fled."

"There's always a tribunal," said Drusus, "whoever sits on it."

He glanced around the room.

"We have to work together, the tribunal, the magistrates, the landowners, merchants… but we need a leader."

The vice-magistrate nodded. It had become every man for himself and trading of favours in place of the rule of law since the legions had gone. Drusus' father would have been a natural leader, but then he had backed the wrong horse in the rebellion, with tragic consequences. So close, so close to success, reflected the magistrate. So many of them had backed the general, hoping for rewards and riches, and instead they had lost their fortunes and their protection. The last hope, perhaps, for a unified Britannia was Vitellus Astrebanus. If not, God help us, he thought.

Ophelia shifted her gaze from the pensive magistrate to Junius' wife, Livia, who relaxed on the next couch around the circle. She was wearing the most peculiar gown, sheer silk, so fine that it was possible to see the outline of her breasts beneath. It might have been fine for pagan times, thought Ophelia, but now, in a Christian town, it was hardly suitable, even for a private dinner party. Had she worn it for the benefit of the men? Drusus, perhaps, or… Ophelia glanced at her own husband, but he was all ears on the discussion.

"We need to unite, under one man," Drusus repeated, "who can provide law and order, good organisation."

"That's what Constantinus was promising," observed Junius. "He took the legions, crossed to the continent, and he was defeated, and where did that get us? All the support we gave him, the treasure, the supplies, and nothing in return except shame and the Empire abandoning us."

"No one knows that better than Vito," said Drusus. "Our father backed Constantinus from the start, and look how he suffered when he failed."

They did not need to be reminded. Drusus' father had collapsed while reading a letter with the news that General Flavius Claudius Constantinus, the usurper, once hailed as co-emperor Constantine III, had been captured and executed.

"But Constantinus was in conflict with Rome," Drusus continued. "Vitellus has learned from his mistake. He'll put Britannia first, yes, but we can be an ally of the Empire, not a rebellious province, not a source of enmity. If we do that, the Empire will welcome us as friends."

Ophelia's gaze returned to Livia, running down the curves of her body to her waist. At least she had covered her lower parts… with a pair of loose trousers, a fashion from the east apparently, but better than having everything on display. Of course, Livia was bored, alone in the house, with her husband away in Londinium or on his estate in the east. She was rumoured to have a lover. *My own situation is hardly better*, thought Ophelia, *but I would never consider taking another man to my bed. It's quite enough with Cornelius.*

She sighed and signalled to the servant for more wine.

"Well-watered," she added, as the man refilled her glass.

"And Vitellus is the right man?" asked Cornelius. "I don't think everyone would agree."

"Your wife's father," said Drusus. "You think he's an alternative?" There was unmistakeable scepticism in his voice.

"He's the governor of Britannia Prima, after all," said Cornelius.

Drusus Astrebanus was on his feet, gesticulating. He paced past the magistrate and his wife, waving his hand, pointing to no one in particular.

"We need a man who'll take care of Londinium, Verulamium, Britannia Superior… the whole of Britannia. Publius Julius will never do that. He's far too comfortable in his position, at the moment, at least."

He came to a stop by Ophelia's couch. His eye must have caught the honeyed cakes on the small table beside her. He reached out and took one, evidently unconscious of his bad manners.

"Excellent cakes," he said. "Where did you get the honey so early in the season?" He seemed to address the question to Cornelius, as if the food were his responsibility.

"From my father's garden," said Ophelia.

Drusus' head whipped round.

"Your father's garden… well, make the best of it while you can."

"What do you mean by that?" she asked.

"Your father's situation may be a little precarious," he replied.

"You're only saying that because your brother's marriage fell through."

Drusus laughed.

"Times are changing, Mistress Ophelia, and your father hasn't changed with them. He made a lot of enemies by failing to support the uprising. If the men of Britannia Prima had joined us, then matters would have ended better than they did."

He glanced around the room, looking for support.

"And," he added, taking another cake, "he's living beyond his means – raising bees when he should be raising taxes." He chuckled to himself. "With the legions gone, business isn't going so well for those farmers your father seems to favour."

Another jab, thought Ophelia. There was a rumour she had heard through her friends, though not, curiously, through her family, that her sister was to marry a farmer. Well, that's what the smart people called him. If the rumour was true then Hypatia's putative husband was the son of one of her father's allies. She half remembered him as a boy, a skinny creature with a northern accent, barely able to speak Latin, who had lived in their house for several years to study with her brothers: a reward, it seemed, to his father, for good service. The whole matter was perplexing and an embarrassment. It was better to change the subject.

"Actually," she said, "things are going so well in Britannia Prima that my father's considering travelling, later in the summer."

"Oh, really?" said Drusus, fixing her with a hard stare.

"Yes… to visit my brother, Gaius, in Arelate…"

"To Gaul, you mean?"

"Oh, yes, and then perhaps even on to Rome itself, now that the troubles are over."

"Gaius survived, then?" said Drusus. "Even though the general made Arelate his headquarters?"

"Oh, yes, and now the emperor looks very favourably on him for his loyal service."

Of course he survived, thought Drusus, just like his father, backing both sides, content to hide behind the authorities, and to look after himself while doing so. He took another cake and popped it into his mouth, honey glistening on his lips.

"Too sweet," he said, grimacing. "I hope your father picks a suitable deputy to delegate his responsibilities to while he's taking care of his leisure."

"He doesn't consult me on such matters, Master Drusus," said Ophelia. "And in any case, I'm sure he'll be pleading for Britannia when he meets the emperor."

"Perhaps he should consult you," said Drusus, turning away, as the others laughed. Then you could advise him, he thought to himself, that the moneylenders in Londinium are concerned about his borrowing – nothing to do with my brother, naturally, nor the records he's begun compiling. What had one of them, Sergentius, said of Publius Julius' pledges to repay? Not worth the wax they are sealed with. Yes, Mistress Ophelia, the chickens will be coming home to roost for the Ursini pretty soon.

He revealed nothing of his reflections as he returned to his place. He flashed a quick smile at Mistress Livia, but it was wasted. Her gaze was elsewhere.

Ophelia had not entirely understood Drusus' comments, but she caught the sting of his tone. Her expression must have betrayed her feelings, and she forced herself to smile, just in time to catch the sympathetic look Livia was giving her, and to see her roll her eyes. Ophelia quickly glanced away, and her own eyes caught the bored and sour face of the magistrate's wife. No doubt the magistrate would hear her opinions when they returned home. Is that my fate, she thought, to become bored and bitter and angry?

She glanced back towards Junius' wife. Perhaps I shouldn't be so hard on Livia. It's not easy to be a wife in these times. None of these men appreciates that I can speak Greek or write poems in several languages, she thought – not well perhaps, but at least the words line up according to the rules. The food we eat is bought in the market. The clothes I wear are purchased from craftsmen, the tailor and the seamstress. No need for weaving or sewing, no spinning or carding, as I was compelled to do, rich man's daughter or not, throughout my childhood. Am I simply meant to be decorative and give birth to children? Perhaps it would be just as well, she considered, if the barbarians come to Britannia and ransack the cities as they have plundered Rome, and we're all forced to fend for ourselves.

"First and foremost," said Drusus, regaining his couch, "as I said before, we must re-instate the rule of law and ensure all the appointments are filled with competent people. Then every man will know his place and what's expected of him. Then we'll defeat the raiders, drive them back into the sea, just as we have done on so many previous occasions."

Cornelius raised his glass.

"I wish you good luck, Astrebanus… and you, Junius."

A slave appeared to light the oil lamps.

"Where's the entertainment?" said Livia, suddenly, with a glance at Cornelius. "Didn't you say there would be music?"

ಌ Chapter 2 ೲ
Gaul, later in the year

Ophelia woke with a shiver and opened her eyes. She was lying on her back. A blue sky dappled with leaves stretched above her. For a moment she was completely disorientated. She wondered where she was, even, for a moment, who she was. Then a paralysing fear, a dread, a panic gripped her, swept over her. She closed her eyes again and tried to recollect, to understand. She felt she was merely an actor in a drama she had no control over, that someone else had written the script, staged the play. How had her life been pushed from its track so unexpectedly?

Her father and her brother, Lucius, had appeared at the house in Verulamium just a few days ago. They had taken Cornelius into a back room and closed the door. Her husband had emerged ashen faced, shaking.

"We have to leave immediately," he had said. "It's time to go."

"What's the matter with you? Why the sudden hurry?" She had thought he had been behaving rather strangely, silent, withdrawn even, since he had returned from visiting her father earlier in the summer. "You said it was just a family visit."

"Don't question me, Ophelia," her husband had shouted. "Just do as I say! Collect everything you'll need for the children for the journey. The maids will not be coming with us. You have to make sure the children are ready to go!"

Then he had vanished into the town and not returned until late, stinking of wine.

Two carts had arrived the following day, and the servants had loaded as much of their goods as the carts could carry – the gold, the silver, even the pewter, the best furniture, her jewels and clothes, and last of all, to her surprise, the *lares*, the family saints, as they had become – and they had left for Londinium. Surely, she had thought, taking the *lares* meant that Cornelius didn't expect to return?

Her mother had met them at Lucius' house, hugging her and weeping, as confused as Ophelia. Why had everything been upset? Life with Cornelius might not have been perfect, she thought, but it was a normal life, with a home, with her children, with servants to look after her and take care of the things she didn't want to do. Why was everyone so agitated? She deserved to know, she thought, but nobody seemed to feel a need to explain. Her mother told how their family home, Villa Verdaris, had been emptied and the valuables carried away, some to Londinium, and the rest, she wasn't sure where. When Ophelia had tried to locate the furniture from the house in Verulamium, it and the beautiful pottery and golden vessels she had admired so much had disappeared.

"Sold," said Cornelius, brusquely. "We can't carry them with us."

"But…?" They had travelled before, not to the mainland, perhaps, but to visit friends, to the baths at Aquae Sulis, and they had never needed to pack everything up, to sell their possessions.

"It'll be a long journey, my dear," her mother had said. "We could be away for years. Publius Julius thought it best." But despite the brave words, the older woman could not suppress her tears. The men had merely ordered them to go here, to go there, to keep the children out of the way, while they and a group of rough-looking servants took care of things.

Ophelia and the children were wrapped in woollen cloaks one early morning, placed on a cart, and before she knew what was happening, they were on the south road to Dubris. They stayed at smelly hostels amongst other travellers. They were not the only people journeying incognito, she suspected, glancing around the common dormitory, but that provided no reassurance, quite the contrary. Many people had left Britannia in recent years, some in hope and others in fear. Her neighbour, Livia, and her husband had gone, crossing to the mainland to seek their fortune, so Livia had said. There was nothing surprising or dramatic in people from Verulamium or Londinium travelling to Gaul or Belgica to stay with relatives.

There were even some particularly wealthy families who had estates on both sides of the water and crossed back and forth on a regular basis. Certainly some people had become anxious about the raiders appearing from the east, now that the coastal forts had been abandoned, but Verulamium was nowhere near the coast, and even if the town was threatened, she and the children could always have travelled west to Corinium or Verdaris, to safety. Others, of course, had departed quietly and without any fanfare after the general had been executed. But they had been on the losing side, and that had been last year. And in any case, her father had not supported the rebellion, though he had been careful not to speak against it either.

"Stay out of sight," her father told her. "Don't tell anyone who you are, or what's going on."

"But I don't know what's going on," she had protested.

"It's better like that," said her father. "And keep the children quiet."

The inn at Dubris was full of malodourous people, waiting for a boat to Bononia. She wondered how she looked herself. She was not particularly vain, but she did not like to look untidy. Now she had been seven days on the road. She had not been to the baths. She was sure she must smell awful. Her father and mother were dressed in shabby cloaks and worn shoes. Her mother's hair, usually so carefully prepared, hung in ragged streaks to her shoulders, visible even under her headscarf. Ophelia could not believe her eyes.

"Haven't you brought a maid?" she asked.

"Publius Julius didn't want to," said her mother. "He said we would find new servants when we arrived, servants who are used to living in the south lands."

"Let me tidy your hair, at least, Mother," she had said. "We have to try to look good, even if it's difficult in these circumstances." Fussing with her mother's hair had given her something to do, to keep her occupied.

They had to stay three days, while her husband, brother and father paced up and down, impatient with the boats, at the wind which blew in the wrong direction, at the seas which were too rough, until suddenly, once again, they were bundled up, hurried on board a ship and transported, vomiting and crying, across the sea to an equally shabby inn on the far shore.

Still no one provided an explanation, although by now it had become evident to her that there must be a problem, and it must be serious. Her father was an important man, the governor of Britannia Prima, no less, a Roman citizen of senatorial rank, he had always boasted. He had held house at Villa Verdaris like it was a court, surrounded by servants and officials, guests from all over Britannia, including Cornelius' father, and from the mainland, too. And now they were scrambling, hurrying from place to place, mixing with the *plebs* as if the Ursini were ordinary people. She could not grasp it.

And where was her sister Hypatia? So great had been her confusion that it had taken several days before she had realised that Hypatia was not with them. Of course, her sister was recently married, beneath herself, her neighbours in Verulamium had been keen to point out, though none of them had been invited to the wedding. Ophelia had been there. What had all the fuss been about? Hypatia was only her younger sister, and her husband Marcus, well, he was just Marcus, no one special. She had seen who had been invited. She had had fine people at her wedding to Cornelius, of course, the best people from Londinium, but there was something strange about Hypatia's wedding. Half of the guests she did not know. Top men, she had realised, from all over Britannia Prima, and their wives. That should have warned her something was going on, but she had still been influenced by her friends. She had been foolish enough to put on a mask and pretend she was indifferent. She had been foolish enough not to ask.

Hypatia had decided to remain behind, at Verdaris with her new husband, to take care of the estate until they returned, that's what her father had said.

"If Hypatia could decide to remain, why am I being dragged and bundled from place to place like a fugitive?" she had asked. "Why couldn't the children and I stay at Verdaris, instead of coming with you, since you don't seem to want me anyway?"

Her father had simply sighed and turned away instead of answering.

Why had Cornelius been forced to follow them, for that matter, she had mouthed silently to his retreating back. His uncle stayed behind. I know that. I know his daughter is to marry Vitellus Astrebanus, since Hypatia turned down the match. Has already done so, possibly, she mused, and once I would have been invited. Is that why we ran, because of a stupid family quarrel?

It had to be something more important. Had there been a rebellion in the west? Surely she would have heard something, even if Verulamium was far away from Corinium. She had friends who wrote regularly, and the women were often more honest about events than the men were. They had less to lose. There were always stories, she had heard them as a child when she should not have been listening, of people who had found themselves on the wrong side of a rebellion and had to run for their lives. But her father had supported the emperor all along. He was a good governor, a good man. And had Hypatia been sacrificed, thrown to the wolves, so that the rest of the family could escape?

These thoughts tumbled through her mind as she lay with her eyes closed, trying hard not to be awake, trying hard not to think about what had happened.

Though she tried, she could not stop thinking. She could not block out those memories. But she could not make the connection between those events and where she was now. How had she got here? Why was she lying here, on the ground, apparently in the open air? Why could she smell wood smoke? Why did she ache so much?

She could remember the town of Tricasses. They had arrived with a group of merchants, travelling south from Remis and Catalaunis. They had travelled in the same manner since leaving Bononia, as members of large groups, staying in hostels. It did not seem right. Her father was an important man, wealthy, well-known. Why were they lodging in stinking hostels along with traders and pilgrims and other good-for-nothing people? Why weren't they staying at the villas and houses of the people to whom they had been such generous hosts at Verdaris or at the townhouse in Corinium? In Remis a man had even offered her money. He had mistaken her for a prostitute. She had run to her room, closed herself inside and wept. That had scared the little ones and they had begun crying, too. Cornelius had been furious, not at the importuning stranger, but at her.

"Can't you get a grip of yourself?" he had yelled.

"No," she had screamed back, "no, no, no, not while you tell me nothing."

He had not even told her to shut up. Just as her father had done, he had turned his back and left the room.

When they had arrived in the next town, Autessiodurum, they had also stayed in the hostel. For once it had been clean and comfortable, but after the evening meal her father had quarrelled with the merchants. She had not been able to hear everything, but enough.

"We don't plan to continue on the road south tomorrow," the leader of the group had said. "We've heard reports of bandits on the road to Augustodunum."

"There are bandits reported everywhere. Everyone's frightened of bandits," replied her father. The merchant had shaken his head.

"That's as may be, sir, but we prefer to wait a few days and see if there's better news. Perhaps some soldiers will show up, who could act as an escort, or maybe a bigger group of traders." The merchant did not seem worried, only weighing his options, like any other trading calculation. "If not, we can always take the other route, on the Aquitania side. It's longer, but better safe than sorry."

"I'm the governor of Britannia Prima, a citizen, of senatorial rank. I should be able to travel where and when I like. It's my right!"

The merchant shrugged and ordered more wine.

"Take or leave it, mister, I'm not stopping you. We're not planning on going anywhere tomorrow. Why not relax and have another drink?"

Lucius and Cornelius had tried to calm her father down, and at last they succeeded.

"Father, you can't bully the merchants, and we can't carry on alone. We don't know the roads. It just doesn't make sense to argue."

They waited three days in Autessiodurum, until her father had lost patience. Her brother, Gaius, was expecting them in Arelate. Publius Julius Ursinus was not a man used to being told he could not do something, Ophelia reflected. Instead, he searched around the town, looking for men he could pay to escort him on the road south, and in the end, he found half a dozen rough-looking fellows. She had overheard him discussing it with her brother.

"With me, you, and Cornelius, together with our servants, the cart drivers, and these men I have hired, we will be at least a dozen armed men in the party. It would be a brave group of bandits to attack us."

"I think we should wait for the merchants," Cornelius had countered. "They know the road best."

"Nonsense, these men I've found are locals. They know what they're doing."

In the morning the family had gathered in the hostel yard; the group had formed up and taken the streets to the south gate. The guards had interceded as they left.

"Are you sure you are making the right decision, sir?" they had insisted.

"A few bandits are not going to stop us," said her father, adamantly. "My son's waiting for me in Arelate. We have to push on."

The party, her family and the escort, had set off on the south road, passing through fields and pastures until they had reached a small town, a village really. She remembered the children had been hungry, so they had stopped to eat, and she let them run around. After they had left the village, the forest began to close in, the trees hanging over the road, and then they had heard hooves in the distance, more travellers coming along the road to meet them. She remembered looking round, wondering how they would pass the other group on the narrow road, and realising she could not see the men from Autessiodurum. Had they left them in the village, she wondered, and after that it was really hard to remember what had happened.

Ophelia lay still, trying to grasp at fleeting thoughts, those final memories. Was it all a dream, a nightmare, a vision, a sick delirium? Then why did it all feel so real, the road, the inns, the people, and now the hard ground and the open sky, the shadows of the trees, the smell of fires, the earth beneath her?

☙ Chapter 3 ❧
Gaul

Although she still had her eyes closed, Ophelia's instincts warned her there was someone close by. She opened her eyes and looked up. There was a shadow over her. At first she could not make out who or what. Then she began to distinguish a young woman, one who looked like a peasant or a serving woman. The woman bent down. She was speaking to her. She had something in her hand, a beaker. Ophelia could now make out the worried look on her face.

"Drink, drink," said the woman, slipping her hand under Ophelia's head and lifting it slightly. She was clumsy and inadvertently splashed water on Ophelia's face. A little ran into her mouth and she gulped once or twice, coughed reflexively. The woman took the beaker away and reached behind her out of sight. Now she had a bowl in her hand. She offered it towards Ophelia.

"Eat, eat," she said. Ophelia could hardly make out her words. She tried to lift her head in response to the woman's urging tone. Her body refused to obey. The young woman shuffled around on her knees and lifted Ophelia's head into her lap. Then she tried to spoon some food into Ophelia's mouth. Some sort of porridge. Some of it slid between her teeth. It tasted bitter and nasty, not even like proper food. She gagged and spat it out.

"You must eat, lady," said the woman, stroking Ophelia's cheek gently. She tried again with the food. It was disgusting, like something the pigs would have been fed at home.

I'm not at home, thought Ophelia, not even in the nastiest hostel. I'm outside in the open air. I'm lying on the ground. Can I have fallen ill, she thought? It's the only explanation. That must be why I hurt so much. That must be why I can't remember what happened.

The young woman had the beaker again and tipped it towards Ophelia's lips. Reluctantly she sipped at the water.

"Come along, lady, sit up," said the woman, easing Ophelia into a sitting position. She began to see a little more clearly. She seemed to be in a clearing, among trees, in a forest. There was an open fire close by. That explained the smell of smoke. There were other shapes, other people, perhaps women, too. Further away, different shapes, perhaps horses, horses grazing, on the other side of the clearing. The young woman holding her called out, a loud harsh sound which disturbed Ophelia. Some of the shapes turned towards her. They were coming nearer. As they approached, she saw they really were women, roughly dressed, like poor labourers. One of the women knelt in front of her, took up the spoon and tried again to feed her with the porridge. She could not struggle anymore and swallowed some of the disgusting mixture.

She looked down at her legs, stretched out in front of her. Her travelling cloak was stained and dirty and seemed to have been torn.

"Where are my children?" she asked.

The young woman holding her did not seem to understand.

"Where are my children, Lucia and Titus?"

She felt the woman grip her more tightly.

"No children," the woman said. "Amalric didn't bring any children."

Ophelia understood enough to feel panic rising. She felt nausea. She felt her stomach tighten, the disgusting taste of the food in her mouth. She was ready to vomit. She never vomited. She was a lady. Ladies did not vomit. The more she tried to get a grip on herself, the worse the nausea felt. She leant over and was sick. Her stomach retched again and again, and she coughed. Her mouth was filled with an awful acid taste mixed with the bitter taste of the porridge. Just the thought of it made her stomach tighten again.

The young woman holding her did not flinch. She kept her arms around her.

"Some water, lady," she said softly. "You'll feel better."

Ophelia drank, a sip, a second sip; she leant over and spat the water out to wash her mouth. Spewing like that had shocked her body, shocked it out of the lethargic and paralysed state she had been feeling. Slowly she straightened her back, out of the grip of the woman who had been holding her. Now she felt ashamed at herself, behaving like that in front of strangers, in front of these peasant women. She looked around again: the edge of the forest, up close, two or three fires burning, women bent over them, over cooking pots. One of them seemed to be skinning an animal.

"Where, where am I?" she asked, almost to herself.

"You're in our camp, Amalric's camp," said the young woman. Ophelia turned to look at her. Her words were beginning to make more sense, the way that the speech of the servants in the hostels had made sense if you listened very carefully, a sort of Latin, but all messed up.

"Who… who are you?" said Ophelia.

"I'm Anna," said the woman, deliberately. "I'm Amalric's girl." The other woman, the one holding the bowl, said nothing. Ophelia felt her watching.

"What's your name?" the woman asked.

Ophelia turned her head slowly to look out over the camp.

"Where are my children, my family?" she asked.

She saw Anna and the other woman exchange a look.

"I have two children, Lucia and Titus. I have a husband. I have two brothers and a sister. My mother and father… My father is an important man. No, no," she said, shaking her head, "no, there is something that doesn't fit, something wrong." She stared ahead, took a deep breath and then began again. "I have two children, Lucia and Titus. They were beside me on the cart. I have a husband. I have two brothers…" She could not go on. She took another breath. "My father's an important man. My father's a rich man. He can't leave me here."

The women stared back at her.

"Don't you understand me?" she whispered. "I… have… two… children… I… have… a…" Her voice faded away to nothing.

"We don't know," said the young woman, a worried look on her face. "Amalric only brought you to the camp."

Suddenly she felt a wave of tension inside her. Her feelings washed over her. She could not control herself anymore and only screamed, screamed at the top of her voice, as hard as she could. She could do nothing but scream. If she screamed loud enough and long enough someone would come and wake her up from this nightmare. But no one came. She did not wake up. She only saw the young woman's face close to hers and felt a soft cheek against her own. It was some sort of comfort at least, that the other woman wrapped her in her arms. Ophelia ceased to scream out loud and began to sob, sobbing and sobbing as waves of fear and horror washed over her. What had she done to deserve this?

She could hardly breathe, her chest felt so tight. She began to pant and gasp for breath. Was she dead or alive? She must be alive. Surely her body would not strain like this if she were dead. Through her own tears she could see the young woman was crying with her. She could make out another woman coming towards her. Suddenly, there was a flood of water over her, icy cold water drenching her. She gasped involuntarily and the shock broke her sobbing.

The young woman was soaked, too, but she patiently wiped the water from Ophelia's face with the edge of her tunic. She tried to reach for Ophelia's hair, as if she wanted to dry it, but the cloth would not stretch that far. Ophelia felt a sudden urge to move, to escape from the woman's grip. She reached out her hand and pushed the young woman back. Then she curled up her legs and put one hand down to steady herself. She looked around again, seeing but not understanding the women, the trees, the open sky, smelling but not understanding the smoke, the earth, strange people.

"Are you feeling better now?" asked the strange young woman timidly.

No, Ophelia wanted to say, no… I have two children. Where are they? I have a husband. Where is he? My father… My father has abandoned me. Why, why? she thought.

Instead she simply nodded her head slowly a couple of times in reply. The words which ran round in her thoughts just would not form in her mouth.

"I'll fetch some more water to drink," said the young woman, getting to her feet, "and perhaps Letti has some meat you could have. Better than porridge for a lady," she added, leaving Ophelia sitting alone. She began to feel cold. The water had seeped through her cloak and it was damp, and she edged a bit nearer to the fire. She realised she must have been lying on a bed of leaves and straw, laid out on the grass. There was a rough blanket nearby that might have been covering her. What kind of place was this? Again she looked around to try to make sense of it. She could see no one she knew, just these curious peasant women. Could she have fallen ill, and her family had left her in this place? Why would they leave her in the middle of the forest, with no one but these strangers to take care of her? Just then she caught the sound of hoof beats, soft thumps on a forest path, and riders appeared on the edge of the clearing.

Ophelia looked up hopefully, thinking it might be Cornelius or Lucius or her father. It was simply a group of labourers, she thought, as they dismounted, calling out to the women and laughing. But if they were simple farm people, why were they riding horses?

Anna came back with the beaker, water slopping over the edge.

"You take it, lady, and drink."

For the first time Ophelia really looked at the young woman. She must be about the same age I am, she thought. She seemed like a peasant, a round face, long brown hair and kindly eyes. The young woman smiled and held out the beaker, and Ophelia slowly reached out and took it. She put it to her lips and drank a couple of gulps. It took away the last of the nasty taste in her mouth, but the shock of the cold water in her stomach made her cough once again. The young woman moved towards her, but she held up her hand.

"I'm all right," she said, "Anna." She remembered that the young woman had called herself Anna.

A smile spread across the woman's face. Then she jumped up and walked to one of the fires a little way away, where another couple of women were crouching. When she came back, Ophelia could smell meat. Anna was holding a piece in her hand.

"Eat this," she said. "It's fresh, just cooked now."

She crouched down and handed it out. Her hand was not very clean, thought Ophelia for an instant, before taking the meat. It tasted a little better than the porridge, almost normal. She chewed on a piece, concentrating on moving her jaw, when suddenly she thought of a question. She was forced to swallow the meat.

"Who's Amalric?" she asked. The young woman, Anna, had mentioned the name several times.

"He is our chief," said Anna.

"Your chief?" echoed Ophelia.

"Of the band," Anna continued, "the people who live in the camp. We're outlaws, I suppose," she added.

Ophelia stopped chewing, her mouth half open.

"Outlaws… bandits?" she whispered.

She could see Anna nod, without saying anything in reply.

Then she heard new voices, men's voices, and Anna stood up quickly, glancing around. Ophelia turned her head, following her gaze. Four men had walked into the clearing, talking loudly. One of them was carrying a deer slung over his shoulder. He swung it down, and it thumped on the earth. He looked over towards Ophelia, saw her sitting, and called something to Anna. He left his comrades and strode towards the two women. He glanced at Anna and then smiled at Ophelia. It was not a nice smile.

"You've woken up, my beauty," he said, with an odd tone of relief in his voice. "Very beautiful lady."

He crouched down, reached out and touched her face with his rough hand, and then slid it down her shoulder, inside the cloak, over her tunic. She could feel his hand resting on her breast. The man looked directly into her eyes as he held her. She said nothing, frozen, not moving.

"Amalric," he said, letting go of her breast. He took his hand from her dress and stood up, all in one movement. He looked down at her, laughed, and returned to his friends. Ophelia was shocked. What had just happened? This man had grabbed hold of her breast. Who was he to do that, this man, Amalric, as if he owned her?

Ophelia heard the bandit shouting to Anna.

"Tidy her up, now she's awake. I don't want her looking like she's been dragged through dirt, like she's living in a pigsty."

She heard Anna respond but did not catch what she said.

"And," said Amalric, in a loud voice, "I want her dress repaired, do you understand?"

Now she examined her surroundings more carefully, Ophelia saw that the clearing was really a camp of sorts, with a row of low huts, wooden, with roofs of branches and rushes, the kind of huts that the farmers at home constructed to shelter animals.

Am I not among pigsties, she thought, wherever I am?

She saw Anna struggling along with the bucket, slopping water. For a moment she was worried that it would be thrown over her again, and she cringed in expectation, but instead the young woman took up a cloth and began to wipe her face.

"He wants you clean," said Anna, with a frown on her face. "Can you stand up?" she asked, holding out her hand. "Here, I'll help you."

Ophelia struggled to her knees. She felt weak and dizzy.

"Oh, oh, by Jesus," she said. "I feel unwell."

Anna reached out and took hold of her, an arm about her waist.

Ophelia was on her feet, one leg, then, after an effort, the second, shaking, resting her hand on Anna's shoulder to steady herself.

"You're so tall. You'll have to sit down when I comb your hair," said Anna, gazing up into her face, again with a smile. Then hesitating, she continued, "You must take your dress off if I'm to repair it."

For a moment Ophelia thought she had misheard her. Anna's accent was so strong, but when she repeated the words there was no mistake.

"Why?"

"I need to wash and repair it," Anna said. "Amalric said so. Don't worry, you can keep your cloak on. No one will see you."

Ophelia looked around, almost in panic again. Anna followed her gaze. The men had gone, but she seemed to understand her reluctance.

"Come," said Anna, and gently she took Ophelia's hand. "Follow me. I can see you're still not well. We'll go into the hut. Come."

Ophelia turned slowly to follow.

"This is Amalric's hut. This is our home, your home now, too, I think," said Anna.

Ophelia felt she was shrinking inside, crumbling up into nothing. She let go of Anna and stopped, clutching her arms around herself, almost to reassure herself that she still had a physical existence.

Anna pushed open the plank door. Ophelia hesitated on the threshold. Anna drew at her arm again.

"Come, come, Amalric has gone. You can come in. Take your dress off. I'll fix it."

She's speaking to me as if I'm a child, thought Ophelia.

She took a pace inside the hut, almost stumbling over the step which led down to the hard beaten earth floor. A dim light seeped in through a window, high at the far end and around where the sloping roof met the wall. She had expected it to be muddy, dirty. Was she relieved, she thought, that the floor was clean, sprinkled with rushes, cleaner than some of the hostel rooms she had been forced to stay in on the journey? At the back of the hut was a low shelf, a single plank of shaved wood, a row of earthenware pots and jugs, even a pair of small statues. She screwed up her eyes in the dim light, but even she, in her confusion, could recognise Mars and Venus. Beside them was an earthen lamp and a candle holder. On one side lay a low bed and a mattress covered by a blanket.

Anna was smiling.

"Our home. I'll find the things to make a bed for you. No room for three, here," she said, pointing to the mattress, "and too much disturbance when Amalric comes. Now you can take off your gown."

Ophelia did as she was bidden. There was something in Anna's insistently friendly tone that suggested she could be trusted.

"Sit down," said the young woman, pointing again to the mattress. Ophelia obeyed, crouching down and letting herself drop onto the low bed. It smelt faintly of the herbs she remembered from the kitchen at Verdaris. A familiar, comforting smell. Anna went out. Ophelia closed her eyes, and in a moment her head dropped, her body slumped, and she fell asleep.

She awoke with a start. A hand was shaking her.

"Wake, wake, my lady!"

For an instant she thought she was back in her room in Verulamium, that everything had been one long nightmare from beginning to end, but reality struck her, like a blow to her stomach. The smiling face leaning over her was not Mav, her maid, but the stranger, the young woman, Anna. She was holding the gown.

"I washed it," she said. "It's like new," she added, crouching down to show it.

Ophelia struggled to her feet, adjusting her underwear. She took the gown, and Anna curled her legs around and sat on the bed, gazing up at her.

"You're so beautiful," she said, "so slim, a real lady, like the statues. What's your name, my lady?"

Ophelia slid the gown over her head and let it drop. It did not look like new, just a patched old gown like a beggar would wear. She glanced down at the smiling, curious face peering hopefully up at her.

"Ophelia," she said.

"Ophelia," repeated Anna. "Ophelia, I love that name. I've never heard it before."

"It comes from Greek," said Ophelia mechanically, as she had a hundred times at dinner parties in Verulamium. Instead of saying, "Oh my! How wonderful!" Anna continued to watch her with a blank smile. Ophelia sighed and came to a decision. She knew no one. She had no friends here. She did not know where her family was. She could spurn this young woman, or she could take her as she seemed to be, kind and well-meaning. She had never had a problem with Mav, with the kitchen girls. She turned and lowered herself to the mattress alongside Anna. Anna in turn, in some instinctive manner, seemed to understand Ophelia's decision, gave her a radiant smile and hugged her.

"I'm frightened," said Ophelia. "What happened?"

Anna took a deep breath, hesitant.

"I don't know. Amalric doesn't tell me everything. Ophelia, please trust me. He's not a bad man, not all the time, not to me."

"Where are my family, my children?"

"I don't know," said Anna, patiently. "Amalric brought you two days ago, I think, but no family, no children. Perhaps he found you, lying by the road. You were sick… asleep all that time."

Perhaps, thought Ophelia, perhaps it's best that I believe that.

"What does he want with me?"

Anna sighed again, gave her a slightly hopeless look.

"I don't know, but I suppose the same as me. Someone to do as he says, to make his food, clean the hut." She paused briefly. "Someone to lie with." Her voice sank for a moment, and then she seemed to force a smile back onto her face.

"Maybe he's just planning to ransom you," she said in a hopeful tone. "He did that once with an old lady he caught. She must have had a rich husband. You must have a rich husband, a fine lady like you, or a rich father."

Ophelia felt tears coming again. She wiped her hand across her face.

"I'm sorry," said Anna, "I… I… I don't know…"

Ophelia drew up her knees, wrapped her arms about them and turned towards her companion.

"Once my father was a rich and powerful man. Now I'm not so sure. Recently, he started to seem old and frightened. Everything has become so strange. Even before I woke up in this place it was like a dream, a bad, bad dream. My father has gone away and left me behind. I've been abandoned. Why? Why? Why?"

Anna's eyes were wide open, staring at her.

"My father was a baker," she said. "He died. Someone stabbed him in a fight. I ran away from home. I thought I could work in a bakery in Autessiodurum. What a fool I was!"

"Why?" asked Ophelia, distracted by the girl's chatter, by the effort needed to understand her words.

"Do you think they wanted a village girl in the town bakery? What else was I any good for? I was young and stupid. Luckily I was good-looking still, and what's a girl like me going to do when I get cold and hungry? No one's going to help me for nothing. When Amalric came into town he spent the night with me, and in the morning I left with him. I've been here ever since. Better one man than a whole town, don't you think, if you have to?"

Ophelia felt confused, disorientated, unsure about what the young woman was telling her, why she was revealing this story. Anna must have seen her confusion, since she got to her feet, holding out her hand to help Ophelia up.

"It's a life, here, Ophelia, in this camp. I've seen worse," she said. "It's better than being a whore, better than being dead." She looked at Ophelia thoughtfully. "We all have to deal with it, in our own ways. Come, now, with me, and meet the other girls."

What sort of life, thought Ophelia later, as she sat by the fire, recovered enough to chew on a piece of flatbread, just cooked over the open flames. She was no fool. She could imagine what Amalric wanted. The hand on her breast had told her clearly enough. She had seen it in his eyes. She was a married woman, after all. She had done her best with her husband. She had not chosen Cornelius, but she had done her best, and she had two children to prove it. And now this man would want the same, sooner or later.

He returned to the camp just before sunset, striding out of the woods in the dusk. Anna had made flour cakes, meat with herbs. She served him and then sat down beside him while he ate.

"Don't you think she's pretty?" she said, looking at Ophelia, poking Amalric's arm. The man looked up, grunted, his mouth full of food, glanced at Anna, and continued eating.

"I fixed her dress," she continued. "It's good material. You should get me a dress like that. You could buy it in town, in Senones." She gave Amalric a quick glance. "Even I would look prettier in a dress like that."

Amalric swallowed his food at last.

"Are you starting to get jealous, little Anna, worried that Amalric's getting bored with you, now he's found a classy new woman?"

Ophelia saw a sudden glint of fear in the young woman's eyes, as if Amalric's rough comment could contain a grain of truth.

"You don't get around me so easily," he laughed, reaching out and cupping his hand around her chin, and then he looked across at Ophelia. She tried not to meet his gaze, not to attract his attention.

"Did you eat?" he asked.

"Yes," she paused, "my lord."

"You don't need to call me that, princess. I'm not your lord. We don't have lords in this camp. Just as long as you do as I ask, you'll get along fine." He took another mouthful of stew, chewed for a while and then added, "If you don't ask too many questions and don't get too curious, that is."

Ophelia said nothing.

"Amalric," said Anna, not looking at him directly, "are you holding her for ransom… like you did the old lady? She told me her father's a rich man."

Amalric allowed a smile to creep across his face, his lips twitching, but said nothing for a moment. There was an uneasy tension in the air.

"I know her father's a rich man, my little chicken. You only have to take one look at her to see that."

He turned to Ophelia. The smile, chilling though it had been, had vanished.

"You're not leaving, not now, not ever."

But my father's an important man, a provincial governor, she thought. He can't want me to be here, with a man like you. This is not what he brought me up for. Haven't I always done as he wished? Haven't I always been a good girl? Didn't I study hard, at Latin and Greek, and philosophy and mathematics? Didn't I practise sewing and weaving until my fingers ached, just to show him I was better than the other girls? Didn't I marry Cornelius because he wanted me to? Didn't I leave home when he asked me? Didn't I bear his grandchildren, that he looked on so proudly? I never argued, defied him, like Hypatia. Haven't I been good enough? What have I done to be abandoned like this?

"Cat got your tongue?" Amalric suddenly asked, breaking her train of thought. For an instant she was almost grateful, and then she realised there was something strange about his voice. His tone, his accent had shifted. Until then, talking to Anna, he had spoken in dialect, the same dialect Anna spoke, but now with those words, addressed to her, she realised his Latin was perfect, even educated.

"I'm sorry," she said automatically, shaking her head, as if someone had addressed her at the dinner table when she had been daydreaming. "I… I…"

"…was thinking someone might come to save you," he said. "Don't underestimate me, princess," he continued, getting to his feet. "I know who you are, and I was the one who decided to bring you here. I'll be the one who decides what happens to you and when."

She expected the worst when night fell. Anna had found another mattress and made up a new bed, on the other side of the hut. Amalric's shadow filled the doorway, outlined in the flickering light of the embers outside. He looked down at her, stripping off his clothes. Then he lay down beside Anna, his familiar place, she supposed.

It could not last, of course. On the third night, he turned to her. It was obvious what he wanted. She had already been forced to see what he did with Anna. She had never been in the same room with a man and a woman, coupling together like that. But she had had to listen while he and Anna… how could she even put it to herself?

She did not want to give herself to him. She still just wanted to sleep, to fall into unconsciousness, to try to forget. But he would not let her, not tonight. She was too weak and he was too strong. At first she resisted, tense and stiff, and it had been painful. Then the resistance had ceased, her body had relaxed, more than that, it responded to him in a way she could scarcely comprehend. A feeling took hold of her that she had never experienced with Cornelius. She screamed as much from surprise as any other sensation. When he had finished, he stroked her cheek.

She closed her eyes, blocking him out, blocking the world out. She could not cry. No tears came. She was too numb, beaten, defeated. She lay, sweaty and soiled, awake long into the night.

In the morning she felt dirty, outside and in. At the same time, she felt apathetic, helpless. She was ashamed to look at Anna, who must have lain silently, listening to her scream. She did not dare to show herself to the other women, supposing the noise she had made must have carried to all the other huts in the camp, so loud had it been. She lay almost unresponsive until Anna came with some water and a square of cloth.

"Did he hurt you?" she asked, as she wiped Ophelia's body.

Ophelia kept her eyes closed.

"That wasn't the worst."

"Oh," Anna said, in such a tone that Ophelia opened her eyes and saw the expression on Anna's face.

"It was awful, indescribably awful," said Ophelia.

"Will you clean yourself or do you want me to do it?" asked Anna, softly.

She offered Ophelia the cloth. Ophelia struggled half upright and took the rag from her. Anna patted her shoulder, stood up and left the hut.

Ophelia ate little, drank little, but mainly sat staring into the fire, watching the other women but avoiding their eyes, the men come and go, without taking anything in. It was unspeakably awful the next night, too, when he came to her, the same loss of control, the same incomprehensible sensation, but it seemed only to satisfy him. She felt she had become a thinking soul trapped in an animal. Her body was an animal which, without her willing it, accepted him and responded. Then she had a night of peace, when he went to Anna instead. That night she was able to sleep in peace.

With time, Ophelia was relieved that her novelty wore off. Amalric was not a young man anymore, and he needed his rest, especially as the nights grew shorter and the weather damp and cold. Then he was glad to creep under a blanket and snuggle up against another warm body, without any need to prove his manhood. She no longer felt ashamed in front of the other women. They must have known what was going on all along. Why was she so stupid to think anything else? She lived in Amalric's hut. Of course he was using her. She was no better than them, she understood, hoping she was concealing her scrutiny of the other women as they chatted by the fire.

She had been a faithful wife. Cornelius had been the only man she had ever lain with before now. She wasn't giving herself to Amalric by choice. He was forcing himself on her. She thought bitterly of her neighbour, Livia. Everyone knew that she had been having an affair with an actor. At the time, Ophelia remembered, she had thought, how could she? How could she lie with a man little better than a slave, and having a worse reputation? She shuddered. An actor, a bandit… who was the better woman now?

Just suppose, she considered, that Livia's body had reacted to her actor the way that her own body now reacted to Amalric. She had never felt that way with Cornelius. Might that explain everything? Was that what Livia had been seeking from her actor?

The leaves had started to turn yellow and orange and brown, and a few had begun, twisting and turning in the chill air, to fall. It was no longer comfortable to sit by the fire in the evening. One bright day, the men went away. Ophelia was left in peace. Anna was left in peace. They were gone several days, and they did not tell the women where they were going. Maybe the men had not known where they were going themselves, other than out raiding, but when they returned, they brought with them fresh horses, with saddle bags that bulged and clanked and banged. There were new weapons, new pieces of armour, and over the horses were draped a pair of girls. When they were unloaded and slung to the ground, Ophelia could see that they were hardly more than children, terrified and clinging to each other.

Amalric and his companions ordered the women of the camp to prepare a feast. They ate and drank, sang and danced with their women, and after that the younger men and the boys set on the girls, one after the other, cheered on by the older men. At first the girls screamed and fought, but the men beat them until they were silent and, once they were still, the men had their way. Amalric did not join them. Instead he came to her when she and Anna retreated to the hut. She was trembling with fear, dreading that he would demand she satisfy him with the shrieks of the captives still ringing in her ears, but instead he sat down beside her and stroked her hair. Then he crossed to Anna, lay down beside her and went to sleep, undisturbed by the whoops and shouts outside.

Ophelia lay awake, the sight of the trembling girls still before her eyes, their cries and shrieks in her ears. She wondered why she had not screamed and fought when Amalric first came to her. Why had she just let him have his way? Were those two girls braver, more defiant, than she was? Was she such a coward, afraid of being beaten, that she had let Amalric use her, or had she already been cowed, during her years with Cornelius, even before then, taught that submission to a man was her duty? Was she actually one of those pitiful women she had heard about, who let their husbands beat them, abuse them, who even sought men who treated them that way?

She despised herself. She was contemptible and worthless. Perhaps she deserved what was happening to her. Perhaps she should not have been so obedient all along. Perhaps she should not have fooled herself into believing she could be happy by keeping the men around her happy, and in any case, had she really been so happy… really? No one had beaten her, true. No one had raped her, but she had been offered up, as a bride to a man she hardly knew, because her father needed an ally. She had given herself to him, without complaint, and carried his children, and when he seemed to have lost interest in her, she had thought she was satisfied with the life she was leading, because it was the same sort of life her mother had been leading. And she had never thought there could be a better life and never, never, never in her most horrible nightmares had she imagined she would suffer something as awful as the life she had now.

She never found out what had happened to the girls. They were not in the camp when she woke the next morning. No one said a word about them, not even Anna.

C3 Chapter 4 ᐓ
Gaul

After the night when the girls had been assaulted, Ophelia was unnerved and turned in on herself, speaking rarely, and then only in single words. Had the outlaws done the same to her sister-in-law, Daphnea? Surely little Lucia, her daughter, was too young to have been treated like that, just a baby. What had Anna seen before Ophelia woke, when she, usually so chatty, did not mention the girls? Anna had said that Ophelia was the only person that Amalric had brought to the camp. She had to believe that Anna was telling the truth, that her children had never come to the camp, that the other members of the travelling group, her father, her brother, her husband, her mother and Daphnea were somewhere else, but where? Why had no one returned to find her? Why had no one come searching for her?

"We're leaving," said Anna one day, seemingly without any preliminaries. "The men have decided."

Ophelia had not been paying attention to the chatter. More than that, she had actively tried to push thoughts of Amalric and the others out of her mind as much as possible.

"Leaving?" she asked, looking blank.

"For the village, the winter village, before the weather turns bad. I need your help, Ophelia, please?"

"Help?"

"We have to pack up the hut. I can't do everything alone. It would be so much easier if you would help me. Tomorrow Amalric will come with horses, and then we'll all have to leave."

There was something in Anna's beseeching look that prompted her into action. She rose to her feet slowly, mute, and followed Anna into the hut. She did not feel like asking questions. Unthinkingly following Anna's example, she tied the clothes and blankets into bundles. The few cooking pots, beakers and dishes were gathered together. Even the two small statues were carefully packed into a basket. Nothing was to be left behind. The robbers had no intention of giving others the opportunity to steal their belongings.

That night she and Anna huddled together on a single mattress, with only a blanket to hold off the chill night air. In the morning Amalric appeared, leading a long line of sturdy ponies. The bundles and packs and bags and baskets were slung over their backs and secured. Despite her own sense of misery and anger, Ophelia could feel an unusual air in the camp. Even the grimmest, most silent of the men seemed cheerful as they hoisted the packs and loaded the horses. Amalric inspected the hut, empty and swept clean, exchanged a few words and a laugh with Anna.

"All ready?"

He crossed to where the men were waiting.

"Let's go!"

The men set off through the forest, leading the animals. The women trudged after them. Ophelia simply followed the others, not knowing where she was going, what was going to happen, hardly caring. She just let her body slip into a rhythm, one foot, then the other, one step after the other, following the group. Anna walked behind her. Occasionally Ophelia felt her hand on her back if she stumbled or walked too slowly.

Her body moved automatically, one foot after the other, but her mind filled with disturbing thoughts. She had taken for granted, she recognised, that the bandit camp must have been close to the place where she had last seen her family, close to the road, though no one, she was forced to admit, had ever actually told her that. She had reasoned, furthermore, that the local people must know the location of the bandit camp. She had seen several of them with her own eyes, visiting. She recalled from her childhood that everyone at Verdaris knew where the local out-laws lived, if only to warn their children to go nowhere near them. She had assumed that her father, searching for her, could ask the farmers or villagers for directions. But now, now they had moved away, who could searchers ask? How could they find out where she was?

In the middle of the day they stopped. The men kept to themselves, eating and drinking, and the women sat separately. There was no chance to make up any fire. They ate bread and pancakes they had brought with them. A skin bag of wine was passed around. For a moment, she was tempted to sit stubbornly in place, to refuse to go further, but when the meal was over, she got to her feet as the others did and allowed herself to follow. They walked the whole day, and then they stopped and slept on the ground. Someone made up a fire. Amalric left her alone. He left Anna alone. That was one good thing.

They walked the whole of the next day, on and on, along endless paths in the forest. It was almost impossible to judge the passage of time. The trees looked all the same. The paths looked all the same. A thin grey light filtered in through the branches, through the rustling, drying, dying leaves. It was impossible to see the sun, to tell where it was in the sky.

No one was coming to find her, because no one could find her, not lost in this never-ending forest. If she was going to be reunited with her children she would have to find a way to leave the bandits. She would have to escape, though she hardly dared to contemplate the word. It was no longer any use merely expecting that someone, her father, her brother, her husband, anyone, would show up, looking for her. She turned over each argument, each proposition, again and again.

It was useless being surly and alone, she concluded. She had to talk to, to befriend even, the other women. They knew things she did not – where they were going on this endless trail, if nothing else. She had been reluctant, she acknowledged to herself, because, in part, she still had difficulties understanding the women's chatter. She felt they mispronounced their words in an ignorant manner. She did not want to understand. She did not want to be part of this group of dirty, dishevelled creatures.

That was the path of hopelessness and defeat, she was now forced to admit. Whether she liked it or not, she was part of the group, and unless she did something about it, then she would remain a part of the group for all time. She had to try, however much her soul rebelled against the thought, to satisfy Amalric, not just in bed, but at other times. He knew more than he had told her, had told Anna even. That was obvious. He had hinted as much, too, in less guarded moments. She had to pretend to be his friend. If she was going to escape from the band, she would have to be more cunning and more deceitful than they were.

They camped again that night and walked on through the following day, and again the day after that, seemingly endlessly.

Anna tried to engage her in conversation.

"Soon we'll be at the village. I'm so looking forward to getting there!"

"Which village?" asked Ophelia, forcing herself to appear to take an interest. Her question was all that Anna needed. She took a couple of quick extra steps so she could walk beside her.

"Didn't I tell you that we don't stay in the camp all winter?"

"Possibly," said Ophelia, reluctantly.

"Amalric has a village deep in the forest, where we can live in warmth and comfort when the weather turns bad. How nice it'll be to see Milva, and our cows and pigs! And Grear and Ylva! I've missed them so much! I would have missed them more without you," she added, placing her arm around Ophelia. Ophelia let it stay. She needed Anna's touch, something familiar and comforting in a world on the move.

As the shadows began to lengthen — what few distinct shadows there were in the forest — Ophelia made out a break in the sea of trees, signs of a clearing, and within it a ring of huts, with walls of wood and mud, some square, with long low roofs, others round under cones of thatch, with wisps of smoke rising above them. As the first of the men emerged from among the trees, children came running with cries of joy and shouts of welcome, happy to see their mothers and fathers once again after a long absence. Unfamiliar women came from several of the huts and hurried over to embrace their menfolk, whom they had not seen since the start of summer. An older man, his hands red with clay from making pots, embraced Amalric.

"Welcome back, chief!"

"Thank you, Emeric, it's good to see you again! I hope you have been taking good care of the village."

A moment later, two women came running towards Anna and Ophelia, throwing their arms around Anna with squeals of joy.

"Grear, Ylva," cried Anna, hugging her friends. "Tedric," she cooed, as Ylva held up the child she carried in her arms. "How I've longed to see you! How much you have grown!"

Ophelia felt an impossible conflict of emotions. A small, almost infinitesimally small, part of her was drawn into Anna's joy. She had almost begun to see the young woman as a friend. But part of her, the much greater part, remembered her Lucia and Titus whom she had lost, remembered the cruel torture of the captive girls.

Anna led the way towards one of the huts, a sturdy, square construction with a sweeping roof of reed thatch. Ophelia remembered similar huts clustered around the road junction close by Verdaris. She and her brothers and sister and their friend, Marcus, had sometimes walked down to the village or taken the path back that way after bathing in the river. The village women had fussed over them, offered them fresh milk or small cakes. She had always thought how warm and snug the little houses could be compared to the hard stone of the villa, baking hot in summer and icy cold in winter.

Now this was home, apparently. Amalric's home, Anna's home, and, unwillingly, her home, too. Without any fire lit, the hut was dark and gloomy, slightly damp since no one had been living there while Amalric and Anna had been away. Anna busied around to gather dried leaves and bark to start the fire. She showed Ophelia where she would sleep, where she should lay out her mattress, and where the pots and vessels were stored for the food, carefully arranged around the hut. While she was fussing, an older woman came in and bowed her head. Anna turned and spoke to the woman in a patois quite indecipherable to Ophelia. The woman turned to her and bowed again, a shrewd twinkle in her eyes.

"This is Milva," said Anna. "She takes care of Amalric's cows and pigs while he's away."

Ophelia gave her a small, uncertain smile.

"Amalric doesn't like having animals living in his house," said Anna. "Milva lives with them in the round hut next to us."

Ophelia felt of wave of relief pass through her. It was bad enough with Anna close by, but the old woman would have been too much. As for a house full of animals, she realised reluctantly, perhaps for the first time, that she shared Amalric's opinion. It was a tiny, tiny acknowledgement, that, of course, no civilised person shared a house with farm animals.

☙ Chapter 5 ❧
Remis, Belgica

Belgica had lost a lot of its attraction since Treviri was no longer the northern capital of the emperors, since the praetorian prefecture had been moved to Arelate. Being in the direct path of barbarian invaders had not helped, either. Nonetheless, it had a gravitational pull on exiles from Britannia and was still home to many well-educated men.

The lawyer Quintus Apollinarius sat in the courtyard of Comenius' tavern, the best in the city of Remis. Across the table sat the brothers Vitellus and Drusus, the sons of his old friend, Chief Cassius Astrebanus. He was a spider in a web of correspondence and gossip, happy to be of service.

The lawyer felt he owed the young men his attention, in the interests of his own business, not least, though it meant several days of travel from his home in Treviri. Especially, he reflected ruefully, as it had been his letter that their father had had in his hand when his heart gave way and he collapsed and died, a letter informing the chief of the execution of General Flavius Claudius Constantinus.

"I'm surprised to see both of you on this side of the water," he said, smiling, "in the circumstances."

"Completing some unfinished business… unavoidable," said Vitellus, coldly.

The lawyer arched his brows. He was always curious about business that did not involve him. Neither Vitellus nor Drusus took the hint, or else they chose to ignore it. Never mind, thought the lawyer, I'll find out sooner or later. He let his brows relax again and replaced the inquisitive expression with a smile.

"And you newly married, Vito. Congratulations, a fine match."

Vitellus Astrebanus, the older of the brothers, smiled back, equally sincerely. Beginning to resemble his father, thought Apollinarius, with his dark hair already smoothed down to cover a bald spot.

"You're quite correct," said Vitellus, "with her father at death's door and an entire fortune to be inherited."

"I meant that Milesia is a beautiful woman, and intelligent, too, and a woman who a man might easily yearn for. I remember her from my time in Londinium."

"I need a son," said Vitellus, "for the future of the family. She doesn't have to be intelligent for that."

"Good looking helps," said his younger brother.

"Ah, Drusus, always an eye for the girls," said the lawyer.

"But to no good fortune, Apollinarius," replied Drusus, "especially now your own lovely daughter has remained in Britannia with Milesia."

"Bryna's too young to be marrying," said the lawyer, with a laugh, "yet… but I'll bear you in mind when the time comes."

"Can we get down to business?" said Vitellus with irritation, suspecting he might be the target of the lawyer's humour, not his brother. "I am, after all, eager to be reunited with my new wife."

"Of course, Chief Astrebanus," said the lawyer. "They did elect you chief, in your father's place?"

"Not yet."

"I assumed it would be a formality," said the lawyer.

"I will become Chief of the Durovenes, once those stooges are ready to acknowledge me. But it's not going to happen if I have to sit here in Remis, talking to you. To business!"

"No," said the lawyer, with a wave of his hands, "it won't. Now tell me what happened."

"She burned the documents that Drusus took with him," Vitellus snapped.

"Wait a moment," said Apollinarius, raising his hand, "I just want to make sure I understand. These were contracts you're talking about, instructions to pay the bearer a certain sum, coin or silver…"

"…or gold," said Drusus.

"…or gold," echoed Apollinarius, "on a certain date."

"As repayment of loans," added Drusus. "She claimed the documents were copies, Hypatia did, that the debts had been repaid years ago."

"But they had not, and Hypatia burned them?" The lawyer looked sceptical.

"They had not been repaid," said Vitellus with emphasis, "not according to our records."

"Not according to the look on his face – Silvanus', I mean – when I showed them to him."

"And how much were the contracts worth – face value?"

"Enough for us to claim Villa Verdaris," said Vitellus.

"Which would have been yours," said Drusus, glancing at his brother, "if you had married Hypatia as the governor promised."

A sour expression appeared on Vitellus' face. His voice rose in anger for a moment and then subsided. "I was treated disgracefully. To think I even imagined I would be a suitable partner for that conniving bitch."

"So Hypatia burned the letters," said Apollinarius. "She must be beginning to feel rather secure in her position. I suppose that discourages employment of the same tactic in the future. Have you thought of approaching the merchants? They must also be carrying some of the governor's debts? You would expect them to be willing to support your claims against the family."

"Not while Silvanus can claim he's the legitimate deputy for Publius Julius."

"But the papers you have collected surely undermine that legitimacy? If the governor has been repudiating debts left and right, surely no one could support his daughter or her husband?"

"The facts on the ground say otherwise, Apollinarius." Vitellus grimaced. "Silvanus has put his own people in the administration and has the loyalty of the auxiliaries. I'll give that to him… very effective, unfortunately. The facts on the ground are that we can't touch him without more support." He shot the lawyer a suspicious glance. "Speaking of facts on the ground… you have the documents we left with you safely locked up?"

"In an iron-bound chest, Vito. Would you like me to show you?"

"There's no need." Vitellus frowned. "And are you sure these are all written in good faith? I don't want any more claims of duplicates."

"I'm a lawyer, not a money-changer. If a man from a good family, a man I've known for years, tells me he's owed money by another man, and he has a document to back it up, am I not to trust his word?"

Vitellus frowned.

"Being from a good family didn't prevent the governor from clearing out leaving his debts behind him."

"He wouldn't be the first," shrugged Apollinarius, "nor, I suspect, the last. In any case, given the situation, wouldn't you be better off tracking him down and confronting him directly rather than going after his daughter and her husband?"

Vitellus drummed his fingers against the table.

"I've taken care of that. It won't be necessary."

A look of concern flashed over his brother's face, and Vitellus fell silent for a moment.

"My lawsuit," he said finally. "Claudius Cornelius helped draw it up. The tribunal in Camulodunum voted in support. A letter has been sent to Rome, laying out that Ursinus and his family are corrupt and inefficient, and proposing that, as premier chief in Britannia, I should be appointed governor."

"The tribunal in Camulodunum has no jurisdiction over Britannia Prima," said Apollinarius, without allowing sufficient time to reflect on his choice of words, "not since the province was divided."

"Rome will listen," argued Vitellus, "and in any case, I've argued for reuniting the provinces as a necessity to face the sea-raiders."

Apollinarius sniffed.

"I think Rome may have other things to worry about now, my friend, like rebuilding the city after the barbarians – though, in the circumstances, talk of raiders might catch their attention."

"The emperor will listen. The emperor must know that his will is being defied," said Drusus.

"But will he do anything about it? The Empire is overrun by people defying his will, most of them a lot nearer to Rome than Marcus Ursinus."

"Silvanus," said Vitellus.

Apollinarius continued looking sceptical.

"And Publius Julius, he may also have influence. He's hardly likely to allow a case to be brought against himself or his own son-in-law without speaking up when he has the chance."

"He won't be speaking up," said Vitellus, "to anyone."

Another anxious glance from Drusus froze his words.

"You're right," said the lawyer, noting the exchange. "Some of the people to whom he owes money are very curious as to his current whereabouts since he passed through Remis… incognito, so he thought, though everyone was following his progress."

"They can still their curiosity," said Vitellus. "We're offering them very generous terms for his debts, and that should relieve them of their concern."

"But then the debts become your concern."

"That's my choice," said Vitellus, rising from his seat, "and I can handle it." He bowed to the lawyer, then hurried across the tavern yard towards the gate.

Drusus followed his brother out into the street. Once out of earshot, he rounded on Vitellus.

"You almost said too much. I told you it was a mistake."

"It had to be done. Did you want him to arrive in Rome?"

"No, no more than you, but was it necessary… I mean… the women and children, too?"

"No witnesses, all right?" said Vitellus, grasping the edge of his brother's cloak. "No one blabbing and crying, even if they got no further than Arelate. That would be as bad, if not worse."

"We could have sent a messenger ahead, to pre-empt him, with your request, with your testimony."

"What, and still allow Ursinus to stand in front of the emperor and defend himself? No, it had to be this way. Just keep it to yourself."

"I'm not the one blurting out," said Drusus.

"I'm not blurting," replied his brother. "I'm dropping hints, Drusus, to keep people on their toes. So long as no one uncovers the truth, let them speculate. It'll only make them nervous, and nervous people serve my purpose."

❧ Chapter 6 ❧
Gaul

The village settled into a slow, winter pace, governed by the shortening days and the chill in the air. Even Ophelia no longer felt as tense and wretched. In the camp she had always felt an air of threat. It had been inherent in the environment around her, in the sight and sound of the men, in her memory of their behaviour. In the village, with their wives and children, even the hardened bandits appeared a little softer. The nights passed, and the days, too, one by one. The clothes Ophelia had been wearing when she first arrived had become torn and dirty. The village women provided her with new ones. She no longer stood out from them, however much Amalric might have liked to preserve her appearance. She was a little taller, a little lighter haired, but she had begun to resemble a peasant. She was still aware, still well aware, that she was not. But what was she? Just as she still perceived the women as ignorant rustics, they despised her, Amalric's pet, a useless mouth to feed through the winter.

Was she any better than that? She had burned the porridge when she was set to watch it. She had picked the wrong berries in the woods and spoiled the efforts of others. At first she had even spilled the water when she fetched it from the pond. In the camp she had not cared. I don't belong here, she had thought. She had been so bound up in pitying herself that she had not cared what she did or how she looked. No one else cared about her in return. Well, Amalric was proud of her, in his rough way, as men are of trophies. She was a status symbol, a Roman woman for the chief when the other men in the band had to be content with humbler companions. Otherwise, the only person who gave any sign of affection was Anna.

In the winter village, compelled to keep company with her, day after long day, Amalric's attitude towards her began to soften. He began to reveal a little more of himself, to treat her a little more as a confidante than as a mere decoration.

"My mother," he said, one day, quite suddenly, "used to be a maid in a big house." He chuckled to himself. "Maid… servant, whatever, she didn't get to choose what she did. She milked the cows and fed the chickens. My father was away at the war. We had to eat. And even when he came back to visit us… can you eat silver or gold, which was all he brought with him? He buried the treasure behind our hut. Being buried, that's all it was good for to us."

He looked thoughtful for a moment, and then he gestured around their own four walls, until he thought she understood.

"I grew up in a hut like this, sharing it with a cow and a pig." He glanced at Ophelia. "At least my life has improved a little since then." He chuckled again before continuing.

Had he expected her to find his comment amusing?

"I was allowed to run in and out of the barns and stables around the yard, jump on the haystack, beg for scraps from the kitchen, but I never set foot in the house, a dirty little boy like me." He glanced at Ophelia again. "I remember in the summer, the children from the big house came down to the village." He laughed, a low ironic laugh. "I say village, but it was a cluster of little huts, not even as much a village as this one. I remember them, a boy and a girl, with their tutor. She appeared like an angel, floating over the ground, not treading on it." He rolled over on his stomach and looked at Ophelia. "Smelling of perfume, golden sandals on her feet, and in such a dress… like the one you used to have. I'll get you another when we return to the summer camp." He paused. "Yes, like one of the goddesses my mother and aunt told stories about round the fires at night, come down to earth to tempt mere humans. And she did torment me." He laughed again, the irony replaced by a sad wistfulness. "Not in person, of course, but in my daydreams."

Ophelia listened to his talk but said nothing. Is that how she and her brothers had appeared to the villagers around Verdaris? Not real boys and girls, but beings of a different order? She had never given a thought to how the villagers looked on her family. It seemed ridiculous. Could there be some boy, among those village children, still thinking of her? She glanced at Amalric and shivered at the thought. What a fool, then! How many other men walked around with such ridiculous ideas? She wasn't an object. Or was she? Had Cornelius considered her any more than an object, a prize he had been awarded by her father… for what? For nothing more than being who he was? Maybe that's why her marriage had gone the way it did.

"When the time came," Amalric began again, "I joined the army, just like the old man. I was in Italia, in Hispania, along the *limes*. You name it, Amalric has been there."

"Were you ever in Britannia?" she asked, hardly daring to break his train of thought, but happy to interrupt her own.

"Before your time, my dear," he replied, gazing up at the roof. "I was with the federates in Londinium, and then up on the Wall for a while, but they recalled us before we could settle in. Trouble on the Danube, though we never got there, that time. They sent some other poor bastards to get massacred."

He looked at her.

"Good morning, miss, how much?" he suddenly said in British.

She scowled, rolling away from him, not liking his comment. He reached out for her, his hand grasping at her waist.

"I'm sorry, Ophelia. It's the only words I know."

"They say a lot about you," she said, stretching herself out beside him again. The air was chilly, and there was no sense in discomforting herself over a few foolish words. Imagine, she thought, he could have marched through Verulamium with the legionnaires, ogling her as he passed by, and she wouldn't even have noticed. He could have been among those rough men who had whistled at her in the street, when she had been a child in Corinium, made vulgar gestures that she had pretended not to see. She had noticed them, well enough, and knew what they meant.

"I never saw her again," Amalric said, confusing her for a moment.

"Who?" Was he still talking about some British whore?

"The girl from the villa, Astraea, her name was. One day men came, men on horses. My mother hid us away. It wasn't like here, no forest to hide in, just a wide flat plain, criss-crossed by ditches. We ran as far as we could and dived into a ditch. We stayed there all day, and the next day, too, hungry and drinking ditch water to keep alive. We could smell the smoke. They burned the farmyard, and everything they could in the villa. The master had gone, the mistress, too, the children. We never saw them again."

"What happened to you?"

"After a while a new master came. It wasn't the same." He stopped. "I never found out what happened to Astraea."

She felt anger rising inside her. She was about to scold him that he and his men were no better than the raiders who had attacked his childhood home, but her thoughts jumped ahead too quickly, too precipitously.

"Where are *my* children?" she suddenly asked. "Where is *my* husband? Where are *my* parents?"

Amalric frowned, opened his mouth as if he were about to speak, and then closed it again.

"Where are they?" she repeated. "I know you know! You brought me here!"

"To the camp," he corrected her.

"What does it matter?"

"What does it matter where your children or parents are… now? Or the husband who has abandoned you?" He grimaced. "And besides, I told you already, Ophelia, don't ask those questions. Please," he added.

I know you know, she thought again, looking at him looking at her, a small battle of wills. How can you look at me like that and speak so sentimentally about your own past, some stupid memories I'm supposed to listen to, and you think I should feel sorry for you, you bastard, when you won't tell me the truth?

But no words came. His look had silenced her, and this time silence would have to suffice, and a look of as much contempt as she could muster. To spite him, the cold air, the drizzle outside, would have to be suffered.

"I have to get wood for the fire," she said.

Spring came… eventually.

"Ophelia, I'm expecting… a child," said Anna, her hands folded round her belly.

I should be grateful it's not me, was Ophelia's first thought, mean spirited though that was, she recognised.

"Congratulations?" she said, giving her friend a hug.

"I'm so happy," said Anna. "I've so much wanted a child, so much wanted to be a mother."

"Wonderful," said Milva. "Then you can stay here, in the village, all summer."

Ophelia's heart sank. Anna would stay in the winter quarters with the child and leave her alone with Amalric. How could she survive? She couldn't cook. She couldn't find food in the forest. She could barely keep the hut tidy. She wasn't nice to Amalric like Anna always managed to be. She made no effort to keep him in a good humour. To be alone with him would be hell on earth. And without Anna, she would have all his attention.

"I couldn't leave Ophelia," said Anna.

"You'll have to, eventually," said Milva. "You can't have a baby in the camp."

"I know, but that's still months away," said Anna.

Still months away… Ophelia felt a selfish surge of relief, gratitude even. But it simply postponed the problem, and supposing she got pregnant herself? She lay with Amalric far more often than she ever had with Cornelius, and she had had two children with her husband. She knew women, even older than her, who had had many more. How could she have Amalric's child? What would she do? She felt a wave of panic sweep over her. Anna had become a protection against all sorts of horrible eventualities. She had even managed to be the one of them to get pregnant.

"We're not going back to the camp we used last year," announced Anna, more cheerful, more buoyant than ever.

Thank God, thought Ophelia. Only remembering the place brought on such awful feelings.

"We're going to a spot nearer the Aquitania road," said Anna. "Amalric thinks I don't know his plan, but I overheard him discussing it. They think it's too risky to return to last year's camp, and if there are any travellers on the Lugdunum road, they'll probably have an escort of soldiers. Travellers in a hurry or stingy merchants will take the Aquitania road, and Amalric plans to be waiting for them. We were in that other camp two years ago. It's a nice place, Ophelia. You'll like it," she added.

They set off again, to the west this time, through a river valley, across a range of hills, until they found a clearing, one the band had used on previous years, with a stream running nearby, plenty of game in the woods, and convenient for the road. The huts needed cleaning and repairing, but there was a certain pleasure in that, the satisfaction of good work done properly. There were villagers nearby who knew them from old. Amalric was certainly no saint. He did not believe in taking from the rich and giving to the poor, but he was a professional and knew the value of making a deal: you help me and I'll help you. A tip about travellers passing by, or an accident on the road which would force a merchant to halt or take a path through the woods. That might save a villager from having his animals stolen, perhaps even provide a few coins or cut silver in a bag on his threshold. You scratch my back and I'll scratch yours… a universal principle to live by.

It was a principle, Ophelia realised, that she had singularly failed to follow. Anna would be leaving, and with Anna all the practical skills of camp life she had hidden behind would be gone. She would have to deal with the other women alone, and she could not face the humiliation.

Once I was a person others looked up to, she thought, the mistress of the house, but here I'm useless, a person who gets in the way. What's so wonderful about being able to read and write where there are no books, about mathematics and geometry in a place with no numbers, about being able to speak perfect Greek and Latin, quote poetry, when no one's interested in listening, when food needs to be found and prepared, animals slaughtered and cooked? All the skills and abilities that I have been so proud of are utterly useless. Did the servants at Verdaris despise me, despite my pride in my talents? Did they laugh at Father and Mother behind their backs, knowing they couldn't survive a day without someone to run after them? I've treated Anna like a servant, like one of the servants I used to have. She's cooked the meals, tidied the huts, cleaned the clothes and bedding. She's even comforted me when I have been feeling low. So long as I make no contribution to the group, I'm not even the other women's equal, and they know it.

"I wish I could be useful," she said to Anna. "I've never learned how to bake bread, even to cook porridge. I'm just a person who messes up but who no one can criticise openly."

"You can spin," said Anna.

Ophelia's mouth turned down. That did not help her feel better. Every woman could spin, whatever their background. Every woman had to spin to provide thread for the weavers.

"You can grind flour," continued Anna, who was working away at a hand mill.

"That's all, the simplest stupidest labour."

"It's necessary," Anna pointed out, trying to be encouraging.

"But I only grind half what the other women do."

"You're learning," said Anna, "getting stronger. Soon you'll be able to grind as easily as any of us."

And so she ground and ground, until her arms ached, until tears came to her eyes, but she knew all the grinding in the world would not be enough when Anna left.

She was Amalric's woman, his favourite, and the women were anxious to avoid his anger. She had exploited that, she knew, to be lazy, selfish, a backwoods version of Livia, her old neighbour from Verulamium, enough to open her legs, pleasure the master, and let others do the work. Not much difference, she thought bitterly as she ground and ground, between what I do now and what I did then, except that when Cornelius grew tired of me, I still had food to eat and a roof over my head. She did not dare to think what might happen if Amalric tired of her.

You have to help me, Anna, please, please, help me, she first begged in her own thoughts, and then, finally sinking her pride, she had pleaded openly with her friend.

"Watch, Ophi, what I do, follow where I go, remember what I tell you." Anna had sat across from her, cross legged on the floor of the hut, looked at her with large brown eyes. "I know you can do it. Believe in yourself. I know how clever you are. I've heard you talking to yourself, and in your sleep sometimes, all sorts of strange things I've never heard of before or can't even understand properly."

"I have to be able to take care of Amalric," said Ophelia. "All that other stuff doesn't count. I have to be able to take care of Amalric, if that's all I do, if I'm going survive in the camp."

And so she followed Anna, and watched what she did, and copied her. And sometimes, much to Anna's wonder and amusement, she took a flat piece of wood, or a strip of bark, and painstakingly scratched out notes to herself, using tiny letters marked with soot, and stacked them in a heap in the corner of the hut.

"For future reference," she said to Anna, "for when you aren't here." I haven't forgotten, she said to herself, as she made her notes. I'm still Ophelia Ursina. I haven't forgotten.

And Anna was always kind, so practical, so busy, despite her belly now swelling with his child, always a soft word, always a word of encouragement like a favourite sister should. Ophelia found herself becoming one of those figures, the same type of shadow she had picked out on her first day, moving among the camp-fires, looking after the men, tending their wounds, turning a deaf ear to screams and cries in the night.

Not far away from the camp was a river, and a little way upstream a small lake where the women could wash. In the spring the water was cold, and it was enough to step into the shallows and splash yourself quickly. As the summer drew on, Anna recollected that it grew pleasantly warm, and every so often the two women took the path through the forest. At the edge of the pool, they would strip off and, shrieking happily, Anna would plunge in. Ophelia could see it was a relief for Anna to take the weight off her legs. She, herself, had never been fat, if anything rather a little too slim for conventional taste, like her mother, though her long arms and legs had obviously made her especially attractive to Amalric. Now with the walking and grinding and fetching and carrying, she could feel the muscles ripple beneath her skin. The two women laughed in the dappled sunlight, splashing water on one another. It was no bath house, but it was wonderful to be clean. For a moment no camp, no Amalric, no work, no worries, just the joy of being together.

Towards the end of the summer, when they were making their way down to the bathing pool, Anna told Ophelia she would have to leave, to return to the winter camp.

"I can't have the child here," she said, as they took off their clothes. "It's too risky, and if I wait, I'll be too big to travel, and Amalric says I should go. Letti can come with me, and maybe Baric." Baric was Letti's man, her husband.

"Baric must go with you," said Ophelia. "It's a long walk to the winter camp, and it wouldn't be safe for just two women. Amalric should go with you, too. It's his child, after all. I'll persuade him."

"I wish you would," said Anna, easing herself into the water.

"You're so round," said Ophelia, touching her hand to Anna's bump. "I hope you haven't left it too late."

"I have another month if I have counted right," said Anna.

"I'll miss you," said Ophelia. Once that would have been hard to admit, but being less dependent had made her appreciate Anna all the more.

"When you come back to the village there will be two of us, me and the baby. Aren't you excited?"

Anna took a piece of soap that the women used for washing.

"Let me wash your back, Ophi," she said. Ophelia turned her back to her friend and felt her gentle hands rubbing her.

"Stay still, Ophi, I'm washing you."

"No you're not, Anna, you're tickling me."

Ophelia felt Anna's bulging belly bump against her back, and Anna's hands against her thighs.

She turned around, slightly agitated, and she saw Anna's bright brown eyes looking up at her.

"What is it, Anna?"

"I'm so sorry we'll be apart, Ophi," she said, in a trembling voice. "I'm a little worried about having the child."

"Don't be sorry, don't worry. If I could do it, you'll be fine," said Ophelia, concerned. "Come on, let's get out. You must be cold. You're shivering."

"No," said Anna, "I'm not shivering from cold. I need to tell you something."

There was a strange tone in her voice.

"I'll miss you so much. I think I love you, Ophi."

Ophelia put her arm around Anna's waist and began to guide her towards the bank.

"I love you, too, Anna. You're like a sister to me."

She felt Anna sigh.

"Come and sit by me, and we'll dry off together," she added quickly. There was a flat rock by the river, where the women left their clothes, where they could rest, dry off and comb their hair.

Anna sat down beside her, placed her head on Ophelia's breast, and Ophelia could have sworn she was weeping.

☙ Chapter 7 ❧

Gaul, a year later

By the time the bandits returned to the winter camp once again, Anna's child had been born, a little girl. Amalric had named her Fredagunda after his own mother, and Anna had not objected. Ophelia was pleased for her. She remembered the first few weeks with her children, Lucia and Titus, in Verulamium. How strange it had been, feeling the child inside her, the birth, the pain and the strain, and then feeling like a cow, with the baby sucking at her breast, and then, almost immediately, Cornelius had found a wet nurse, and the little one had been taken away. Perhaps that had been a mistake, she thought, watching Anna as little Fredagunda suckled joyfully. Perhaps I would have been a better mother if I had kept them with me longer. Perhaps if I had looked after them better, then they would still be with me now, but that was not what women did in Verulamium, not women like I was.

"You've survived, too, Ophi," said Anna, once they had a little time together, "even though you were worried you wouldn't."

"It was hard, Anna, after you had gone," she admitted. "I can't count how many times I wished you were still with me."

"Did you use your scribbles? I always thought they were a scratched-out version of me to have with you, like a magic charm."

Ophelia laughed. "Of course they were, and I did need them at first, and then after a while, I didn't need them anymore, and..." She raised her finger. "I don't plan on going back to relying on you now. I'm going to do my share of the housework, my share of looking after the animals, and I have had plenty of time to consider that I'm not going to waste my time all winter in the village like I did last year."

It took a day or two to get settled, and another to pluck up courage. There was an older woman in the village, a woman who, amongst the villagers, was one of the most important, a woman who seemed to regard her the most disdainfully, and who, in fact, she had come to fear. That woman held the key to her using the winter constructively, held the key to her gaining a better status in the band, one that she might use in the future when she needed to. It had taken her many hours of worrying to bring herself to take the steps she was now planning to take.

She raised the hood of her cloak and pulled it tight, almost as a protection, and knocked on the door of the woman's hut.

A sharp voice, without opening the door, asked who was there.

"Amalric's Ophelia, Mistress Ilana."

There was a rustle from inside and a creak as the door opened. A thin-faced, sharp-nosed woman stood in the opening, looking her up and down.

"I wondered how long it would be, Amalric's Ophelia, before you came to visit me."

Ophelia took an involuntary step back at the tone in the voice.

"I've heard your story," Ilana continued. "I could see what type of a woman you are, or once were, should I say."

Ophelia's heart sank. She began to wish she had never come.

"I'm sorry, Mistress Ilana. I don't understand. I only came..."

"I grew up in a big house, one of the house slaves. Now do you understand? My mistress was a woman like you… used to be."

Ophelia could say nothing. Ilana turned her back on her and took a couple of paces into the interior of her hut. Ophelia felt an almost overwhelming desire to flee, but she held her ground.

"Come in and close the door, Amalric's Ophelia," said Ilana, without turning round. "The cold is getting in, and I feel it all the more as I get older."

Ophelia followed her cautiously. Ilana pointed to a wooden stool.

"Sit down and listen to me," she said sharply.

Ophelia sat. She was trembling and wondered if she showed it.

"Yes," started the woman again, "I was a house slave, far away from here, and you can guess what my life consisted of?"

Ophelia could say nothing. At Verdaris, in her own home, there had been many such slaves, and they had a variety of tasks. How could she guess? And then an idea struck her… of course she knew.

"You were made to weave?"

"I was made to weave," sighed Ilana. "I was the best bloody weaver in all of Dacia, and did I get any credit for it? No… just a slave, made to work, while the mistress, who did nothing, took all the praise."

"I can weave," said Ophelia quietly.

"You can weave," said Ilana. "All you fine ladies claim you can weave."

"I can weave well," said Ophelia, a little more firmly. "I practised hard. I was proud of my skills. I was as good as any of the slaves."

Ilana came towards her, bent over her as she sat.

"Do you know what this is?" She showed her hand, stiffly curled.

Ophelia nodded.

"I used to be the best weaver in Dacia until Rivaric came by, and then I said, fuck it, I'm not weaving for this bitch anymore. I'm leaving, and they can hunt me throughout the Empire, but I'll die before I come back here."

"You're not dead."

"Not yet, anyway," said Ilana, turning away and taking something from the fire. "I suppose you're hungry listening to an old woman ranting?"

Ophelia was far from hungry.

"I… I…"

"Share my meal with me, Amalric's Ophelia, and I'll give you a chance to show me how good you are at weaving. I'll see if you can live up to your boasting. Do we have a deal?"

If your cooking is as good as my weaving, thought Ophelia.

"We have a deal," she said.

"With these hands, and these eyes," said Ilana, as she scooped a little stew into a bowl and handed it to Ophelia, "it's become difficult to do anything but the simplest work. Do you know I wove the cloth for the dress you're wearing?"

"Yes," said Ophelia. "Anna told me. That's why I came to see you. I can see the quality."

The woman snorted. "Once I could make such beautiful patterns, but now… it's all I can do to weave plain cloth." She coughed and wiped her hand across her face. "I would need someone with keen eyes and nimble fingers who could assist me. Someone with real skills and not just an exaggerated opinion of herself. I've seen too many of those over the years… snotty villa girls, mostly."

"Mistress Ilana," said Ophelia, forcing herself to eat from the bowl. "I'm a snotty villa girl. I admit that. Or rather, I've been a snotty villa girl. But I promise you, when I was younger I worked at the loom until my fingers ached and my eyes burned… to be the best I could be. I wanted to show them I was the best. My promise is not an empty promise."

"We'll see, tomorrow. When the sun's up, come to my weaving shed, and show me what you can do, and then I'll judge whether your abilities match up to your promises."

Ilana had a loom in a shed behind her hut, a tall frame which stretched from the floor to the ceiling. Ophelia had always loved to weave as a child. It was the shapes and the colours which fascinated her, watching the different threads pass back and forth, until the pattern built up in the cloth, or just letting her fingers do the work, seeing diamonds or zig-zags ripple across the material. Ilana sat her on the weaving stool, gestured for her to start.

The shuttle felt strange in Ophelia's hand after all these years. She had been just a girl the last time she sat in a weaving shed, before she was told she had been chosen to marry Cornelius. At first she felt nervous and clumsy under Ilana's gaze. She could hear the changes in Ilana's breathing, almost as a critical commentary on her work. And then the outside world faded away, and it was just her and the thread, her and the rhythm of the loom.

Ilana continued watching as she worked, adjusting the thread, guiding her hand now and then.

After a while she spoke.

"You'll do," she said, "for a villa girl, but there's a lot I can teach you… if you show me you deserve it."

It was even fun when there were two, she and Ilana, working together, setting up the pattern, handing the shuttle back and forth, singing together to keep the rhythm. Through her work with Ilana, bit by bit she became one of the group. Her ears became attuned to the dialect of the villagers. She learned their stories, often harder and more bitter than her own. Her mood lightened as the winter season passed by, though she remained a little special, a little different, still Amalric's Ophelia, though Anna was never Amalric's Anna.

In the village there were no wet nurses. It was the mother's own responsibility to feed her baby, and to wean it when the time came. Anna would stay in the village with Fredagunda all summer. Ophelia would be on her own with Amalric again with no Anna to share the burden. It was a trying time. The good humour that he had shown in the winter village, even dandling Fredagunda on his knees in a clumsy way, had gone. He was once more tense, wary, monosyllabic. She wondered whether it was only leaving Anna behind that upset him. She was lonely without Anna. He must be too, she thought. Anna's so warm and caring, knows how to handle him when he's irritated or stressed, and I'm not that way. He's surely worried about my cooking, whether I can repair his clothes, how well I'll take care of him, everything Anna does so perfectly. Ophelia did her best, and it was a lot better than she once imagined she could.

It was almost the end of the summer when the worst of Ophelia's fears became real. At first she hoped it was not true, that somehow the impossible had happened, and that she had simply missed her monthly bleeding. That some other cause, illness, tiredness, poor diet, had prevented it. She counted the days. There was no doubt; she must be expecting a child, Amalric's, of course. It was natural that it would happen. Even though Amalric was often away, and moody and irritable when he was home, they had lain together often enough that summer. She could not avoid the truth. It was not as if it were the first time she had expected a child. She knew what to expect, not like some silly girl… herself, in fact, the first time. Then, though, her pregnancy had been part of a plan, long before it happened, long before, if she dared admit it to herself, she was even capable of becoming a mother. She had been born to be a mother. Then she married Cornelius. They lay with one another. She became pregnant and gave birth, as a wife should do – a son, then a daughter. She had done her duty. Cornelius became a father as a man should, and that way his family would carry on to the next generation. But the child inside her now, its father was a bandit, a robber, a thief, who had stolen her from her family and forced himself upon her. This little growing being was not part of any plan of hers.

There were herbs and plants, she knew, that women could use to provoke their bodies into rejecting a child, but she did not know what they were, or where they could be found. There were ways, she was unsure exactly how, of poking and prodding inside herself that would get rid of the child, but they were wrong and dangerous, and, in any case, they required someone who knew what to do, and while there might well be such a woman among those who lived with Amalric's band, it would be very, very foolish to let it be known that she wanted to kill their leader's child.

She said nothing to Amalric. She had no Anna to confide in, and she was unsure if she could have confided such thoughts to Anna, seeing how much Anna cared for her own child. A child, a child would tie her down, tie her to Amalric, tie her to the band, to the village, to the camps. If she was unable to escape on her own, how could she flee with a child, unless she abandoned him or her? Her thoughts went round and round in an almost perpetual loop. Though she revealed nothing, Amalric was so disturbed by her silence he began to wonder if she was unwell.

"You seem out of sorts. Is there something wrong with you?"

Yes, yes, she wished to say, I'm carrying your child. That's what's wrong with me.

"I'll be away a few days," he went on. "I have to go to Senones to meet a friend. I'll buy that dress I keep promising you."

As if that will solve my problem, she thought.

"I'll be fine," she said. "I can take care of myself. I've done it before."

She waited until he had gone, then she lay on the bed until she was sure that he was not coming back, and her thoughts edged closer and closer to a decision.

If I don't run away now, she concluded, then I'll never escape, ever.

It was no problem to leave. No one was watching over her. She could come and go as she pleased, and so she went, taking the path which they had travelled to the camp.

I'll go south, she thought, and when I'm well out of sight, I'll turn to the west, and eventually I'll find the Aquitania road, and then I'll find a way south and then… but her train of thought could not stretch further than that.

And so she walked and walked along the path, until her legs began to get tired. Then she sat for a while, and then she walked again, and eventually twilight began to fall, and suddenly it was dark among the trees, and it was difficult to see the path, and so she sat down again. She was hungry and thirsty. She had hastily packed a little meat and bread before she had left the camp. She had eaten most of that earlier in the day, but she had not packed anything to drink. In a landscape of trees and streams, it would be easy to find water, she had thought, and, indeed, when she had halted earlier, she had seen a stream nearby, a little way from the path, and she had drunk her fill. But now it was dark, and there was no stream by the place she had stopped. No doubt there was one nearby, but in which direction? And how far from the path, and how would she find it, and how would she find her way back? And she hadn't seen a path to the west, not one that was sure to go west, and anyway, how far was the Aquitania road from the track she was following? Supposing she had been wandering away from the road, deeper into the forest?

I really don't know where I am, she thought.

It was dark in the forest. The wind rustled in the trees. Creatures rustled through the underbrush. What sort of creatures? There were bears and wolves in the forest, so Amalric claimed, and poisonous snakes. And Anna said the same, and she should know.

She huddled at the base of a tree, her arms wrapped around herself, and the darkness closed in, and the air became chill, and she began to feel cold, and lonely and lost and helpless, and eventually she began to cry, first softly, a few tears dribbling down her cheeks, and then the full awfulness of her situation took over her, and she began to sob uncontrollably.

She was a stupid city girl. She was lost in the forest. She was a failure who couldn't bear to stay and couldn't run away either.

"Oh, Lord Jesus," she prayed as she wept, "what am I going to do?"

There was no obvious answer to her prayer, no flash of light, no still small voice of calm, but nonetheless, in putting her desperation into words, she began to feel a little better, as if someone might be listening to her. There is a message in this after all, she thought, one that's not very comfortable to face. Is this where my life has been leading? Is this, Jesus, what you wanted to show me? Once I was proud, conceited, lazy, privileged and took my life for granted. I thought I was better than others because I could speak Latin and Greek, and do mathematics and recite poetry and quote philosophy, and… no one cares about that. I thought I was better than Livia because she had an affair with an actor, and I was a chaste married woman, and now I'm bearing the child of a thief and robber. And I took it for granted that I had a powerful father and a rich family, and now I'm alone, no riches, no food, no water, no shelter, no way to go on. Even now, I thought because the women are no longer hostile towards me, because I have a role in the band as Ilana's helper, I could survive in the woods.

I've been a fool, she thought, to have run away like this on an impulse, alone into the endless forest, but perhaps I have a little wisdom left, enough to recognise my mistake. So far, I've not come to any harm. I've not run from Amalric into the arms of a far worse beast, animal or human, which I could easily have done, probably would have done, before too long. Perhaps you have been watching over me, Lord Jesus, though I never asked you to. Her tears began to dry up. She sniffed and blew her nose on the sleeve of her cloak. Tomorrow the sun will come up and I'll still be alive. I'm not even really lost. If I only follow the path I can get back to the camp safe and sound. I'm hungry and I'm thirsty but I shall just have to put up with that until morning, until I can see my way, and then I'll find a stream, and then I'll turn my steps north again, back to the camp, back to Amalric. I think… I think… I'm beginning to understand. I think I begin to see what you've been trying to teach me.

"I've learned a valuable lesson, Jesus," she acknowledged, speaking out aloud to listening void. "I must accept your plan for me, to be patient, to be resilient, to bear the child, because you have planted him or her in me to be part of my future. But, Jesus, next time I run, because there will be a next time, I promise you, I'll be well prepared, even if I have to take the child with me."

She edged around the tree so she would be concealed from the path, and eventually she fell asleep.

❖❖❖❖❖

"I'm expecting your child," she said to Amalric when he returned.

"They said you disappeared from the camp while I was away." He sounded as if he had not heard what she had said.

"I had to have time to think, to pray," she said, "when I found out."

"What?"

"That I'm pregnant, going to have a baby," she almost shouted at him.

His head turned slowly towards her, a look of surprise on his face.

"Don't you think I needed time to consider, to think over my situation, when you were away and I was all alone?"

He accepted her word, her lie, because for him it was a triumph. Proof of his manhood, despite his years, and a fulfilment of a wish, to have a child together with the mistress of his dreams, or anyhow, her substitute.

He did not say as much then, but she knew it. Instead he kissed her, more gently than she had expected, and held her in his arms, and stroked her belly. He would have sent her to the winter camp right away, had they not been planning to leave soon, had she not said she didn't want to go and, in any case, pregnant or not, pointed out he still needed her.

When they finally reached the village and Anna heard the news, she was as excited as Amalric. They would be mothers together.

"Fredagunda will have two mothers, and your baby, too," she said, placing her hands on Ophelia, though there was nothing in the least to feel.

Ophelia reached out her arm around her. What a strange world, she mused. Once the life she was leading had seemed like a nightmare, an episode she could force herself to sleep through, and then she would awake, and everything would be as it was. Now it began to seem more and more that her old life was the dream, almost as if it had never happened, that Lucia and Titus, her family, her own childhood were things she had imagined. It was so difficult to know what was real, what was true, what was just a story, and really, most of the time, it seemed better not to care.

☙ Chapter 8 ❧
Britannia Prima

Vitellus Astrebanus had ridden over to the neighbouring villa, a couple of miles to the north of Agridurnum, through the green woods and lush fields of his estate, where his tenants and slaves could be seen tilling his land, tending his emerging crops and caring for his animals… if he had bothered to look. His mind, however, was on other things than the state of his land. He rewarded other men for taking care of such mundane matters. He had been reluctant to visit his neighbour, Chief Bredonius, before he started out and it had been as frustrating as he expected. His mood was no better on the return journey. Wearily dismounting, he handed his horse off to a stable boy and tramped his way through the outer yard, across the inner yard, up the steps and finally through the pillared portico into the house. He saw a servant, hovering in one of the passageways.

"You there, make sure the bath is hot. I'll be needing it later." He had no intention of being rude to the man – it was a man, he was reasonably sure – by failing to address him by name. He had great difficulty in distinguishing faces in poor light and at that distance, and the servants at Agridurnum all wore the same uniform.

"Hey, Vito, how did it go?" came a voice from behind him. He swivelled and saw the smudgy outlines of three figures hurrying across the inner yard towards him. From his gait the one in the lead must be his brother, Drusus, and the other two, those good-for-nothings, the Tullianus brothers, he sourly reflected.

"Not good," he answered. "I'll meet you in my work room once I've got my boots off." He jerked his head towards the Tulliani, trying to signal to his brother that what he had to say was better said out of their earshot. It was best not to insult them too blatantly, though. There still might come a day when he would need their father's money.

Between his dressing room and his work room, Vitellus dispatched another man to fetch wine, and, before his brother put in an appearance, that man returned, placing a flagon and glasses within reach on a low table. Vitellus poured himself a generous amount from the flagon. He needed it.

"So what did our dear neighbour, Bredonius, have to say?" asked Drusus, entering the room, spotting the wine flagon, and pouring himself a drink in one fluid sequence.

"He said he would be going," said Vitellus.

"To Silvanus' festival?"

"Where else, to hell?"

"One can always hope," shrugged Drusus.

"To Silvanus' goddamned independence festival, like all of them. The bishop had been there again, he told me, talking the whole thing up."

"What's the bishop got to do with it?"

"How am I supposed to know what the bishop thinks he's doing? But you know as well as I do that he has been all over the province rallying the indecisive."

"Him and Hypatia," said Drusus.

His brother gave him a cold look.

"The odds are stacked against us. If Silvanus pulls off this 'declaration of independence' from the Empire, we're screwed. They'll just claim that the Empire's laws aren't valid anymore and they can do as they like. Only an invasion would force him back into line, and what's the chance of that happening? We have to act before he makes the declaration, force him to hold off, to admit he must still obey the conventions of the Empire. And how the fuck are we supposed to do that? Even if I gathered every man jack from Agridurnum, they don't amount to an army, and in any case, Silvanus and his gang have been training their own men, claiming they need to defend themselves against the Welsh, when they've been paying them off all along, using our money."

"And the money we have, and the treasure, and the papers…" Drusus hesitated. "We made sure the old man didn't get to Rome."

"Shut up about that," said Vitellus brusquely. "You don't know who might be listening. And the treasure and papers are no good buried in Gaul, are they? Not that they would be much use here, with everyone lining up behind Silvanus. We've only got days to do something, and everyone's against us, telling us to accept reality, that it's best to go along with it. What the fuck! Can't they see it's not the best for us?"

"Perhaps they don't care what's good for us?"

There was a soft voice from the doorway.

"Vito, Drusus, I heard you talking."

The brothers turned towards the door.

"What do you want, Milesia?" asked Vitellus, impatiently.

"I thought you might be a little more welcoming to your wife, Vito," said Milesia, calmly, as if she had not noticed his emotion. "Especially as I've come to tell you something interesting."

"What's that," growled Vitellus, "the second coming of Christ? Is that the solution to our problems?"

She smiled, a smile to stop a man's heart if he had been any other man than Vitellus and Drusus Astrebanus in their present mood.

"A man came to the villa earlier, a messenger from Londinium."

"What the hell did he want?"

Milesia held her smile, apparently unperturbed by her husband's ill humour.

"He had a bundle for you, a document carrier, carefully wrapped and waterproofed."

Vitellus frowned.

"He said he had ridden from Rome, my dear, with a message for you. He had expected to find you in the city, but our housepeople in town sent him on here."

"Where the heck did he expect to find me, except in my own villa?"

"He was very sorry for the delay," said Milesia, affecting an apologetic tone.

"Well, where is he, then?"

She sighed.

"I asked him to leave the roll with me, since you were out. He was very reluctant. He insisted it was to be delivered to Chief Vitellus Astrebanus. I said, I'm his wife, you can trust me. Who can pass on the message better than his own wife?" She smiled, an innocent-looking smile. "Of course, he understood."

"Well, what was his fucking message after all this?" asked Vitellus.

Milesia raised her eyebrows, the merest remark on his impatience.

"In that case, he said, you can tell him it's a message from Rome, from the emperor, confirmed by the Senate. Your husband is appointed governor of Britannia in the name of the Empire."

"Are you sure?" asked Vitellus, his mouth suddenly dropping open, his eyes staring. Drusus placed his goblet unsteadily back on the table, after almost letting it drop.

"He said he had been sent by the Senate itself."

Vitellus frowned.

"But… but surely there should be a delegation, an announcement, in Londinium, a feast, a celebration."

Milesia frowned in return and took a deep breath.

"I thought so myself," she said. "That would normally be the case, but then the circumstances aren't normal, are they?"

"You can say that again," commented Drusus.

"It seems the messenger had been told to wait until the rest of the delegation caught up, but he realised that there was an emergency once he arrived. He said he had found out that there's a usurper, a traitor, who has proclaimed himself governor and worse, almost as soon as he stepped ashore. Londinium's abuzz with the news, he said. Well, we know what it is, that Marcus intends to declare that he no longer accepts the emperor as his sovereign."

"It's true," said Drusus. "There *is* no time to lose!"

"Exactly, so the messenger didn't bother waiting for the delegation, and hurried here at once."

"Extraordinary," said Vitellus, almost struck dumb by the news.

"I told him he had done well to make haste," said Milesia. "I assured him I would make sure that you got the message at once. If you're quick, you can reach Corinium before Governor Ur… Silvanus makes his move."

"What happened to the messenger?" asked Drusus. "He deserves a reward for his initiative and discretion."

"I sent him on his way… with silver in his hand, of course. He was worried that Silvanus might hear he'd arrived with the message and try to intercept him and destroy it before it got to your hands. He was worried he could be apprehended and held or worse, to undermine your position."

"It's very possible," said Vitellus, his reason beginning to function once again. "Silvanus must not know we have received the news until I'm ready to proclaim it in public."

"I told him to leave the notification with me, and I would give it to you. I told him he must hurry back to Londinium immediately, find the delegation and return to the mainland as quickly as he could without raising any suspicion. I strictly instructed him not to stop and not to speak to anyone. I pointed out to him that Silvanus has many friends, and there's the possibility of violence, even against you, Vito, if he learned about the message."

"I'm sure that put some fire under him," said Drusus.

"If you judge by the speed with which he left, I would say it did," replied Milesia with emphasis.

"Well, where is this damned message? Let's get a look at it," said Vitellus, recovered sufficiently from the shock to refill his glass.

"Wait a moment and I'll fetch it. I put it in my room for safe-keeping."

Once his wife had left, Vitellus turned to his brother.

"Well, Drusus, it looks like you were right after all. There's life in the old Empire yet."

"Let's hope that Silvanus recognises it," said Drusus, unable to suppress a tone of doubt.

"He'll have to see the truth, and I'm not going to give him the chance to avoid it. If this message turns out to be what Milesia says it is, then I'm going to ram it down his throat."

At that moment Milesia returned, bearing an ornate document carrier, closed and sealed. She handed it reverently over to Vitellus. He broke the closure on the cylinder hurriedly, extracted the message and unrolled it. A beautiful scroll, elegantly written, with a row of seals along the bottom, the Senate of Rome, the Emperor Honorius, the consuls, everything in place.

"In the name of the emperor and Senate of Rome…"

Vitellus' eyes scanned the scroll from top to bottom. He was an experienced reader of legal texts. Then he let out a long breath.

"We've succeeded. We've fucking succeeded, in the nick of time! Would you believe it!"

Vitellus wrapped his brother in an embrace.

"Call for another glass and more wine, Milesia. Tonight's the night for a party."

"And tomorrow," said Milesia, as she turned to leave in search of a servant, "is the day for action."

It was a happy house that night. The celebration went on late, and not just in the main building, but Vitellus sent his retainers out among the servants, the maids, the stable hands and the field workers, with orders to celebrate along with them, though he was careful not to let anyone know what it was, in fact, that they were celebrating. The Empire, with its order and sense, had reclaimed them. Under his intelligent and generous guidance, the good times would be returning.

○ Chapter 9 ○
Gaul

From once being almost an outcast, the pregnant Ophelia, a more humble and useful Ophelia in their opinion, was enfolded and supported by the women of the village. They smiled as she made her way to the weaving hut, enquired how she was feeling, proffered well-meaning advice, asked whether she thought the child was a boy or a girl, and if so, what names she was considering. Even Ilana laughed and made little jokes about impending birth. Ophelia remembered the previous occasions when she had been expecting, the tension and anxiety as the day came nearer, the visits of the *medicus*, openly, and the wise woman, more surreptitiously, the enquiries after a wet nurse. It had been an event, a ceremony almost, at which she had just been a spectator. Could she now be a natural mother, she thought as she sat weaving, accept Amalric's child, forced on her, take the little creature and place it to her breast? For the first time since the dark night when she had run away, she bowed her head and prayed. She prayed that Jesus Christ and his mother would take care of her through the birth and afterwards. Mary would surely see that Ophelia was far from home, and practically living in a stable, and that she needed all the blessings she could get.

"It's a boy, Ophelia! You're mother to a little boy, look, look." She heard a scream and crying. Was it her own scream and crying or was it the child's, or both, mixed together in a bond of pain and shock?

She opened her eyes and saw Milva holding a small pink bundle. She saw its screwed-up face, red, its tiny hands and feet perfectly formed. For an instant she thought of rejecting it, this child who she did not want, this little bit of Amalric that had grown inside her, who had caused her so much discomfort and pain, but then Milva placed him against her, warm and soft. She remembered the children she had lost, but she was too tired to cry. No, damn you, Amalric, she thought, I carried this child. I have suffered to bring him to the world. He's my son, my son, not yours. She wrapped her arms around the boy and held him to her.

Her son or not, there was no missing Amalric's pride. He named the boy Alanaric, but Ophelia, to herself, called him Lanius, almost a proper Roman name rather than a barbarian one. She was surprised by Amalric's response to the boy. He must have other sons, she thought. A man of his age and living his life. But where could they be? He had never given an indication that any of the young men in the camp were his sons, or relations of any kind. Where, then, had he come from? Where had they all come from? The women had fled, she knew by now, from war and starvation and violence, to seek safety in the forest, but the men, who were themselves so often violent and destructive…

"We'll be leaving for the summer camp again," said Amalric, as the time drew near. "You'll have to remain behind, Ophelia."

Amalric and the men met together, arguing and shouting about what was the best plan for the year, until they agreed they head towards Biturges or even Lemovices, taking care not to enter the territory of one of their rivals. Amalric could not be expected to travel without female company.

"Anna will have to come with me," he announced.

"Will she take Fredagunda?" asked Ophelia.

"No, I can't allow that. You know I won't have young children in the summer camp. They're a distraction, and in the way of business. Fredagunda must stay behind with you and Milva."

Ophelia was anxious about being left behind. It was true she had not liked travelling while pregnant, and she did not like the idea of living in an improvised camp with a newborn baby, but the children would be dependent on her in another way than Amalric, demanding though he could be. Supposing something happened to one of them? In her old life she had always had servants she could rely on in an emergency.

She had not reckoned with the collective wisdom of the women, the experience of Milva, the ironic, but ultimately uplifting, criticism of Ilana, and the acceptance and caring of the other mothers. With the men away, they sat around the fire on warm summer evenings sharing their stories. Ilana had arrived with her man, Rivaric, an auxiliary who had fought with the Romans and against the Romans in the wars between various generals, until he had been forced to flee in the company of Amalric. Then Rivaric had fallen from his horse when it tripped on a forest path and broken his neck and died. Ilana had been left alone.

Grear had also been left alone, alone with her father, when her mother had died. He had taken out his bitterness and lust on his daughter, until she had become pregnant with his child. When the infant had been born dead, Grear fled to the forest, away from the evil man and her miserable existence. She had heard rumours of the outlaws living in the forest, and, hungry and tired, had stumbled into their camp. When Amalric had heard her story, he had led a group of men to her father's farm. They had dragged him, screaming and begging, and hung him from a tree in the centre of the local village. Then they had gathered up his few possessions, his animals and his crops, and carried them away to help Grear start her new life. The cottage and the barn had been burned to the ground.

Ylva did not know where she had come from. Most of the time she remained silent, but it was easy to see that her origins must be from far away. Her hair was blonde, almost white in the summer, and her eyes were blue. She half remembered having followed her parents, clinging to their backs on endless rides. Somewhere along the way they had become separated. Her exotic looks had made her a target for men's lusts, even as a child. It had been a relief to be taken by the bandits.

These women know no better life than with Amalric and his men, reflected Ophelia. The world had treated them cruelly. Women like her had been a part of that cruelty. Ophelia was forced to recognise that she herself would have treated them cruelly, had they ever crossed paths anywhere else, begging at her door, or carrying a dirty child in the street, but here, here she was no better than anyone else.

For Ophelia time seemed to stand still, not because there was nothing to do, but she focused on small matters, on Lanius and Fredagunda, on the spinning and weaving, grinding corn, assisting Milva with the animals, occupations she once would never have imagined she would care about, and which she now took pride in doing well. There were long periods when she almost forgot her old family, her fate, only to be reminded of the children she had lost by something that Fredagunda or Lanius said or did. There was no Amalric, there were no bandits and thieves and drinking and fighting and rapes and robberies. Just the life of a village, which could have been any village, even the village huddled beside Villa Verdaris.

When Anna returned with the falling leaves, she laughed to see them. It was always a delight for her to find Ophelia behaving like a normal woman. Her friend had taken care of Fredagunda all summer, and the little girl had almost come to think of Ophelia as her mother. It did not seem to disturb Anna. She knew what a challenge the role of mother had been to Ophelia and was happy to see she had succeeded so well.

◌ Chapter 10 ◌
Treviri, Belgica

Apollinarius assumed an expression of cautious condolence. "I'm very sorry to hear about your brother. It's still very hard to believe what happened."

"My brother was murdered…"

"I understand," said the lawyer in a consoling whisper.

"…by Silvanus and his cronies," continued Drusus.

"He'd received a letter, I heard, a commission from Rome, naming him governor?" Apollinarius' tone implied a desire to hear Drusus' explanation.

"He did. I saw it with my own eyes, sealed and stamped," confirmed Drusus. "A man came to Agridurnum, bearing the message. I wasn't there when he arrived, but Milesia met him. He had ridden from Rome, she said."

"You never saw the man?" Apollinarius had already heard the story, at second hand, and there were parts he still had difficulty in understanding. "A single man, alone?"

"Yes, so she said. By the time I returned to the house, he had already left, returned to Londinium. He had ridden ahead of the delegation as soon as he heard of Silvanus' plans. Milesia brought us the bundle he left, a scroll, elegantly written, with a row of seals along the bottom, everything in place. We had succeeded!"

Apollinarius nodded, puzzled. He had received no news of such a messenger, travelling to Britannia or returning. A delegation of that status could hardly have remained hidden.

They would have been guests of the authorities, the church, if nothing else. They would not have travelled alone. It was far too risky in these times… unless, unless, perhaps, they had taken a boat down the Rhenus, though that would have been a peculiarly roundabout route. My man in Colonia said nothing, he thought, though it's unfortunate I never did brief him to look out for a message concerning the governorship of Britannia.

"It was fortunate timing, or at least seemed so," said Apollinarius thoughtfully. After all, he reflected, the consequences had been most unfortunate for Vitellus Astrebanus. "Even in Treviri we heard the news that Governor Ursinus intended to declare that that the rule of Rome would no longer extend to Britannia Prima."

"He was already a usurper when he proclaimed himself governor," hissed Drusus.

Apollinarius could not help frowning.

"And your brother decided to confront him in public?"

"He had to. He had to stop the madness, the treachery."

"And he rode to Corinium, right into the traitor's nest."

"He didn't ride alone. He took twenty of our best men with him."

"And you?"

"I stayed at Agridurnum, with Crassus and Flavius – you know them, Tullius' sons. We were to ride to Londinium with the news once Vito had taken control, and then here to Belgica, to spread the news of Silvanus' fall."

"And what happened in Corinium to make your plan fail? Surely Ur… Silvanus, I mean, should have obeyed the emperor's notice?"

"I don't know exactly. I just know they grabbed Vito and killed him."

"I suppose it was a trap," said Apollinarius, feigning a sudden insight. "Silvanus must have known about the message. It must have been a trap all along. I heard your brother was arrested when he handed over the document, that he was tried by their tribunal on charges of rebellion and executed immediately he was found guilty."

Drusus looked suspicious.

"How did you hear these details, from who?"

Apollinarius smiled, a small, slight smile.

"I have to keep communications open, Drusus, with everyone. Isn't that why you and others employ me?" The lawyer paused. "And you, what happened to you?"

"A troop of Silvanus' cavalry appeared and rounded everyone up. I managed to escape, me and Crassus and Flavius, after we hid all night in a stable."

"It's fortunate, then," said the lawyer, "that you are standing here before me, hale and hearty. You don't think they may still come after you?"

"Me, why, how? Silvanus has no friends this side of the water, no more than Publius Julius had, despite all the palms he had greased over the years."

"And Mistress Milesia?" Apollinarius wanted to hear Drusus' version, though his daughter, Bryna, Milesia's companion, had already written.

"Taken away, so I hear. I don't know where."

"And my daughter?"

Drusus shifted uneasily.

"I couldn't do anything, Apollinarius. They took her, too. There was a whole crowd of them, and only three of us."

The lawyer was calm enough. His daughter was safe. Far away, it was true, exiled with Milesia to a holy house in the south-west of Britannia. Whether he would ever see her again was a matter that weighed heavily on his heart, but he did not want to reveal that to Drusus.

"And you are intending to continue your campaign?" he asked to cover his discomfort.

"They may've killed my brother and occupied our home, but aren't I my brother's inheritor?"

"He has a son, doesn't he? Surely Constantinus is his father's inheritor?"

"A child, a mere child, and he's out of the picture, in exile with his mother."

The lawyer shook his head.

"For now, perhaps, but I hear there are plans to bring him to Treviri and place him with the canons and give him an education… which he won't get among a few hermits in Dumnonia."

"A child can't be the Chief of the Durovenes. A child can't be the master of Agridurnum and governor of Britannia. It takes a man to do that."

A child can be a symbol, thought Apollinarius, a rallying point.

"And you're the man?" he asked.

"Why not? I haven't lost everything," said Drusus, aggressively. "Vito was not so stupid to bet everything on one throw, good though it seemed. There's gold and silver deposited here in Belgica… with friends. There's the chest you have been guarding for us, the one containing the letters of debt."

The lawyer's frown deepened.

"But the governor's disappeared, no one knows where, and the means to repay the debt with him. People have been searching all over. How do you intend to press for payment?"

Drusus hesitated for a moment, considering whether to reveal what he knew, before continuing.

"I'm not as helpless as you take me for," he said quickly, "and besides, I have copies of all the correspondence with Rome that led up to Vito's nomination. Milesia's quite a scribe, and she even made a copy of the letter of appointment. I just have to choose the right time. But that's not, in fact, the reason I came to see you."

The lawyer's frown, which had momentarily vanished, reappeared.

"Bryna," Drusus said. "She has travelled with Milesia, but she was never included in the banishment."

The lawyer nodded in agreement.

"And she's still not promised to any man?" Drusus continued.

"She's still young," said Apollinarius. "For now, she's going to stay at the holy house with Milesia. Perhaps she will never marry."

A flash of annoyance crossed Drusus' face at Apollinarius' complacent tone.

The lawyer frowned.

"My daughter would need a home, a place to live, if she were to accept a husband."

"I've not given up my claims, Apollinarius. I've just said that. Your daughter can still be mistress of Agridurnum, and if not, then with a wife like Bryna, I could settle… here in Belgica, if necessary."

"I don't see why not, then. If she must have a husband, why not you?" said Apollinarius. "You're an intelligent young man, and in the family business, so to speak," he added with a smile, but then his tone turned sharp. "I'll consider it, Drusus, but I want to ensure that she'll be treated well, have the kind of life a girl like her deserves. I'm not letting her marry an impoverished exile, do you understand?"

"I'm not an impoverished exile, Apollinarius," replied Drusus in a similar tone. "I'm the rightful Chief of the Durovenes. My brother was appointed governor of Britannia

Prima and was criminally murdered by a rebel. My family have been insulted and my lands, my inheritance, stolen. I don't intend to let matters rest."

☙ Chapter 11 ❧
Gaul

When spring arrived again, as it inevitably seems to at the end of winter, the men finally decided that it was safe to return to the camp near Autessiodurum. Ophelia had played a role in their decision during the months of cold and rain, whispering in Amalric's ear. During the long hours spinning and weaving or sitting quietly keeping watch over the sleeping children, she had come to the conclusion that the only way to find the truth about her family was to go back to the place where everything started and confront her fears. The key to the puzzle must lie in the woods around that camp, and in finding the right questions to pose to Amalric, questions to which it did not matter what he answer he gave, but to which his reaction, the tone he used, the expression on his face, would give away the true answer, however much he tried to hide it.

Ophelia also worked hard to ensure that she would be a member of the travelling group. At first Amalric was hesitant. He had nothing against Ophelia's company, but he once again insisted that he did not want young children in the camp, and Ophelia and Anna agreed with him. Drunkenness, cursing, fighting and fornication were common in a camp with few women and many men, and with long periods of waiting until they were forewarned or spied out suitable victims for robbery. The solution which suited everyone was to leave the children in the village, under the care of Grear, who was herself expecting another child. Notwithstanding the subterfuges she had employed to join the group, Ophelia felt a wrench as she waved the two little ones goodbye. During her time caring for the children, she had developed friendships with the women, with Milva and Ilana, with Emeric and even some of the farmers and villagers who lived round about. She had found her place as Ilana's helper and become used to the rhythm of the village. She was forced to admit to herself there were times when it had begun to feel like home.

Perhaps Amalric's hoping for another son, thought Ophelia.

"Do you want another child, Anna?" she asked, as they tramped through woods on their way north.

"I don't know, Ophi," she said, with a sigh. "I wonder if it will ever happen?"

"Amalric really seems to have lost some of his verve," said Ophelia.

"He seems worried," said Anna. "I think that's what it is."

"I'm not complaining if he leaves me alone."

Anna looked at her sharply.

"Are you sure? You've always sounded like you enjoy his attention."

"You think I enjoy it?"

"It certainly sounds like it."

Ophelia stopped, staring at Anna. There was a strange impulse inside her that she could not control, and suddenly she burst out laughing.

Anna stared at her, first uncomprehending, and then with a look of worry.

"Are you all right, Ophi?"

"No, no," choked Ophelia, trying to get herself under control. "Oh, my God. I don't know what came over me," she panted.

"Ophi, you really are the strangest person sometimes," said Anna. "Why do you have to make everything so complicated? Why can't you just accept simple facts and leave it at that?"

"Because I don't want to be here, Anna. I don't want to be with Amalric, however good he is in bed, and he's not that good, only occasionally. I don't know any more," said Ophelia. "That's what makes me so confused. There are times when I hate everybody, and there are times when I don't care anymore. There are times when I wish I could find my children, and maybe even my old husband, and there are times when I'm not sure... about my husband, anyway."

"You mean you don't want him back?"

"I mean, sometimes I wonder whether it isn't best to forget that old world, let it go. I have a new child and I've begun to realise that Cornelius wasn't much of a husband. Maybe it's healthier to look towards the future than to cling to a past that isn't going to come back."

"Are you sure? Are you sure that it isn't going to come back?"

"I don't know, I don't know, that's the problem. Years have gone, and no one has come to find me, and when I tried I couldn't even run away. I was too frightened. What's worse, to look back to my old life or forward to the new?"

"You have Alanaric, and you have me and Fredagunda. We can be a family for you, if you let us."

"Can you two get moving or let us past?" came a sour voice from behind them.

Anna reached out and put her arm around Ophelia's waist, and feeling her touch, Ophelia reached out and slipped her arm around Anna, and together they walked on, side by side, tripping over roots and dodging branches, until at last they had to admit that it was not a very practical way to make progress along a forest path and let go of one another and went back to walking in single file.

The clearing which Ophelia had hated during her first year with the gang seemed just a little less threatening. Then it had been a place of horror, a nightmare to her. Now it just seemed like a collection of ramshackle huts, barely visited by the men during the long absence, and half-overgrown with weeds. She would not ever think of this place as home, but it did not affect her so much anymore. The people around her, Anna and the other women, were her friends now. Even the men treated her with respect by their own standards.

Amalric had never been particularly talkative, and now he became more and more secretive, though occasionally, when Ophelia managed to catch him unawares, she could be quite surprised. One day she caught him bent over a wax tablet, scratching away with a stylus. She came near and leant over, curious to see what he was doing. There was a column of numbers, and he was carefully adding them together – II then IX, crossed out and replaced by XIII, she noticed about halfway down.

"You made a mistake," she could not resist pointing out. "Two plus nine doesn't add up to thirteen."

"Shit," he said, glancing up at her, "then the whole sum is wrong."

"You should use an abacus or counting stones. Do you want me to help you?" she offered.

"No," he answered stubbornly, smoothing out the wax with the flat end of the stylus and starting again.

"I always found subtracting rather difficult, myself," she said, watching his effort, "and calculating ratios." For once she laughed out loud.

He looked at her again, with a quizzical expression, unused to her amusement.

"We had to do ratios in the army," he said, with a note of triumph. "They were easy. How could we lay out the camp, otherwise?"

"They didn't just teach you how to kill people, then?"

"Read and write," he said. "Do you think I would have ever learned that, growing up as a swineherd?"

His eye suddenly twinkled, and she recognised the sign that something vulgar, which would annoy her, was coming.

"Old poetry, too, Ovid…" He paused for effect. "*Nothing else to say, but I pressed her naked body against me. Who doesn't know the rest?* We knew. We learned that in the army. How about we follow the poet's advice?" He tugged playfully at her dress.

"Oh, shut up," she said, half in annoyance, half playing along. "That's not in Ovid!"

"It certainly is," he protested, and laughed. "I assume they didn't let you read the naughty bits, when you had your fancy tutor, but in camp, they were the only parts we were interested in."

"I never said I had a tutor."

"All you rich girls have tutors. Did he ever try it on with you?"

"No," she said, laughing out loud, a little defensively, "he had one of the cooks."

What the hell are those numbers he's adding, she wondered, scanning the tablet as he laboriously laid out his calculation once again, sounding it out as he did so.

"Curious, are you?" he said, suddenly breaking off from his scribing. "Wondering what old Amalric is up to? Why he's busy scribbling numbers? Two and nine is…" He flicked his fingers.

"Eleven," said Ophelia.

"As you say, eleven." He scrutinised the sum in disbelief, scribbled further, and then stabbed at the result. "A fair price for a farm, wouldn't you say, translated into pounds of silver."

"I wouldn't know," she said.

"No," he replied. "You never had to buy a farm, did you? You inherited straight off. Don't think I don't know, Ophelia, my dearest. But if Amalric wants to live to a ripe old age, he'll have to buy a farm, far away from wars and troubles, and for that he needs silver, and since he doesn't have enough silver, he'll just have to go on robbing people."

"And that," she said, pointing to the final set of numbers, "is the amount of silver you still have to steal, right?"

He gave her an odd, uneasy look, as if she had performed a miracle, read his thoughts.

"It's logic," she said.

"I would have enough if…" he said, looking up at her, and then his mouth tightened. "It's how many people I still have to kill," he said grimly, shutting up the tablet.

Ophelia felt a sudden wave of sadness sweep over her. It wasn't true. There was no need for him to treat her like that. The way he had laid out the numbers was obvious.

He stood up and slouched away to the hut, bearing the tablet with him. But she had read the calculation, remembered the sums. If her reasoning was correct, then he was a rich man, so where was all his silver?

It was shortly after she had caught Amalric with his counting problem that he came to Anna and Ophelia with an announcement.

"I'll be going away for a while."

"How long?" asked Anna.

"Perhaps a month. I'm going to the north. I have some business I must take care of."

It was not unusual for him to be away for a few days, in Senones or some other local town, usually with the other men, exchanging booty for food and other things they needed, but a month was a long time. Ophelia thought of his mysterious calculation. Amalric, with a good horse, could reach anywhere in Gaul or even Italia in a month. Was it connected, somehow, with his talk about buying a farm?

"What do you want us to do," asked Ophelia, "come with you?" There was a touch of hope in her voice.

"I don't think so," he smiled.

"Should we go back to the winter quarters, then?"

"I won't be away that long. You can stay here if you don't get yourselves into trouble." There was more than a touch of seriousness in his expression.

"Will you tell us what you are doing?" asked Ophelia, as mildly and innocently as she knew how.

"No," said Amalric. "Just be here when I get back. I might well have presents."

❧ Chapter 12 ❧
Treviri, Belgica

The rain beat incessantly against the shutters. A pair of candles dispelled, as best they could, the gloom of Apollinarius' dining room.

"As it happens, I'm expecting my daughter here in a short while," said the lawyer. "Mistress Milesia sent me a message saying that she'll be visiting to see her son and will be bringing Bryna with her."

Drusus was a little surprised.

"I thought Milesia was confined to the holy house where Silvanus sent her?"

The lawyer smiled.

"Did you think the governor would be able to confine Milesia Cornelia so easily?" he said. "Heaven high, emperor far away, as the Persians put it… fine so long as no one asks too many questions," he continued, a note of warning in his voice. "You're travelling once again into Germania Magna, I hear?"

"My brother had his contacts, but it's not easy to find trustworthy men in these times."

"I can only agree," said the lawyer. "I mainly have to deal with untrustworthy men, at least that's what their victims claim. When will you return?"

"In a month or so, I expect."

"Very well, I'll have spoken to Bryna before you return, and then we'll see whether we can reach an understanding."

Drusus could not believe his luck. Was Apollinarius ready to give away his daughter to him? Had it really been so easy?

In the fresh air of dawn the following day, he saddled his horse and rode off into the wilds of the east with a light heart, feeling better than he had done for a long time. Perhaps his luck was improving.

Drusus' heart was still light when he returned to Treviri a couple of weeks later, through the east gate, clattering into the yard of Apollinarius' house. The man he had ridden to meet had proved amenable, in his own barbaric way, and agreed to provide proof he had kept the promise he had made to Vitellus. Now, thought Drusus, knowing what he did, he could pursue his claim to the lawyer's daughter. He smiled as he remembered Bryna laughing in the halls of Agridurnum, arranging flowers under Milesia's supervision, blushing at his clumsy approaches. In truth, then he had been in no mood to marry, and Apollinarius was right, she had been far too young and immature. But now, these years later, he could see the advantages of a good wife, not least to give him a more dependable, solid appearance to the exiles, the men he needed to support him. Bryna would serve that purpose admirably.

"Welcome back," said the lawyer, seeing him enter the house. "Was your journey a success?"

"I hope so," he replied. "You know the Germans better than I do. Warlike and uncivilised, but men whose word to their friends can be trusted, I believe."

"They always have a welcome for guests" – the lawyer smiled enigmatically – "but their friends, those they choose carefully."

"Speaking of choosing," said Drusus. "Mistress Bryna, did she pay you a visit?"

"Oh, yes," said the lawyer. "In fact, she'll wait on us at dinner this evening."

It could not be better.

As she served the meal, she looked so lovely, he thought. A sweet smile, elegant manners, soft comments to her father and his guest. He tried to imagine her without her gown – better not to, not at dinner.

When she had left them, he expected the subject to turn to the betrothal, but he was quickly disappointed.

"My daughter will be returning to the holy house with Mistress Milesia in a few days," said the lawyer. "It's been such a pleasure to have her here, for her mother, too, unwell as she is, but the ladies have their duties, Drusus, taking care of the poor countryfolk. But I gave you my word, and I spoke to her. She's ready to consider you as her husband, but I don't want a formal betrothal yet. She asked me for time to consider over the winter, and then in the spring… perhaps the flowers will bloom for you? Let's hope so." He lifted his glass and offered a toast to his table companion.

Drusus' optimism had not lasted long. He would have to be patient. His whole life seemed to be a matter of being patient, carefully moving pieces hither and thither, always keeping his goal in mind, like a chess player. Perhaps it would be unnecessary to foray into Germania Magna again, he thought. Perhaps he should shift his attention to finding a nice country villa, not too far from Remis or Senones, which he could share with Bryna, one with a lot of impoverished rustics around it whom she could minister to, and who would come to admire him as their benevolent lord. He was wakened from his thoughts by the voice of a maid.

"Master Drusus, I have a message for you. Mistress Milesia wishes to speak to you after dinner."

"Milesia?"

"She has been staying in town, in one of the guest houses," said the maid, a little too pertly. "She thought it best to let Bryna have time with her father, but today they're preparing for their journey back to Britannia. You'll find the mistress on the upper floor."

Drusus made his way up the stairs. His dead brother's wife was on her feet when he entered, outlined against the bright light of a window, the shutters wide open to the street outside.

"What the hell are you doing here, you fool?" was the first thing she said.

He blinked in the sunlight, not quite able to focus on her.

"What do you mean? I could ask the same thing. I have as much right to be here as you do, more perhaps, as the suitor for Apollinarius' daughter."

She ignored his words.

"Don't you know he's here, searching for you?"

"Who?"

"Marcus Ursinus, or Silvanus, as he happens to be calling himself again."

"S-Silvanus?" Milesia must be deluded, thought Drusus. He could not possibly be here, on the mainland. He had to be far away in Britannia, safe in his counting house.

"I saw him in the street," Milesia continued, "drinking wine in the forum. There was no mistaking who it was, even though he was pretending to be an ordinary farmer, and he's not alone. He has a squad of cut-throats with him. You don't have to believe me, Drusus, but you will when you get his knife in your ribs."

Drusus hardly knew what to think. Silvanus, the man who had executed his brother, her husband, right here in Treviri! She would not make such a thing up.

"My God, you're serious!" he stuttered, unwillingly.

"Of course I am, you fool! And if you want my advice, get out, get out of town, leave immediately!"

"But... but..."

"Get out, get out, leave! Leave us alone, in peace, for God's sake! Do you want him to realise I'm here, when I should be in Dumnonia?"

He took an involuntary step towards the door, impelled by the force of her voice.

"And," she added, as he stood on the threshold, "don't imagine you're going to take Bryna from me."

By then he had turned, taking the steps to the ground floor, two at a time. On the way down he brushed past Bryna, hurrying up towards Milesia's shouting. He did not have time to stop to exchange even a word with his promised wife. A panic gripped him. They were after him. He had allowed himself to be distracted by emotions, by desire, and it had led him into a trap. The same kind of trap that they had laid for his brother. He had to get out of town. He had to get to Remis, where he had friends and shelter. He found his horse in the stable, untied it and threw himself onto its back. He urged it out through the gate into the street, scattering a few townspeople who got in his way, and, with an extra kick, sped towards the bridge and the road to the west.

As he put the town behind him, glancing around to ensure there was no pursuit, his heart stopped racing and his mind began to clear. What did Milesia have to do with his marriage plans? She had no right to dictate to him who he should marry. She had no right to override Apollinarius if the lawyer thought he would make a suitable husband for his daughter. Did she think she owned Bryna just because the girl shared her exile? Once things had settled down, he would put her right on that matter.

More of a concern was what conditions the lawyer could impose. The very fact he was on his way to lodge with the ex-treasurer of Britannia Prima and his sons only emphasised the tenuous nature of his life after those fateful days at Agridurnum, after the letter had arrived, after Silvanus' men occupied the villa and drove him into exile. He felt his stomach tighten at the memory of having to hide in his own stable, and then the desperate rush to the gate and down the road to Londinium. It was fortunate he and the brothers still had friends in the city. While this sort of life might be bearable for a rebel, on the run for a cause, it wouldn't do, of course, for a married man.

He handed off his horse to Tullius' stable hand and went in search of his friends. He would stay out of sight until the coast was clear, seek their advice, decide his next steps.

Tullius the merchant had once been the treasurer of Britannia Prima, Counsellor Tullianus, the right-hand man of Governor Publius Julius Ursinus. There had come a day when he had realised that the sums did not add up. The outgoings from the treasury far exceeded the incomings. There could be only one inevitable result. The governor would never be able to repay the money he was borrowing. The treasury would be empty, and that would leave nothing for Tullianus himself. Better, then, to take his share while gold and silver remained to be taken, to cut his losses and run. And so he had run, he and his family, his goods and an iron-bound chest. With the proceeds he had set himself up as a merchant in Remis, adjusted his identity, and was well away from the troubles of Britannia, so he thought.

"They're after me, they're after me," the old merchant shouted, running into the atrium, literally running. Drusus had never seen Tullius move faster than a slow amble since he had first met him.

Crassus and Flavius observed their father, usually so dour, with surprised expressions. He came to a halt, breathing heavily, looking around at the three young men.

"You've got to do something. They're after me."

"Who, father?" asked Crassus, still grappling with the strange spectacle.

"Three thugs — they came up to me in Comenius' tavern, threatening me. I thought they had come selling cheap slaves, but instead they threatened to rob me."

"Who were they?"

The old man looked from one astonished face to the other.

"I don't know, that's the point! I just made an appointment to meet them… for business. Who could be after me?"

"Who, indeed?" muttered Drusus to himself, well aware of Tullius' background.

"What do you want us to do?" asked Crassus.

"Get rid of them! Don't worry if you have to use violence. I'll cover for you with the magistrates afterwards."

"But if you don't know who they are, how can we do that?" asked Flavius.

"They're staying at Festus' lodging house. I know which room. They lured me into the meeting with a message that came in the hands of Festus' servant."

The three young men exchanged glances. Festus' lodging house was well known in the town as a place where travellers from Britannia tended to stay, exactly the place where some disappointed lender or cheated merchant might put up while visiting Remis.

They waited until nightfall and a good bit after. Then, accompanied by one of the grooms, a burly man named Braxus, they made their way through the deserted streets to Festus' lodging. They rushed up the stairs to the room which the thugs were occupying, barged in and launched themselves over the sleeping figures. Whoever they were, they were not entirely taken by surprise, and they fought back all too effectively. Braxus took a knife to the belly almost immediately, and Drusus himself was not able to draw before he was being pushed out of the room and towards the stairs. Someone in the yard below was already shouting.

"The watch is coming!"

Drusus recognised the man pushing him in the flickering light. The sight of Marcus Silvanus, the man who had ordered his brother's death and stolen his birthright, distracted him for a moment, and in an instant he was tumbling backwards down the steps.

As he fell, he remembered Milesia's words: "Your life is in danger."

When Drusus awoke, his head was aching. When he opened his eyes the light felt blinding, even though the shutters were closed. He tried to lift his head, but he felt a hand on his forehead, restraining him. He heard a voice, a woman, by her accent one of Tullius' maids.

"Lie still, master, and I'll tell them you've woken."

He sank back on the bed. What the hell had happened? He could remember losing his footing, and then nothing more. He could remember the feeling of recognition, of seeing Marcus Lucullus Silvanus in front of him, feel his hand on his arm, propelling him backwards, backwards, out of the room, onto the balcony, and then a shout, and then… nothing.

"You fell," said Crassus, "down the stairs. Luckily Flavius grabbed you and we were able to get away."

"Get away? From what?" he asked, his eyes still closed.

"Don't you remember? Father sent us to take care of those thugs who were threatening him."

"Thugs, ah, yes, but one of them was Silvanus."

There was silence. He opened his eyes. Crassus and Flavius were standing by the bed.

"*The* Silvanus?"

"I recognised him."

"But…"

"Milesia warned me. She said he was in Treviri. He must have followed me here."

Crassus swore.

"They let them go."

"Who?"

"The watch. Since it was only Braxus who got killed, they told the foreigners to get out of town at first light. The magistrates preferred it that way, better for business," said Flavius.

"We thought you were going to die," said Cassius.

"You've been knocked out for five days, totally out of it!" said Flavius. "Matty had to spoon gruel and water into your mouth to keep you going."

Now, when they mentioned it, Drusus began to recognise the feelings in his body, hunger and pain, and not necessarily in that order. And behind them, a faint feeling of relief.

"So he's gone?"

"Who?"

"Silvanus."

"If you say it was him. The man we took on was a big black bastard. You could hardly see him, stark naked in the dark. We were lucky to escape with our lives."

On the third day, Drusus got up from the bed and dressed. This is all too much, he thought. My enemies have taken everything from me, now even my dignity. This is no way to live, hunted from pillar to post. I deserve better. I deserve a home. I deserve a wife and children. The German promised me, and I'll take him up on the promise.

Before then he had other business to take care of. He searched through the house until he found a piece of vellum, one of Tullius' old business letters, and a scraper. Carefully he scraped the surface clean, smoothed out the vellum and took up his pen. It was better to keep the matter short. There would be fewer opportunities for misinterpretation.

> *My honoured Magister Apollinarius,*
> *Your daughter deserves a husband who has dignity and wealth. I promised you I would not abandon my family's cause. Our rights and our property have been stolen from us and I intend to ensure they are restored. I have taken a decision to travel to Rome to make my case in person. I shall return in the autumn.*
> *Your servant and future son, Drusus C. Astrebanus.*

◌ Chapter 13 ◌
Gaul

The weather changed suddenly after Amalric had ridden away. It was hot, very hot, almost better to sleep outside, under the bare skies, to catch a little of the breeze, but Anna had other ideas.

"I want a bit of privacy," she said, stripping off and lying naked in the hut.

"I'm not surprised," said Ophelia, standing by her mattress, looking down at her. She was no prude. That was impossible in the camp, and they had sat drying by the swimming hole in the other camp many times before. Sleeping outside would have been going too far, particularly considering the risk of mosquitoes and flies.

"Ophi, come and lie down with me, please. It's nice, just us two, without Amalric, without the children."

There was something in her tone that persuaded Ophelia to do as Anna wanted and stretch herself out beside her friend.

Anna put her arm around her.

"Thank you," she said and kissed her cheek. "For once it's so peaceful. I wish we could be like this forever."

Ophelia curled up with her back to Anna. Amalric's unpredictable moods and silences, his calculation, his talk of buying a farm, his sudden lengthy absence, preyed on her mind. She needed to think. The touch of Anna's body against hers was a reminder that she was not alone, a reminder that they both had children to think of as well as themselves, that she could not attempt to run alone, as she once had done, that she had ties that held her back. She felt Anna's hand on her thigh. She half turned and saw her friend's brown eyes looking back at her.

"Anna, you have me here, even though it's so hot. Amalric's away. Go to sleep now. We have a whole month without him, he said, even if that's not forever."

When Amalric returned he brought new gowns and new jewels for them. These were no gowns and no jewels he could have purchased in a provincial town like Autessiodurum, but he deflected every attempt to find out where he had been and what he had been doing there. They gladly wore them, for their own delight more than his.

Searching for roots and places where berries could be found in the autumn was a good excuse for Ophelia and Anna to disappear from the camp. They could talk and speculate about what Amalric might be planning, what they might do if he decided to leave the camp, matters which they could not discuss within earshot of the other women, their master or his cronies.

"I never had to search for food in the bakery," protested Anna, half-heartedly poking amongst the undergrowth with a sharpened stick, looking for wild onions, while Ophelia was supposed to be spotting trees which would bear nuts they could collect in the autumn before they returned to the winter camp.

Anna sat down on a fallen log.

"I don't mind doing practical things, keeping the hut clean, growing vegetables, cooking the food. It makes me feel useful. It keeps me busy. But digging for roots seems an awful lot of effort when it is so hot."

Ophelia had broken off her own search and sat down beside her.

"They taste nice, when we cook them," she pointed out, "but I was remembering the garden at the house where I grew up. All the plants and herbs were organised into little plots, so it was easy to find what you needed. I never really learned what the plants looked like, but I can still remember where all of them were."

"I'm not clever and thoughtful like you. I haven't had the schooling to be like that," said Anna. "I don't have a lot of nice things to remember from my life before I came here, like you do. Not that it helps much just now."

Ophelia frowned.

"I'm sure you had good times, too," she said, "and my life wasn't always so easy, now when I look back." She stood up. "Let's follow the path a little way. Aren't there some fields further on? Maybe we could find something to steal. We're robbers, after all!"

Anna threw the stick into the woods and joined her.

"I like listening when you recite the poems," she said as they meandered along the path, "and when you talk all strange in different tongues like a real lady. It's almost magic. It makes me dream of a different life than just being here in the camp. Do you think we could have a different life, if Amalric went away, or even if he took us with him?"

They were chatting and laughing so much that they came to the edge of the forest without intending to and found themselves looking out across the fields. Close by the crop was stunted by the shadow of the overhanging tress, so they decided to walk a little further in the hope of finding something that could be added to the cooking pot.

Amalric discouraged any temptation for the women in the group to approach the road, and Ophelia and Anna had never strayed this far before. But Amalric and the men had ridden off the previous day and he was far from their thoughts, and his warning slipped their minds. The path carried on beside the trees, and they were inquisitive, so they followed it until they reached the road.

As they stood on the edge of the wood, Ophelia began to feel a strange sensation take hold of her. She suddenly stopped and fell silent. She began to glance from left to right, and then she stepped out into the middle of the road, staring along it as it disappeared amongst the trees. The road stretched out before her, like the road in her memory, the one she travelled along in her nightmares. She grabbed hold of Anna's hand and began to walk along in the middle of the highway, pulling her friend reluctantly behind her. Soon the trees formed high walls on either side, bending over, almost cutting out the light. Ophelia walked as if she were in a dream. She was no longer conscious that she was holding Anna's hand, not even that Anna was beside her. Instead, she was seated in a wagon, rolling along the road, her brother and husband riding horses in front. Her father at the rear, with his servant. Two small children, silent and anxious, gripping tight to the luggage piled behind.

Suddenly Ophelia halted and began to stare around, her eyes blank.

"What's the matter, Ophi?" whispered Anna, breaking the silence. "I'm frightened. Is there something wrong?"

"Shh, my darlings, I can hear horses," said Ophelia in a far-away voice.

"Ophi, are you ill? Do you feel dizzy?" There was panic in Anna's voice. "You're not going to fall down and start shaking and foaming at the mouth like the crazy girl I once saw growing up?"

Ophelia's eyes travelled back and forward, as if she were looking for something. In her mind she was still on the wagon, hearing the sound of horses' hooves approaching. She desperately tried to see the men they had hired in the town, but they seemed to have vanished into thin air. Then the vision clouded over; she could see nothing. She just felt arms holding her and someone whispering in her ear.

"It's all right, Ophi, it's all right. You're safe, you're safe with me."

She looked around again, and there was only the open road ahead, with trees stretching on around a slight curve, and the arms holding her belonged to a round-faced, brown-eyed woman, her eyes glistening with tears.

"Oh, Anna," she said, lifting her hands to her face and covering her eyes. "Oh, Anna, it was here, right here, that it happened."

"What are you talking about, Ophi? You sound unwell, like you do sometimes in your sleep. I've heard you cry out, tossing and turning."

Ophelia was staring once again up the road. She could have sworn she had heard horses, but none came.

"Is there something I can do, Ophi, that will help you?"

"It was here, Anna," she whispered, "where Amalric and his band attacked my family. I've seen this place in my dreams, but I didn't know where it was, or even why I saw it, but now I know. Whatever happened to my father and mother, my husband, my children, it happened right here. Where could they be, Anna?" she asked plaintively, staring down the empty road.

"I don't know what to do, my darling Ophi." Anna was crying. "Have you gone mad? Have you been touched by the sun while we were walking?"

"No," said Ophelia, her voice calm, "no, something awful happened here. I can feel it, but I can't remember. I don't know what it was."

She turned to the tearful Anna.

"Let's say a prayer together," she said. "We can pray that one day we can still find them. That one day the memory will come back, and I *will* know. Let's make a little cross beside the road in memory of my family. Perhaps when people passing see it, they'll wonder who it was made for and give them a thought."

While Ophelia found two straight pieces of wood, Anna gathered together a bunch of summer flowers, and some lengths of tough grass to plait into a string. The two women bound the wood together into a rough cross which they planted at the edge of the trees. Then they made a garland of the flowers, which they placed around it. They grasped each other's hands and knelt and prayed. Ophelia prayed for her family, for those she believed she had lost, and especially her children. Anna prayed to the Christian God and every other god she could think of that Ophelia would return to the happy, laughing version of herself that she had been just a short while before.

The women stood up and climbed back across the ditch to the roadway, where they remained for a moment, brushing dirt from their clothes. Then they turned their backs on the fateful corner, on the little memorial they had created, and began to pick their way through the trees towards the path. They had only gone a little way when they heard a sound on the road.

"Now there really are horses coming," said Anna in a whisper.

Then there were voices, men's voices.

Ophelia felt her chest tighten, her heart began to race and her blood pound. She could hardly breathe.

"Suppose it's ghosts or spirits," she muttered. "Supposing I prayed too hard, and now God has sent a messenger. What shall we do?"

"Suppose it's Amalric," said Anna, rather more practically. "If he finds us here, he'll be furious, especially after what you just told me. We should never have come this far."

She pulled at Ophelia, who stared half-bewitched towards the road, pulling her back amongst the trees. They crouched down and peered out. Three men came riding along, serious and stern men, armed with swords and spears.

"It's certainly not Amalric," whispered Anna, giving the men a careful examination through the undergrowth, while trying to calm Ophelia, who was shaking and ashen faced, "and they look too solid to be spirits."

The men's clothes, their hair and beards were trimmed in the Roman style. One of them was dark-skinned. There was no one like that in Amalric's gang. Ophelia stared at them between the stems of a bush. They were the first Romans she had seen since that tragic day she had just recalled. She stood up, almost as if she were going to reveal herself, although Anna was clutching at her tunic, trying to make her hide. She watched the horsemen come nearer. Should she call out? She felt an almost irresistible urge to run towards them, but Anna was holding her tightly. She could almost feel the cry for help forming in her mouth, but it died away unuttered. Her eyes followed the three men as they trotted by, just a few yards away, and disappeared up the road. She stood like a statue as the sound of the horses faded away into the distance.

"Come, Ophelia. It's dangerous. Let's go home before Amalric finds out where we've been," said Anna, pulling at her. And the two women turned, drained of emotion, and started to pick their way among the trees until they found the path that led back to the camp.

❧ Chapter 14 ☙
Gaul

Amalric and the men returned the following day, burdened with plunder, goods they could sell, food and drink. They were very pleased with themselves. The tip-off they had received had been faultless, a fat caravan of merchants and their families. The bandits' horses were laden, and they had with them packhorses and riding horses which they had taken from the travellers they had ambushed and slaughtered on the Lugdunum road.

Ophelia was nearly sick as Amalric boasted of their success. She and Anna must have been on the same road, at almost the time that Amalric and his band had been doing their evil deeds. Amalric claimed they had taken the convoy completely by surprise, and none of the band had even been injured. Surely the three Romans she had seen would have put up a fight. They were well armed, and they looked like they knew how to use their weapons. Even if they had died, they would have gone down fighting. She examined the horses the bandits had captured. Did any of them look like the ones the three Romans had been riding? She did not want to feel that more of her people had been dying on that stretch of road, though she felt a slight twinge of guilt. She had not given a thought to the people who had actually died, whom Amalric was boasting of killing, only the three strangers.

Despite his boasting, Amalric's survival depended on an equal measure of reckless ferocity and caution, and he decided to lie low for a few days and see if there was any reaction to the ambush. When there were no alarms, he and the men loaded the booty onto the captured horses and set off to town to sell it.

"We need to offload this stuff," said Amalric. "We'll be away for a few days. We can't risk being seen in Autessiodurum or Tricasses, so we'll cut across country to Senones. Everyone must stay in camp until we are back," he added. "It's possible that a search party will be sent out, and I don't want them finding you."

Anna and Ophelia huddled together, holding one another, their thoughts on Ophelia's vision, of the realisation that they had been on the Lugdunum road just as Amalric had been engaged in assaulting a group of innocent travellers.

But there was more than that. Ophelia was unusually lost in thought. The appearance of the three horse riders had reminded her of her previous life, that it was not a dream that she was the daughter of the governor of a province, that once she was a rich woman. She felt torn apart. One half of her told her she should have tried to escape. She should have called out to the riders. The other half warned her it would be futile. How could she leave without Lanius? Anna would not have come, could not have come with her. Anna would have remained behind to face Amalric's wrath. Ophelia knew she could not leave Anna and Fredagunda behind, but how could they all escape together, assuming Anna even wanted to escape? Sometimes Anna sounded as if she enjoyed the life with Amalric, would be ready to follow him wherever he went, yet at other times she sounded very different, as if there was something else on her mind that she could not quite say to Ophelia.

Where would they go? She had to find out what had happened to her family. Her brother was in Arelate. Perhaps if she could make her way to Arelate, she could find him, but where was Arelate? She knew they had been travelling south, so the city must be somewhere further south, but how far, and how to get there with no money and no transport? It seemed impossible unless she found help. She had seen her reflection in the lake. She was no longer Ophelia Ursina, citizen of Verulamium, daughter of Governor Publius Julius Ursinus. She looked like a peasant, dressed like a peasant. No one would believe her. Supposing she had called out to the three men, how did she know they would treat her in the way she hoped? And not all men meant well. Even rich men could behave no better than Amalric if they got their hands on a good-looking peasant woman.

Anna turned to Ophelia and whispered into her ear.

"I took one of my favourite brooches and walked down to the washing lake today. I stood on the edge and threw the brooch as far as I could. I offered for us, Ophi. I made a prayer to the old gods to match the one we offered to the Christian God by the side of the road. I prayed that we would find a way out of this, that we would find a place where we would be safe, together."

Ophelia snuggled a little closer; there were tears in her eyes. Had she heard correctly?

"You mean, Anna, that you really want to leave?" she whispered, almost frightened to say the words aloud, even to Anna.

"I'm tired of these men," said Anna. "I know what they are. In the end they're just cruel and nasty. I know they could turn against us if they thought we were doing wrong. I want a decent life, Ophi. I want Fredagunda to grow up as a normal child, not in a robber's camp. Despite what happened before, I just believe our lives could be different and better if we could get away together. That's what I prayed for."

Ophelia struggled not to sniff and reveal her feelings to Anna, the thoughts that had been tumbling through her mind, her calculation that all the prayer in the world would not help them unless something changed, and then slowly, slowly, she was overtaken by sleep.

On the following day the men returned. They looked grave, but they brought with them a cargo of food, drink and enough silver coins to ensure that no one would go hungry during the winter. They called the women together. They were uneasy. The people they knew in Senones, the ones they trusted, had said that there had been men enquiring, asking a lot of questions, checking records at the hostels, interrogating the guards. One result was evident: the inquisitive strangers had stirred up the authorities.

"The bishop's been preaching against the iniquities of the bandits. Christian men and women should be able to travel the roads of the Empire in peace. Something has to be done, the old fool had said," grumbled Amalric. "What's it all about, I wonder? Nothing, probably. This kind of uproar has blown up previously and dribbled out into nothing." He shrugged, downing a mug of ale. "Of course, there's always the risk that they'll take the whole matter seriously, and if they do, that'll be very inconvenient."

Amalric knew. He'd hung plenty of bandits himself in his time.

The depressed mood in the bandit camp did not last. Such moods seldom did. A few days later – Ophelia had long given up counting the days, so she could not say exactly how many – Amalric interrupted her and Anna while they were grinding corn.

"I'll have an important visitor coming tomorrow," he announced. "I want a special feast prepared for him. Anna, you must organise the women to do their very best."

"Will you want me to serve?" asked Ophelia.

Often when Amalric had special visitors, other bandit chiefs or the corrupt merchants from neighbouring towns who bought his stolen goods, he demanded she dress up in Roman clothes, wear polished sandals, and Anna would braid her hair, Roman-style. It amused Amalric and flattered his guests when she served them. He liked to see her dressed in her finery, and his guests imagined themselves a lot better than they actually were. Now he had bought her new clothes she thought this would be an occasion when he would want to show her off, but he was curt.

"You're to stay out of sight, Ophelia. Anna will serve. You'll remain inside the hut and don't show yourself under any circumstances."

His abrupt dismissal only made her more curious. Who was this prestigious guest, so sensitive that Amalric wasn't prepared to play his usual games? Why did he order her to hide so vehemently? She kept her thoughts to herself then and during the following day, as she helped Anna and the other women to prepare the feast. Eventually, as evening fell and the men began to assemble, Anna urged her into the hut.

"Do as he says," she implored. "He seems so nervous. I've not seen him like this for a long time."

Ophelia closed the door as Anna left, but she was careful to leave a gap so she could peek out. Shortly, she was rewarded by the sight of Amalric striding to his place at the leader's table, followed by a trio of strangers. Their clothes betrayed that they were Romans, or at least imagined they were. From the hut it was impossible to see any details of the visitors or hear what was being said over the laughter and shouts of the feast. However, after a while Amalric stood to offer a toast to the visitors. The men and women around the fires quietened down. They listened to his words of welcome and cheered. Then it was time for the guest to reply. A quiet, if not quite silence, spread through the clearing as the young Roman got slowly to his feet. From her hiding place Ophelia could see him more clearly, pale and dark haired, though in the jumping light of the fires, the smoke wafting across the clearing, she could not make out his features clearly.

He raised his glass, looking at Amalric.

"To my comrades in arms, good health and the blessings of the gods," he announced in a strong voice which carried across the encampment. It was not his words that surprised Ophelia, but his accent. He was not a Roman, not a real Roman, not a Gaul, one of the locals, but a Briton, one of her own people. And even in those few words she could tell he was speaking Latin, clear, educated Latin, the language you only spoke if you belonged to a certain class in society, the class that she had once belonged to.

What was a man like that doing in a bandit encampment? She stared at him through the gap in the doorway as he stood beaming around the gathering, his glass held high. He was not one of her family, not even someone she knew well, but there was something about him that seemed familiar, a vague memory deep in her mind. Supposing this stranger would know her from her past? That would not be surprising, given his age and style of dress. That would be why Amalric had ordered her to hide. The visitor might recognise her, even in her humbled and altered state. Supposing, even if he did not know her, he might be willing to help someone from his own province, so cruelly held by the bandits? Her curiosity had already been high, but now it became unbearable. She had passed up the opportunity to approach the three strange horsemen. She could not simply hide and let this chance escape as well, but she could not be rash, defy Amalric in front of his men. If she was going to reach out to the stranger then it would have to be done carefully, stealthily, and only once she was sure it would be safe to do so. But first she had to get a better look at him. If there was a risk he would recognise her, then there was a good chance she would recognise him, and if she knew who he was, then she would know how likely he would be to help her.

She waited until the man had sat down and the noise of the feast rose again, and then she pushed the door aside and quietly slipped out into the shadows. She did not dare think what would happen if she were caught sneaking around in direct disobedience to Amalric's orders. She doubted even she, his favourite, would be spared his anger, but she had an overwhelming desire to get a better look at this mysterious Briton.

She was not so foolhardy as to show herself amongst the people sharing the feast. They probably did not realise she had been told to hide herself and would have greeted her loudly. Instead she slid back along the wall of the hut, thanking God that the noise of the party would cover the sound of any breaking twigs or stones rattling underfoot. From the back of the hut, she turned and walked into the forest. The gloom amongst the trees was dispelled intermittently by the shifting flames from the fires, so she could see her way. Once she was sure she was far enough off, she began a long trek around the woods, all the while praying that Amalric did not change his mind and suddenly call for her.

No, she thought, he did not need to impress his British guest with a half-feral Roman woman. The man she had seen was far too well-dressed and well-spoken to fall for that illusion, unlike the local establishment. And even then, though he might not be impressed by her appearance, as soon as she opened her mouth she would be revealed, and there would be questions and answers, and Britannia wasn't such a large place – two and two might easily make four or even five, for good or ill. And Amalric might be bluffing that the only words he knew of British were vulgarities.

For seemingly ages, she threaded her way among the trees, stopping now and then to ensure that no one had been alerted to her progress. Fortunately they were all too interested in the food and drink, the same food and drink that had been bought with the loot taken from the travellers just a short time before. Had Amalric known the guest would come already then? Is that why he had carried out the raid in the first place? Someone began to play on a pipe, and soon there was a drum accompaniment, and to her relief the sound of the feast grew louder.

At last she reached a point in the forest directly behind the high table, where Amalric sat beside the guest. Anna was serving wine, bending over the guest and her master, her breasts nearly bursting from her low-cut gown. At least that would keep them distracted, thought Ophelia sourly. Slowly and carefully she made her way from tree to tree until she stood just a few paces from the two men. It was difficult to make out their words, but she dared not move any closer. She held her breath and listened.

Amalric laughed. To Ophelia it felt like he was standing next to her, that at any moment, he would turn his head and look straight into her eyes. She only heard one sentence of their conversation, but it was enough.

"Don't worry, Drusus, it'll be waiting for you when you return."

Her eyes were opened. She knew who the stranger was. She could see the outline of his father in his face: Drusus Astrebanus, the son of Cassius Astrebanus, her father's enemy. Her breath almost failed her, and she had to take a step back and lean against the tree, placing the trunk between her and the feast. No wonder Amalric had hidden her away, she realised with horror. Drusus Astrebanus would recognise her immediately, and it did not matter what was his motive for being in the bandit camp, she would be in desperate trouble if he saw her. Feelings of panic began to wash over her. Her chest was heaving as she struggled to breathe. She began to feel faint. How stupid she had been to creep out into the night!

She forced herself to take a deep breath, and then another. After a moment, her head began to feel a little better. Slowly she began to creep back into the shadows. She was shivering and terrified as she circled around the clearing to her own hut. Well inside, she threw herself down on the bed, gasping, clutching at her arms in an attempt to comfort herself.

How strange that he, Drusus Astrebanus, was sitting at the table with a bandit chief as if it were the most natural thing to do in the world, and she, Ophelia Ursina, was creeping through the woods, with dirty feet and ragged clothes like a savage. She was unable to suppress an almost hysterical laugh. And then she stopped, frozen by a thought. What, in fact, was Drusus Astrebanus doing here in Amalric's camp, sharing a meal, laughing and joking with him, staring at Anna's breasts while Amalric looked on complacently? What was their relationship? The Astrebani had been her father's rivals. She had known that as a child. She knew her father had hoped that her sister would marry the older brother, Vitellus. But then Hypatia had refused, and her father had given way to her desires, and she had married Marcus Silvanus. That would scarcely have pleased Vitellus, or his younger brother, unless, of course, after their father had died so suddenly, they had not wanted the families united. Amalric gave all the appearance that Drusus was an ally, a partner – in crime – if not a friend. In crime… in the crime… She had not come to Amalric's camp because she was sick, because she had been abandoned. That assumption, that convenient rational-isation she had abandoned long ago, and the feeling that had come over her on the road, she recognised it now, primed by the appearance of this enemy of her family. Something awful had happened, and Amalric had been involved, and she knew his way of life and his habits well enough to guess what that could have been. He had attacked her family the way he had attacked the travellers on the road just a short time before, and somehow, it was just too much to be a coincidence. Drusus Astrebanus was involved, but how and what had happened, and how had she survived?

☙ Chapter 15 ❧
In the same place, at the same time

Drusus' gaze wandered around the encampment. He, at least, was sitting at a crude table, on a stump of log. Most of the bandits were sprawled on the ground, clustered around campfires. Somewhere out in the dancing orange shadows were the two men, retainers of the merchant Tullius, he had hired to accompany him, taking the opportunity for food and drink and maybe a girl to lie with. Perhaps they were among the group to his left who were laughing and cheering, or the other, over to his right, tearing at a roasted carcass. This life in the woods might be all right for Amalric, he thought. Amalric had grown up in the wilderness. He was used to it. One overnight halt will be quite sufficient for me, he thought.

Drusus' mind wandered away from the encampment to his home, the Agridurnum Estate overlooking the gentle grass slopes of southern Britannia; to the feasts his father had organised, May Day, Harvest Home, Saturnalia; the bonfires in the outer courtyard, the players, the dancing, old and young together. He felt his stomach clench, gripped by a sudden anger. His home and lands had been stolen, his brother cut down in cold blood. He should not need to be hiding in a forest in Gaul, the guest of a bandit, surrounded by men who were no better than thieves and women no better than sluts.

I should have been living in the Villa Verdaris, thought Drusus as he chewed on a mouthful of half-cooked venison. Not

Marcus Silvanus, and that treacherous hussy Hypatia Ursina. And Vitellus, he should have been governor of Britannia, from the palace in Londinium. The emperor had promised it. The emperor had recognised who were the true leaders of Britannia. Well, that jumped-up provincial's day of reckoning will come, thought Drusus, just as soon as I reach Rome with the news and find the help I need.

There was a burst of laughter from around him which lifted him out of his reverie. A buxom young woman was serving meat, her tunic cut so low that her breasts were barely covered. She whispered something to Amalric and he patted her on the rear.

"More meat?" said his host, as the young woman sidled around and nudged up against him. "There's no shortage here."

"I suppose," said Drusus, trying to keep a note of disparagement out of his voice, "there's no shortage. We're in the middle of a forest, after all."

Amalric laughed.

"Excellent hunting, plenty of meat, eh, Anna," he added, patting the young woman on the rear again.

She bent over to serve Drusus. He turned away, once more surveying the encampment. He had expected the bandit group to be a strictly male preserve, like a military camp, but there seemed to be no shortage of women, laughing, drinking, flirting, jumping up and fetching and carrying.

Amalric must have noticed the direction of his gaze.

"You want a companion for later, Drusus? You think you can manage that, if you don't drink too much of this excellent wine I took from the bishop's vineyard?"

Drusus turned to the bandit and shook his head. He did not want one of the half-drunk peasant women. He did not want to lie with one of them on a dirty bed in a wooden shack, or perhaps even worse, out in the open air. There was only one woman in his future, Bryna Apollinaria, and he was enduring this journey because he needed to make it for her.

He remembered her in Agridurnum, a thin little girl then, merely one of Milesia's companions. He had not taken much note of her to begin with. She had just been a child. There was something about her that had grown on him. She was, after all, Apollinarius the lawyer's daughter, a respectable young woman in fact, a very suitable companion, and her father had evidently thought so too. Now, when he had seen her again, she had filled out, grown into a woman, someone who would grace Verdaris, whom he would have been proud to be seen with on the streets of Corinium, intelligent, not really what you would call beautiful, but easy on his eyes and with a warm look in hers, a kind tone to her voice. She was just the type of woman he needed.

"More wine?" said Amalric, pushing a flagon towards him. "You seem very thoughtful."

"I was reflecting on luck, on Fortuna," said Drusus. "She is such a fickle mistress. We should all beware of relying on her too much."

"I try to avoid it," said Amalric. "I try to pick fights when the odds are heavily in my favour."

"It's not fighting I was thinking of," said Drusus, "it was love."

"The same principle applies," said Amalric.

Perhaps if your ambitions are no higher than a peasant girl, thought Drusus, but mine, at least, are higher. As for fighting, he had seen what that achieved. His brother had picked a fight with Silvanus, taken twenty of the best men, and he had lost – God knows how, but he had lost, not just the fight but his life. And he, himself, he had hardly done better. He had stumbled into a brawl because he was helping his friends, and it had almost cost him his life, and at the hands of the same man. Perhaps that was a characteristic that he and the bandit shared. They both preferred fights with the odds in their favour. It was simply that Amalric relied on his sword, and he, Drusus, trusted his wits and his training. The law, when you learned how to use it, was as effective as a sword, just as deadly, and with far less risk to yourself. His enemy, Marcus Silvanus, evidently understood that, but he doubted Amalric would.

Out among the shadows and flickering flames, the drum and the pipe had become louder, more frenetic. A dance had begun, men and women assembled in a ring, twisting about each other, clapping in time to the rhythm. Drusus watched, almost hypnotised.

"Women," he said to no one in particular, "you just can't trust them."

Amalric laughed. He found it easy to laugh apparently, even though living in a foul mud-pit in the middle of endless woods, thought Drusus.

"You're a fool if you trust men either," said the bandit.

There were few men he could trust, thought Drusus, and those he did… he only had to look around him to see where that could lead, and worse. He had been forced to flee from Apollinarius' house, and just when he thought he had a safe refuge with Tullius, fate had caught up with him. And what about Milesia and her threats? He had to trust the lawyer would stand by his word, but his sister-in-law, why had she put herself in his way? Didn't she see that her chance to escape from exile depended on his success?

"You can't trust anybody these days," he said, "not even family."

He must have let his emotions show in his face, because when he turned he saw Amalric scrutinising him.

"Oh, you can trust me, Drusus," said Amalric, quickly. "Your brother trusted me, and I didn't let him down."

"And the hoard?"

"The hoard's where I buried it. Only I know the place, and tomorrow, before you leave, I'll show you where it is, just as I promised. Don't worry, Drusus, it'll be waiting for you when you return."

It had better be, thought Drusus.

"Very well, but how can I be sure of how much is there?"

"You don't trust my calculation?" smiled Amalric. "Better not, perhaps. I didn't get the schooling that some others did."

That's enough, thought Drusus, the drink is starting to go to our heads.

"Time to call it a day, Amalric," Drusus said. The dance had come to an end; the dancers collapsed into a laughing heap and, sweating from their efforts, called for more wine and ale. "I had a long ride today and I have further to go tomorrow."

"Are you sure you wouldn't like company for the night?" asked the bandit again.

"Quite sure," said Drusus. The memory of the fall down the stairs, waking in Tullius' house, the pain and humiliation, the drums and the shouting had brought on a headache. He needed rest, he needed sleep, he needed all his energy directed towards one purpose: revenge.

❧ Chapter 16 ☙
In the same place, on the following day

The visitors left at around midday. Amalric had been asleep when Ophelia woke, but she did not dare to leave the hut. A little later, when the sun had risen, there were noises from outside as people began to stir. Now Amalric woke, shook himself and glanced down at Ophelia. He saw she was awake.

"Stay here," he said, "until I say you can come out."

Ophelia now understood she had good reason to obey him without any protests. She heard a yawn from Anna, who stretched her arms above her head, rolled onto her side and smiled across to Ophelia.

"I could really go on sleeping," she said, "but I'll go out and fetch you some food, Ophi. Wait a moment." She got to her feet, straightened her robe and followed their master out into the open air. She was gone a long time it seemed to Ophelia, and when she came back, she was a little flushed and breathing heavily.

"Are you all right?" asked Ophelia.

"Yes," said Anna, abruptly, and placed down a couple of oat cakes and some water. "They're just getting ready to leave. You can probably come out before too long."

Ophelia could hear laughter, loud voices outside in the camp, and after a while Amalric returned with a grunt to Ophelia that she should go out and help with tidying up the remains of the feast. Then he turned and called crossly through the door for Anna to come back.

"I don't want to lie here alone, woman."

Anna came running, flushed with anger at Amalric's tone, meeting Ophelia's eyes for a moment as she brushed past her.

The camp was quiet as Ophelia made her way among the smouldering hearths, the half-chewed bones and discarded flasks. She was left to consider her new knowledge, that Amalric's guest had been Drusus Astrebanus. Her dreams had been confused. She had woken several times with the impression that her mind was trying to arrange all sorts of pieces of information, like a worried housewife trying to arrange shards to repair a broken pot, and that no matter how she tried, though they should, the fragments would not fit together. After a while, she gave up her tidying and sat down on a log, beside the embers of an extinguished fire. She had not been sitting long when she heard a rustle, and Anna dropped down beside her.

"He's fallen asleep, and the way he was yesterday, I don't think he'll be awake for a while," she sniffed. "There was really no need for him to be so mean."

Ophelia studied her friend. How much did she trust her? Enough to tell her what was in her heart? She glanced up to make sure no one else was nearby and could overhear.

"I recognised him," she said at last, in a quiet voice. She felt Anna lean against her.

"Who?" Anna whispered, her lips against Ophelia's ear.

Ophelia turned towards her friend, their faces almost touching.

"The man, the visitor."

Anna did not move.

"I know who he is," Ophelia repeated.

"Who is he?"

"My father's old enemy… and mine."

Anna was still and silent for a moment, and then she spoke almost inaudibly.

"I followed them. They went out of the camp together this morning, Amalric and the stranger, down the path towards the pond. I followed after them."

Ophelia turned back to the ashes of the fire, feeling her brows furrowing almost involuntarily.

"What did they do?"

"Nothing to begin with. They walked a way down the path and then stood for a while, pointing and talking."

"And then?"

"Then they walked off the path, towards the forest, and stood again, looking at the ground. Then they returned to the camp, but I didn't. I hid, and after they had gone, I walked down to the place where they had been standing."

Ophelia felt Anna's breathing, heavy, almost panting, against her ear.

"Their pointing began to make sense. There's a large stone and a tree beside the path. It was those they had been discussing, and they had walked out to a place just beyond them. I could make out their footsteps in the earth."

"Did you hear what they were saying?"

"No, but I know something even better. Follow me, quickly, now," said Anna, glancing around, "and I'll show you."

Suddenly she was no longer there, no longer crouched beside her. Ophelia stood up. Anna was already halfway towards the edge of the woods, but not in the direction of the pond. Ophelia followed after her, caught up to her once they were hidden from sight.

"Where are we going?"

"Shh, just follow me."

The two women began a long circle around the camp, further even away than the one Ophelia had taken the night before, until they overlooked the path to the pond.

"There's where they stood," whispered Anna as they squatted behind a low bush, "and there's the stone and the tree I mentioned. Now come with me."

They quickly crossed the path, and slipping among the trees on the other side, began another long, concealed circle that brought them to a point midway between the two landmarks. Anna turned her back to the path and began to pace away into the woods. Suddenly she stopped and dropped to her haunches. Ophelia slowly followed after her.

"Here, here's where they were standing… and look, there's something strange."

She glanced up once again to make sure no one was coming, then reached down to the ground and began to brush back and forth with her hand. The soil was loose, and she easily pushed it aside. She looked up at Ophelia bending over her, then she made another sweeping movement with her hand. There was a glint of metal, dulled but recognisable. Anna swept again. Ophelia recognised the motif, Bacchus, the god of wine, with a bunch of grapes in his hand.

"Enough, Anna," she said with a shudder. "Cover it over, cover it over and let's get away. If he sees us here, he'll kill both of us."

Anna brushed the earth back into the small hole she had dug and then lightly drew her hand across it. She doubted Amalric would see that someone had disturbed the earth, and if he did notice, it could have easily been a curious wild animal.

The two women made their way back to the path and then turned towards the camp. There was nothing unusual about them emerging together from the forest, walking back from the pond, not even their silence, the serious looks on their faces. Nearly everyone felt grim, and looked worse, after the night of feasting.

Ophelia said nothing about what she had seen, but she had seen enough.

Anna said nothing about what they had seen, but she, too had seen enough. She reached for Ophelia's hand and squeezed it to signal that they shared a secret, but Ophelia's mind was elsewhere.

♋ Chapter 17 ♌
The Lugdunum Road

Drusus was well on the way south by the time the sun began its descent through the trees. The two hired men followed him. All three of them let their horses choose their own pace. Drusus still felt uneasy after the meeting with Amalric. The others were suffering from the after-effects of the feast. It would have been foolish to quarrel with the bandit. He was just about to take a long journey, and Amalric could easily dig up the treasure and vanish before he was back. They had to trust one another and stick to the deal Amalric had made with Vito. Half of the buried wealth belonged to Amalric, and half to the Astrebani, to be retrieved in an emergency, and only when enough time had passed that no one would suspect where the coins had come from or recognise the origin of the objects.

Amalric had kept his word so far. The details of the ambush had been kept quiet, despite attempts by nosy individuals to dig them out – dig them up might be more appropriate, thought Drusus. There were only a few people who knew that the attack was anything more than a regular robbery. Of these, Radagus, Amalric's deputy, had been paid off and taken the hint to move elsewhere. Another man, Amalric had recounted, had been talking too much in the taverns of Autessiodurum, and he had been found in the morning floating in the Icauna River, his tongue cut out. That seemed to have been sufficient to ensure further silence, Amalric assured him. Drusus hoped that it was.

He did not have the means to confront the bandit leader if he did break his word, and Drusus knew Amalric well enough to understand that if he tried any trickery himself, Drusus Astrebanus could be the next man dredged up from some waterway.

He remained uneasy because he was unsure exactly what was buried in the pit behind Amalric's camp. Of course it had not made sense to start digging to check. Who might come trotting down the path, who might be watching? The fewer people who knew that a fortune was buried in the woods behind Amalric's camp the better. Nonetheless, what exactly was half of an unknown whole? It sounded like a problem for the philosophers to chew on, though it had worrying practical implications. Vito's sources had been equivocal about how much Publius Julius Ursinus had been carrying with him, and Amalric had provided vague justifications over the intervening time concerning the need to pay off members of the band who had participated in the ambush. He had to trust Amalric's assurance, but even bandits grew old and tired, and he was increasingly concerned that Amalric was beginning to fall into that category.

Supposing he was unable to recover Agridurnum? How much would an estate cost, he wondered, in Belgica? Were there citizens still anxious after the barbarian raids, still fearing further wild hordes piling over the Rhenus as they had a few years before, still ready to sell their farms for whatever they were offered? He would need a town house, too, within easy distance of the forum, in Remis or Treviri, where he could meet clients, maybe do a little trading. A woman like Bryna would expect silk and jewels, and he would need good horses, for himself and his sons. Such luxuries cost money. Nonetheless, however much the bandit had stuffed away, it would never be sufficient to expunge the humiliation he had suffered at the hands of Silvanus. To eradicate that feeling would take more than gold and silver.

Drusus dozed in the warmth of the sun, rocked by the gentle pace of the horse. When the animal missed its step where a chunk of the road surface had worked loose, it jerked him back to the present. Drusus felt the leather cylinder tapping against his thigh. Though it was unprepossessing in appearance, he knew it should be worth more than all the silver buried between the tree and the stone to the right person at the right moment. But how quickly that could change he knew very well. He had carried a similar set of documents to Corinium, to confront Silvanus directly. Hypatia Ursina had burned them in front of his eyes. Vito had been apoplectic.

"I'll get even with that bitch," he had shouted. Well, he never had. In fact, you could say, if you considered the matter carefully – and, on a long horse ride, Drusus had time to do that – the bitch had got even with them. An eye for an eye, a tooth for a tooth, a fortune for a fortune, a father for a father, and now a brother for a brother. The Ursini and the Astrebani were equally balanced, but he intended to shift the reckoning in his favour. The leather cylinder attached to his saddle contained a second set of debt letters, "pay the carrier in silver or gold", with the stamp of Publius Julius Ursinus, Governor of Britannia Prima, and they were the ones he planned to use to confront the governor's son, Gaius. He must have laid his hands on the share of Publius Julius' treasure that was not buried by Amalric's camp, the share that Vito's sources said had been sent ahead, by sea. Even so, he doubted whether Publius Julius' son would be able to repay one tenth of the amount he was carrying, but he could be forced into compliance, into some payment. He would not want to lose face with his masters.

But those were not the only documents in the cylinder. He also had a copy of his brother's petition, the one that had led to his nomination as governor. The emperor's authority had been defied. Now he would present the case in person, to the Senate and people of Rome, or at least the emperor and his court. He had a copy of the letter which had been sent to Vito, a copy which Milesia had managed to scribble down the day after they received the original. It was rough and ready. Vito had intended to send the copy to their town house in Londinium, ready for posting in the forum, but it would suffice as evidence. He had also written speeches, practised them over and over again until his rhetoric was polished. He was no Cicero, he knew that, but the authorities in Rome would have to listen.

When he was done with Gaius Ursinus, when he had obtained the recognition from Rome, he would return to Britannia and claim his rights, backed up by the emperor, the force of law and the might of the Empire. Once he had finished with Hypatia and her husband, he could afford to ignore Milesia. Then she would be dependent on his good will. He chuckled to himself. *She's always been just a little too clever for my taste,* he thought, *and it would serve her right to have to do my bidding. I'll marry Bryna and have a horde of children and live happily ever after. Maybe the tables will turn sufficiently that Milesia will have to return to Agridurnum and take care of them.* But first things first, it all depends on the other pieces falling into place.

Drops of rain began to fall. He felt them first on his face, and then dampening his hair. *Gods,* he thought to himself, *how difficult everything has become.* He reached around to the bag slung over the horse behind him and pulled out a broad-brimmed hat, straightened it the best he could then stuffed it onto his head and pushed it firmly down. The last thing he wanted was a gust of wind to take it and blow it away.

There was a sudden sound from the man riding beside him. Drusus looked up. A little way ahead, a break in the trees through the drizzle, the linear shape of a building — their lodging for the night. How he hated these lodgings, day after day, these endless miles of road, but soon, soon there would be an end.

❧ Chapter 18 ☙
Gaul

It had not been simply bad luck, thought Ophelia, that her family had fallen into the hands of the bandits. The pieces began to drop into place, like small coloured stones in a mosaic – first a jumble, small heaps, neat but separate. Then, in the hands of a master, a picture begins to emerge. In this case it was the picture of a monster, a many-armed monster, but with how many heads? Ophelia sat by herself, on the stone by the path leading down to the pond. Behind her, she knew, lay the buried treasure. She would have loved to take those few more paces, to scrape away the earth again and confirm what she had glanced, but it was too risky. In any case, in her heart she knew it was unnecessary. She had seen enough when Anna had dug in the soil and exposed the corner of the drinking vessel. It was not just that she had recognised the figure of Bacchus. It was the small, almost unnoticeable mark that lay a little further down the sliver of metal that Anna had unearthed, her father's mark, her family's mark. The buried silver was her father's silver.

Drusus Astrebanus had no need to see what was buried. He knew it was there. Elementary logic led to the conclusion that Drusus Astrebanus must have been involved in the attack. Her family had been fugitives, running away, and now she had a better idea of whom they had been fleeing from. Now she knew why they had not been guests at any friendly houses during their journey. Her father must have already feared the Astrebani, and quite rightly if they had been ready to participate in highway robbery. She also thought she now understood why Amalric had been so adamant that she should keep hidden. She was stolen goods, just like the silver and other treasure, but stolen goods that Amalric wanted to keep for himself. If he had seen her Drusus would surely recognise her, and he would want to know what she was doing there. He would have seen that Amalric had broken his word, that he could no longer trust the bandit. Drusus would have his own ideas about what should happen to her. Perhaps he would have demanded to take her away, to ransom, to threaten the rest of her family, or even just have her killed as an inconvenient witness to his wrongdoing. Instead, for his own gratification, his own strange purposes, Amalric had kept her hidden, safe, if you could call it that, given the price he had exacted on her body and on her soul.

She stood up, glanced behind her and then turned and watched as Anna came up the path from the pond with a heap of washing. She felt a new determination to survive until she could get away, though she had no idea what she would do if she succeeded. Time would tell. Just now survival was everything. Just now she might know more, might understand more, but what was she going to do with that knowledge? She could not confront Amalric directly. That would reveal what she knew. Worse, it might throw suspicion on Anna. Amalric could be unpredictable, despite all his soft words for both of them. Patience, patience was of the essence.

She gestured to Anna to put down her burden and sit beside her, checking that no one else was within hearing distance. She was hesitant. What more should she say to Anna? The more that Anna knew, the more her friend would be in danger. On the other hand, she would already have to keep quiet. She already knew about the treasure, so why not tell her the truth?

"Anna," she said, leaning over and whispering in her ear. "I have to tell you something important. The treasure you found, it may be Amalric's treasure now, but once it belonged to my family, my father. It must have been stolen the day I was taken and brought here."

"How do you know?"

"I saw my father's mark on the piece you showed me. I would have recognised the beaker anyway, but the mark took away any doubt I might have had."

Anna was silent for a moment, seemingly apprehensive.

"I've been thinking about it myself," she said, "while I was doing the washing. I'm sure he buried it the same day he brought you here. The others got drunk, I remember, but he was strangely sober. I thought he was just keeping watch on you, making sure none of the men tried anything, but he went down to the woods for a long time on his own that night."

Ophelia placed her hand on Anna's as reassurance to her friend.

"Anna, you told me that Amalric took Drusus and showed him where the treasure was hidden."

"That's how I knew where to search."

"I must tell you something else. The night of the feast, I crept through the woods and hid behind Amalric and Drusus, listening to their talk."

Anna's face was taut and white.

"You never told me."

"No, it was too dangerous, and you must never, ever speak to me or anyone else about this. I heard Drusus ask Amalric about the treasure. He knew it should be here even before Amalric showed it to him."

"This man, Drusus, you called him… I've never seen him before. I don't understand. What does he have to do with Amalric, with you?"

Ophelia sighed, tightened her lips for a moment.

"Drusus and his family hated my father, back in my old life, when we lived in Britannia. My sister was right. Dear Hypatia, I didn't believe her. I thought she was silly and immature, fearing conspiracies. I thought she just wanted her own way, to marry the man who she chose, and not the man father wanted her to marry. But now I can see she was right, Anna. I wish I could meet her again to tell her."

Anna reached out and placed her hand on Ophelia's knee, stroking her gently.

"I'm worried, Anna," Ophelia continued. "I think I'm supposed to be dead. I don't know what happened to my family, but you've heard the men boasting. They don't like to leave witnesses to their deeds, and why would they make an exception for my family… unless they were going to try to ransom them, and we have never heard any talk of that. No, I'm beginning to fear they are dead, all of them, and I was supposed to die alongside the rest of my family. I think Amalric saved me. I'm not sure how grateful I am to him for that. He's given me a chance, but what am I going to do with it? What would happen if Drusus was to find me? And he will, in the end, if he is an ally of Amalric's. Amalric can't keep me hidden forever, and I don't think he wants to, either, not for much longer. Somehow I have to get away, to somewhere where Drusus and his friends can't find me. But I can't see a way, not alone, not with Lanius."

"You don't have to leave alone… you can't go and leave me behind."

Ophelia looked at her, worried.

"You're not happy to stay with Amalric, not even if he gives up being a bandit, living here in the woods?"

Anna's gaze was firm.

"No, Ophi. If you leave, I'm coming with you… not just me, but Fredagunda, too. We'll be safer together."

Ophelia let out a huge sigh.

"You give me a reason to keep on living, Anna. You are the reason that I am grateful that Amalric saved me, that he brought us together, and you've showed me what really caring and really loving means."

Anna got to her feet, put her arms around Ophelia and kissed her.

"Together, Ophi, together we'll win. Can we use the treasure, your family's treasure to help us escape? There must be pounds of silver hidden in that hole… and, Ophi, I know where Amalric has other treasure buried."

Ophelia could have wept. For the men in her life loved her in their own way, she knew, like a man loves his favourite dog, until it gets too old for the chase, and then… From her father onwards, she had been a tool, which they could use for their own purposes. Anna had accepted her as she was, with no hope of gain except to be her friend.

"That's easier said than done, Anna," said Ophelia. "How far do you think we would get if we just walked away with Amalric's savings? Especially when we have to take Lanius and Fredagunda."

Amalric would set the hunting dogs on their trail, track them down in a day, and then their lives would not be worth living. If he was on their trail it might be better to kill themselves right away, better than being ripped apart by the dogs. Once she might have thought that death would be a relief, but not anymore. Now she was determined to live. Every moment she lived, every moment Lanius lived, was a moment taken back from the Astrebani.

Amalric remained uneasy, frequently absent from the camp during the summer. He was never away more than a night or two, and Anna began to wonder if he had found a new woman in one of the nearby villages or even Senones. Maybe his plans for a villa, for a farm, did not include them after all. On the other hand, if he had a new girlfriend, she was having no good effect on him. His mood remained gloomy and his performance in bed was lacking. The chief complaint he made out loud was that traffic had dried up on the Lugdunum road in the aftermath of the band's attack on the travellers and, unlike in previous years, it had not returned. The guards on the south gate of Autessiodurum resolutely prevented any further commerce in that direction. What was worse, according to the gossip Amalric had picked up, the Christian leadership had persuaded the authorities in Lugdunum to do the same with the northbound traffic.

"The road's still being used by locals, but there's no profit in risking our necks for a cartload of roots or a couple of scrawny cows," he complained.

Ophelia was occupied with her tasks in the camp one late summer morning, when a youth appeared from out of the forest. She recognised him. He was one of the go-betweens Amalric used when he wanted to send a message to Senones. The youth looked around, slightly bewildered until, noticing Ophelia, he came over.

"Miss," he said, "miss, I need to speak to the chief."

"The chief's sleeping," said Ophelia.

The youth's face took on a miserable expression.

"It's important."

"That can't be helped," she said. "You daren't disturb him and neither do I. You'll have to wait. I'll fetch you some beer and bread."

Ophelia ducked into the hut and collected a pitcher of beer and some bread and brought them out to the boy, who sat quietly eating and drinking while she busied about. When Amalric finally emerged from the hut, yawning and stretching, he found Ophelia and a couple of the other women chatting to the youth, catching up on the gossip from town.

"He needs to speak to you," Ophelia said, when she saw her master from the corner of her eye.

Amalric took a step back, scratched his belly absentmindedly, examining the silent youngster.

"Speak, damn it," he said at last.

The youth touched his forehead before beginning.

"Martius sent me, chief."

A frown crossed Amalric's face, but he said nothing, simply waving a hand for the youth to continue.

"He sent me with a warning, chief," continued the boy. "There is talk of a new man in Senones."

"There are many of them, all the time, these days."

"No, chief, one in particular. A soldier, Constantius, named to the post of *magister militum*, a general who has sworn to root out the bandits."

"Let him try," laughed Amalric.

"The bishop gave his blessing," the youth continued.

Amalric shook his head, clapped the youth on the shoulder, dug out a small coin from a fold in his tunic and sent him on his way.

But the bandit was no fool. He had already picked up the same rumour elsewhere. There was no sense in ignoring good advice. The gang had enough money and supplies for the winter. There was only one realistic thing to do, and that was to break camp early and return to the village.

"It feels bitter to retreat," he explained to Ophelia and Anna, "bitter to give up when there are still weeks of summer still to go

– but," he added with a wry smile, "even bandits have wives and children to think of."

⚘ Chapter 19 ⚘
Arelate

Drusus, or rather his horse, walked tiredly in through the north gate of Arelate. His two companions followed at a respectful distance. He had friends in the city, men he had known since his childhood, who had bet, or whose parents had bet, on Constantinus' success. When the general had declared himself emperor and set up his capital in Arelate, they had flocked after him. Of course, since then they had been forced to turn their coats a few times, run for their lives now and then, but most of them had survived with their heads still on their shoulders.

Inside the walls, peeking above the roofs of the houses, he could see the high shape of the amphitheatre, and over to its right, the theatre. A real city, he thought, grateful after days on horseback. He dismounted and stood for a moment. His arse was sore from sitting and his legs were stiff. He took his horse by the bridle, and the three men crossed the forum in the direction of the amphitheatre and then took a right turn into a small side street. The sign of the Golden Goose welcomed them, with food and beds, two in the common dormitory and a private room for himself.

"You two keep yourselves busy while I attend to my business," Drusus said.

When it came to tracking down Gaius Ursinus, it would be better to rely on old connections than to wander round the town making a public proclamation, especially as poking into Ursinus' business might arouse suspicions. He had one person in mind to talk to, an old acquaintance of Vito's, named Tacitarius, whose father had been a business associate of their father. Apollinarius had provided the name of his house in Arelate. Tacitarius, he thought, should be able to put him on Gaius Ursinus' trail.

Tacitarius was at home when Drusus called. A servant showed him through the public rooms into the quiet of the atrium, where the two men greeted one another, a little awkwardly, given the play of history. To be confronted with the son of Cassius Astrebanus after all these years clearly brought back uncomfortable memories.

"Past times, past times," mumbled Tacitarius, "well-intentioned but ultimately misguided. We don't want to talk about that. People have moved on. The new regime has need of talented men."

Like you, thought Drusus. Like Gaius Ursinus.

"And what about Britannia? What's the view of your master, the praetorian prefect of the Gauls, the man who governs the western part of the Western Empire? Is he planning to take control once again?" Drusus asked, hopefully.

"Britannia?" said Tacitarius, his face a question mark, as if he had never heard of the place.

"Y… yes," said Drusus, his tone now tinged with uncertainty.

"Ah, Britannia, yes, well, in the circumstances…" said Tacitarius, but he did not follow on with a more complete explanation. "Have some more wine, dear Drusus, and tell me about your problem. You're trying to find Gaius Ursinus, I believe."

"I am, exactly."

"A fine man, a gentleman," said Tacitarius.

That was not what Drusus had hoped to hear.

"Well worth his promotion," Tacitarius continued. "Yes, a good candidate. We were glad to support him. Left more for us to do, of course, but…"

"…he had always been loyal to the emperor… of Rome, I mean," said Drusus.

"I couldn't have put it better myself, Drusus. I see you understand."

"You needed to get him out of the way?"

Tacitarius looked astonished.

"Not at all. Gaius was the best man for the post, and we must all make the effort to get on with the emperor, especially given the turmoil we've had here in Arelate. Luckily there's a new man in charge, General Constantius. Fine man, new broom, make a fresh start. I can introduce you if you like."

"I think I'll pass," said Drusus, the memory of the bandits all too fresh.

"Well, don't say I didn't offer. Now," he mused, "Gaius Ursinus, yes, well you've left it a bit late to find him here, I'm afraid."

Drusus frowned.

"Apollinarius was unable to provide me with directions. I know his family were on their way here to meet him, but that was a while ago."

"It must have been, what, several years ago now, that he told me? Yes, I remember him telling me his father was on his way. Most strange altogether."

"What do you mean?"

"We were at the baths. I remember him mentioning that his father would be paying a visit. I thought it odd, but, well, with all the turbulence that there has been in recent years…"

"Go on."

"It was about the time we heard he had been promoted, engaged, too, to a very nice girl, Cecilia. I rather fancied her myself, but he got in first. Of course, her father was only too keen to get her attached to a man who would have connections in the court, not someone like me, still stuck in the provinces. Had to pack up the house and leave before the old man arrived, and then, oddly enough, I don't think he even did."

"No," said Drusus, rather more definitively than he should have done.

"Took the route over Vesontio, everyone assumed."

"And Gaius?"

"He was in a hurry to be off to sunnier climes and better things. Up and up, from all I've heard."

"To Rome?"

"No, why should he go there?" said Tacitarius, astonished at his friend's slowness. "Haven't I been saying that? No, he left for Ravenna. It must have been four or five years ago. I've lost track of things a bit."

"Ravenna, you say, successful?" said Drusus, a feeling of despair growing within him. That meant he would have to visit Ravenna as well as Rome. "Well, I had hoped to have a chance to meet my old friend while I'm visiting Arelate. I suppose I shall have to put it off until I reach Ravenna, if that's where he is."

"Friend?" said Tacitarius. "I thought your father and his were at each other's throats."

"You said it yourself earlier," said Drusus, "in these times, we all have to be able to adapt to the circumstances."

"Ha, ha, very well put."

A slave appeared, padding silently along the paving, and bowed as he came up to Tacitarius.

"Master, it's time for you to proceed to the baths. Have you forgotten your meeting with Aelius?"

"Ah, yes." Tacitarius turned to Drusus. "Why don't you come with me, Drusus? Aelius is a fine fellow, and very funny.

He also owes me dinner, and rumour has it that he has hired in some new dancing girls, straight off the boat from Syria."

Drusus was drawn reluctantly into the party. When he woke in one of Aelius' guest rooms the following day with a terrible headache, the last he could remember was slipping coins into the knickers of one of the dancing girls. If she had ever accompanied him to bed, she must have left already. She would have been terribly disappointed, unless, that is, she had been in need of a good night's sleep.

He was making his way past the theatre, towards the bridge over the river Rhodanus. He was on the hunt for a ship-owner who was said to organise regular traffic with Rome, when he heard a light laugh. He looked around and saw a young woman smiling at him.

"You don't recognise me," she said.

Drusus shook his head. "No."

"I'm not surprised. You fell asleep like a log. Can you believe I slept next to you the whole night, and you were snoring like a baby? I didn't have the heart to wake you when I left."

Drusus squinted in the bright sunlight. The girl confronting him was pleasant-looking enough, but the one he vaguely remembered had bright red lips, coal-dark eyeshadow, and gold dust sprinkled on her cheeks. She also had a small mole on one of her breasts, which had been an irritating distraction when she had been dancing. Drusus felt frustrated. He wanted to find the ship captain. It would just be his luck that this female would get in his way, and when he got to the port he would find that the man had sailed that very day and would not return for three months. Everyone just seemed to have gone before he got there.

"The girl I remember had a mole on her left tit," he said, ungraciously, hoping to drive her off. "About there," he added tapping the girl on the breast.

"You mean like this," she said, sliding her hand under her cloak and drawing back her gown with a smile.

"Well, I'll be damned," he said, taking a closer look at her face. It was hard to make the connection without the paint, but there was no mistake about the mole.

"I'm not engaged tonight, if you would like a do-over, same price," said the girl, "and no falling asleep if we get together a little earlier."

"I thought you were a dancer?" he said, annoyed at being drawn into a conversation.

"With extras, for men I like," she smiled.

"I'm at the Golden Goose tavern," he said thoughtlessly, not wanting any further discussion, but simply to get rid of her and get on with his business.

"Very well," she said, kissing her fingers and then pressing them against his lips. "My name's Xancha, and yours?"

"Drusus," he said distractedly, taking a few steps along the street. "They know me at the tavern."

"Until sunset, then, Drusus," she said, pulling her shawl respectably about her head and vanishing into the anonymity of the crowd. He swore to himself, put her out of his mind and began pushing his way in the opposite direction.

The main dock was on the other side of the river, and to reach it he had to cross a swaying bridge of boats and take a left turn onto the quayside. About two-thirds of the way along, he found the man he was looking for, Otosius, the ship-owner.

"Of course, master, a passage to Rome, nothing could be easier," said the merchant, accepting his money and making a note of his name. "Unfortunately, the ship has not yet arrived from its last voyage."

"When will it be here?"

"Three or four weeks, I expect, depending on the winds."

"I see."

"You have to have patience, master, in this business," said the ship-owner with a smile, pocketing Drusus' coins.

Or walk, thought Drusus, as he glumly crossed the bridge back to his lodgings at the Golden Goose tavern. He was not even sure how far it would be by horse from Arelate to Rome, and he was not planning to make the journey by land, anyway.

As he crossed the threshold of the Golden Goose, his attention was caught by a voice calling his name.

"Hey, Master Drusus!"

He swore. He had forgotten about the girl, Xancha, sitting with a glass of wine, evidently waiting for him. He had never promised he would pay her for another night, so why was she bothering him? How long had she been there? Who had seen her? Fortunately, she was dressed in civilian style and not the topless attire and leopard skin she had been wearing at Aelius' dinner.

He did not want to create a scene in front of the tavern, so he mastered his irritation and kissed her hand when she held it up for him. He was about to open his mouth to send her on her way, when she spoke instead.

"What do you say about dinner?" she asked.

She was already off the bar-bench before he could reply, her arm through his.

"There's a cook shop, two doors along, selling fresh seafood," she said merrily. "I've heard it's excellent... and good value," she added, with a reassuring smile.

She was still dozing beside him when he woke. She was pretty and well-shaped even without make-up, toilet preparations, or the leopard skin, he could admit that. He nudged her until she stirred.

"I think I paid for a turn I never got," he said.

She looked up at him with a sleepy smile and rolled onto her back.

"Take what you want, just don't hurt me," she said, her hands sliding down his back.

Drusus was not a man with extravagant desires, and one night with Xancha would have satisfied him and given him enough pleasant memories to keep him going for a long time. He was, however, a man with a need to reach Rome, and that goal had been temporarily frustrated. He had no wish to spend more money on dancing girls, not even Xancha, not even when she left a note at the tavern reminding him of her services, not even when, increasingly desperate, she wrote that she would meet him for free, just for the price of dinner. He wasn't interested. He did not need her, but despite that, the two of them found themselves together more and more.

He had three weeks to kill, maybe four. He did not dare leave town in case the ship turned up while he was away and sailed to Rome without him. He was novel enough to Tacitarius and his circle to be able to cadge a seat at the theatre or join a group visiting the baths without being boring. He had a fund of stories to tell, and he could even make them up if necessary. He was not especially worried his welcome would run out yet, but he was impatient. There was a reason he had come south – to reach Rome, and he had been thwarted.

At the end of the third week, he took the bridge to the port again, to look up Otosius. The man was apologetic.

"There's been no sign of the ship yet." He shrugged his shoulders. "The time of the year, master. It's in the hands of the gods."

"You'll send me a message when the ship docks?"

"Of course, master."

Four weeks passed, and the fifth, and no message came, so he passed by the ship-owner's booth again. The man smiled weakly, looked uneasy. The ship had still not come.

"The winds," he said, "the storms. It's easy for it to be delayed."

"But you promised me, you took my money."

"I can't do anything, the Fates…" said the man, shrugging his shoulders. "Do you think I like it? My cargo, that I already paid for, somewhere out on the sea, and winter almost here? Any moment to be dashed against the rocks, or sucked down by a whirlpool?"

"Are you trying to deceive me?" asked Drusus.

The man shook his head sadly.

"No, sir. I can see you don't know this business."

The following week, the man was cheerful, optimistic once again.

"The ship's come in. All's good. Full cargo. I'm all set up for the winter."

"What about me?" asked Drusus. "When's it leaving?"

A serious expression expanded across the ship-owner's face.

"It's late in the season, sir, you know the risks."

"No, I don't," said Drusus, his irritation boiling over, "otherwise I'd be a fucking ship-owner, and not a lousy landowner."

"Sir, please, don't get upset. I'm only thinking of your best, of your safety. We can't sail at this time of the year, too risky. *Mare clausum*, we call it. The sea is closed, by government orders – four months."

The ship-owner tried to look sympathetic.

"Don't worry, sir, you still have your berth… on the first boat out in the spring."

"Four months! What am I going to do until then?"

She was delighted, of course, Xancha. She had attached to him more closely than a limpet to one of Otosius' hulks. He had already earned an unwanted reputation for being her lover. He had had to dismiss the hired men and send them on their way. He could hardly afford to keep retainers and buy the expensive wines and baubles that Xancha demanded when she was at her worst. It had gained him great credibility among the men, Tacitarius, Aelius, the exile Britons and their Gaulish friends. He could not believe the others were jealous that he had managed to pull one of the best-looking, sexiest dancing girls in Arelate, without even trying. Nonetheless, he recognised that, illicit and exotic as she was, she helped him gain access that he never would have done alone.

He did not understand what she saw in him. He supposed eventually that he must be as strange to her as she was to him and his friends.

"I love your British accent when you try to speak Greek," she said.

"I am speaking Greek, not trying to speak it," he answered testily, "the best Greek money can buy in Britannia."

The only reply he received was a tinkling laugh, her dark eyes sparkling as she hid her mouth behind her hand.

She spoke Greek, of course, but not the kind of Greek that you read in Homer or was any help for understanding the works of Plato. On the other hand, if you wanted to curse someone in the fish market in Alexandria, or hire a donkey to ride into Jerusalem, then he learned all the vocabulary necessary.

He could not keep himself adequately occupied gazing at Xancha, nor she with him, for that matter. She slept around, he was sure of it, but she always came back, especially when the weather got chillier and the cold winds blew down from the mountains. Then she was happy to curl up with him and share a meal fetched by the tavern-owner. And if he was honest with himself, just those evenings he was pleased she was there. The other days, when the weather was warmer, she disappeared into the town.

"I'm going to have my hair done," she claimed, "and then I'll go to the baths with the girls."

"Have fun," he said, as she waved to him over her shoulder. He could not help feeling she was meeting other men, but he would believe her to keep the peace.

He was grateful to get a break and would make his way to the library. There was a good stock of law books, and men willing to discuss cases. He gladly shared his experience, and, in turn, by careful questioning, learned from them. Italia, it seemed, was infested with Goths, the same barbarians who had held Rome to ransom a few years earlier. Now they were filtering through Arelate on their way to Aquitania and Hispania where they hoped to settle, to the consternation of the local lawyers. Nothing was known about their customs and laws. Everything passed along by word of mouth. How could you ever do business with them that way? You never knew when this sort of arcane knowledge can come in useful, Drusus thought, listening to their complaints. If he ever needed to discuss Visigothic inheritance rights with a camel-driver from Antioch, between Xancha and the denizens of the law library, it would be no problem. The gods save him from ever having to do so.

It was another evening of this seemingly endless winter. They had dined, but a cold drizzle had chased them indoors, into his rooms, and to his bed. They were lying beside one another, when Xancha spoke.

"You could always stay here," she said. "I could give up dancing. I could be with you."

If he had revealed how he felt on his face, he must have looked sceptical.

"Do you think I like putting myself out for men, just for a meal and a bed?" she continued.

She swung a leg over, so she was sitting astride him, pinning him down. It was comforting to feel her weight pressing against his hips.

"What would you do instead?" he asked.

"I could teach the women, the barbarian women, to do their hair and make-up in the Roman style."

She looked earnest. "Eastern fashions are all the rage. You should know that by now. There's a lot of them want to learn," she insisted. "You can't believe how many of them admire the way I look. I just know I could do it."

"They're admiring the way you look because you are pretty," said Drusus.

"Seriously, Drusus," she said. "Some of those Visigoth girls are pretty too, and they'd look a lot better if they followed the fashions, I promise."

He smiled.

"And what would I do?"

"There'll be plenty of need for men like you, Drusus, here or in Italia, men who are quick-witted and not hung up on the old ways."

She began to massage his stomach.

"We could leave Arelate and move to Narbonna or Tolosa. There'll be plenty of opportunities."

Her expression shifted to one of sadness.

"I know you can't marry me, a man like you, a woman with my past, but I could be your lover, until you found a wife…" She paused, a half-smile on her face. "And maybe even after that." She bent down, her breasts pressed against his chest, and gently bit his ear.

Drusus sighed. She did not understand. She could not understand. What was the prospect of a life as a small-town lawyer together with a former dancing girl compared to becoming governor of Britannia Prima?

"I have to leave," he said. "I've told you what I have to do. You know I have to try."

She straightened up, slid her leg back, kneeling beside him, and then leaned over, an arm each side of his chest, her face inches from his.

"You mean you are stuck in your old ways after all. You only see one thing… clinging to the past."

Better she thinks that, thought Drusus to himself, than suspecting I don't want to be with her. Then she might leave me for someone else.

"Yes, I suppose so," he said, "but I have a past worth clinging to."

"The past is over, Drusus. Even I can see that. I've heard enough. Don't you think I keep my ears open at those dinners I get dragged to, the men I've been with… before I met you," she added hastily. "I'm not giving up," she insisted. "If you don't want me, if you won't come with me, I shall go to Narbonna or Tolosa myself. I can change my own life without you."

Why couldn't I stay here in Arelate with Xancha? thought Drusus, crossing the forum a day or two later. Why am I leaving? There's nothing wrong with the place. The people don't get on my nerves the way they do in Remis or Treviri, always reminding me of my past, hoping for favours, expecting me to avenge Vito. In Arelate everyone has a past they are only too ready to forget: backed the wrong candidate at some point, lost a fortune and a position and scrambled to find a new one. And Xancha, there's really nothing wrong with her. She's pretty enough, sharp-minded even, in her own way. Maybe she's right, too, maybe the past is over, and there is a new future for a woman like her, for a man like me.

He turned a corner.

No, no, this was dangerous thinking, complacent thinking. A surge of guilt came over him. What was he doing, imagining a life in Arelate, in the south, with a woman like Xancha? That was not why he was travelling, not why he was on the way to Rome. He thought for a moment of Bryna. He had given his word to Apollinarius that he would be back in the autumn, and he had already failed to keep it. Supposing the lawyer would not wait. Supposing he found another husband for his daughter. He, Drusus, wouldn't be able to show his face in Belgica. He couldn't give up. He had to go on. He had to continue. He had to return as a success. He couldn't fall into the same comfortable, coat-turning ways as Tacitarius or Aelius, or that bastard, Gaius Ursinus. The honour of his family was in his hands. It was his life's goal to restore it, whatever it took. His ancestors expected it. How would he be able to look them in the face, when, one day, he met them in whatever afterlife he and they had earned? To abandon that goal would make his life meaningless. It would be… it would be to be less than a man, to lose all honour, to be a failure.

❧ Chapter 20 ❧
Gaul

The winter felt unending. For Ophelia and Anna that meant caring for their children, making sure they got enough to eat, keeping them strong and healthy to resist the diseases and illnesses which took so many. Amalric, on the other hand, had little to do. He did not have the skills or interest for handicrafts, wood carving or leather working that some of the other men had. He did not care to sing or tell stories around the fire.

"Once," he said, grudgingly, "I had the reputation as the best story-teller in the legion, but that was long ago."

Ophelia was alone with him as he stared into the fire. Anna had gone with the children, visiting Milva to listen to her stories. She told the same ones, of life beyond the frontiers, the old ways, the doings of the gods, over and over again. They probably did not understand her tales, especially little Lanius, but they never seemed to tire of listening to her.

Ophelia, on the other hand, had had enough. She was tired of guessing, tired of trying to calculate, from pieces, from fragments. There was one story she wanted to hear, and she wanted to hear it from Amalric.

"Tell me what happened that day," she said, "when you killed my family."

"I didn't kill your family," Amalric said, "and haven't I told you not to ask questions, not to be so curious?"

She turned and looked him full in the face.

"You're not the only one who had another life before this one. I haven't forgotten my life either."

She half-expected an angry outburst, but when none came, she continued.

"You talk now about giving up this life. What about me, what about Anna, what about the children? What choice do we have?"

"You're my women. They're my children…"

"And you expect us to accompany you to wherever you decide to go?"

"Why not? Do you want to continue living this life on your own?"

"Do you think we can trust you? Do you think I can trust you, a man with blood on his hands, my own family's blood…"

"I told you, I didn't kill your family."

"Then tell me the truth, tell me the truth. I'm the mother of your son," she said. "I deserve to know."

He lifted his hand and stroked her cheek. "I was riding beside you, Ophelia," he said, "all the way from Autessiodurum. You didn't even glance at me. I was just another a dirty peasant, I suppose."

"I had nothing to do with it," she replied. "My father recruited men in town, as an escort. What had they to do with me?"

"It wasn't hard to volunteer."

"No," said Ophelia, suddenly, staring at him. "You knew who we were, didn't you? You were waiting for us, specifically for us."

There was a look of surprise on Amalric's face, a moment of hesitation which she first interpreted as an attempt to come up with a good lie.

"I didn't know who your father was, who you were. It was just a job to be done," he said at last, "but once I saw you, I only had eyes for you. You had such poise, so much class. You still do. Anyone can see that."

He looked away.

"I had received a request, against payment. I arranged matters to the best of my ability."

She did not press her point. She was not stupid. She had long ago put two and two together.

"Go on," she said.

"I rode beside you, beside the wagon you sat on, together with your children. Yes, I know all about them, Ophelia, but I promise I didn't harm them. Please don't think that of me."

She said nothing.

"Of course, I knew when we would meet the rest of the band, Radagus and the others. I had told them where to wait, and me and the boys hung back just before the place we had agreed on."

"I remember," she said, "the men in the escort had vanished. That's the last thing I can remember."

"I saw what happened," said Amalric, a dreamy tone in his voice. "The wagon driver panicked. The oxen swerved. One of the wheels ran down into the ditch. In a moment the whole wagon rolled over. I was already galloping up. I saw it happen."

He looked so earnest, as if willing her to believe this to be true.

"You were thrown out. I saw you fall, but the little ones – what were their names? – they were trapped under the cart. The whole weight came down on them. There was nothing I could do. Honestly, Ophelia, we never killed your children, not me nor Radagus nor any other of the men."

But you would have done, she thought.

"Why didn't you kill me?"

"I told you," he said, "I had been riding beside you for almost two days. I had been watching you. I imagined how Astraea – you remember, I told you about her once – I imagined how she must have looked if she had grown up… just like you. How could I have killed you? How could I have let any of the other men kill you? It would have been like killing my dream, like killing part of myself."

"So what happened?"

"You were thrown off the cart as it toppled, tumbled down into the ditch. I jumped off my horse and scrambled after you."

He lay back and stretched out, staring up towards the roof of the hut, as if the scene were playing up among the rafters instead of in his own mind.

"What have you got there, boss? Something valuable?" Radagus, his deputy then, came towards him, striding along the road.

"A woman, Rad! She fell from the cart. She's lying down here."

"We were to kill them all, boss. That's what he said, and you agreed to it."

"I can't kill her, Rad."

"I got rid of the others, and Bellarius took care of the old woman. You've got to do it."

"Check all the men are dead, Rad, the carters and the servants, too. We can't afford to leave any witnesses."

Radagus scrambled back up to the road, gave a kick at the lifeless corpse of the carter and crouched down to try to see under the cart.

"There are a couple of kids under here," Radagus called back.

He put his ear against the woman's chest. He was trying to hear her heart. He licked his finger and held it in front of her face. Was he imagining, or was the side closest to her mouth a little cooler? A tiny, tiny hint of life.

"What did you say, Rad?"

"There are a couple of kids, trapped under the cart."

"Are they still alive?" They must be her children, a little boy and a little girl. They had been riding beside her the whole way. She must be their mother.

"Can't see," said Radagus. "What d'you want me to do?"

"Get some of the guys and roll the cart back. We need to get the stuff out."

She was breathing, faintly. When he looked carefully he could see her chest rising and falling. There was no sign of blood, but that didn't mean much, he knew. He'd seen enough dying people in his time. He had to take his chance that she would live. He put his arms under hers and began to drag her up the side of the ditch. He was breathing heavily, not just from the effort of dragging her, but from desperation.

"Don't die, don't die!" he said, half aloud. She couldn't die now, not when he had just found her.

"You say something, chief?" said Radagus. He had his back to him, waving for help to tip the cart over.

He let the woman gently down on the edge of the road, slipped his hand inside her gown, his finger searching for her heartbeat. He could not help touching her breasts, warm and soft, alive. He was not going to let her go, not now, not to the gods or to any other man.

A couple of the other bandits came over, cursing about the overturned cart. For a moment he was forced to leave the woman where she was, to help his companions tip it over. At Radagus' command they put their shoulders to the weight and heaved it onto its side. Radagus crouched down by the children. The boy's neck was bent at a peculiar angle. The girl had blood dribbling from the corner of her mouth.

"They're dead," said Radagus.

"Poor bastards," he said. "I'm glad I don't have that on my conscience."

"Too late to have a conscience in this business," said his partner, "but I'm with you. It would have felt heartless to have to kill the little sods out cold."

"What about the horses?" he asked. "Are they injured at all? We'll need some of them to carry the stuff back to camp."

"I'll check, and I'll loosen the oxen, and we can drive them back with us. There'll be a few meals on those if they are not too tough."

"Better still, Rad," he pointed out. "You remember that farmer over by Aureasilva who was asking after oxen? He'll owe us a few favours for these."

"His daughter, for example," said Radagus, with a wink.

That reminded him of the woman. He went back to her, knelt down beside her again and felt her heartbeat, checked her breath. No change. She was still alive. Every moment looked more promising, as long as the men did not get over enthusiastic when his back was turned. He saw his horse, grazing a little way up the road, where he had leapt off when he first saw the wagon rolling into the ditch. He called. The beast knew his master's voice and looked up, considered for a moment, and then began to amble towards him.

Hurry up, you stupid animal, hurry up, he thought, impatient. When it drew near enough, he patted it on the nose and let up a silent prayer. If he lifted her up onto the horse, and if she had an injury inside, it could kill her. On the other hand, if he left her here, he or one of the others of the band would have to make sure she was dead anyway. On his horse, she had a chance of life. And as for him, he didn't give a damn about some farmer's daughter. Radagus could have her if he could only keep this woman alive.

Suddenly he was back in the present, glancing across at Ophelia.

"I carried you back to the camp," he said, "slung over the horse."

"Wasn't Radagus angry?" Ophelia asked, "when he saw what you'd done?"

"Nah," said Amalric. "It was my deal anyway, and I let him take the oxen over to Aureasilva, so he was soon distracted. Worth two oxen for a new wife, don't you think?"

Normally she would have been annoyed by a comment like that, but now she did not react. She could not react.

"Do you promise me you're telling me the truth about Lucia and Titus?"

"I promise, as an officer and a gentleman," he said, with a peculiar smile. "The gods took them. Perhaps it was for the best."

"Perhaps," she said. "But what about the rest of my family… they're dead, aren't they?"

"Radagus told me. He had done what we'd agreed."

"Agreed with who?"

"The man who gave us the job."

She was about to name Drusus Astrebanus, but she managed to inhibit herself.

"And after? Did anyone ever come looking for us?"

He lay thinking for a moment.

"There were people curious about what happened, a few, but we'd agreed to keep silence. A nosy lawyer," he said at last, "far too fucking nosy for his own good, and once I heard that three men came, years afterwards… not long back, actually."

"Do you know who they were?"

"No idea, two Britons and an African, I heard, on horseback. There was a rumour going round town that they were something to do with the church. You know how easily the bishop can get worked up."

She stared at him. She could not stop herself.

"I think saw them," she said, "from the edge of the woods. I was this far away from them, three men, on nice-looking horses, young men, about my own age. I could have gone," she said.

"But you didn't," he replied. "You couldn't have left without the boy… without Alanaric, could you? Despite everything, he is your son."

"Despite everything, yes, he is."

He sat up and looked across at her.

"Listen, Ophelia, I'm not a fool. I know you're not here because you want to be. I want to offer you a chance to leave… to leave with me, to find a new life, away from this, from the forest, the robbing and murders. Anna and the children can come too. Somewhere nice, like you were used to before."

She watched him. She saw the sincerity in his eyes. If she spoke she would have to lie, so it was better that she said nothing, reached out for him, taking him in her arms. Let him interpret this whatever way he wants, she thought, as her lips met his.

Ophelia said nothing of Amalric's revelation to Anna. Her old life did not concern Anna, she felt. Only their future life, whatever future Amalric thought he might have as an honest man. She found it hard to believe it would be possible for her to be part of that, whatever he imagined. Even if she stuck by him, and God knows, there was little enough reason to do that, whatever he promised, sooner or later someone would become curious. Who was this woman? Where had he found her? Or Drusus or his brother, or some acquaintance from Londinium or Verulamium or Corinium, would pass her in the street, and there would be a flash of recognition.

"Ophelia, isn't it, Ophelia Ursina? I thought you were dead?"

And, from that moment, to all intents and purposes, she would be. Once the word got back to the Astrebani and their friends, to her father's enemies, to the people who would want her silenced.

Beyond the frontier, the *limes*, perhaps she would be free of that risk, but at what cost? At Amalric's mercy, as much as she was now, for the rest of her life.

❧ Chapter 21 ☙
Rome

Drusus set off through the narrow streets, past shop fronts, in and out of market stalls, and around a trio of temples until he reached the forum, the heart of Rome, the heart of the Empire. He would have been lying if he said he was happy to be there, but there was no describing his relief when Otosius had finally told him the boat was due to depart. He had gathered his few belongings, spent one last night with Xancha and, with a light heart, left her and Arelate to their fates.

"I promise," he said, one foot over the threshold, "I'll be back in the autumn." In the moment he had forgotten that he had made a similar promise the previous year, five hundred miles to the north.

Now he glanced suspiciously up and down the street, his eyes passing over the famous buildings on each side without really taking them in. There was only one which interested him, the Senate House. He took a guess and began to climb the shallow slope until he reached what he thought was his destination, then he turned off the street and up the steps into the portico. The high rectangular doors must lead to the chamber, he surmised. He did not suppose it would be appropriate to walk right in. He would need an introduction to a senator willing to promote his case. Arranging that at a distance had been beyond even Tacitarius' capacity.

At the guest house where he was staying, an institution for visitors from Gaul, the other residents had already tried to persuade him to leave at once for Ravenna.

"Everything happens there now."

"No one's in town anymore."

"But he'll have to find a patron."

"Postumus," suggested one voice.

"Collonius," said another.

"Aedilius," added a third.

"He'll need a fistful of gold, patron or not."

"Bagful more like."

Their voices had buzzed around him like annoying flies.

"Visit to the chamber?" came a sudden voice from behind him. A portly, middle-aged man rose from a stool where he had been sitting, half-hidden in the shadows. "I know all the stories."

"I have important business," said Drusus. "I need to see a member of the Senate."

"You won't find them here," said the man, with a chuckle. "Nobody's been doing business here since the Goths came through."

"I need to ask someone about a document," said Drusus, brusquely, "about a position my brother was promised. It was approved by the Senate."

The guide's face acquired a cunning expression.

"Well then, you're definitely wasting your time here. None of the senators are ever in the city, and they don't listen to strangers' petitions anymore. They've got their own problems to worry about. The man you need's Aedilius."

Drusus recognised the name from among those suggested by his acquaintances in the guest house.

"Where can I find this Aedilius?"

"Information costs money in this town, my friend. Access costs money. Getting stuff done costs money. Do you understand?"

Drusus understood, reached for his belt and pulled out a coin. He could not say he had not been warned.

The man held out his hand with a smile, glanced at Drusus' offering with approval and slipped it into a pocket inside his tunic.

"You'll find Aedilius at Caracalla's baths. Ask for Justus' stand. He sells perfumes. He'll point you in the right direction. My cousin," he added by way of explanation.

"Thank you," said Drusus and turned to leave. The guide retreated into the shadows and lowered himself heavily to his stool.

"You want to cut through there," he called out, pointing across the street, "past Castor's temple, and through the houses, round the Capitoline. After that it's easy. Big building, the other side of the stadium."

Drusus followed the guide's instructions as best he could. He had no idea which temple was which. Most of them appeared closed up and abandoned. The houses the guide had so casually referred to consisted of a large range of buildings, a palace which would have covered half of Londinium. He could easily lose his way if he took the wrong turning. The path the guide had suggested led him around the palace until he could see a long white wall ahead, and when he stepped out into the sunlight, he realised it was one side of a stadium, stretching as far as he could see between two low hills. He turned to his left and made his way alongside the arena. Above him loomed the high walls of the palace, glistening in the sunlight, pink and yellow flowers poking here and there from among the stonework, bees and other insects circling unpleasantly close to his head. A worrying thought began nagging at him. He was heading towards the baths. He recalled the baths in Londinium, full of sweating merchants and money lenders. He had known most of them. Getting anything done was a matter of friendships and favours. Was he going to have to press his business in a pool, on a man he had never met before, amongst a lot of naked strangers? How would he be able to show the document, make his case? It was one thing to have a chat, shake hands on a deal with men you knew, but in this city, where he knew no one?

When he reached the end of the stadium, he found he was standing in a large irregular piazza. He stopped a man passing by.

"The baths?"

The man pointed across the piazza towards an enormous building, longer and higher even than the stadium. He set off across the open square. Two slaves were brushing the flagstones in a half-hearted manner. The sun beat down, and he was sweating before he reached the other side. The entrance to the baths was a huge arch, stretching high over his head. The space inside was almost the size of the square outside, but as he gazed around he noticed that one end of the building was blocked off, a trio of workers standing idly and chatting by an untidy stack of planks and a heap of marble blocks. In fact, the giant building was almost empty. Only at the far end of a long aisle could he see clusters of people, standing around. He increased his pace, passing by statues in niches, images of gods and emperors, archways and arcades, until he came to the busy area. Here at last there were shops and a taverna. He looked around, trying to spot the perfume shop, then followed his nose into an alcove, where a waft of lavender and myrrh drew him on. A man he took to be Justus was leaning on a marble counter, observing him with apparent disdain. It wasn't hard to pick Drusus out as a foreigner.

"I'm looking for Aedilius," said Drusus, not wanting to waste any more time.

Justus' expression did not change.

"The senator, I mean," said Drusus. "I came from the Senate House."

The shopkeeper's expression changed from one of disdain to one of amusement.

"Aedilius isn't a senator. He's just a freedman who takes care of their business."

Drusus was not interested in a further explanation, though the man seemed primed to provide it.

"You've got urgent business with Aedilius?" he enquired, no longer leaning on the counter-top, beginning to take a more active interest in the stranger. "But how do you intend to find him?"

Drusus recognised the hint, reached into his purse and slapped a couple of coins onto the counter.

"Aedilius usually comes here around the third hour," said the shopman. "He conducts his business in a suite of chambers through the second archway."

"Not in the baths?" Drusus felt a surge of relief pass over him. The perfumer laughed.

"Only his closest cronies get to meet him in the baths." He glanced down. "I hope you've got more in that purse of yours. His help doesn't come cheap."

"I'm looking for my rights," said Drusus stubbornly.

"So's everyone, mister, but round here money talks."

A rich freedman, Drusus expected, would be fat, bejewelled, slow and lazy, so he failed to react when he saw a small group enter the baths at a brisk pace, advancing down the aisle in his direction. In the lead was a grey-haired man with a nose like a hawk, tall and slim, wearing a neatly tailored gown and silk cloak. Behind him strode an almost equally tall, equally elegant individual, bearing a small bag, and behind him, another short man, obviously a scribe, lugging an enormous holdall. The group was completed by a pair wearing military-style uniforms, glancing from left to right as they vanished under the second archway. It was only when he overheard someone greet the group with a "Good day, Magister Aedilius," that Drusus realised he had been mistaken in his expectations and began, himself, to hurry towards the arch through which they had disappeared.

"No further!" said one of the military men, emerging from behind a pillar, holding out a hand.

"I wish to see Magister Aedilius," said Drusus.

"There are many who do," said the man flatly. "Do you have an appointment?"

"No, I was hoping he would have time for clients who were willing to wait."

"If he worked like that," said the second, "we would have the entire baths filled with people."

"Arms up, my friend," said the first, laughing. "I'll let you in to speak to Decius, since you are obviously a stranger." He briskly patted Drusus down his sides, shaking his head when he reached Drusus' purse and the leather document cylinder.

"No swords or daggers on you, very good," he said, indicating with his thumb that Drusus could now pass through the doorway. Once inside, Drusus saw he was in an antechamber containing two ornate desks, one on either side of the doorway. Behind one desk stood the taller of the men who had been following the magister. The smaller clerk was sitting behind the other, his head in a sheaf of documents. Drusus, assuming that the tall man was Decius, took a step towards him and opened his mouth to speak to him. The man, with an almost imperceptible direction of his gaze, indicated that Drusus should, in fact, consult his sitting colleague.

"I wish to see Magister Aedilius."

"Your name?"

"Drusus Astrebanus."

The scribe reluctantly set aside his documents, glanced at a sheet of papyrus which lay on the table in front of him and began mouthing to himself.

"Pontius, Cassius, Claudius and Agememnon, Cognidubnum… no, I don't see any Astrebanus here. Did you have an appointment?" he asked finally, looking up.

"No, I wish to make one."

The clerk made a humming noise and flipped over the document to consult the backside.

"I can't fit you in before the Ides."

Drusus took a deep breath and reached into his purse. He slid a coin across the desk in the direction of the clerk. The man observed him closely but said nothing, merely scratching the back of his neck and raising his eyebrows. For a moment Drusus was nonplussed. Was he now in trouble for attempting to bribe an official? The clerk sniffed, and with a deliberate and slow gesture tapped two fingers on the table. Drusus extracted another coin and slid it to lie beside the first one.

The clerk caught his eye with a cynical smile.

"Magister Aedilius is taking his bath now," he said. "If you come back at the fifth hour, I'll see what I can do for you." He pushed the papyrus sheet towards Drusus. "Write your name here, and the reason you wish to speak to the magister."

He wrote his name, passed the sheet back, and with a brief nod, left the chamber and returned to the main hall. At least it was cool inside. He crossed to the taverna and ordered a glass of wine and a pastry. A flock of sparrows fluttered around in the dome, keeping a sharp eye out for unguarded food. He sat down to wait, with a certain sympathy for the tiny creatures.

In Britannia, in Belgica, he was an important man. The name Astrebanus meant something, opened doors, got people's attention. A tribal chief – at any rate, he could think so. He had a justifiable claim to be named governor of Britannia. He could not imagine having been treated that way by a mere clerk or being forced to wait by an official. But here, here he was obviously nobody, dependent on the assistance of a tourist guide and a perfume seller to get access to a freedman, to kick his heels while the man took his bath. He felt sick inside, but not so sick that he would miss this opportunity. When he judged the fifth hour had come, he downed the last of his wine and made his way back up the aisle until he reached the second archway once again.

The guard recognised him and, with a brusque gesture, let him in. The short clerk was sitting where he had been earlier, talking to a well-dressed man.

"Please wait, Master Astrebanus," called out the clerk, causing the well-dressed man to rotate his head and scrutinise him. "Magister Aedilius will speak to you momentarily." The other man gave him a nasty look and returned to his conversation with the clerk.

Presently, the taller of the two appeared from the archway at the rear of the anteroom and beckoned Drusus over.

"Magister Aedilius will see you now."

Aedilius stood up when he came in, stretching out his arms in a form of greeting.

"Master Drusus, or should I say Chief Astrebanus," he said with a smile, "how can I help you?"

Drusus reached into the cylinder at his waist and drew out the copy of the letter that he and his brother had drafted all those years ago.

"My brother petitioned for the governorship of Britannia," said Drusus, "to the emperor. Here's a copy of the letter."

The tall clerk took the sheet and passed it to his master. Aedilius took it, sat down and, holding the sheet close to his face, began to scan back and forth. Then he put it down on the table.

"You realise," he said, "that this petition is several years old."

"I do," replied Drusus, "but we received a reply, a letter of nomination, with the emperor's seal, with the seal of the Senate."

He extricated Milesia's copy and handed it over.

"Really," said Aedilius, laying it on top of the letter and placing his elbows on his worktable, his hands together, his fingertips against his mouth. "Then your brother was a lucky man."

"Far from it," said Drusus. "A traitor murdered him."

A look of concern spread across Aedilius' face.

"So very sad," he said. "All too many usurpers, infesting the Empire, claiming others' rights, destroying the organisation and legitimacy – so many of them, apparently, from Britannia," he added, glancing up at Drusus.

"I was hoping," said Drusus, "to obtain a replacement appointment letter, so that I can claim the position for myself in place of my dead brother."

"I have to be honest with you, Chief Astrebanus," said Aedilius deliberately, "I am not familiar with this matter." He paused, as if considering carefully what to say next. "You must be aware that the Empire has allowed the province of Britannia to take care of its own affairs in recent years. No governor has been appointed that I can recall."

He paused again.

"Of course, I'm not omnipotent." He smiled in a self-satisfied manner. "This appointment could have been made before the time of the Goths, before I was called in. There was a certain amount of confusion and disorganisation… which I have had to make an immense effort to rectify. You said the document had the seal of the emperor?"

"Yes, Emperor Honorius, of course."

"Of course," said Aedilius, a slightly chilly tone in his voice. "In that case it is possible the appointment was issued from

Ravenna. Some of the stamps were carried there during the disturbances, and the emperor may have chosen to make the appointment in the name of the Senate without consulting it – entirely understandable given the circumstances."

"I am planning to travel to Ravenna," said Drusus, a little too quickly.

"Then I suggest you pursue your case there. There's nothing more I can do."

"But without the support of the Senate…?"

He reached once more inside the document case.

"I have a speech here, ready prepared, to plead my case."

Aedilius waved his hand dismissively.

"If you can obtain clarification from the emperor, then the agreement of the Senate would be a mere formality… no need for speeches."

"But without it, without at least recognition that I have a case…" Drusus was trying hard not to sound desperate.

Aedilius glanced again at the documents that Drusus had handed him and then slowly began to roll them up.

"The honour of my family is at stake," said Drusus.

"The honour of your family," said Aedilius, slowly. The documents were a neat cylinder in his hands. He glanced across at the tall clerk, who still had the ribbon that had tied the letter dangling from his fingers.

"The honour of your family," repeated Aedilius, rising to his feet and rounding the desk with silent steps. "You think, Chief Astrebanus, because your brother received this letter, this supposed nomination" – he waved the scroll at Drusus – "that you, a mere provincial, also have a right to this position. Am I correct?"

Drusus nodded in disconcerted silence, not liking the change in Aedilius' tone.

"Your brother was murdered, you tell me." Aedilius' voice began to rise in volume. "Do you think I inherited my position from my brother? If only my brother had lived to be murdered!"

He took a breath before continuing. "Look around you! What did you see as you made your way among the glories of Rome?"

Aedilius paused for a moment, as if he were anticipating a reply, but he began again before Drusus was able to collect his thoughts sufficiently to provide one.

"Shuttered temples? Plundered palaces? Statues and monuments torn down and smashed? How many brothers do you think died at the hands of the barbarians… and sisters, and mothers and fathers and sons and daughters? And you come here asking for favours, thinking you can call on my time, on the emperor's time, on the Senate's time, because of one dead brother in a far-off province?"

He thrust the scroll towards Drusus, clearly expecting him to take it, an unavoidable indication that he was dismissed.

Drusus had half-extended his hand to take it when he had an inspiration, as if one of the gods had whispered into his ear.

"I… I… can always go to Collonius," he stammered.

Aedilius froze, then he slowly withdrew his hand, still clutching the roll. A frown crossed his face. He glanced down at the documents and then up at Drusus. He pursed his lips, took a step backwards.

"Perhaps," he said finally, "I can be of a little assistance to you. I will have a letter of introduction made out for you." He glanced across to the tall clerk. "Pompeianus would be the right man, I think."

The tall clerk gave a brief nod of agreement.

Aedilius stood up. He held out the documents once more, the faint hint of a smile on his face.

"It has been a pleasure to meet you, Chief Astrebanus. Unfortunately, I was never able to visit Britannia myself, but I understand it's a green and pleasant land, well worthy of a young governor… full of initiative."

Drusus returned his bow. The interview was clearly over, and he followed the tall clerk out into the antechamber.

The well-dressed man had gone, and two merchants now stood leaning over the short clerk's desk. They looked up when Drusus emerged from the archway.

"Decius… Pompeianus," said the clerk from behind him.

Decius bent down underneath the table and selected a rectangle of vellum from the large bag which lay half-concealed below. He flattened the sheet out on the desk, while the two merchants, the tall clerk and Drusus peered down at him. With great care he selected a thin brush, dipped it in some ink and, with a great flourish, began a series of strokes across the top of the page.

"Your name again," he said.

"Drusus Astrebanus, Chief of the Durovenes."

The scribbling continued until the clerk replaced the brush, picked up the sheet, sprinkled sand on it and then waved it in the air a couple of times before handing it over to Drusus. The eyes of the two merchants followed the transaction.

"Be careful you don't smudge it," said the clerk.

Drusus eyed the document.

"My Best Magister Pompeianus," it began, with the first three words and Pompeianus written in different hands. "May I recommend the bearer of this letter, Drusus, Chief Astrebanus, to your attention. His errand may fall within your purview. Your faithful friend, Julius Augustus Aedilius."

Is that all? thought Drusus. But enough, I hope.

The gaze of the two merchants followed him as he left the antechamber. A man who received a letter of recommendation from Magister Aedilius was worthy of a little respect.

❧ Chapter 22 ❧
Gaul

The bandits did not return to the camp on the Lugdunum road that year. Amalric judged it was preferable to keep a low profile, to avoid unnecessary provocation of the Bishop of Senones. Instead they took the path to the Aquitania road. Ophelia had fully expected to travel with them, but Amalric took her aside when he saw she was beginning to pack.

"I don't want you coming with us," he said. "Anna can come, but not you."

"But Alanaric does not need my breast anymore. He's old enough to stay in the village on his own."

"That's not why I want you to stay."

"Are you hiding me from someone again, Amalric?"

He glanced around to see if anyone could overhear him and dropped his voice to a whisper.

"Stay here and keep your eyes and ears open, Ophelia. Look out for outsiders, for people asking questions. You understand. You've travelled more. You've seen more of the world than Anna."

Ophelia felt a clutch at her heart, her feelings conflicted. Strangers… they could mean an escape for her and Lanius if they were people who could be trusted but, if not, they could also mean death to the friends she had made, to Anna, to the children and to herself.

In the morning she gave Anna one last embrace and watched her leave on the heels of Amalric. Where did her loyalty lie, she wondered as she watched the band disappear amongst the trees. She had no love for the bandit, no love for the men with him, but she had also come to see that the village offered a refuge of sorts, even a sense of freedom, for girls like Anna, Grear and Ylva, for men like Emeric, and, hard as it was to admit it, for herself. If Drusus Astrebanus and his brother had been prepared to slaughter her family, how many others were there who would do the same? How many other families were there who had suffered the same fate? Livia, for example, and her husband, had they survived or died?

She looked up and noticed Fredagunda was crying. She opened her arms and called to the girl.

"Here, Freda, come to Aunty," and she wrapped the sobbing child in her embrace.

Ophelia was glad to be able to throw herself into the weaving, glad to be able to help Milva with the animals, to scratch out letters in the dirt and try to teach Fredagunda to recognise them, to scold little Lanius when he trampled on her improvised school, kicking the dirt angrily to capture his mother's attention. She found she was busy, useful, had a sense of purpose. Sometimes when she lay down in the evening, tired, reflecting on what she had done during the day, she could almost imagine she was happy.

She was milking a goat when she heard footsteps behind her.

"Almost done, Milva," she said without turning around, and then she realised the steps were not Milva's but someone heavier, louder. She spun around and was astonished to see Amalric standing behind her.

"I'm only visiting," he said, "passing through."

Was it only a feeling of surprise that persuaded her to take him in her arms and let him kiss her?

"What are you doing here?"

He said nothing as she bent down and picked up the bucket of goat's milk, untied the goat and slapped it on the rear to encourage it to amble away. He picked up the stool she had been sitting on and tucked it under his arm.

"What are you doing here?" she repeated, as he took her elbow and walked beside her to the cottage where Milva would be waiting to start the process of turning the milk into cheese.

"Have there been any messages for me?" he asked.

"No," she said, still surprised, "why should there have been? Were you expecting a message?"

He shook his head, neither a denial nor a confirmation. They had reached the hut. Milva's eyes were wide when she saw him. The old woman ran to embrace him, but there was a look of concern on her face when she stepped back, as if she had an uncomfortable intuition despite the smile he gave her.

"I'll remain for the evening meal, for the night," he said to the women, and then, taking hold of Ophelia's arm, steered her out of the hut.

"There was no one here, looking for me, asking for me?" he began again, a worried tone in his voice.

"No, Amalric," she replied.

"I'm worried," he said at last. "He never came back."

"Who never came back?" she asked, but before the words had even left her mouth, she knew the answer. "The man," she said, "the man who came to visit you last year, the man you didn't want me to meet."

"I didn't want him to meet you," said Amalric, suddenly harsh. "But, yes, him. He promised to return, to complete our business. It's a long way to Rome, and there can be accidents, mishaps on the way, I know." His voice was full of doubt.

"Rome," she said. "Is that where he was travelling?"

"So he told me. He had business with the Senate, he said." Amalric spat. "I once had business with a senator. I cut his throat and took his purse. It's all they deserve. Too many good men died for the sake of their quarrels."

She placed her hand on his arm.

"You take their gold, you must accept the risk," she said.

He gave her a confused look and then laughed.

"By the gods, I wish I had come across you earlier in my life! But…" He shook his head again and looked away from her, letting his gaze wander over the village, the huts, the people.

"You've only ever known me as a thief and a robber, a dishonourable man, an outlaw, living from hand to mouth, but I haven't always lived like this."

He glanced back at her, searching her face for comprehension.

"Do you think I have wasted all the riches I have gained in stealing from travellers? It's hardly the island of Capri or Tivoli here in the forest! The fucking Golden House of Nero! A life of luxury and waste!"

"I know you haven't," she said quietly.

"Once I made my living by killing on behalf of the emperor, and now I suppose I've been doing the same on my own behalf," he said, "but I'm tired of this life, especially when the winter winds begin to be felt in my bones, and my teeth are tired of chewing on sinewy oxen or half-rotten vegetables."

"And now these rumours?" said Ophelia, trying to sound innocent and worried.

He said nothing for a moment.

"I don't like to break my word, once it has been given, but…"

She held her breath.

"I don't want to be too late again. That's the story of my life." He sounded wistful, melancholy. "I've always seemed to be a little too late. If I had run to the villa when I had noticed the horsemen coming, I could have warned them and then none of this would have happened. If I had been quicker to see the writing on the wall at Arelate, after Gerontius was defeated, then Tertius wouldn't have died, and I might have been able to get the boys away. I could have remained an officer, serving out my days, with a fat bonus at the end, and riches and stories to take back to my own country. Instead, I had to scuttle for the forest. One fucking thing after another, and now… now, I'm beginning to worry I'm going to be too late again, and again everything will be lost."

He wiped his hand across his face, as if he were trying to clear his vision, and looked down at her.

"Enough," he said tetchily, turning away and disappearing into the dusk.

He came back later, but when she woke in the morning he had already left.

❧ Chapter 23 ❧
Ravenna

The only merit with Ravenna, concluded Drusus, was that it was so remote from civilisation that the invading barbarians had passed it by. A provincial small town, now packed to bursting with courtiers, officials, and all the fawning tradesmen and servants needed, or desiring to be needed, to supply them. He found an overpriced room that would have been unfit for a slave in any other town. Rome had been expensive, but this place was outrageous, and he examined his purse with disquiet. His reserves were falling fast. He was no trader who, with a secret handshake or by displaying a certain token, could have access to credit. He was no mover-and-shaker from Rome whose name alone was enough to open men's purses. He had already realised that he had left both his treasure and his reputation in Gaul.

He needed to complete his business with Gaius Ursinus as soon as possible and start on his way home, but first he had to locate Magister Pompeianus. A few enquiries in his lodging soon clarified the matter. "The Duke", as he was known, turned out to be one of the most influential people in the court, second only to the emperor, at least in his own opinion. In any case, an audience with the Duke was as good as an audience with the emperor, better in fact, since the emperor never did anything without consulting his mother, and Mother did nothing without consulting the Duke. It was not difficult to locate him, Drusus understood, in a town this size, but gaining access could be another matter.

"A letter of introduction from Aedilius," mused the clerk, scratching his chin, when Drusus had located the imperial offices, "and addressed to Magister Pompeianus. Those bureaucrats in Rome do not seem to be abreast of the Duke's new status," he added, sniffing. "I shall have to ensure they're informed right away."

"What about my case?" asked Drusus. "Can you do anything about that right away?"

The man observed him doubtfully.

"That depends… I'll take your document and let the officials have a look at it. If the case is open or shut, then we can probably slip you in, but if it requires some consideration…" He shrugged his shoulders. "Who knows? It could take months or years, depending on whether anyone has an interest in dealing with it."

He smiled at Drusus, reaching for the precious copy of the petition letter.

"Of course, for a donation to the church… our emperor's mother…"

"It seems to me that this is a fairly obvious case of injustice. I'm only looking for a confirmation of the nomination we received," said Drusus. "It should be straightforward. I'll take my chance."

"Very wise," said the clerk, a professional flatterer.

Drusus doubted his wisdom, but the truth was, he did not have a choice. He only had to look around at the dress worn by a mere scribe, at the mosaics and tapestries in the basilica, at the procession of dignitaries he had seen out of the corner of his eye, making their way into a church, to realise that a fee, a fee that would make a difference, was way beyond his means until he had obtained what he was owed by Gaius.

The clerk, impervious to the financial concerns of petitioners, sucked in his lips and scratched his ear.

"Let's say you return on Jove's Day, and I'll see what progress we've made."

Drusus, promising to return as suggested, took his leave.

Locating Pompeianus had been easy. Locating Gaius Ursinus, he assumed, might be a great deal more difficult. He would be just one of many court officials, and there did not seem to be any shortage of those. In fact, his best hope might be to ask the clerk he had just been talking to.

"I say," Drusus said, turning back. The clerk, in the process of filing his document under pending, turned reluctantly once again. "Do you happen to know where I can find Gaius Ursinus?"

The clerk regarded him sceptically.

"You're not planning a lawsuit over this?" He waved vaguely and slightly uneasily in the direction of his filing system.

"Not at all," said Drusus with a smile, suddenly realising he had the clerk on the back foot. "It's a private matter, with my fellow countryman. I was hoping to meet him at home."

A faint expression of relief passed over the clerk's face.

"I suggest you enquire at his workplace, through the arch and behind the church. Tell them Mercurius sent you."

Drusus was momentarily taken aback. The man had not asked for a bribe. In fact, he seemed to be keen to be brought to Gaius' attention. Slightly astonished, he made his way under the arch and round the church, from which the sound of chanting could be heard, presumably emanating from the distinguished group he had seen processing inside. At the rear of the building was another arcade, similar to the one he had just visited, and a quick enquiry told him where Gaius Ursinus typically met clients.

"He won't be there now," emphasised Drusus' informant, eyeballing the church to indicate where Gaius was currently to be found.

Most convenient, thought Drusus.

A young man, a Greek, was sitting bent over a writing table when Drusus arrived at his destination. The man looked up as he approached, brushing back his black curls.

"I'm looking for Gaius Ursinus," Drusus said, unsure if he should speak in Latin or try a few of the choice words he had learned from Xancha to supplement his schoolroom Greek. "I'm a fellow countryman of his, and I hoped to catch up on old times, share some stories."

The Greek smiled, evidently fluent in Latin.

"I'm sure he'll be happy to meet you, but just now he's in the church, and when that's done, we must attend the law court."

"I can meet him at home," suggested Drusus.

"Wonderful, I'll let him know. He's always generous with his time."

Drusus slipped the young Greek a coin, quite unbidden.

Gaius Ursinus' house lay inland, away from the sea breezes. Once it had probably been a courtyard for artisans, but with the influx of imperial courtiers, it had been tidied up, the workshops converted into living spaces and the yard dug out to make a small garden. While not luxurious, it gave a very comfortable impression and, given the lack of space in town, was probably a signal of the prestigious position occupied by its owner.

That owner, however, was not at ease to be meeting Drusus Astrebanus. That was obvious. Far from being a convivial chat between two Britons a long way from home, an atmosphere of frigid tension dispelled the warm, southern evening air.

"I did not expect to see you here," said Gaius. "You must feel it worthwhile to travel such a distance."

"I do," said Drusus. He wondered for a moment whether Gaius had any inkling of his involvement in the fate of his family. It couldn't be possible, he decided, surmising he would be occupying a berth on the floor of the Adriatic before dawn if Gaius had any such suspicions. A man in his position would probably have few inhibitions dealing with an outright enemy.

"Then tell me your business."

"Your father," said Drusus, extracting a couple of sheets from his document carrier, "was a man with expensive tastes."

"I don't think so."

"It's not a matter of thinking," said Drusus. "It's a matter of adding and subtracting. Adding very little and subtracting a great deal."

"I'm not sure what you are implying."

"I'm not implying anything," said Drusus. "I'm informing. Informing you that your father, in order to fund his lifestyle, his beautiful villa, his town house, his gaggle of clerks and bag carriers, his luxurious food, his Christian church building, your education and a leg up in your career, his daughter's extravagant wedding – I don't mean Hypatia's, that was done on the cheap at the last minute, but Ophelia's, the envy of Verulamium – had to borrow considerable sums." He tapped the sheets in his hand. "These documents list his debts, those debts, in any case, which my brother and I were able to collect in our hands before..."

He hesitated.

"Before what?"

"...before your sister's husband, Marcus Silvanus, had Vitellus murdered."

"That had nothing to do with me," said Gaius. "I had left long before that happened."

"I'm well aware of that," said Drusus, with emphasis.

"In any case, Marcus must take responsibility for his own deeds. My father delegated authority to him before he left. It's only a sad mystery how the family were lost, otherwise none of this might have happened."

"Indeed," said Drusus, "a very sad mystery." Only your sister Hypatia left of all the family, he thought, and perhaps it's better not to admit any relationship to her in your circles, married, as she is, to a renegade.

"So what do you want from me?" asked Gaius.

"Cast a glance at that list," said Drusus. "Every item is backed up by a contract, with your father's sigil at the bottom." He tapped on the cylinder. "You are the eldest son. You must preserve the honour of your father. It would be a shame if you were exposed as a man willing to sacrifice his family name to dodge his obligations to his creditors." Drusus looked around him, with an ironic smile. "This fine house, your position at court, in church with the emperor, I believe, kissing his mother's hand, I can imagine. All would be gone."

Gaius' face was tight, pale in the lamplight.

"You know I can't pay these sums. Even with my position here. I'm not a corrupt official, but a respected member of the court."

"I'm not a fool, Gaius. I know you can't pay these sums, but I'm willing to cut you a deal."

It was a no-lose proposition. He had come upon it while riding over the mountains from the Eternal City. Money alone would not be sufficient, and his encounter with Aedilius had left him uneasy. His confidence in the bureaucracy of the Empire had been shaken, his respect for the Empire undermined. The whole edifice, which looked so imposing from afar, was distinctly shaky when viewed close up. His impression of Rome, the city and the people, had been disappointing. He was well aware that an army of barbarians had entered the city, looting and raping. He had taken that to be an aberration, a glitch in the normal framework of how things had been, were now and would be in the future. He had left with the unavoidable sense that there might not be any going back, that some unfixable change had taken place. That, in fact, galling as it might be to admit it, Silvanus might be right. The answer to the question of who ruled in Britannia might not lie in the Senate and people of Rome, but rather in the Britons' own hands. And, if that was the case, he needed a few more tools in his armoury than an appointment letter from the emperor, which after all, had not done his brother any good. He would need something that would specifically appeal to the Britons.

"My proposal is this," he continued. "In return for a generous interpretation of the loan terms, one which, shall we say, does not threaten your position in court too much, you'll prepare some letters for me which state the following... you might want to take notes."

"I'll hear what you have to say first, Astrebanus," said Gaius.

"Very well. Item one, you grant me the lands and property of the Verdaris Estate, to be inherited in perpetuity by my descendants without claim." Drusus smiled. "You aren't planning to return to Britannia, I'm sure, so that will cost you nothing."

"But my father made the property over to my sister Hypatia, and when she married..."

"You are head of the family, your father's inheritor. You can dispose of the family property as you will. I'm not asking you to argue the claim on my behalf. I'm well enough schooled to do that myself, and the estate will be fair compensation for the expenses and inconvenience my brother and I have accrued in settling with your creditors. May I continue? Item two, you resign your rights in the inheritance of the governorship of Britannia Prima and make them over to me."

"I don't have any such rights. My father made them over to Marcus Silvanus, at the time he took him up into the family."

"Then you lose nothing by preparing such a letter. Item three, you recognise me as Chief of the Durovenes and paramount chief of Britannia Prima."

Gaius could not help laughing.

"What do you think I care about this foolish tribal nonsense? It was all posturing even in my father's time."

"Then prepare the document as I ask, Gaius. And item four, last but not least, and this should not hurt you too much either, you assert your right to the chiefdom of the Dumantes in your father's place."

That should fuck it up nicely for Silvanus with his allies. They won't know which foot to stand on, thought Drusus, but he was careful not to say as much.

"That's ridiculous," said Gaius, with a frown. "I've never made such a claim. I live here in Ravenna, serving at the court. What do I want making such a claim?" Drusus could see that Gaius smelled a trap, but that he could not put his finger on where it lay. On the other hand, with Publius Julius' fate unknown, Gaius Ursinus' word, on parchment and with the proper seal, would weigh significantly in Britannia. It wouldn't necessarily permit Drusus to ride unmolested into Corinium while girls threw garlands at his feet, but it would make his task a good deal easier.

"In return," said Drusus, "as far as these letters of debt are concerned, let's say a select few will be returned to you at a rate of one tenth. I'm sure there are men, Jews and Greeks, in Ravenna, who would be willing to forward you the money. They would want security or favours in return, perhaps, but that's not my problem. My problem is to have my fair share of these debts for which my brother and I have so carefully and expensively taken responsibility."

Gaius' eyes were still, his mind clearly working overtime.

"It will take some days," he said finally, looking down at the papers. "These are large sums you are expecting, and the letters you require… my clerk is busy."

"I'll be patient," said Drusus. "As you said, I've come a long way, and I've been waiting a long time. Three days should be enough, I think, for you to inform me of your progress. I've already made the acquaintance of your clerk. He seems very efficient, and I'll be happy to meet him again when my other business has been completed, or perhaps it's better for us to meet more discreetly here. Yes, let's say in three days, here at your private residence."

Drusus replaced the lid on the document carrier.

"In the meanwhile, these I intend to deposit with the magistrates," he said, placing his hand on the case, "unless I get a token of your goodwill in dealing with your commitments. I know you have friends, many friends in this city, but if any harm comes to me, then you'll be exposed, I promise, and your success and prominence will come to an end. Am I clear?"

"Clear enough, Astrebanus," said Gaius coldly. "Now, if you will excuse me, though I haven't much appetite anymore, my family and staff expect me for dinner. I hope you are not insulted if I don't invite you to join us."

"Not at all," smiled Drusus. "I'm looking forward to dining at your expense for many years to come."

When Jove's Day came around, Drusus made his way back to Mercurius, the clerk.

"My good sir," said the clerk, rubbing his hands together. "I have excellent news for you. Your case has been reviewed already and you are requested to attend upon the Duke tomorrow. Arrive at noon and take your place. You will be called when it's your turn to be presented."

Drusus took his place in the audience hall on the following day, a feeling of hope in his heart. The officials must have seen at once that all that was needed was to ratify the previous decision. He was one of many in a crowd of supplicants, and not the most important by any means. Pompeianus sat on a throne at one end of the hall. Behind him were arranged a row of solemn dignitaries. Their clothes revealed their status: religious, military or laymen. They appeared to have no other role but to affirm that the Duke spoke for the emperor.

Drusus bowed when it was his turn. Others had fallen to one knee, but he was too tense, too strained, too unpractised to carry it off. He might not be able to rise up again. The Duke, himself, stood up as Drusus approached and greeted him. Drusus took a deep breath, straightened himself, ready to begin the speech he had prepared, tactfully modified to suit his audience. Pompeianus, however, raised a hand, causing him to hesitate. The Duke glanced to his side, catching the eye of a retainer, finely dressed, who handed him a scroll. When he turned back, his expression was enough to still Drusus' tongue.

"Your petition has been reviewed, Chief Astrebanus. A search has been made in our archives." The Duke nodded towards the retainer, as if to suggest the man was the one who had carried out the search.

"We find no record of having received this petition, and thus no record of having appointed your brother governor of Britannia, either any part, or the province as a whole."

Drusus' heart sank to the pit of his stomach. His knees shook. He almost slumped to the kneeling position without meaning to.

"Of course," continued the Duke with a smile, "it is possible that the Senate might have acted without consulting the emperor. Unfortunately, this has happened on occasions, but we believe you have enquired with the Senate already, which is why our friend Aedilius recommended you consult with us. We can, therefore, find no support for this petition, and so, regrettably, it must be denied."

Drusus was about to speak, but one look from the Duke silenced him.

"You may be, must be, aware, Chief Astrebanus, that the Empire has withdrawn its forces, albeit temporarily, from the province of Britannia. If we might speak frankly, we consider this to be a most appropriate course of action. The province has been draining us of manpower and of wealth, and in recent years it has contributed little in return, except a series of rebels and traitors."

"But…"

Pompeianus held up a hand to indicate that Drusus should hold his peace. He had not finished his exposition.

"There is nothing more that the Empire desires at present than peace on the frontiers wherever possible. It is to our satisfaction that Britannia is at peace and our hope is that the province remains at peace. Until we are able to re-assume our responsibilities, we need leaders, competent local leaders, whom we can trust to maintain order in accordance with our desires for the best of the Empire and the people of our provinces. Governor Ursinus, though he may never have been our first choice" – Pompeianus waved the scroll in his hand – "this governor, Ursinus, appears to be ensuring stability, and we see no reason to disturb him or our provinces by offering incentives or support to any rival or competitor."

Drusus could barely maintain himself standing. It was all he could do not to break out in tears. His bladder felt like it was ready to burst, though he had drunk hardly anything before attending the convocation.

Pompeianus smiled once more.

"Of course, though it is to be deplored, the Empire has little control over events beyond the frontiers. Supposing some other contender was to emerge as governor of our former province, then, of course, that would be the time to review the circumstances and ascertain whether that man deserved our support."

Drusus realised he was being given a sop at the end. Was that all it was? Was that all it had come to? The Empire was not going to lift a finger to help him in his struggle against Silvanus, but, if he could unseat the man himself, with his own means, then he need not fear retribution.

Pompeianus gave him one more bland smile and handed the scroll to his attendant. The attendant took half a dozen steps towards Drusus and extended the scroll for him to take. Drusus took a deep breath and bowed towards the Duke. He had said only one word in the entire encounter. He took three steps back, bowed again, and turned to walk, to hide himself, among the waiting throng. A hundred pairs of eyes watched him go, thankful that it was not their petition which had been so brusquely and decisively rejected.

Behind him Pompeianus resumed his seat, there was a loud shout, and the next petitioner was called forward.

Drusus stumbled out of the audience hall. He could not orient himself for a moment in the heat and the bright sunlight and could do no more than collapse on a nearby stone bench, his head in his hands, his eyes closed. He had never even been given an opportunity to speak, to deliver the words he had so carefully crafted, neither to the senators nor to this so-called Duke. They had not wanted to listen to him. They had not given him a chance.

The tears that had seemed so ready to fall in front of Pompeianus had dried up. Instead, he was seized by a bitter thought. Somehow, by some means, Silvanus must have got here before he had. Silvanus must have lured the emperor into giving his support. Silvanus must be responsible for the "forgetting" of Vito's petition for the governorship, of the letter of appointment. Nothing else made sense. And who could have been the channel for this communication? Who other than Gaius Ursinus, that weasel, that worm, that snake? It was a good fortune that he had the means for a quick revenge. Tomorrow, tomorrow he would see. Tomorrow, if that man did not give him the letters and pay the money, then Drusus would destroy him. They might have been able to hide the truth about the petition, but no one, not Ursinus, not Silvanus, not Pompeianus, not the fucking emperor's mother herself, would be able to hide from the truth that Publius Julius Ursinus was a criminal, a swindler, a thief and a disgrace to the Empire.

Drusus made his way, at the appointed time, through the streets of Ravenna to his meeting with Gaius Ursinus. In the smaller alleys, it was shaded, cool and quiet. The atmosphere suited his mood, cold and determined. He came up to the house and tapped at the door. There was no reply. Siesta time, he thought for a moment, but he had an appointment. He rapped again: still silence, strangely echoing silence.

"Are you looking for Counsellor Ursinus?" He wheeled round in surprise. There was an old woman peering from the darkness of a door across the alley behind him.

He had no time to answer that this was indeed his intention, before the old woman spoke again, with a sort of malicious glee.

"You won't find him. He's gone."

"What?" spluttered Drusus, knocking again.

"Knock all you like, sir, but you'll get no reply. I'd be surprised if you couldn't walk right in."

Drusus took the crone at her word and pushed against the door. It swung at his touch, revealing a stretch of unencumbered tile before him.

The old woman had by now joined him on the threshold.

"Came yesterday, they did."

Drusus took a tentative pace forward into the house. His boots echoed on the floor as if he were beating an empty drum.

"Cleared the place out, they did," observed the woman, following him, stretching her neck to peer into one of the rooms leading off from the entrance. "Took everything, wife, kids, servants, the lot."

Drusus courage grew, and he advanced further into the house. The only noise was the dribbling of a fountain, and even that sounded more like a waterfall, echoing and re-echoing through the empty building. He stopped to orient himself, to identify the room where he had met Gaius on the previous occasion.

"Came as quite a surprise," continued his companion. "Nice woman, Cecilia Ursina. Not that I knew her, of course, but her cook was nice, and if the cook's nice, then usually the mistress is, too, that's my experience."

"Be quiet," said Drusus. He would have used stronger language, but he had a tinge of gratitude towards the old woman. Somehow the discovery of the empty house was a little less traumatising with her banal observations in his ears.

He crossed the small courtyard. Here, here was the place where he had spoken to Gaius. He stepped inside, his eyes taking a moment to adjust to the dark of the room. It was bare, empty, empty as any of the other rooms they had passed on the way.

"Here, Tibs!" he heard the woman calling. When he came out, she had a cat in her arms. "They left Tibs," she observed. "Naughty Tibs, you must have been out in the town when the master went away. Now you'll have to come and live with me. Luckily I have got plenty of fish for you." She stroked the cat's head, and it turned and looked up at her.

"Tibs is evidently less bothered about the master leaving than I am," said Drusus suddenly.

"Ah," said the old woman, "did you have business with him?"

"I did," said Drusus, "most important business. I wonder where he could have gone."

"He couldn't have gone far," said the woman. "All the stuff they took with them. The wagon couldn't get into the street. They had to carry it all down to the crossroads to load it on."

Drusus remained frozen for a moment. The old woman and the cat stood in front of him, but he did not see them. He saw instead the thoughtful, calculating face of Gaius Ursinus, already plotting to escape while they sat talking.

"By Christ," he swore, glancing around for a final time. "I suppose I will have to find Ursinus at his work."

"Down by the basilica," said the old woman, helpfully.

"I know," he replied sourly, beginning to tire of her.

He made his way to the administrative quarter, circumnavigated the church and paced down the arcade until he reached Gaius' workplace. The same young Greek sat outside, bent over his writing.

"Good day," said Drusus, unnecessarily loudly. The Greek looked up with a smile.

"Good day, sir," he said. "Did you manage to meet my master before he left?"

"He left?"

"Why, didn't you know, sir?" said the Greek, all smiles. "Master Gaius received a most unexpected opportunity to join our embassy to the court in Constantinople. Rumour has it the emperor's mother pulled strings to get him included."

"He's gone… to Constantinople?" Drusus voice was a weak stutter.

"Why yes, his whole family, too. The galley left yesterday. It's remarkable! What success! What a promotion!" Drusus could have throttled the man for his effusiveness.

"How unfortunate… for me… that I missed him." His words came stumbling out. "And how… fortunate… for him. I wish him good luck."

The Greek smiled, then waved towards the space behind him.

"This office will be vacant at the end of the month, sir. It's an excellent position for business. Will you be looking for a clerk, sir?"

"I'm only passing through," said Drusus, turning his back on the youth and walking away, not knowing where he was going. The documents, the letters of debt that he had carried all this way, were worthless. There was no point taking them to the magistrate now. Who would believe him, him, a rejected petitioner, against a man who was under the protection of the emperor's mother, who had been appointed to the embassy to Constantinople at her express request? It would look like he was a vindictive failure, striking out in a futile and pathetic manner. Perhaps the scrolls were worth no more than Hypatia had said, that day she burned the first bundle in Corinium? Nothing. For a moment he felt like throwing the entire container into the sea, but hope held him back. Destroyed they would be out of his reach, and Gaius and the Ursinus clan, too. While he had them, who knew how Lady Fortuna could change?

He found he had reached the city gate, so he turned and traced his steps back, carefully avoiding the basilica, until he reached his lodging. He had a few coins left in his purse, enough to justify one more night in his miserable room. He felt a surge of rage, though rage was useless. He was beaten, almost destitute, in a foreign city, and had the most powerful persons in that city against him. There was no sense in remaining. He had to make his way back to Gaul, to his friends, where his influence and position still meant something. He had to conserve his remaining silver for the journey. Hoping for a boat was out of the question. He was not ready to wait another winter, and he would have to cross the peninsula even to find one. He would take the land route, horseback where he could find a mount to hire, stay in modest accommodation, stick to the simplest food.

At dawn he set out, passing through the gate without looking back. The law, the institutions, that he had trusted had let him down, let his family down, let down everything that his forefathers had believed in and stood for. The Roman Empire did not care what happened to the Astrebani, their faithful allies and servants. The Roman Empire did not care what happened in Britannia. Very well. He, Drusus Astrebanus, alone, hungry and thirsty, trudging the Via Aemilia, did care. The Duke had pointed the way. If they were not willing to help him make a change, then he would have to do it himself.

෯ Chapter 24 ๛
Gaul, the following year

In previous years the signs of spring had been a time of excitement. For the men there was the prospect of new opportunities for enrichment. For the women, their minds were on the newborn lambs and kids, on the need to plant the crops for the coming year, the gathering together of the handicrafts produced during the winter and the plans to sell them at the Spring Fair. This year the excitement was tinged with concern. The previous year had been gruelling for Amalric and the men, for Anna and the women who had travelled with them: few travellers on the Aquitania road, and those that were, armed and alert. Now, everyone was on edge when at last the first flowers appeared in the woods, the green leaves on the trees, anticipating the coming season. At first incessant rain turned the open ground in the village into a swamp and the paths between the houses into streams. Rain kept travellers from the roads, and there was little reason to leave the village. Then, as the weather turned, the mud dried up and the puddles and pools which had hindered transport drained away.

"I'm not going to let them think I'm beaten," announced Amalric, giving the order to prepare the move with more bravura than he had often displayed during the winter.

"We can't remain where we are," he said to Anna and Ophelia. "There's nothing to do here, no prospects. We have to go and see what the authorities are intending."

"Are we going back to the camp by Autessiodurum?" asked Anna, when Amalric gave the order to start the journey.

"Why not? It's as good a place as any, and they can't keep the road shut for ever." He looked at the women. "A year of enthusiasm from the bishop should have been enough. With a bit of luck by now this new officer will have lapsed into the same indolence as all the previous ones. And then… we'll see…" He did not complete his thought, almost as if he were unwilling to hear his own words now that he was confronted with action.

"You two should come with me," he said at last. "I'm going to need you. You can leave Fredagunda and Alanaric here with Milva."

Ophelia felt a tug at her heart. The previous summer had been too good to last. Anna had already had to suffer the tension and threat which she had been able to avoid. Anna's loneliness and desperation had been so obvious when she returned. It would be unfair to put her through that again alone. On the other hand, without the children they would be tied to Amalric and his plans, though it might be just as well to be in place to see what he decided at first hand.

Once they arrived at the summer camp, the huts had to be repaired, aired out and tidied up, vegetable patches replanted, forage gathered. Amalric came and went, visiting his contacts, listening in the markets and taverns, fishing for information about the intentions of the officials. The men hunted and kept a look out for unwary travellers. The women cooked and cared for them. Through repetition of the daily tasks, life started to take on a routine. Above all, they waited for the big prize, an unprepared caravan, a train of mules with valuable goods or perhaps a group of rich and foolish pilgrims, trusting God to protect them in a land he seemed to have forgotten. What the bandits saw instead was worrying. Magister Constantius had retained his zeal and ambition. God had not forgotten Gaul, not this year, anyhow.

"The bishops have put pressure on the army," Amalric said to Ophelia. "Constantius has to buckle under, at least for now. The travellers are in escorted groups. We can't take them on."

He needed someone to talk to and Ophelia served that purpose, not because he expected advice in return, but to be able to put his thinking into words. He could not reveal his fears to the other men. They might simply melt away into the forest, or worse, they might decide he had become weak, lost his authority. It would be a short step to disposing of him entirely or betraying him to the authorities. Ophelia was conferred the role of his confidante. The more difficult the situation, the more he began to treat her as if she were really his wife, a partner in his life.

"Your fate is linked to mine," he said. "If I fall then you fall with me."

There was some truth in what he said, she knew, but she held her tongue. Perhaps if he had shown her respect and been truthful with her from the start, she might have felt more loyalty to him. Might have, but that opportunity had passed long ago. He had always said he admired her. Sometimes it seemed he almost worshipped her, but he had shown it in a very strange manner. Too late, as you always feared, coming to me now, Amalric, she thought. Too late to think you can treat me like your wife when all this time you've acted like I'm a slave and a whore for you to use. I'm not your wife, and I never will be.

"These escorts are not the usual urban thugs that can be bribed to run away at the first sign of danger," Amalric went on. "They're uniformed soldiers, from across the frontier, maybe, but acting under orders, willing to fight, and unbribable."

"You've tried it?" she asked.

"I've asked around the usual places. People look the other way, pretend they don't hear me."

Are you losing it, she thought, your influence, your position in the vicinity?

Worse was to follow. Waltrude, one of the women, appeared from the forest, tired and limping. Her husband took her by the arm and led her to Amalric. "Tell him what you saw," he said.

"I was out collecting eggs at Vetrus' farm," she gasped. "He's always been a friend of ours. Then I saw soldiers among the trees. I was frightened, so I left the path and hid until they'd gone."

"What were they doing?" demanded Amalric.

"Following the trail, that's all I could see," said the woman.

"How far away were they?" he asked again.

"Not far," she said, "about halfway to Autessiodurum."

He left with a pair of his men, slipping into the woods in the direction Waltrude had indicated.

"Fucking idiots," he said, on returning. "They're marking the trails in the forest. You'd think they were surveying a road."

But he was not so sure of himself the following day.

"You can't stay here, I've decided," he said to Anna and Ophelia. "If it comes to a fight, I don't want a bunch of women around the camp. You must all go back to the village. You'll be safe there. It's just a village like any other."

"And you?" asked Ophelia.

"We have to stay, we men. There are riches buried around the camp, our gains, built up over years of raiding. All that will be lost if the camp is taken over by soldiers. We can't afford it. We'll follow after as soon as we can. I'll send you a message if anything happens… and if it does, go to the Fox Tavern, in Autessiodurum, through the stables. Ask for Martius."

Ophelia, genuinely alarmed, nodded in confirmation that she understood.

"But you could come to some harm, all of you?"

"Do as I say," said Amalric, suddenly angry. "Anna, Ophelia, you and Waltrude, and all the women, pack up your goods and leave at daybreak. I'll send Crassix and Philo with you as escort, at least until you're within a day's march of the village."

Ophelia listened to what he was saying and knew he was trying to convince himself. His anger simply betrayed his own anxiety. She and Anna knew of one hoard of buried treasure. Probably there were others. Wouldn't it be better to dig it all up now, and for all of them to retreat to the village, out of harm's way? He's frightened of his own men as much as the soldiers, she thought. How long would they remain united if greedy eyes saw the profits to be gained by treachery?

Waltrude already seemed to be trying to hide, crouching, looking anxiously from side to side, as she scuttled around the camp, gathering her few possessions together, and she wasn't the only one.

"I'll go and help her," said Anna when she noticed. "She needs encouragement now. They all do." Anna sprang up and hurried over to the frightened woman. Amalric and Ophelia watched her go.

"What do you want with me, Amalric?" said Ophelia, alone with the chief, seized by a strange feeling of calm.

"Pack up the hut and go back to the village," said Amalric. "Take care of the children. I won't forget you. I've always loved you above anyone else, Ophelia. I'm a rough man. I haven't always followed the ways of civilised people, but I can, I will, if you'll help me. Once I've understood what's going on here, I'll come for you, you and Anna, and our children."

She stood up, kissed him on the forehead and ducked into the hut.

⋈ Chapter 25 ⋈
Gaul

For Anna and Ophelia the days in the village were a time of eerie peace. Crassix and Philo, the men Amalric had sent as an escort, returned to his camp, and the only men who remained were Emeric and a couple of other old timers, injured soldiers, and a few youngsters who had neither women nor treasure to worry about. The men sat in the sun lazily, played dice, threw daggers at targets, slept, and occasionally went out hunting. They ate the food the women provided and played with the children when the fancy took them.

Ophelia and Anna ground corn and baked bread, carded wool, anything to keep themselves occupied, listening to the talk of the other women, waiting. The extra bread they baked, the extra meat they smoked were packed carefully away. They would be starting a journey sooner or later, but in which direction, and with whom? Would Amalric come for them, or should they make a run for it themselves? Should they leave now while they knew he was distracted? Ophelia felt torn. There had become, despite everything, a certain security, a certain familiarity in Amalric. He had told her he loved her, and there was no doubt he was telling the truth, but she did not love him; perhaps at best he had begun to earn her respect as he had shown himself to be more human. On the other hand, she had not loved Cornelius. Love had never been part of the discussion when she married. She had simply done her duty. And what was her duty now, and to whom? There was no one to tell her, no one to steer her way. She had already lost two children, two children she could have saved if she had dared to ask more questions, to challenge her father and her husband, in the way her sister had done. Now Lanius needed her. She could not, she would not lose another child. And… and… there was something else. In those last few days in the camp, Amalric had turned to her with a desire and a desperation he had not shown for a long time, and she was beginning to suspect there would be consequences. If he came for them, she would have to go with him. What was the alternative?

The days passed, and no news arrived. The tension rose. No one could utter aloud what they were thinking, not even Ophelia and Anna to each other. It was as if they were walking across a narrow bridge, with an abyss on either side. Only by keeping quiet, by staring ahead, by steadily placing one foot in front of the other, could they hope to continue on their way. A distraction, a look to either side, and they would fall into the depths, to an inevitable doom.

Then the sound of hoof beats, approaching along the forest trail from the north, broke the silence. The young men dropped their dice and stood up, reaching hesitantly for their weapons. The women emerged from the huts and turned towards the path with anxious looks. Whoever was coming was in a hurry, galloping in fact, which could be dangerous on forest paths, criss-crossed as they were with roots and studded with stones. The horseman emerged from among the trees and cantered into the clearing occupied by the camp. He pulled the horse up sharply and began to shout.

"Flee, flee, the soldiers are coming!"

At first they did not realise the man was Philo. For a moment they could not take in what he was saying. They crowded up to him with questions, but he only grew more agitated.

"Run away, run away, as fast as you can!"

"What's happened?" asked Milva, trying to sound calm.

"They came for us in the night… soldiers! They must have waited. We began to gather up our things… to dig up the treasure. Then they came out of the trees. We fought. Everyone fought. There were too many!"

Philo was nearly screaming.

"I was the only one to get away. I grabbed a horse… left all my stuff behind." He drew a breath. "I managed to jump over them, out into the woods. I headed this way until I found the track. Then I galloped as hard as I could."

"But what should we do?" asked one of the young men.

"Run away, flee, as fast as you can! They're coming after me!"

"But you must have left them far behind?" commented Emeric, trying to restore a little calm.

"Did they have horses?" asked Ilana. "Did you see any?" Her tone was sharp.

Philo looked around, catching his breath.

"No, no, I didn't see any horses."

"What happened to the other men, Amalric, Crassix?" asked Milva, trying to sound more soothing.

"I saw Crassix fall, trying to reach the horses."

"And Baric?" asked Letti, tearfully.

"I don't know."

"And Amalric?"

"I didn't see him. We were all trying to save ourselves."

The cold truth began to dawn on the villagers as they exchanged worried looks. If the soldiers knew which way Philo had taken, they could be here at any time, even if they didn't have horses, and they could easily have hidden those, the way they had hidden themselves. The young men began to glance around, looking at each other. What did they have to lose by clearing out, compared to the risk to their lives if they stayed? Ilana could read their thoughts. She had seen men routed, running, fleeing for their lives so many times.

"If you run, and soldiers are coming, you'll die, just like Crassix and the others."

"Are you going to stop us, you women and Emeric?"

"If there are any men left among you," said Ilana, "you can save yourselves and help the rest of us. And you too, Philo, if you ever want to think of yourself with honour again."

"I'll stay," said one of the youths. "And me," said another.

"Thank you, Nardo, Irgun. Now you two go with Philo, on foot quietly, back along the path and listen. If you hear anything, men or horses, creep back here, through the woods, and warn us if you can."

"But if they come galloping, Ilana?" said Nardo.

"If they come galloping, Nardo, hide in the forest. Don't run. Hide. Save your life, and pray for us. Take your swords, men. I hope you don't need them. The rest of you," she turned to the youngsters who had not volunteered, "you cowards are no use to us. If you're not willing to help, leave."

"What will we do now?" asked Anna, as the young men slunk slowly away.

"We're village people, innocent country folk," said Ilana. "Why would any soldiers bother us?"

Emeric looked at her.

"You think we can just sit here, and wait till they turn up and bluff it out?"

"If they turn up," said Ilana, shrugging. "I think they'll have better things to do than hunt through half of Gaul for a bunch of miserable serfs like us. You and me, Emeric, we'll go up the path later on and find Philo and the boys. Kiss them goodnight. If no one has come by then, we're probably safe."

"What about me?" asked Grear, her eyes wet with tears. "He said my Crassix is dead, what will I do?"

"Stay here with me, my dear," said Milva. "I'll take care of you."

"I can't stay," said Ophelia, in a whisper to Anna, as they lay huddled together in Amalric's hut in the dark of the night. "We can't stay."

"What do you mean, Ophi?"

"If the soldiers come," she said. "I've read the histories, the stories the generals wrote of their lives. I know how the Romans treat rebels. In the soldiers' eyes we're Amalric's whores, and if we're lucky we'll be quickly converted into soldiers' whores. If we are unlucky, we'll be dragged into the circus at Autessiodurum or Arelate and ripped to pieces, and Freda and Lanius the same, if they survive that long. They're bandits' children, and who needs more bandits? We can't expect any mercy."

Anna's eyes were fearful.

"But you're a citizen, Ophi, aren't you? They couldn't kill you like that."

"No one's going to take the time to listen if I claim I'm citizen," said Ophelia. "It might even make things worse, and it wouldn't save you, Anna. In any case," she continued, "you know there are people who would be only too glad to see me dead, humiliated and dead, Drusus Astrebanus and his friends, and perhaps others."

"But we promised Amalric we would stay… we would wait until he comes."

"If he comes," said Ophelia.

"He could be dead for all we know," said Anna, looking at the ground.

All the talk about what they would do came flooding back to her; brave thoughts when no danger threatened. And now, now…

"Then we have to leave, don't we," said Anna, looking up at Ophelia, "without waiting for Amalric?"

"Yes, we have to leave, tomorrow, at daybreak, you and me, and Lanius and Freda."

"But we were going to go with him. That's what we agreed. He told us he would come for us. You said so, too. Oh, Ophi, where will we go?"

"I don't know," sighed Ophelia. "Away from here, away from the soldiers, and when we are far away, then we can decide what we do next."

Anna leaned over and kissed her.

"I trust you, Ophi. I'm not going to wait for Amalric. I'm coming with you. We're not going to die."

"No," said Ophelia. "We're not going to die. Try to get some sleep, Anna. We're going to need all the strength we can muster tomorrow."

Ophelia lay awake a long time, thinking, calculating. Where would they go? She had imagined this moment many times before, but after that one miserable night alone in the forest, it had only been a hope, a dream. Supposing her sister was still alive, in Britannia, could they reach her by going north? Britannia was far away, over the sea. They had no money for a boat.

The soldiers had come from the north. When they had travelled, she and her family, they had come from the north, and her father had made them stay in hostels, and even then he had been betrayed. Her enemies, the people who wanted her dead, they were all in the north between here and the sea. Then her brother, Gaius, he was living in the south. They had been on their way to meet him, but that had been years ago. She knew the name of the town, Arelate, knew it was an important town, knew it was in the south, but she had only the vaguest idea where. She had only the vaguest idea where they were now. She knew the nearest towns to the village were Bituriges, Pictavis, Limovic. She had even been to Biturges once, with Ilana, to the fair, but otherwise they were just names, and they were places where Amalric might find them, or Drusus or the soldiers. But Gaius, he wouldn't be waiting. He would have gone on with his life, not even thinking she still existed. In the end, Anna was right, and even Ophelia had begun to consider it would be best to leave with Amalric. Now they had no more time to think, to dream, to wonder what would happen. Tomorrow, tomorrow they had to leave.

We can't go north, she thought, right into the arms of the soldiers, of all my enemies. There's only one way we can go: south, away from the threat we know. We have to go south and hope no new dangers lie in that direction. We have to reach Arelate, and when we do, we'll find Gaius.

"Wake up, wake up," came an urgent voice. It was Anna. To Ophelia's surprise a shaft of light was piercing the darkness of the hut, and she could see Fredagunda and Lanius shovelling porridge into their mouths with their fingers. She must have fallen asleep eventually.

"You let me lie here," she said, struggling to sit up.

"You looked so peaceful," said Anna, "and you need your strength, too. Here, I've made enough porridge for you."

Ophelia sat cross legged on the floor, facing the children.

"We must go on a walk after breakfast," she said.

"Oh, great, can we pick flowers?" asked Fredagunda.

"Later, after lunch. We must look out for new flowers that we've never seen before."

She felt Anna's hand on her arm.

"We've a job to do before we leave."

"We must pack the food we prepared," said Ophelia, still only half awake.

"I already started on that," said Anna, "before I woke you, and I added some extra clothing. It'll get chilly when we're out after sunset. But no, there's something else we must do before we go. Come with me."

She drew at Ophelia's arm until she stood up and followed her to the corner of the hut where her bed lay, the one she had always used when Amalric was at home, the one they had now given over to the children while their master was away. Anna pulled at the mattress, dragging it across the floor.

"Look, in the corner, can you see?"

There was a flat stone, set into the earth of the floor.

"All his treasures in one place, you and his pot of gold, that's what he said to me once, when you first came here."

Ophelia gave Anna a sharp look, but her friend was already on her knees, tugging at the stone. With an effort she pried it up.

"Look!"

Underneath was a small pot, black clay, made blacker with use, and against the black glinted silver.

"Amalric was a very cautious man," said Anna. "This was his emergency store, if he was ever caught in the village. He showed it to me the first year I came with him, and when you came, he told me to place your mattress over it."

"What are you proposing? That we take it?"

"We'll have to take it," said Anna. "We're going to need money, you always said that. Don't you think he owes us something after all we have done for him?"

Anna scooped out the coins, the small pieces of cut silver. At the bottom of the pot were even several fragments of gold.

"We have to hide these," she said. "I'll put a couple of coins in my purse, and you can take some, but the rest we have to hide, in our clothes, in our belts, in the packs, in the children's clothes, so no one can see or find them."

They gathered up the children, collected together as much food as they could carry, and checked they had the valuables well hidden.

"We're going to leave, Milva," Ophelia said. "We have to. If anyone wants to come with us, take their chances on the road, they can."

"We daren't stay," added Anna. "We're Amalric's women. These're Amalric's children. We can't afford to be taken."

"And if he comes for you?" asked Milva.

Ophelia hesitated. Should she tell the truth or a falsehood?

"We're going south, Milva, to find my brother. Tell him that. He'll know what I mean, if he comes." To anyone else she could have lied, but she could not lie to Milva, who had sat with her, cared for her, taken care of the children, been more of a mother to her than her own mother had been.

She could not lie to Ilana, either. She embraced the woman who had become her friend, tears in her eyes.

"Goodbye, Ilana, and thank you. Finish the cloth we were weaving and make yourself a dress from it and remember me when you wear it."

"You were always planning to leave," said Ilana, looking grave. "I always dream of leaving when I sing songs from my homeland, and you sang so many you had to have the same dream." She smiled. "I couldn't understand the words, but I understood the meaning."

"Aunt Ophelia, you said we were going on a walk, come along," came a child's voice. Ophelia glanced round the anxious watching faces for a last time, barely able to make anyone out through the tears, and turned and followed the children as they ran and skipped down the path away from the camp.

❖❖❖❖❖

Ophelia expected to hear the sound of hooves on the path behind them, the soldiers, Amalric, even Philo come to tell them that their master had arrived in the village and was looking for them. There was nothing, only bird song and the rustle of leaves. No one was coming behind them, but they kept on moving. Ophelia carried Lanius, who was lighter, but Fredagunda was a heavy burden. Her little legs did not allow her to walk fast enough or long enough to keep up, so Anna had to carry her on her back, held in place by a cloth, for as long as she had the strength.

When they stopped to eat in the middle of the day, Fredagunda asked the question that must have been on her mind for a long time, the obvious question.

"Aunt Ophi, when are we going home?"

Ophelia cringed inside, but she did not want to deceive the child any longer.

"We're not going home, Freda. We're going to look for a new home."

There was a silence, and then Fredagunda spoke again.

"But I want to go home." She began to cry.

Anna folded her in her arms, bent over her, kissed her head and stroked her as she sobbed. Ophelia watched them. What was she doing? Of course the village was Fredagunda's home. It was Lanius' home. They had known no other. She watched Anna. It had been Anna's home, too, she thought, longer than it had been hers. What was Anna thinking now they had finally set out? Was she regretting it, perhaps? She felt a tear coming to her own eye. Milva and Ilana had become her friends, too. She shook her head. Even if the village had become a sort of home after all these years, it could not be any longer. Whatever Amalric had been calculating, whatever was his fate, they would have had to leave sooner or later, he had made that clear. And now the decision had been taken out of his hands, out of their hands.

"Anna, dear, we must make a few more miles before it gets dark," she said softly.

Anna released her daughter.

"I'll carry her," said Ophelia, and before Fredagunda had a chance to protest, she hoisted the girl onto her shoulders.

Anna had been crying too. She saw that now clearly and reached out to her.

"We all left something behind, even me," she whispered, "even after all I've said over the years."

They walked and walked until their legs ached and they could walk no further, until nightfall. Then they stepped off the path and crouched in the forest, sharing bread and meat, and slept, huddling together more for comfort than warmth in the summer night. When the children woke up, they shared the carefully rationed food. At dawn they set off again, stopping now and then to listen for the sound of horses. This time, instead of forcing the pace, they began by letting the children walk. Little Lanius toddled along, and Fredagunda skipped and jumped, gone for a moment the regret for the village, glad to be able to stretch her legs instead of sitting scrunched up, bound to her mother's back.

The women, too, were content to be relieved of their burdens for a while at least. It did not last, of course. The children became tired and wanted to be carried, first Lanius, and then when she saw the little boy sitting on Ophelia's shoulders, remembering the perch she had had the day before, Fredagunda, too. But Anna and Ophelia took their time, and the pace was easy. If there were cavalrymen tracking them, they would have seen them long ago, and by now they were so far from the camp that a suspicious patrol might take them for local women. If Amalric had followed them, they would have heard the sound of his dogs on their trail, and no dogs came. Slowly a feeling of hope began to suffuse them, a feeling that they might have escaped.

❧ Chapter 26 ❧
Arelate

It was summer, thought Drusus, sourly, and Arelate again, though no Xancha. The dancing troupe had long moved on. She had gone with them, he assumed. There was a part of him that missed her, but another, larger part which was selfishly grateful. She would have been a luxury he could no longer afford. He had not really grasped how thoroughly his purse had been plundered in Rome and Ravenna until Gaius Ursinus had slipped away into the Adriatic and he had been left clutching the roll of worthless promises.

In the autumn he had plodded the length of the Via Aemilia until he had reached Placentia, a down-at-heel town of dilapidated wagon stops, and the only horses for hire he could find were in worse condition than himself. He had felt tired. He had felt sick. He had felt the gods, every single one of them, were against him. He had been forced to admit that he could not continue trudging the high roads in winter weather. There were the mountains to cross, whether he travelled north or west to Arelate. Either way, even if he found a fit horse, he would not have been able to reach Remis before winter set in, supposing even he could find others going in the same direction at this time of year. He had had no desire to chance his life on the way, to risk getting caught in a storm alone. He had had to find somewhere to rest and recuperate before the illness overtook him, an inexpensive place where he could gather his forces until the passes opened in the spring.

On an impulse he had taken the road to Mediolanum. The city had seen better days before Emperor Honorius had moved the court to Ravenna. Perhaps that was for the best. The lodgings were cheap, and he had not stuck out amongst the miscellany of people who had gathered in the city, Romans and barbarians, citizens and refugees, fortune seekers and folks escaping from ill-fortune. In Mediolanum he had had a minor stroke of luck, two really. He had been searching for a *medicus*, in need of a treatment for fever, and had run across an old Jew who prescribed him warmed wine with willow and a comfortable bed. When he complained of his dwindling purse and the reason for it, the true cause, he suspected, of his sickness, the doctor had helpfully mentioned he had a cousin, Simonus, who did business with the east, and who might be willing to accept a couple of the governor's letters of debt.

"You say this man's son's in Constantinople?" Simonus had interrogated him when Drusus had sought him out.

"As far as I know. I was told by an authoritative source, and I've no reason to doubt it," said Drusus. "The man was fleeing from me, after all."

The moneylender had looked sceptical.

"I doubt he'll pay my partners any more than he was willing to pay you. I'll give you one hundredth of the face value," the man grumbled. "I wouldn't give that much if I didn't have a cousin in Constantinople who might possibly be able to use these. If this man, Ursinus, has accepted a post in the city he can hardly flee again, and my cousin will find him out. I'll take the chance."

Drusus had pocketed the coins bitterly, one hundredth of what should have been a fortune, but still a small sum that would tide him over. The amount would keep him from going hungry. Perhaps he could even buy a decent horse. But since he was not planning to move on until spring, a horse would have been a useless expense. Instead, he had bought himself a new gown and a new cloak and hired a room. If he had been religious, he would have made an offering, but Mediolanum was completely under the influence of the most fanatical Christians, and he had no intention of donating any of the remaining silver to them.

Instead, with the comfortable bed obtained, he had gone down to the forum in search of the second component of the doctor's prescription. The place was alive with rumours, he had soon discovered, of yet another peace treaty between the leaders of the local barbarians and the Roman authorities. The Romans, not surprisingly, were keen to see the back of the troublemakers once and for all, and the barbarians, while holding out for as much as they could, were well aware of the numerous times the Romans had deceived them and turned against them and were keen to close the deal.

"The Romans haven't understood yet," one bearded gentleman had muttered in Drusus' hearing, "that their days of glory have gone, and it's us who represent the future – but they will."

Some future, thought Drusus, but he had begun asking around. Was there anyone who needed a lawyer? In Latin, in Greek, in British, or any one of several Germanic dialects? The men hanging by the law court had laughed in his face in the first week, until there came a knock on the door: an undistinguished middle-aged man, looking shifty.

"My daughter, she got herself pregnant…"

"Not by a Goth?" enquired Drusus.

"How did you guess? You are the man who was talking in the marketplace, who understands the laws of these uncivilised ruffians?"

"The Goth in question had a stock of treasure even though he was uncivilised?"

"That's what I'm trying to find out," grumbled the man.

And that had been his first client of the winter. It seemed that the boys and girls, not to mention the older men and women, had made the most of their relationships with the foreign visitors, unwelcome as they had been at first. However rough and uncouth to the sophisticated citizens of Mediolanum, there had been a fascination which drew people together, for profit and pleasure, more often than not with predictably disappointing results. And that meant teasing problems for a lawyer's mind and tinkling silver for his pocket. Drusus had been almost sorry when news came that the snows had melted and he had had to make good on his decision to purchase a horse and take to the road again.

And that had led once more to Arelate.

He found Tacitarius in the city. There was something strangely different about him. He stood straighter, held his chin a little higher. Above all, he was wearing a woollen military cloak instead of the silk one which had been his favourite the previous year.

"Tacitarius, you look positively martial," Drusus exclaimed as he greeted his old friend.

"Drusus," came the reply, "you seem to have lost weight. You have a lean and hungry look."

"Has there been another revolt while I have been away?" Drusus enquired cautiously.

"On the contrary," said Tacitarius. "Just now we are all loyal troops of the emperor, following the excellent example of Magister Constantius, intent on setting Gaul to rights!" He scrutinised Drusus' shabby appearance with a critical eye. "I take it your mission failed. Not governor, not wealthy?"

Drusus shook his head.

"You take life too seriously, my friend. That can be danger-ous." Tacitarius slapped him vigorously on the back. "Let's move over to a tavern, and I'll see what I can do to help fatten you up. Then you might resemble a noble Roman a little more."

"I need to leave as soon as possible for Remis, now that I've been obliged to put this Rome affair behind me."

"Well, you won't need to fear for bandits on your journey north. Our efficient magister has cleared them all out, at least according to his own reports."

For a moment, Drusus did not catch the implication of his words, but as they sank in, he felt his legs sag beneath him.

"Cl... cleared them out?" he managed to croak.

"Yes, hung them along the wayside from Lugdunum to Autessiodurum," continued Tacitarius nonchalantly. "Mopping up operations are continuing, I've heard, as a few of the master-minds are rumoured to have slipped away."

"There's hope then," Drusus muttered, letting out a deep breath.

"What did you say?"

"...that he'll finish the job effectively."

"Yes, yes. And what a flood of treasure has appeared on the market! I've managed to secure a few delicate silver pieces myself."

Drusus, stumbling, felt his chest tighten once again.

"Are you all right?" asked Tacitarius, grasping his friend by the elbow.

"Yes, yes, just tired from my journey. I hope I won't miss the chance to acquire a few items," he managed to gasp out.

By then they had reached the tavern, and Drusus was glad of the opportunity to sit down. The evening had not started well.

As Drusus realised over the next few days, news in the town was hardly clearer or better. Despite the magister's boasts, it seemed the route from Arelate to Autessiodurum was far from secure.

"I wouldn't travel north if I were you, just now," said Aelius. They were seated in the baths, in the caldarium. "Even with these convoys the military have organised." Tacitarius nodded, sweat dripping from his brow.

"Stay with us! There's always work to be done, opportunities to be picked up, here and there."

"But I can't stay," said Drusus. "I have to get back. I have business that needs taking care of."

He was acutely aware that he could not say what sort of business he had in mind, least of all that it was directly threatened by the activities of the admirable Magister Constantius.

"Then perhaps you should cross to Aquitania," suggested Aelius, "and then take the road to Senones. I've heard it's been quieter in the west."

"It's easy enough," said Tacitarius, "and I've crossed over to Burdigala several times in recent years, Nemausus to Carcasso and so on. I'll write you a pass if you stop by in the morning. It's fine, if you don't mind the Goths. They're taking the place over… results of that treaty you were talking about."

Drusus looked doubtful.

"It's out of your way, I know, but how much does a man value his life?" said Aelius. "I value mine sufficiently," he added "to have had enough of this steam."

He got to his feet.

"Oh, and by the way, Drusus, you might have some luck if you travel west," he continued from the doorway. "That dancing girl you took up with, the pretty one with the mole on her tit, what was her name, Xancha? She took the west road too. Perhaps you can hook up again."

"Uh huh," said Drusus, unenthusiastically.

"Well, you know what, maybe you're right to dump her," Aelius added with a frown. "Rumour had it that she was expecting a child when she left town."

Drusus sat silent for the moment and then let out a string of oaths, solid Gothic oaths, picked up on the streets of Mediolanum. Xancha expecting a child? It could be his, should be his, if she had been telling half the truth. A son even; something might have been achieved by this misery of a journey. He relapsed into silence, staring at the floor, unmoved by the trickles of sweat running down his face.

"You speak our language well," said a man sitting further along the bench, shaggy haired, his beard streaked with grey, his face and arms covered with scars.

"A little, sufficient," said Drusus, glancing at him, speaking Latin.

The man nodded, a wily smile on his face.

"You speak ours," said Drusus, seeing the look.

"A little, sufficient," replied the man, the wiliness shifting into friendliness. "You're thinking of going west?" he continued, switching back to Gothic.

"Seems like it could be a good idea," replied Drusus, now in the same tongue.

"It's a long journey, alone," observed the Goth. "Dangerous, even."

"To reclaim my ancestral lands," Drusus added. "I have to do it."

"The family lands… in Aquitania?" chuckled his neighbour. "You'll need some luck. They're being reallocated, to folks like me."

"My family lands are in Britannia!"

"Ah… so far away, just like mine. Do you know what my ancestral lands consisted of? A patch of swamp between the river and the endless forest. Enough for two cows and an eel trap."

He laughed. "And I was in Rome with Alaric and took more gold than I could carry! Can you believe it? You ever been there, Rome, the Queen of Cities?"

"I just came from Rome. It didn't look much like the Queen of Cities, more like the outhouse of cities… you didn't leave much."

The old man shook his head, then gave Drusus a shrewd look. "Made my fortune it did, and the Roman girls… they weren't too willing at first but when they got a taste of Goth performance there was no holding them back." He pumped his fist.

"You sound like my friend, Amalric the German," said Drusus.

"It's a new day and a new way," said the Goth. "We poor boys're taking over, and you rich ones, you're going to have to whistle for your fortunes."

"I've heard that before," sighed Drusus, "but I'm not planning to give up so easily."

The Goth laughed again.

"Are you going to put up a fight, or rely on the lawyers, like your friend here?" The Goth nodded in the direction of the dozing Tacitarius.

"If you two are going to keep talking in tongues, I'm off to join Aelius in the frigidarium," Tacitarius interrupted, suddenly noticing the man's tone and expression. He rose to his feet and made his way through the arch.

"Pompous idiot," muttered the Goth to Tacitarius' retreating back, then catching sight of one of the bath servants called out, "Hey, you, throw more wood on the fire, you idle bastard."

"Your Latin is quite serviceable," said Drusus.

"Like I said, sufficient." The man grinned again. "But I don't like to rely on it. The pen is mightier than the sword, they say, right?"

Drusus nodded in acknowledgement.

"Don't believe it, son. Sword wins all the time, in experienced hands, of course."

The Goth's face took on a self-satisfied look, and then, seeing Drusus' sceptical expression, he went on. "Man of the law yourself, I suppose." He scratched at his beard. "Then maybe you could do me a service."

"I don't plan to stay in town, arguing cases, if that's what you mean."

"That's not what I need… on the contrary. My son and his cousin, they're setting out tomorrow… in the same direction you're taking. Going to make their fortune, so they say." He nodded. "Yes, like I said, there's a lot of empty land out there, estates once owned by mighty senators, and now… they daren't set foot in the place because if they did we'd wring their balls off."

Drusus nodded with a certain amount of sympathy. If he caught a Roman senator unawares, he might also be overcome by a desire to wring his balls off.

"The lads are going out to see what they can find in the way of bargains, and they're taking a bag of my hard-earned treasure with them. You wouldn't be able to keep an eye out, and make sure they aren't swindled, if it doesn't delay you too long, you understanding Latin and our words?"

"I'm a lawyer, as you say," said Drusus.

"I don't expect anything for free," laughed the Goth, getting to his feet. "Be at the west gate tomorrow, early. I'll send a man with your fee."

It was the middle of the morning before Drusus walked his horse up to the west gate. He had had to stop by Tacitarius to pick up his pass.

"No point in taking risks with Constantius," Tacitarius said, fixing the administration's seal to the document. "Just wave this at any officious minion, and you should get by."

Half a dozen men were waiting by the gate. The "lads" the Goth had spoken of were two men of his own age. They were accompanied by an older man, grizzled and bearded, one of his arms severed at the elbow, and a trio of mean-looking individuals. Veterans of the wars, thought Drusus.

"Took your time," said one of the "lads", without introducing himself.

"Drusus… Astrebanus," said Drusus, deliberately. He had not spent a winter in Mediolanum without encountering the arrogant ways of the younger generation of invaders.

"The old man said early." The lad spoke again. "We've been waiting so long it's almost tomorrow." His Latin was impeccable.

"This is early," said Drusus, deliberately speaking Gothic, "for me." His accent, he knew, could be better, tinged too much with Frisian, but he was fluent enough to surprise his audience.

"Thormond," said the man who had spoken, "son of Athmond." He turned to the older man, evidently a servant. "Give him his commission, and let's get on our way."

"Sismond, his cousin," said the second young man, with a smile and a glint in his eye.

☙ Chapter 27 ❧
Aquitania

Far, far to the north, Ophelia carefully cut up the last of the bread and cheese and shared it out, but reality was staring them in the face.

"We're beginning to run out of food," observed Anna, seeing the tiny portions. They had no idea where they were, though they were not wandering, like the wicked people in the Bible, in a completely trackless waste. They had been careful to stay in the woods, out of sight, and they had stuck to the smaller paths, sometimes just the tracks of animals, but always trying to keep moving south. They had crossed streams and climbed ridges, but they had passed no villages, just a few isolated and deserted huts. Once they had heard the sound of an axe, far away, and they had chosen paths to avoid approaching what must be a man. If there were people living here, to find them they would have to take the wider paths and the risk of leaving the trees. The woods had meant safety for them, for the children. The dangers lay in the open space, the fields, the grassy slopes, where they might be spotted and questioned.

They talked it over that night, both feeling a little foolish. They were grown women. They had both led normal lives before becoming part of Amalric's band. Why were they so concerned about emerging from the woods and acting normal again? And anyway, the silver coins they had taken from Amalric's hoard had no value in the forest, only in a town. Perhaps there was something else holding them back from leaving the familiarity of the woods. Within the trees they knew who they were, what role each of them played. Outside, that would change.

Anna watched as Ophelia took the lead on the path, tall and slim before her, the bundle strapped across her back, and her son perched on top. How long, she wondered, would she be satisfied with walking around like that, like a peasant woman, when she returned to the town? How long would Ophi be satisfied to have her, a mere baker's daughter, as a friend when there would be so many other possibilities? If only she didn't have to keep on hoping, hoping that one day Ophi would turn to her and look at her, and she would see her feelings returned. She had tried to tell her, tried to show her, so many times. But once they left the little tracks and took the road out of the forest, once they entered the outside world, she dreaded that her hopes would evaporate, gone like the dew in the morning, like the birds in autumn.

Ophelia was aware of Anna, steadfastly marching behind her, carrying by far the heavier burden. She was painfully aware that once they left the shelter of the trees they would enter a world where she could no longer hide behind her friend as she had done so many times in the forest. Even if people did not know exactly who she was, whenever she looked them in the face, whenever she opened her mouth, she would reveal the type of woman she had been, and they would have questions, they would make assumptions. And now, confronted with that prospect, she was no longer quite sure what answers she had. How could she explain matters to her brother and his family? He would be sure to have a family, a nice polite, well-brought up family, when she, what did she have? She had a son, who would need to become a man she could be proud of, but what did that mean when his father had been… well, what had he been? A thug and a rapist, that was true, but he had been clever, a survivor, in a hard world.

Would Lanius inherit those traits from his father, or her own doubts about herself? And she had Anna. What would her brother and his wife… she could only imagine his wife, the wife of an imperial officer! What would his wife make of Anna? Anna, whom she owed her life to. Anna, who had given her comfort on so many lonely days and nights. Anna, whose daughter she felt was almost as much her own daughter. They could hardly accept her as equal, as a sister. She would never have done so herself, back… back when she had been the wife of an imperial officer. And every step away from the forest, every step towards the town, towards the *civis*, towards civilisation, would be a step back, back into her old life.

They had no choice. The landscape was ever more unfamiliar. Their food was running low. So the following day they kept their eyes open for glimpses of light through the trees, and while they still maintained a steady course, as best they could, to the south, whenever they had a choice, they turned away from the deep forest, in the hope of finding open countryside.

Towards the middle of the day, they were climbing yet another seemingly interminable hillside when they heard a noise ahead, the clanging and tinkling of bells. They stopped and listened. Ophelia was unsure what the sound meant, but Anna recognised that there must be a flock of sheep or goats nearby. They continued walking, cautiously, holding the children tightly. Suddenly they heard a dog barking and a man's voice. They looked at one another anxiously.

"Courage, Anna," whispered Ophelia.

"Halloooo!" Anna called out.

The dog began to bark again, and they could hear it coming towards them along the track. They scooped up the children and sat them on their shoulders. Suppose it was a hunting dog, like the ones in the camp, or a giant watch hound, kept by the shepherd to scare off wolves? It could tear them apart in a moment. The man shouted and the dog stopped, somewhere ahead of them, barking over and over.

"Halloooo!" Anna called again.

"Who's there?" answered the man, still unseen, a little uncertainly.

"Two women, lost in the forest," replied Anna. Ophelia looked at her doubtfully. That sounded like asking for trouble.

"Fido," shouted the man. "Stay!"

Anna and Ophelia continued to walk on, cautiously, down the path, watching for the dog. Then they saw it, standing ahead of them, blocking the way. Thank the gods it was obedient, since it was as least as large as they were, white and shaggy, a match for any wolf. Faced with the women and the order from its master, the dog appeared confused, alternately growling and wagging its tail. Anna and Ophelia stopped, viewing it warily. How far off was the master? Not far, fortunately.

The shepherd was an older man in a rough tunic. A battered straw hat sat on his head, and he carried a stout pole. He came to a halt beside his dog and scrutinised them.

"We're two women, lost in the forest," repeated Anna. Ophelia let her talk. She had a dialect that sounded honest.

"Where are you from?"

"We are from a village to the north. Our children ran off, and we could not find our way back."

The man looked sceptical. He took a step towards them.

"No men?"

Anna hesitated. What could they do but trust him? He was little threat on his own, but his dog could take down all four of them.

"We're quite alone, with our children."

The man took another step forward, the dog following at his heels, sitting every time his master halted.

"You're not from around here," he pronounced finally.

"No, we're not," admitted Anna. "That's how we got lost."

He grunted, still not sure of the situation.

"Follow me," he said suddenly. Fido, the dog, jumped up, turned around and began to trot off down the track, in front of his master. The two women followed along behind. Presently they came across a flock of goats, grazing on the sparse vegetation and the low-hanging branches of the bushes and trees.

"I would offer you food," said the man, "but I have just eaten my midday meal." He shrugged almost apologetically. "The rough wine I have will hardly be suitable for children, but if you follow that track, to the right, it's steep but it'll lead you downhill, until you reach a village. There's a well, and when you get there call out for Petra, that's my wife. She'll give the children something to eat and point you on your way."

He grasped the dog and eased it off the track.

"Thank you," said Anna. Ophelia held her silence but gave the old man a smile as she passed him.

"Nice doggie," said Fredagunda, and the wolfhound wagged its tail. If its master was sure of these strangers, then the dog was ready to accept them.

Anna led the way down the track, which presently left the forest and followed alongside a small stream. In the distance, down a steep slope, they could see a cluster of huts, and beyond them farm fields spread out into a valley. As they walked into the settlement and began to make their way among the houses, another dog began to bark. A large pig appeared to investigate the fuss, followed by an ageless peasant woman.

"Good morning, mistress," said Anna. "We're to ask for Petra. We met the shepherd in the forest."

"My husband," said the woman. Fredagunda had wriggled down from Anna's shoulders and run over to a low fence where there were a couple of ducks penned up. They had had no ducks in the forest. These were new to her.

"You've come far?" asked the woman.

"We're lost," said Anna.

"We told your husband our children got lost in the woods," said Ophelia. "I don't think he believed us, and he was right not to. We ran away. My husband was a cruel man, and I could stand it no longer, so I escaped, and my friend came with me."

"Where are you going?" asked the woman.

"To my brother, in the south, at Arelate."

The woman shook her head.

"I don't know that place, is it a town?"

"A big town in the south."

"The only town I know is Pictavis, and that's way up to the north. My husband travels there sometimes, once a year."

Anna's eyes suddenly opened wide.

"Pictavis! I've heard of that city!" She turned to Ophelia. "Ophi, we've come a long way if we've passed Pictavis. We must be safe."

Pictavis was a town Ophelia had heard of, a place that Ilana had occasionally visited, and although it was a little cruel to think so, if the town was in Anna's mental map, then they had not come far enough. The further south they travelled the safer they would be. To a land where no one knew them, where they would be a threat to no one.

"Come in, and I'll find you a little to eat," said the woman, Petra. "Those children look starving. I've only porridge and some greens but it will fill them up."

"That would be wonderful. Thank you," said Anna, as they followed the old woman into a low hut. She asked no further questions but only fussed around finding four bowls. She was a poor woman, and there were now only her and her husband in this hut, so that was quite a task. After days walking in the woods, even porridge and rough vegetables tasted wonderful, and Anna and Ophelia were grateful to the woman. When they had finished, she showed them, pointing away across the fields into the distance, which route they should take.

"With an hour's walk, if you carry the children, you should reach the road," Petra said. "You should make for Pictavis," she insisted, giving the children a kindly look. "That's the nearest town, everyone knows that."

"My husband, too, unfortunately," said Ophelia, with a sigh. "We must continue south if we're to escape from him."

The woman sounded sympathetic.

"You won't get there this evening."

She gave them some crusts of bread and suggested they fill their flasks from the well.

And they did not get anywhere, not even to the road. They decided to sleep in a field to gather their strength. They hid in a dried-out ditch so they could not be seen by people passing by. They need not have worried, as no one came, but they were stiff and a little cold in the morning. They ate the bread and drank the water and continued on their way.

While they had been in the forest, they could walk in the shade. Once they reached the road they were out in the open and began to feel the heat of the sun. Despite the shadow of occasional trees, they grew tired and thirsty and hungry, and Fredagunda began to complain. They saw more and more people working in the fields, and a couple of farm folk wished them good morning as they passed by. When Anna asked how far it was to the town, they waved vaguely, and said not far. To Anna and Ophelia, half dragging, half carrying the small children, it seemed to take for ever, but just as they began to offer up desperate prayers, they saw a smudge across the road ahead of them, which gradually took on the shape of a cluster of houses.

To the shepherd and his wife, it must have been a town, and to Anna, too. But to Ophelia's eyes it was no more than a meagre village. Certainly, they had money, but could they use such money in a small spot like this? In the marketplace there was a well, so at least they could slake their thirst without having to answer the question. Anna's practicality did the rest. She took out the smallest silver coin in her purse and offered it to the baker with an apology. The baker examined the coin with suspicion, turning it in his hands, perhaps wondering how a poor-looking woman had come by an object of such value. Then he took a large knife and banged it down twice on the coin, cutting it into quarters. For one quarter they were given two large loaves of bread, and for another a cheese and some cooked meat. They had enough food for today, and for tomorrow too. They ate, drew up water from the well and filled their leather bottles. The sun was now high in the sky, so they sought out the shade of a large plane tree which stood in the town square and let the children sleep, curled up in the shadow.

They saw she's a lady right away, thought Anna sadly.

Anna's so wonderful, thought Ophelia. How will I ever be able to repay her?

⊂ Chapter 28 ⊃
Narbonnensis

The men took the road to the west, Thormond, Sismond and Drusus in the lead, and the three veterans, Scan, Norm and Auri, riding behind. There was nothing to detain them in the next town they reached, Nemausus, no cheap land to be had, and, for Drusus, no word, no sign of a woman named Xancha. They began a long sweep, south and west, through Betterae, and then up into the hills until they reached Carcasso, always with the same result. On the road, they recounted their histories. To their chagrin, the young cousins had not been present in Rome but had been suffering under the hands of a tutor, beating into them the basics of Latin, reading and writing, at Athmond's order. For all the old Goth's disdain for the pen, he had made sure the younger generation could use one competently. Identifying their contempt for the Romans, Drusus gave a heroic air to his own tale of deception and disappointment.

When they finally reached Tolosa, their luck changed. A distant relative of Athmond sought them out. At first he had only disappointment for Thormond and Sismond.

"The best lands, in the valley along the Garunna towards Burdigala, have already been taken by men who arrived earlier and by friends of the king — but," he added, "there are lands between Carcasso and Tolosa that the king's ready to recognise as part of his territory if his supporters take them over. They'll be borderlands, it's true, and no one can guarantee there won't be conflicts."

"We can deal with that," said Thormond, grimly.

"Best to get the arrangement down on parchment, or a sealed tablet," said Drusus, "but how are we supposed to do that when the current landholders are in Italia? I had difficulty enough trying to catch them there."

The relative smiled a knowing smile, his gold jewels betraying that he understood quite well why the senators of Rome were not keen to have any further encounters with strangers.

"They have an agent in the city, charged with exchanging their lands for gold," said the cousin, "first come, first served."

"Our man, here," said Thormond, indicating Drusus, "can take care of the business, if we can meet this agent."

The land agent's office was close by the forum.

"I have here," he said, indicating a shelf of scrolls, "the titles to several select estates, signed and sealed by the owners, ready for sale."

He handed one to Thormond, who glanced at the document and passed it over to Drusus.

"No well," said Drusus, inspecting the first he was shown.

"There is a very good stream," insisted the land agent.

"In the summer?" Drusus remembered the thirsty ride from Rome to Ravenna the previous year.

The agent rolled up the scroll again and selected another. Drusus scanned the details and then began to read them out to Thormond and Sismond, doing his best with the translation.

"Two springs and a stream which does not run dry even in the hottest summer, a villa with farmyard, three resident slaves and two free tenants still remaining. And the right to a share of the tax from the neighbouring properties."

"If the king permits," emphasised the agent. "And more slaves will be needed," he added, rubbing his hands together, "to run the farm and the house, but" – he shook his head sorrowfully – "with the anarchy there has been, one of your… countrymen… stole several of them, and some of the others took the opportunity to run off."

"You mean we've been left with those that are either worthless or completely lack initiative?" asked Thormond.

"The situation can easily be remedied, my lord," said the agent. "The property's a day's ride, my lord, towards Carcasso, and on the south slope. Very good for grapes… might even be worth trying olives."

The agent's clerk rode with them, carrying the roll which described the boundary marks for the estate, the locations of the springs, the names and conditions of the tenants, the slaves and their families, their animals and the tax assessment of the neighbours.

"I don't understand," said Thormond to Drusus, as they descended the hills from Tolosa. "You should do the same as us. Why waste your time and effort on trying to regain your lands in Britannia, when without effort you could purchase at least as good here in our kingdom?"

"It wouldn't be the same," said Drusus, not willing to admit his current shortage of treasure. "My family have owned our lands for centuries. My name, Astrebanus, there's honour attached to it in Britannia. It means a great deal to me."

Thormond shook his head. He had spent his entire youth moving from one place to another, sometimes as a result of a victory, equally as often in a hurry, during the night, as a result of a sudden defeat.

"Thormond, you want to buy lands here," Drusus pointed out, "to create a legacy for your children and children's children. I inherited a legacy, and my enemies have stolen it from me. I intend to return and get it back."

They reached a dusty track leading off the main road, and after riding about half a mile came to a bridge over a swift-flowing stream. The clerk called a halt and unrolled his document.

"Here," he said, "is the southern boundary, and there," he added, pointing up a barren and stony hillside, "is the estate."

Leaving the others by the bridge, Thormond and Drusus took the path along the river. Drusus had with him the property roll. The valley bottom was promising, small fields with growing crops adjoining a cottage where a man and a woman watched them ride by.

"Atresius and his wife, twenty-five years old approximately, two children and three goats," said Drusus, quoting from the scroll. "A free man… the slaves live up by the villa, apparently."

They rode on, higher into the hills, until they reached a more level area, with several fields and, beyond them, a small villa shaded by trees.

"One of the springs rises just beyond the house," said Drusus, scrutinising the document, "supplying water and carrying away the waste."

They rode up to the building, dismounted and walked up to the portico. The house was empty so far as they could see, tiles missing here and there from the roof, and the shutters needed repairing, but the view down the valley was stunning.

"Master," came a voice from behind them.

"Syntix, fifty years old, slave," said Drusus.

The man began to speak, but his dialect was so strong that neither of them could really understand what he was saying. His gestures, however, were sufficient to persuade them to follow him round to the rear of the house and into the yard, where two younger men were in the process of repairing one of the barns. They stopped their work and stared at the newcomers.

Drusus nodded and, without thinking, said, "Carry on," and he and Thormond did likewise, round the house, and then on, riding up the path until the villa was a mere outline below them. From there Drusus could see several of the landmarks which were listed as indicating the outer boundaries of the estate; he pointed them out to Thormond, showing him the corresponding lines in the roll which described them.

They took their horses by the bridles and began to walk back down the hill. As they passed the villa once more, Drusus could see Thormond smiling to himself.

"Wouldn't be a bad place for children to grow up?" he said.

"I would prefer my own home," said Drusus, gazing out over the burned brown acres, the scrubby trees, a cluster of scrawny goats munching at a tough-looking bush. He thought of the Tamesis, the water meadows, the fat beasts, the rippling fields of corn, the cool woods, the yards and gardens of Agridurnum.

"But your enemy took your lands," said Thormond, in an irritated tone. "So how *do* you propose to get them back?"

"I… I'm not sure," Drusus admitted.

"Take him to the courts, some tribunal," grunted the Goth, "or" – and he tapped his hand against his sword – "see how he likes to be on the other end of a sharp point… huh?"

"I… I…"

"Look, Drusus, you've been complaining the whole ride how you got fucked over in Rome and Ravenna. That's what they do… those people, with their fancy words and laws." He waved his hand towards the stony hillside. "Do you think we would have got even this land that way? Didn't they try their best with clever arguments? Why do you think Alaric and my father and men like him plundered Rome? It was the only way to get those double-crossing bastards' attention."

He prodded Drusus' chest with his finger.

"If you ask my advice, you should do the same."

Drusus had no words to reply.

"Listen, my friend, I think you're standing at a crossroads. Stay with me and Sismond here, find your girl, buy an estate like this, or a house in town, if you prefer, build a new life with her, or cling to your fantasies about returning to your old home, but if you take that road, make sure you find some good men to ride with you."

With that he continued on his way back down the sheep path to the bridge, where the rest of the group were waiting.

The clerk watched the two Goths nervously.

"What do you say, Drusus?" asked Sismond. "I walked up the path a little way. It looks like it could easily be defended."

"The description of the land fits what's written here," said Drusus. "The landmarks are quite clear. The house is in poor shape, but it's not beyond repair."

A look of relief spread over the clerk's face.

"There's only two more steps then, my lords."

"And what are they?" asked Thormond. "Assuming we're willing to agree a price."

"To obtain the king's sanction to collect the taxes and ensure that the exchange of ownership is registered." He smiled weakly. "We don't want any more visitors riding by and claiming the land is theirs."

"Certainly not," said Thormond, "and since you raise the subject, I'll stay here with Scan and Auri and make sure no one gets that idea into their head, while you, Sismond, you and Norm can ride back to Tolosa with our lawyer friend and get the exchange confirmed. Shouldn't take more than a day or two?"

The last question was directed at the clerk, who smiled humbly and bowed his head.

"In the meanwhile," added Thormond, "perhaps we'll pop in for a chat with the neighbours and let them know who's the new master."

❧ Chapter 29 ☙
Aquitania

Ophelia, Anna and the children walked on through the afternoon and evening, slept the night in an empty barn and continued the next day. Around midday the road they had been following arrived at a junction with another, larger road. Now they were no longer alone on their travels but part of a steady stream of walkers, riders, men leading horses and carts, and even the occasional wagon which came rumbling up behind them, enveloping them in a cloud of dust as they stood to the side to let it past, and then rumbling off into the distance. One of the wagons they saw had a woman and children sitting in the rear.

"Why can't we ride in a wagon like that?" whined Freda-gunda. "I'm tired of walking, and I don't get carried as much as Lanius."

"Hush, my dear," said Anna, "and I'll carry you for a while," her expression of exhaustion belying her willing words.

Towards the end of the day, they reached a town, a real town this time. It reminded Ophelia of Corinium: a couple of rows of shops, a proper forum with a basilica to one side and a fountain in the middle. Anna was nervous, but Ophelia had seen how tired her friend was. It was a time and place for her to take charge. She marched into the travellers' hostel and asked for a room for the four of them, and dinner. The woman who greeted them regarded them in a dubious fashion. They were none too clean, and their clothes were ragged.

"We don't have a room spare," she said, almost immediately, turning her back to them.

"Wait," said Ophelia sharply. It was almost as if she had laid her hand on the woman's shoulder and pulled her back. The woman was about to open her mouth with another dismissal, when Ophelia reached into her purse and pulled out her hand. She opened it out to show the hostel keeper the coin. The woman looked at it sceptically, then held out her hand to take it. She peered at it, inspected it. Money was money, after all.

"Perhaps we might have a room," she said, reluctantly, after a long delay. "I'll see what's available. Otherwise, our dormitory's clean enough."

"If we have to sleep in the dormitory, we will," said Anna, only thankful it would not be a ditch or in the shadows of some alley for the night. "We have to get somewhere to sleep, to rest," said Anna, as the hostel keeper disappeared into the building, leaving them waiting in the entrance. "We can't walk any further, not tomorrow."

The woman came hustling back, a sour look on her face. Evidently there was a vacancy and she would be obliged to take in these two scruffy women and their brats.

"We can't stay here, Anna, not for long. We have to move on," said Ophelia, once they were in the room.

"We must, just for a couple of days," said Anna. "Look at the children! Look at their feet, in their eyes!"

Ophelia did not need to look. She knew only too well. The children sat blankly, almost ready to fall asleep if they had not been hungry as well.

"Can't we stay for a day or two, to rest and get some proper food?" Anna insisted.

Ophelia hesitated. It was tempting to take a break from the road, but here in the hostel they would attract attention. There would be questions. Not least, how had two poor women come across enough money to hire a room?

"We haven't come far enough," she said. "We still have to reach Arelate and find my brother."

"Your brother!" yelled Anna, her tiredness suddenly transforming into anger. "How do you even know where your brother is? Do you think he's still waiting for you?"

Ophelia was shocked. She had never seen Anna so tense and furious.

"I'm sorry, Anna," she said, hardly daring to look at her. "I'm frightened. I'm worried we'll run out of money before we reach safety."

"But where will we be safe? How far will we have to keep going before you're satisfied?"

"We have to keep going," said Ophelia, not having a better answer.

"We can't walk any further," Anna repeated. "I'm shattered, at the end of my tether. I can't carry Fredagunda anymore, and she can't walk. Just look at her little feet! It's hot. We're dirty and disgusting, worse off than we ever were in the camp."

We would be dead in the camp by now, thought Ophelia, but she was not so tired and angry herself to say it. She remembered Fredagunda's words earlier in the day.

"I saw some of the wagons that passed us on the road today, pulled up in the yard, wagons that are travelling south."

"Do you think we could get a ride?" asked Anna, sullenly, disbelievingly.

"I think so," said Ophelia, a hard edge to her voice. "I think I can get us a ride, but before that I'll need to have a proper bath after walking in the dust and heat."

"You're thinking about getting a bath! What about us?" cried Anna, sounding almost pained.

Ophelia realised she had spoken thoughtlessly, but she did not want to tell Anna what was on her mind. It would be hard enough for herself, and she knew Anna would object.

"Anna," she whispered. "I have an idea that will get us a ride on a wagon tomorrow, but I need to have a bath and you'll have to act as my maid. Can you do that? For us, please?"

Her friend looked confused, her fury mixed with exhaustion and desperation.

"Am I to be your maid now? Is that what it has come to, now we're in town? Is that all?"

Ophelia crouched down, tried to take Anna's hands, but Anna pulled them away quickly.

"No, Anna, I promise. It's just I need to act the lady, just for a while. Please, Anna, follow me to the bathhouse. Pretend you're my maid for a moment, I beg you, and we'll all ride tomorrow. I can see you're hurt, but please, please, don't be offended for a little while."

She said no more, shutting the two children in the room as they left. When they arrived at the baths, she assumed her most perfect Latin.

"I say, miss," she addressed the attendant, "is there space for a lady in the bath?"

"Wait a bit, dear," said the attendant, "I'll go and check, 'cause there's a lot of them wagon drivers just gone in." She shuffled off inside.

"Perfect," whispered Ophelia, putting her lips to Anna's ear.

After a moment the attendant returned.

"If you can wait for moment, you'll get a spot of privacy. The men're in the warm room, but they said they would be moving on soon. They'll be glad to be getting to their dinner."

"Thank you, miss," said Ophelia, taking a towel from those supplied by the hostel and beginning to remove the clothes she had been wearing for days, if not weeks.

"Anna," she suddenly said in a commanding tone, "take these travel clothes and wash them for me. I want them absolutely spotless, do you hear!"

Anna's eyes were already wide with astonishment, first at seeing Ophelia strip naked in a public place, and then at the way she was speaking. She, herself, had never set foot in a bathhouse and had no idea of the customs. She felt annoyed, out of place, worried. She did not understand what had come over Ophelia. She had nothing against doing laundry. If that was what was needed she would do it. She snatched up the dirty tunic and underwear that Ophelia had dropped and rushed away. Inside Ophelia felt awful to see Anna upset and having to take this humble role, but she could not show it. This had to be done if they were going to take the weight off their feet and ride in comfort. She wrapped herself in the clean towel provided by the attendant and waited.

After a little while, the woman appeared again.

"The gentlemen're moving on to the cold bath now. You can go in if you're ready. Are you sure you don't want me to take care of your clothes?"

"No, thank you," said Ophelia, in a haughty tone. "My maid will deal with them."

The truth was she did not want the attendant to realise they were her only clothes. Recalling her life in Verulamium, and trying to give herself the same air, she hurried towards the warm bath. Four naked traders were just stepping out when she came in. She recognised a couple of the men who had passed them on the road with wagons earlier in the day. For a moment she hesitated on the threshold. The traders noticed her and turned to get a better look. They laughed and continued on their way. She unwrapped the towel and folded it neatly beside the bath, and then she slipped into the warm water, very, very slowly. It was not just to enjoy the experience of stepping into a warm bath after so long, but, as she suspected, men being men, the traders could not resist the temptation of turning back and watching her slim form descend into the water. There was more laughter, and she was left alone.

The hot bath was not entirely clean, not like the pool where she and Anna had occasionally bathed, but it was warm, and she was filthy. She sat for a while and let her thoughts run. Her plan was distasteful to her, but she had put up with Amalric for long enough. She knew she was capable of tolerating for a wagon ride what would once have disgusted her. She cleaned herself all over and washed her hair. What a luxury, she thought, after all these years. Just to have hot water, oil, perfume.

She could still hear the men's voices for a while from the cold pool, but when she was sure they had moved on, she got out, took the towel and herself, and plunged into the chilly water. It was cold, cold enough after the hot water. Her body was tingling when she climbed out and wrapped herself in the towel. She did not want to go through the whole routine with the hot room, so she called the attendant and asked her to rub her all over and apply some oil and perfume. The attendant braided her hair and piled it up on her head, fastening it in place with a comb.

"Where's my maid, now?" she muttered to the attendant. "She should have come with clean clothes. That girl's hopeless."

"You can borrow a robe, if you like, miss, then you can dress in your room."

"Thank you. You're so kind," she said, dropping an extra coin into the woman's outstretched hand.

"Just keep an eye out for the gents," said the woman. "They've gone round by the stable yard to take a beaker of wine before dinner."

She tightened the robe around her waist and accentuated her breasts. She left the bath house, with the appearance of returning to her room, but was careful to take the long route, deliberately walking around the stables, until she was certain she could hear the voices of the traders a little way ahead. As the attendant had predicted, they were sitting at a table in their towels, enjoying their wine. She walked out of the shadows and came to a halt.

"Oh," she said, trying to sound bashful, grasping the robe tightly around her. "I think I'm lost."

The men's conversation came to an abrupt stop. Their heads swivelled towards her.

She smiled, glanced around as if seeking a way out, and then began to make her way past them. She could almost feel their eyes following her. She hoped the perfume from the bath would drift over them. Then she stopped and turned back.

"Excuse me," she asked, "but would any of the gentlemen be taking the south road tomorrow? I'm travelling to my brother in Arelate. The children are tired, and I don't want to delay the journey if I can." The men eyed her all over, mentally stripping off the robe, no doubt, she thought. Her eye caught a suitable target, a middle-aged man, short and round, tidy looking, with a well-trimmed beard. She flashed him a heart-melting smile.

"As it happens," he said, caught in her trap, "I'm travelling south, and I would have space for you and a maid, if the maid doesn't mind sitting in the back with the goods. Have you eaten? Could we discuss it later over dinner, when I'm more suitably dressed?"

"I haven't eaten," she said, her voice like honey.

"Would you care to join me in the dining room?"

"Thank you," she said, her smile fixed in place. "I'll be happy to… and then I'll be more suitably dressed, too." The men laughed. No doubt they had their own idea of the state of her dress they would prefer, she thought, but that suited her purpose this evening.

Ophelia hurried back to the room, hoping that Anna had managed to clean her clothes and get them dry. Anna's expression when she entered told all, as she sat on the floor still wearing the same stained and dirty clothes, still grimy except where she had been doing the washing. Ophelia could have burst out in tears just seeing her, but tears would not get them a ride.

Her clothes were still damp from the wash. She could not join the traders for dinner in a tunic like that.

"Think of your tired feet, and the children, Anna," said Ophelia, taking a deep breath to control herself and kissing her on the cheek. "I'll be back in a minute. I just have to run an errand."

"What are you doing?" asked Anna, now with concern.

Ophelia did not want to say. This was the town. This was her life. Anna had guided her and cared for her all the time in the forest, and now it was her time to make a sacrifice.

Anna watched with surprise, her anger and disappointment melting away into bafflement and concern, her brow furrowed with worry. She had never seen Ophelia quite so agitated.

Ophelia picked up the purse with its few coins and dashed out of the room, out of the hostel, and into the town. Now she needed luck and speed. She spotted a tidily dressed woman and stopped her.

"Ma'am. I would be so grateful if you tell me where I can find a tailor. My clumsy maid has torn my best tunic and we need to travel on tomorrow. I'm desperate."

"I'm sorry," said the woman, "these maids can be so careless." She rolled her eyes. "If you take that street, you'll find that Remus the clothier may still have his stall open." She pointed down a side street and Ophelia hurried in that direction. It was getting late, and she prayed the tailor would not have closed his stall. She found him standing at the door of his shop, looking up and down the street, just on the verge of shutting up for the night.

"Master Remus, the tailor?" She tried to sound hysterical. It was not difficult. It was how she felt. She gave him the same story she had given the woman in the street. He looked her over. She was clean and smelled good, but there was something rustic about her clothes and they looked damp.

"I'm travelling through the town. My maid tore my tunic," she explained. "I had to borrow hers and she had just started to wash it. It's so urgent. I leave tomorrow, and I can't travel like this."

"Well, I was just about to close," the tailor said, "but for you…" He smiled and directed her into his shop. "Normally it would take a couple of days to stitch a lady's dress of quality, but if madam is only needing a simple tunic, I'll take a look and see what I can find that might suit her."

He sized her up and vanished into the back of the shop. After a moment he reappeared, together with his wife, carrying a couple of tunics. Ophelia examined the quality. They would not have found a place in her wardrobe in Verulamium, but here and now she could not be picky, and she could not waste the contents of her purse.

"That one looks very suitable," she said, choosing the one with the best quality cloth.

"Madam has excellent taste," said the tailor, holding it up against her and measuring. "It'll need the length adjusting a little if it's going to show off madam's figure well."

She hesitated. "Can you do it while I wait?"

He grimaced for an instant, thinking perhaps of his own evening meal, and then smiled once more.

"Of course I can."

There goes another of the precious coins, she thought.

The tailor's wife brought her a glass of wine while she waited. A real glass, she thought, how long since I've seen one of those? The man worked away, stitching quickly but carefully, until he was satisfied.

"Would you like to try it on?"

"Of course, how wonderful!" She stepped through into the back of the shop, pulled off the old tunic and pulled on the new one. The tailor might only be a small-town craftsman, but he knew his job. The new robe fitted like a glove and was sewn just right to show off her figure.

"I'll take two new sets of underclothes, in linen, and a new belt," she added, while agreeing the charge. The old dress was wrapped into a bundle, and she set off back to the hostel. On the way she passed a shoemaker packing away his stall.

"Those would be absolutely perfect," she called, spotting a pair of sandals on the table in front of his booth. With a quick adjustment, they fitted her perfectly.

When Ophelia returned to the room in the hostel, Anna could only stand in silence when she saw her.

"Ophi, what have you done?" she said at last. "You're making me frightened."

"Why, my dear?"

"I remember when you had just been carried into Amalric's camp and dropped onto the ground in front of me. I sat with your head in my lap when you were sleeping, wondering who you were and where you had come from. I saw at once you were a real lady, your hair and your clothes gave it away. But you were hurt, and dirty, and sorrowful. Now I'm so frightened of you. You look like the mistress of the big house where I grew up. She was tall and beautiful, her hair arranged just so, just like you are now. And your dress, like a second skin, your perfume and such elegant sandals."

Anna could not move. She was transfixed by a dream and a nightmare mixed into one.

"It's me, Anna, only me, still your Ophi, even if I look a little different," she whispered, handing Anna the bundle from the tailors.

Ophelia held out her arms and hugged her.

"Think of me, Anna, because now I have to go and earn our ride. If I do a good job, I'll see you in the morning."

Anna looked at her blankly as she realised what Ophelia had planned, what all the washing and perfume and dress and sandals were about.

"No, no, Ophi! You can't, you musn't," she burst out. "Let me go. I've done it before. You're too fine! You're too good! Please?"

She grabbed at Ophelia's arm, but Ophelia pulled away.

"Shh, Anna, I have to go. I have to do it for you, for the children. Take care of Freda and Lanius while I'm gone and pray for me it isn't too bad."

Anna stood in stunned silence. She felt sick inside. She had been so angry with Ophelia, so worried about being abandoned, and now she felt ashamed, jealous and longing and more ashamed. It was all too horrible. She tried to call out again as Ophelia walked away, but her voice never came, and before she could find it again, Ophelia had left her and the children alone in the room. She was still clutching the new underwear.

Ophelia threaded her way through the maze of the hostel to the dining room. She could hear the raucous sound of men at dinner on her way. No worse than the chat around the fire in the camp, she thought. Taking a deep breath, she stepped into the room, and all eyes turned towards her. She could almost hear their intake of breath. She hoped she had not overdone it. The southward-travelling trader waved her over and made a space beside him. She sat down, squeezed up close to him. There was roast fowl on the table, a pungent stew. He leant across and served her, cleaning his hands on a napkin. She ate carefully, not wanting to look greedy, and not wanting to get food stains on her new dress. She could feel his arm around her waist, his fingers beginning to slip downwards towards her thigh. She played a bit uncertain for a moment and took another glass of wine. After that she let him do as he wished.

❧ Chapter 30 ☙
Tolosa

Drusus and Sismond returned to Tolosa, together with the land agent's clerk. While Sismond took advantage of his kinsman's hospitality, Drusus found quarters in a room above a tavern.

"I intend to have some fun in this town," said Sismond, as they parted company. "My arse is sore, and my throat is dry, and I heard the best girls in Gaul have been flocking here."

"I won't disturb you too early, then," said Drusus.

One girl, one particular girl, was all that Drusus needed, and he began his enquiries in the tavern, as he had at each stop along the journey.

"A girl… named Xancha, is she known in town?"

Until now, whenever he had asked, the answer had always been no, a blank shake of the head: "There are many girls who have passed through, seeking their fortune, just like the men."

But she has a mole on her right breast, and another just above her left buttock, thought Drusus. You'd know her if you'd seen her, but then, of course, only if she had been naked, he glumly reflected.

"I think I know the one," said the tavern keeper. "She goes to the baths, to assist the women with their hair and cosmetics. They say she's very good. Can take years off your age, or add them, whichever's necessary."

Drusus swallowed hard.

"At the baths, you say."

"You can't miss her," said the man. "Our baths are still pretty modest. This isn't the new Rome, not yet, and the newcomers prefer to bathe in the river, when they bathe at all."

I'll check out the baths tomorrow, thought Drusus, after I deal with the land agent and the king's officials. If Xancha has been in town long enough for a tavern-owner to have so much gossip to share, she'll hardly be on the point of leaving.

The land agent was no trouble, happy to take care of the gold that Drusus handed over, and to collect his fee, but obtaining the royal approval ran into a hindrance.

"Wallia the king left Tolosa, just a few days ago, and his officers left with him," said the land agent, "to go hunting with his friends. You'll find him on the way to Burdigala. I doubt they're in a hurry, and with a few days' hard riding you and Chief Sismond should be able to catch up with him."

Drusus had heard the name. Wallia, king of the Visigoths, the warlord who had signed the peace with the Romans and made his headquarters in the city of Tolosa, who made the city a magnet for ambitious men of all tribes and religions.

"He's a Goth, after all," said the land agent, by way of building a bond between himself and Drusus, "and prefers to be in the saddle."

Drusus gathered up the documents once again and set out in search of Sismond. He was hurrying towards the forum when he heard a voice call out, a female voice that almost made his heart stop beating, a voice that had once stopped him cold in the street in Arelate.

"Drusus Astrebanus…"

He came to a halt so suddenly a man barged into him from behind, gave him a glare and a curse and hurried on his way. Drusus turned and saw her, standing in the middle of the street.

At least he assumed it was her, cloaked and scarfed as the woman was in the cool of the morning.

He took a step towards her. She made no attempt to meet him. He froze again, two arms' lengths away.

"I thought it was you," she said. "I heard a rumour a man was looking for me, though I hardly expected to see you in Tolosa. I hardly expected to see you again, ever, in fact."

"I heard you were here."

"Did you?" she said, ice in her voice. "Then why did it take so long for you to get here?"

"I came as soon as I knew," said Drusus.

"But you must have been in no hurry to find out. It was more than a year ago you left me."

"But we agreed, we agreed I should go, and it's taken all this time to return."

"You promised to return in the autumn," she said, looking him up and down. "Your business didn't turn out so well, I take it, otherwise you would hardly have been bothered with me now, Chief Astrebanus."

"Don't say that, Xancha…"

"You did try to press your claim, I take it, after all your talk?"

"Yes, I went to Rome, I spoke to the emperor's right-hand man."

He could not look at her directly, staring instead at a spot on the ground at her feet.

"But you failed, and so you left me for nothing, alone and pregnant, for nothing, which any fool could have told you."

"Xancha, I didn't know you were pregnant, not until I returned to Arelate."

"Would it have made any difference if I had told you before you left?"

"It's made a difference now."

"Oh!" She laughed bitterly, utterly falsely. "It makes a difference now, not because of me, little Xancha, but because you imagine you fathered a child. Well, you did, Drusus, for a while."

"For a while?"

"How easy do you think it was for me? Do you think anyone wants a dancing girl with a bulging belly? Or to be advised on fashions from a woman so obviously a whore? No, Drusus, I only survived by selling myself to two men with special tastes, and when I got too big and disgusted with myself for that, I was compelled to beg in the streets. I left for Nemausus and hid myself. I had the child and then the winter came, the rain and the cold, and I moved on to Narbonna in the hope I might find shelter and pity. Your child, your son, was taken from me, and perhaps it was for the best, since then I was able to return to my dancing, the only way I could survive."

She paused, collecting her thoughts.

"I didn't expect you to love me, Drusus. I could see that already in Arelate. I did hope you might protect me, take care of me, when I was faithful to you, when I was carrying your child. I waited for you, I prayed for you, but you broke your promise."

"I didn't know you were expecting, Xancha… and… and… I fell ill. I… I couldn't cross the mountains in winter."

She turned away from him.

"And what happened to our child, where is he?" he asked.

"With a caring father's help, our son might have lived."

He stared at her, mouth open, disbelieving.

"There's no need to look so hurt, Drusus," she said in an accusing tone. "It wasn't you who had to carry the child through the heat of the summer. It wasn't you who had to suffer the indignities of lustful men while feeling sick and swollen, who had to look into the boy's little face as he faded away."

Drusus could only stand, stunned.

"And… and…"

"And nothing," she said, "nothing more, as far as you're concerned."

Only then did she take a step towards him, so that he could catch sight of her face within the folds of her scarf.

"I've rebuilt my life, Drusus. I've made myself something I never was before, a respectable woman. I'm not risking that for you. I offered myself to you in body and soul. You could have had me to love and cherish, to be the mother of your son, but you chose your own vain glory. Well, you can live alone with that thought. I have moved on."

He was speechless. She took a step nearer so that her mouth was close by his ear. He could smell her perfume and, beneath that, her own odour, the odour that brought back memories. He could feel the faint contact of her body against him, a body which had comforted him so often when they had been together.

"And now, I'll give you a friendly warning. I never want to see you again. I never want to hear your voice again, or have you enter my thoughts again if I can help it, and to ensure that there's a chance I'll succeed, I advise you to get out of town as soon as possible. I know how quickly you can scuttle away when it suits you, but for old time's sake, since you did keep me sheltered and fed for one winter, I'll give you a couple of days. After that, I have friends in this town, powerful friends, close to the king. If I was to hint to them that I was being harassed by a deceitful, disappointed former lover, your life would be very short and even that little not worth living, I promise you."

"Ah, there you are Drusus," called Sismond, hurrying towards them. "I was waiting for you by the fountain."

His eye fell on Xancha. Her back was still towards him.

"I thought you didn't know anyone in town," he said.

She turned to look at him.

"Oh… hello," he said, catching sight of her dark eyes, her exquisitely outlined eyebrows, her chiselled nose, her sharply defined lips, and nothing better or more sensible coming into his mind.

"I'm going anyway," said Drusus, and, glancing at Sismond, added, "If you need a guide to the town you couldn't find a better one. On the other hand, I was on my way to tell you we need to leave tomorrow to catch up with the king to complete the transaction. Goodbye, Xancha, for ever, this time." He turned his back on them and strode away.

"I'll meet you at the tavern, at dawn," called Sismond, watching him depart with a puzzled expression.

Xancha watched him go too, her heart heavy, the temptation to call him back, to forgive him, on her lips. She had not meant to be so bitter, but it had been a hard summer, a hard winter which had almost cost the life of the child, until… until she had found a place for the baby where he could be nurtured and cared for. Despite what she had said about protectors, though that much was truthful, despite the fact she had a home, four walls and a roof, she was lonely, lonely without a man.

She looked up at Sismond's concerned face, his expression of wondering why his friend had so suddenly walked off.

"I can't assist you now," she said softly. "I have a client who's expecting me – a woman who needs my guidance," she added for clarification, thinking he might have got the wrong idea. "Perhaps some other time?"

"I'm sorry, but you heard what he said. I must leave tomorrow. I have business with the court," said Sismond, "but I'll be back."

"Then leave me a message when you return, at the Fox Tavern. Do you know it?"

"I shall certainly make sure I do," he said, still straining after Drusus' vanishing figure. He glanced down to take another look at the woman, but she had already gone. He had not even caught her name.

Drusus took alleys and paths until he reached the bank of the Garunna River and could wander no further. He found a cheap wine shop for boatmen, ordered a pitcher and a beaker and sat gazing out over the water.

He had had a son. He had lost a son. He had had a reputation. He had been mocked and ridiculed, and almost lost that. He had had a position in society, property, power. The property had been stolen, the power had been lost, and his position… he was no one. No one in Rome, no one in Ravenna, no one in Arelate, no one even in a provincial hole like Tolosa. A man whom even a cheap whore could despise and turn away. No, no, he sighed to himself… she wasn't a cheap whore, because what did that make him? She had been his companion, his friend, his lover, and the mother of his child. He emptied the beaker and refilled it. A man who had a position in society, property, power could afford to look down on a woman like that, but a man in his present situation had to be grateful for whatever comfort and care he could find.

Even the Goths had mocked him, a lawyer and Roman citizen. Not openly, of course. They were too cunning for that, too practised in flattery. They had mocked him because they had taken from others what he had lost. Chief Sismond, the land agent had called him. He had referred to Thormond as "my lord", a mere barbarian, a generation or two from a hut in the swamp, while he, whose ancestors dated back before the Conquest, he was reduced to doing their bidding. They had mocked him because he believed in the rule of law, while they believed in the force of arms.

He called for another pitcher of wine.

But they had been quick enough to learn from him. It was he who had picked out the property, guaranteed the details on the hillside above the Carcasso road. He who had managed the process with the land agent and would have to put his heels to his horse again tomorrow to make sure the king granted permission for the Goths to share the tribute from their neighbours. At the end of the day, it was he, Drusus Astrebanus, who would place the land into the hands of Thormond and Sismond and their family, because they were clever enough to understand that was necessary. And wasn't he clever? Could he learn nothing from them? It was the only way to gain the Romans' attention, Thormond had said, to invade their city and burn down their houses and palaces and take their gold and silver.

Vitellus had always had a mean streak in him, thought Drusus. He took after Father that way. And me? I was always the conciliator. The one who had to persuade angry men of the rightness of his arguments, despite the tone of his voice. That was my role then, a comfortable role when someone else was making threats, was raising their voice. But now, now there's no one to do that for me, and so no one needs to listen to my words, my pleading, when they know there's no threat of force to back them up. My role is played out, finished.

Drusus swallowed the last of his wine, slammed a pair of coins on the shop counter and staggered away in the direction of his lodging.

They left at dawn.

☙ Chapter 31 ❧
Aquitania, on the road

nna and the children had washed by the well and dined with the humble travellers. Anna had hardly been able to swallow a mouthful, though she knew she was almost starving. Now, clean and full, the children were asleep, but she lay awake. She could not help thinking of Ophelia. Years ago, in her first days in Senones, she had sold herself for food and shelter. She had hated herself for being such a fool for running away from home, thinking she would be welcome in town. Life with Amalric had not been easy, but he had rescued her from that existence. Only one man to satisfy, instead of whoever slapped a coin in her hand. She felt sick at the thought of Ophelia doing it now, her lovely, wonderful Ophelia. She felt lonely, although she could hear the two children breathing on the bed beside her. How innocent they were and how difficult life seemed to be. She could not get the picture of Ophelia out of her mind, her slim arms, the body-hugging tunic, and her sandaled feet peeping out of the bottom, and above it all her face, so elegant, so wonderful, and yet so sad.

She must have fallen asleep, because she woke with a start as Fredagunda pulled at her arm.

"There's someone at the door, Mum."

Anna got up, rubbed her eyes and went to the door. It was one of the maids from the hostel.

"Got to get up, love," she said. "Your mistress caught me in the yard and said you have to pack the things and meet her there. She's ready to leave."

Anna gathered up their few belongings, stuffed them into the packs, tidied the children, ran to the kitchen to grab a few crusts and a little cheese for the day, filled a bottle with water from the well, and finally made her way to where the wagons were already being drawn up. She saw Ophelia standing by one of the traders. He had his arm around her while he talked and laughed with one of his friends. Ophelia saw her coming and waved. She eased her way out of the man's grasp and came over.

"Are we going to ride on the wagon?" asked Fredagunda, with a voice of wonder. Ophelia could have cried to hear her. What we have to do, she thought, perhaps you will too, one day, little girl.

"Yes, Fredagunda. Today we don't have to walk. Aunty will sit at the front with the driver, and you and Lanius can sit back here with Mummy."

"Oh, wow!" said Fredagunda, with a hop of joy.

Anna gave Ophelia a look, a look combining admiration, thanks and pity in equal measure.

"Not so bad," Ophelia whispered and then turned back to the trader. It was time to leave. The man swung her up onto the wagon, his hands grasping her by the waist, and at the rear, one of the stable boys helped Anna up and lifted the children to her. The trader cracked his whip, the mules took the strain and the wagon creaked out of the yard.

The trader was a decent enough man, kept himself clean, no peculiar desires. He was even kind enough to pay for food and a room for Anna and the children, just so he could get more time with this wonderful woman who had dropped out of the sky into his lap. He had only made a wish as he had seen her slide down into the warm water at the bath, and his wish had come true.

"Your accent," he said suddenly, halfway through the second day, "it reminds me of someone."

Ophelia froze, her mind working quickly. Could this man have crossed her path earlier? It hardly seemed possible, but on the other hand he was a merchant, crossing the province transporting his goods. She had hardly set foot out of the camp or the village. Had he been one of the men who had visited Amalric? Or… she remembered she had gone to the fair with Ilana. They had needed new dyes for their cloth, new needles which could not be made in the village. When the other women had heard of their plans they had been inundated with requests for ribbons and buttons, glassware and beads, and they had spent the entire day going round the stalls. Could he have seen her there? Would her accent have stood out so remarkably that a man like this could remember it?

"It took a while," he continued, "to come to mind, because it was a few years ago. She looked just like you, a young woman travelling with her family. I was part of a group of traders coming down from Remis to Autessiodurum. We were planning to travel on to Lugdunum, but they said that there were bandits active on the road. The old man, the father, was furious, demanded that we continue, but it wasn't worth the risk." He looked across at her. "From Britannia, they were, really posh people, governor or something the old man claimed, and I could've believed it." He shook his head. "Real pretty young girl that, with two little kiddies, nice as anything." He glanced at her again. "You have her looks, though. What was her name now?"

Ophelia's stomach cramped so hard she could have vomited her midday meal into the ditch by the side of the road. She clutched at the bench to steady herself, tried to say something, anything to distract him.

"Cecilia…" he mused.

"Maria," she suggested. "Hypatia, my sister's called Hypatia."

"No," he said suddenly, "no, I've remembered, her name was Ophelia, just like yours."

"Hypatia," she repeated.

"The man, the family… there were rumours," the trader continued. "They travelled on the next day, despite our advice. The father insisted. They were never seen again, swallowed up in the forest. I often thought of them after that, on lonely parts of the road. She must have come to my mind when I saw you yesterday," he said, shaking his head again and giving her a weak smile. She patted him on the knee.

Look at me, she thought, look at me. Once, not long ago, then, when you saw me last, I fell weeping because a man mistook me for a prostitute when I thought I was a fine young woman, and now, what have I become, just that, a hostelry whore.

"That young woman," said Ophelia, "perhaps you're right and she's dead, but I'm alive, that's what's important."

As the thought crossed her mind, she expected to experience a feeling of depression or anger at empty words, at the denial of her old self, but instead she felt filled with joy, a sense of freedom.

I'm dead, she thought, dead and… pardon me, Lord Jesus, who rose again. Nobody gives a damn about me, she thought, here on the road, even a man who thinks he saw me before. I can do what I like. For so long I've been frightened of Amalric and then of being discovered by Drusus. Now, who cares who I am, just another anonymous tavern pickup, a woman no longer young, having to earn her food with the only thing she has left.

"You're right," she said. "There was a young woman, Ophelia Ursina, I remember her from my childhood. I heard the same, that she did die along the road to Lugdunum."

She laughed aloud and he turned to look at her with a quizzical expression.

"It's sunny," she said. "There's the road stretching ahead. Who knows where it will lead?"

He grimaced, slightly embarrassed that he had appeared a fool.

"For you maybe, love, but for me, tomorrow I have to turn west, to my home, to my wife."

She lay beside him in the dark. Despite his sudden disquiet during the day, her laughter, her teasing him at the evening meal, the warmth and comfort of her body, had reassured him. He was only the third man, she reflected, that she had lain with: Cornelius, Amalric and now this trader, Marius. That hardly makes me a whore, she thought, but how many more men will I have to sleep with before we reach Arelate?

Her friend, her neighbour from Verulamium, Livia, came into her mind. The women of the neighbourhood had scorned her for sleeping around, for being a tart, a trollop. She tried to remember if she had joined in their accusations. She had certainly nodded in agreement, even though Livia had been her friend, even though she knew it was more complicated than that, that Livia's husband was often away, that Livia felt lonely, that she needed to feel love, perhaps not even that, just someone to notice her.

Once, she remembered, she had decided to drop in on Livia unannounced. The maid had stepped up to hinder her, but seeing who it was, she let her in. The actor, Livia's lover, met her in the atrium on his way out, wishing her a good day as they passed. When she reached Livia's private room, Livia was still lying on the bed, naked. She got to her feet, a little surprised, when Ophelia barged in.

"You caught me…" she said, as they embraced.

Ophelia had seen her naked before, of course, at the public baths, in their own bathhouse, but this was different. Her hair was tousled, and behind her perfume she smelt faintly of sweat, of bed, of just having been with her lover. Ophelia held her slightly longer than necessary, unthinkingly sliding her hand down her back. Livia had smiled in return, tightened her grip and nestled against her, or had she just imagined it? Then Livia had reached up on her tiptoes, kissed her on the mouth and stepped away with a laugh, reaching in one movement for a gauzy shawl that was lying on the bed.

They had not had a chance to meet again. Livia's husband had suddenly returned from the mainland, and they had left just a few weeks afterwards.

In her tired head, Livia's features were indistinct, unclear, and it took her a moment to realise they had morphed, morphed into those of Anna, the same long dark tousled hair, the same brown eyes, the same breasts, a little too large for a slim body, the same curve of the hips.

She was suddenly wide awake. She felt her mouth open, as if to speak aloud, and she could just manage to stifle herself.

"Oh, my God!" she whispered.

The trader beside her shifted uneasily in his sleep.

How did I not see the similarity before? she thought. Perhaps it was because their personalities were so different? Livia was so light-hearted, witty, frivolous even, whereas Anna was serious and calm and caring. I know who I would rather have as a partner if I was a man, she thought, and stopped herself. Is that who I am? A woman who…

"Anna, really?" she whispered to herself, and the trader again stirred at the sound of her voice. "I'm not sure I'm ready for this." She edged towards the man, until she felt the touch of his body against her, and forgetful sleep overtook her.

In the morning Ophelia had a sense of unease, not for having slept with the trader, not even that she half remembered a peculiar dream that seemed to have some significance she could not quite grasp, but about what they would do after they left the man. Where were they going, and how were they going to get there? It was a good ruse to say she was on her way to her brother's. It answered any obvious questions about why a woman and her maid were travelling the roads with a couple of children and very little baggage, but would her brother still be in Arelate, even supposing they were able to reach the city? Anna might be right. Wasn't it just a fantasy to think they would join him there? And supposing they didn't find Gaius, what would they do so they could get food and somewhere to live?

It was one thing sleeping with a stranger for a couple of nights so the children did not have to walk, but it would be quite another thing doing it again and again at every rest stop. Even in the bandit camp there had only been Amalric. She looked across at the trader as he sat beside her on the bench of the wagon. He had already told her he was married and had three children, so she had to be realistic that he would have to drop her off somewhere before he got home. He had acted kindly so far, but suppose he became ashamed or frightened that he would be given away? Nobody knew who they were or where they were. They could just disappear, and no one would care because everyone who might care already thought they, she anyway, were long dead and buried.

The trader broke into her thoughts.

"This afternoon, we'll come to a town, Agininum. I can't take you any further. I have to turn west, towards Burdigala, towards home. I can drop you off by the traveller's hostel. The road over the hills to the east leads to Arelate eventually. Maybe you can find another ride that will take you to your brother."

She thanked him, kissed him on the cheek, and settled her arm around him for the last part of the journey. She was not simulating. She was really grateful. It had been a luxury to sit and watch the landscape pass by after tramping through the forest and along the dusty road, even if she had to pay for the privilege. In the end, getting fucked by a trader was no worse than getting fucked by a robber, or a husband she did not particularly care for, and the beds had been a great deal more comfortable than in Amalric's hut.

The wagon rumbled in through the city gate and came to a halt. She kissed him goodbye, and by the time she had extricated herself from his embrace, Anna and the children were already standing in the road with the sad little bundles which were all they possessed. She sighed to herself. Some fine lady, daughter of the governor, she thought, but then she remembered the words she had exchanged with the trader. That woman, that Ophelia, had expired long ago. She watched the wagon go, waving to the trader as it rolled out of sight.

Once again she was back with Anna, and the two women embraced and held each other tight.

"Thank you, Anna, for taking care of the children, and for playing the maid," she whispered into her ear. There was something about that dream, something she had concluded in the middle of the night that she could not quite retrieve.

"I missed you," said Anna. "I just couldn't help thinking of what you were doing."

"Anna, my dear. I hope I never have to do that again, but if I have to, for us, for Freda and Lanius, I will every night. You never know, I might even get used to sleeping with strangers," she tried to joke.

The look Anna gave her made her wish she had not.

With a sigh, she picked up Lanius, and they headed in through the gate of the hostel.

❧ Chapter 32 ☙
On the road to Burdigala

The tavern was packed. Drusus and Sismond found two places at the single table and sat down, shoulder to shoulder with the other guests. Sismond slapped a coin on the board and a servant handed them spoons and bowls. In front of them was a common dish, meat stew with beans again, but it smelt good after a long ride.

"Can you pass the bread?" said Drusus, nudging the trader sitting beside him.

"Of course," said the man, grabbing the loaf with his fist and handing it over. "Briton, are you?"

"What's it to you?" said Drusus, sourly.

"The accent, I can tell. Don't get many of you Britons around here. Not like in the north."

Drusus tore off a piece of bread and dipped it in his stew.

"Just wanted to say," said the trader, "'cause I gave a ride to another Briton a couple of days ago."

"Uh, huh," said Drusus, stuffing the bread into his mouth.

"Yeah, a woman about your age, had the same sort of accent as you. Said her name was Ophelia."

Drusus stopped chewing and turned towards the man.

"It was uncanny," continued the trader, after taking a gulp of wine, not his first, evidently. "She reminded me of another Ophelia I crossed paths with… years ago… up in the north. It couldn't have been the same woman, of course. I heard that one had a nasty accident. Bandits in the woods." The trader nodded, smiling to himself at the memory of Ophelia.

Drusus felt the dough in his mouth slip towards his windpipe and was seized by a sudden fit of coughing. Sismond turned behind him and thumped him on the back until he stopped.

"Thanks," he muttered, still half choked, before turning back to the trader.

"This… er… woman… Ophelia, you say?"

The trader nodded, his own mouth full.

"A Briton… light hair… slimly built… tall for a woman… about my height?" Drusus asked.

The trader nodded again.

"With her servant and a couple of kids, a little girl and a toddler," he added after he had swallowed his food.

Drusus frowned and fell into silence. Ophelia Ursina had a couple of children, two of them, he remembered, but by now they would be ten years or even more. That did not fit the picture. On the other hand, Ophelia was not a common name. In fact, Ophelia Ursina was the only one who he had ever come across who was called Ophelia. Vito had once joked that Publius Julius must have been intending to call his daughter Orphea, after the legendary musician, but had been drunk at the naming ceremony.

He continued chewing automatically, spooning stew into his mouth and staring absently at the table. Just suppose the odds were against him, and this woman really was Publius Julius Ursinus' daughter. Could it be possible that he had been lied to? Everyone would have had to have been lying to him, to him and Vito… for years. Supposing the governor wasn't dead! He wouldn't put it past Gaius Ursinus to have lied to him, and it would explain the fiasco in Italia. But then… then Amalric must have lied to him too. Amalric had assured him, assured Vito, that the governor and his family were dead. Amalric had taken him to a place in the forest where he claimed the silver was buried, pointed to a spot in the earth, and he, Drusus, had believed him. Amalric was a bandit and a robber, and lying came naturally to him, but even so, this would be one hell of a deceit. It didn't add up. If the governor was still alive, why hadn't he surfaced somewhere? The man was hardly modest. Why had Gaius run away if he knew everything was a bluff? And if this woman was Ophelia Ursina, where had she been? Why was she here in the Narbonnensis?

He jabbed his elbow into his neighbour, who was now chatting to the man on his other side. The trader twisted towards him.

"This woman… she could be my long-lost sister," said Drusus. "Where did you last see her?"

The trader frowned.

"I dropped her off in Agininum, at the travellers' hostel… safest for women there, I think. She said she was heading in the opposite direction, over the hills to Arelate. She did mention that she was hoping to meet her brother."

The meat stew suddenly felt heavy. The wine tasted as if it were sour.

"Thanks," said Drusus, a feeling of nausea coming over him. "Thanks, that means a lot. If I could find my sister, it would change my life."

The trader smiled.

"Glad I said something. She's a fine woman, mister, classy… and…" He stopped. Better not mention to his table neighbour that his sister had been fun to share a bed with. That might provoke him, and who needs trouble? The trader smiled again, and as he did so, a voice rose from his far side.

"…wool cloth you said, Marius. How much do you think you'll get for that in Burdigala?"

Drusus let him return to his business and turned towards Sismond.

"I just had some disturbing news," he said. "Seems we may have passed a relative of mine on the road, back in Agininum, and if it is her, then she's in some sort of trouble. Do you think you can manage the business with the king on your own if I turn back and check things out?"

Sismond wrinkled his brow for a moment. Drusus could read his thoughts. If he messed up the business of obtaining the king's approval for the taxation, then that would be an irritation to Thormond and his uncle. On the other hand, if he could get in front of the king alone, without his lawyer, then it would be too good an opportunity to miss. A moment to come out of his cousin's shadow. Drusus saw the frown fade away as he made his decision. The ambition of a young man won out.

"Very well, Drusus, I suppose I can manage it. And if I screw up, then I'll meet up with you in Agininum afterwards, and we'll cook up some other strategy?"

"Sounds good to me," said Drusus, with relief.

The two men parted next morning with hugs and wishes of good fortune. Sismond saddled up and continued on down the river valley, to catch up with the king. Drusus turned his horse to return to Agininum. He pressed on and reached the town in the late afternoon. He had no desire to lodge in the travellers' hostel, no desire to risk revealing himself too soon. Instead, he chose the same tavern he had stayed in with Sismond. He was even able to get a bed alone. With his horse stabled and in the hands of the groom, he made his way through the narrow streets towards the hostel, down beyond the marketplace, backed up against the warehouses that lined the river. He had nothing to hide. He was looking for his sister, a deed any decent man would do in the circumstances.

"Mistress Ophelia," said the hostel servant, "why, yes! She's taken a space in the women's room. I think she just popped out, but I'm sure she'll be back in a short while."

Ophelia had visited a merchant to exchange some of the gold pieces for silver. She was unsure if she had been given a fair deal, but the man had a kind face and had given her a friendly smile. She had seen a string of packhorses in the yard of his warehouse. Perhaps tomorrow she would return and enquire about travelling over the hills towards Arelate. Then she had bought food for the evening meal from one of the cook shops in the town.

She was about to enter the hostel when she heard talk in the atrium. There was nothing unusual about that, but her ears pricked up because one of the voices had an evident British accent. Far from being a welcome reminder of her home, it was a warning signal in her mind. She slowed her pace but continued in the direction of the sounds: two men, engaged in conversation. They were standing beyond the archway, in the yard. She stopped behind the corner of the wall, took a deep breath and looked round. It was just as well she was close to the wall, because otherwise she would have collapsed. The one man was a hostel servant, she knew, but the other, the other she had seen before, not so long before, as a shadow in the dancing flames of half a dozen fires in a forest clearing. She leant her back against the wall, gasping for breath, a dribble of cold sweat trickling down her spine. How had he come here? How had he found her?

The conversation in the yard ended, and she could hear the steps of the hostel servant coming towards her. She had to get away before he saw her, otherwise he would call Drusus back.

Her feet felt like lead. It felt she could hardly lift them, hardly move from the spot, hardly take a step. One, two… and with an effort she was back out in the street. She stopped again, panting desperately. What was she going to do? She dared not go back through the entrance. She would have to force herself to go round the building, and in through the alley at the rear that led to the stables. She would have to hope that Drusus was not looking for her there, that he was not staying in the hostel and his horse not in one of the stalls. She took a couple of deep breaths to calm herself, pulled her scarf tightly around her head and set off.

There was no sign of Drusus in the stables. No sign of him in the yard. No sign, thank God, of him in the women's room… they would not let him in there, at least. She stumbled in through the door, and at once Anna saw that something was wrong.

"What is it, Ophi? You look sick!"

"We have to leave," said Ophelia, "right now!" She reached for Lanius and took him in her arms. "Come with me, Anna, right away, and Fredagunda."

Anna had the sense not to quibble but took her daughter by the hand. Ophelia stood by the entrance, checking the yard was clear and then, almost at a run, disappeared into the huddle of outbuildings that made up the stables. As she did so, she glanced back and saw a shadow, the shape of a man, outlined in the archway on the far side of the yard.

"Come, Anna, now," she hissed.

The two women threaded their way through the buildings and out into the alley.

"Where are we going?" gasped Anna.

"I don't know," replied Ophelia, hurrying ahead. She reached the corner. In front of her lay one of the main streets of the town, which led from the river gate up the hill to… to the church… the church, they could seek sanctuary in the church. Surely Drusus wouldn't dare confront them in a holy place. But to get to the church they had to cross the marketplace and make their way up the long open street.

In the lower town there were people out and about, making last-moment purchases or hanging by the market taverns. As they pushed their way through the throng, Ophelia glanced around. She could see no sign of Drusus, but then, any one of the men in the square could be him or a retainer. On the far side the crowds thinned out. People kept to the alleys and passages rather than the main street. Ophelia was not familiar enough with the town to risk getting lost. They had no choice but to take the route straight up the hill.

"Come on!" she called back to Anna, who was having a problem with Fredagunda. The little girl did not understand why they had to run. She did not want to leave the market. She was hungry and the food for sale smelled good.

Ophelia was forced to stop and wait. To her horror she realised that she was isolated in the middle of the street. Even if Drusus were blind, he would see her. It was too far, too far to go to reach the top of the hill if Anna did not hurry. She looked around. On one side of the street was a maze of paths among myriad houses and workshops. On the other was a blank wall, but about halfway along the wall was an iron-bound gate. If they could make it through the gate, they could hide for a moment, try to spot what Drusus was doing, see without being seen. Soon it would be dark, and then it would be safe to creep out again and make their way to the church.

She slipped into the shadow of the wall and tried the latch of the gate. She could lift it, push at the gate and swing it open with an effort. She looked back and saw Anna had finally persuaded Fredagunda to follow her up the hill.

"In here, in here," she called, not sure whether to shriek or to whisper. Luckily Anna spotted her and pushed her daughter through the opening. Ophelia swung the gate shut and dropped the latch, and then she sank to the ground, her head in her hands.

She felt Anna's arms around her.

"Tell me, tell me, Ophi, who, what are we running from?"

Drusus was standing under the arch when he saw a couple of figures leave the women's quarters and cross to the rear of the yard. Two adults and a child, and they were in a hurry. He hesitated for a moment, considering whether it was better to remain at his post or to follow. If Ophelia was here, and unaware of him, then she would most likely still be here in the morning. On the other hand, if someone had told her there was a man looking for her, and she was the slightest bit suspicious, then of course, she would flee. Nobody knew better than he that Ophelia Ursina would have every right to be suspicious, and that running away would be her best strategy.

He left his post and trotted across the yard and through the passage where the women had vanished. Beyond was a jumble of buildings, and beyond that he could see an opening leading out into an alley. He crossed to the opening and glanced out. There was no one to be seen. Which way had they gone? To the right, where the last remains of the sun lit up an open street, or to the left, into the dark and narrow lanes of the town? He knew which direction he would take and headed to the left. The alley came to an end at a cross street, narrow and twisting among the houses. He cursed. If they had gone this way he would never find them in that maze. Better to head back and try the other direction.

He ran down the alley and reached the open street. Once more he let out a string of curses. The marketplace, of course, he had crossed it on the way to the hostel from his inn. You could lose a dozen women in this crowd. He looked around desperately and then noticed, far across the square, a woman detach herself from the mass and begin to make her way up the hill. She was tall, taller than average, taller than the dumpy southern women, and she seemed to be carrying something, an infant perhaps. He watched for a moment as the woman stopped and looked back towards the crowded market.

He lowered his head and began to push his way through the crowd.

"What the fuck are you doing!" yelled one man, as he barged against him.

He glanced up. The tall woman was making her way up the open street, and then he saw a second hurrying after her. There had been two of them who had fled. If the tall woman was Ophelia, then the other must be her servant.

A woman beside him backed away from a stall with a large basket of fruit and knocked him sideways.

"Sorry, dear!"

It took a moment for Drusus to regain his balance, and when he looked up again the woman who might be Ophelia had disappeared. The servant, too. He stopped and let out another curse.

"They can't have gone far," he said to himself and resumed his path through the crowd.

When he reached the bottom of the open street, there was still no sign of the pair. He began to make his way up the slope. The women had reached about halfway up by the last time he had spotted them. They couldn't have vanished into the streets lower down the hill, so he pushed on to the point where there was a long wall on one side and a number of lanes leading off on the other. He stood for a moment staring up the street. It was hopeless. If they had ducked into one of the lanes, he would never be able to find them now that darkness was falling, and he had yet to see a woman who could leap a high wall. Better to save effort and return to staking out the hostel. With the hurry they had left in, they must have abandoned their belongings, and those wouldn't be safe for long in that environment if they didn't come and collect them.

Ophelia and Anna realised they were in an overgrown garden. Above them, further up the hillside, they could discern the shape of a building, outlined by the last rays of the sun. The garden appeared long neglected and the house dark and lifeless. Anna took Fredagunda by the hand and began to walk carefully along a rough path that led towards a flight of steps.

"At least we could get some shelter," she whispered. "It'll get cold now the sun's setting."

Ophelia followed her reluctantly, but some of her hesitation disappeared when she noticed that what once would have been a beautiful fountain was dry, and the basin was filled with leaves and branches. No one had tended this garden for years.

Anna was already forging ahead, up the steps and under a portico and then through an arch into the courtyard beyond. Her footsteps echoed among the empty rooms. Then Ophelia saw her freeze suddenly, look back over her shoulder.

"There's a light," she whispered when Ophelia caught up with her, "over there." She pointed. A faint glow danced through one of the windows, and an unmistakeable smell of cooking. The house was not completely deserted.

Ophelia felt anxiety begin to rise again. The type of people who lived in abandoned houses were unlikely to be welcoming to two lone women and their children, or, worse, they might be welcoming in altogether the wrong way. On the other hand, to turn back was to risk running into Drusus, and the nature of his welcome was simpler to foresee.

Suddenly their decision was taken for them, as Fredagunda pulled herself free from Anna's grip and began to run towards the light.

"Come back," yelled Anna, but the girl ran on, disappearing into a passage at the far side of the courtyard. The glow in the window appeared to move and grow and extend into the passageway. Anna took to her heels in pursuit of her daughter, almost crashing into another woman as she dived into the passage. The woman had Fredagunda by the hand.

"Who have we here?" she said, eyeing Anna cautiously.

"I'm sorry we disturbed you," said Ophelia, hurrying up. What the hell am I going to say now, she thought? She took a deep breath and plunged in. "I'm so sorry. We were escaping from a man. He means to harm us. We hid in the garden."

The woman frowned, obviously confused by Ophelia's words.

"You had better come in," she said, evidently judging them harmless.

"I'm hungry, Aunty," said Fredagunda, as she followed the stranger.

"You shall have some bread and vegetable pottage," said the woman, with a kind tone, and then turned to Anna and Ophelia. "You two had better sit down and explain yourselves," she said, sharper and less friendly. There were only a couple of small oil lamps in the room. It was almost impossible to see where the door might be, and where could they go if they found it? They had no choice but to do as they were told.

From the shadows, an older woman appeared, leaning on a stick.

"Mother," said the woman who had spoken to them, "can you find this little girl a bowl and a spoon… she can manage that?" she asked, glancing at Anna.

"Yes, ma'am."

"You needn't address me like that. We have no airs here," said the woman. Her mother, meanwhile, dished up a helping of savoury mash to Fredagunda, and then without asking leave of her daughter spooned shares out for Anna and Ophelia.

"The little one need some?" she asked, eyeing Lanius.

"Thank you, if it's not too hot."

"Won't be if he don't eat it too fast," said the old woman.

"Now you had better explain yourselves again, in words I can understand," said the younger woman, looking at them sternly. "It's unnerving to have strangers appearing from the garden. My mother was quite shaken up."

"I was not," said the older woman huffily, and she returned to her stool in the shadows.

Ophelia took them through the story once again: how they had run away and a friendly carter had dropped them off in Agininum. How she hoped to find her brother, but she was beginning to despair, and now she realised a man had been following them and she was worried he might harm them and the children.

"You need to find somewhere to shelter for a while," said the woman, whose name was Aija, "but you can't stay here more than a night or two. My husband and I take care of this house for the owner, and who knows when he might come back?"

"Don't know what you're worrying about," said the old woman from her corner. "He hasn't been here for years."

"My mother and father took care of the house before us," explained Aija, "before my father passed over."

"Ten years ago it was," said the old woman, giving Anna a confidential look.

"Yes, Mother," said Aija impatiently, her mind obviously on how to get rid of the unwanted guests as soon as possible.

"We don't want to stay," said Ophelia firmly. "The man'll surely be searching for us, but we left our belongings in the traveller's hostel."

Aija sighed.

"I can see you're at your wits' end," she said. "These're no times for women to be out on the roads alone. You were lucky that carter didn't take advantage of you."

Ophelia could feel her face burning. Thank goodness the light was so dim.

The sound of boots could be heard in the hall outside, and the cloth covering the doorway was pushed aside to reveal the shape of a man. Aija jumped to her feet to embrace him.

"My husband, Tygon," she said in a hurry.

"We have guests?" said the man, puzzled. The woman began to talk to him in a patois that was fast and incomprehensible, accompanied by many gestures and pointing. Ophelia could only watch the exchange while shovelling the vegetable mash into her mouth with a feeling of shame.

"My husband has an idea," said Aija, turning to them with a smile. "Tomorrow morning he's taking the cart up to the monastery with a delivery of vegetables. If you were to ride with him, then the sisters who live there would give you refuge for a while, I'm sure."

The man smiled in turn.

"If either of you can bake," he said, making an obvious effort to be understood to the strangers, "you'll be especially welcome. I know Mistress Claudia has been praying to find help in the kitchen."

Ophelia suddenly felt Anna squeeze her hand under the table.

"I would have taken the job myself," said Aija, dismally, "but we're bound to the master of this house and must keep to our duties."

"It's our home here," said the old woman defiantly. "We've a right to stay."

☙ Chapter 33 ❧
Agininum

Drusus slept badly even though he had the bed to himself, tossing and turning, almost convinced that the woman he had seen hastening across the yard, standing in the street, had really been Ophelia Ursina. Why else had she run like that, and not returned to the hostel, even though he had lain in wait most of the evening? Unfortunately, his reasoning ran on, if she was Ophelia and she had run from him purposefully, then she must have recognised him, must have drawn the conclusion he was a threat to her. On the other hand, there were probably plenty of women who had good reason to skedaddle at the sight and sound of a man asking after them, women who had run off with money, escaped slaves, women who had been raped and traumatised, even wives trying to get away from their husbands for one reason or another. The whole world appeared to be made up of half the people trying to run from the other half, and at times it was difficult to discern which half was which. Wasn't he, if he was honest to himself, on the run from Marcus Silvanus?

He must have fallen asleep eventually, because it was light when he opened his eyes the next time. With a start he rolled off the bed and got to his feet.

"By the gods," he said to himself, "suppose those women have got back to the hostel and taken their packs and gone. They could be wherever by now." He pulled on his boots and clattered down the stairs and out into the street. Quick steps took him across the marketplace and down the side street leading to the hostel, in under the arch and into the nook where he had been hiding the evening before.

"Still looking for your sister?" enquired the hostel servant, sympathy in his voice. "She'll have to come back and fetch her stuff before too long, because that bed's going to be needed this evening."

"Nobody's been to fetch it?" asked Drusus.

The man shook his head. "Not that I've seen."

Drusus quickly shushed him. Two figures had appeared from the passage leading to the stables, though neither of them was the woman he thought was Ophelia. One was a big-breasted young peasant woman, and the one with her could have been her mother.

"That's your sister's serving girl," whispered the hostel servant, "but I don't know who the other is."

"A thief, perhaps, in league with the slave," said Drusus quickly. "Stay quiet, and I'll follow them when they leave."

Anna and Aija unwittingly crossed the yard and disappeared into the women's quarters. A few moments later they appeared bearing a couple of bundles and began to walk in the direction of Drusus. He squeezed back against the wall as they passed, chatting between themselves, and watched as they caught the hostel servant and exchanged a few words. The man could not help himself looking towards Drusus.

Don't say anything, Drusus thought desperately, watching the women from the shadows. He had a feeling about the younger woman which sparked a memory – the shape of her shoulder, the way she turned her head – but not one which he could bring fully into his mind. And then they were on the move, out into the open. Drusus hurried after them, but not before he had pushed a coin into the hand of the grateful servant.

The two women made their way along the street and then turned into the market square. Drusus could guess the direction they would be going and could afford to saunter along a good distance behind. They crossed the square in the direction of the main street and began to make their way up the hill, chatting and laughing the whole time. Drusus followed after, wondering what he would do once he got to the far side of the market. It would be impossible to hide. He would just have to watch them from a distance and see where they went, and then dash to catch them up. Now, in daylight, it would be much easier to navigate the alleys of the town. This wasn't Londinium or Rome, after all!

Not that the two women seemed to care. They trudged up the hill until they had almost reached the top, and then they suddenly turned left down a side street. Drusus set off after them as fast as he could. When he reached the place where they had turned, they had vanished. For a moment he stood dumbstruck, cursing under his breath. Then he saw his luck was in. At the far end of the street, there was only a curtain of vegetation, the stream valley he had crossed riding back the day before, and which cut down the west side of the town. To his right was a blank wall, the lower garden wall of the next house up the hill. That meant the two women must have entered the gateway he could make out halfway along the street, a gate which must lead into the town house looming above him. Excellent, he thought, I have them trapped, but I can't just walk in, I don't know who lives there, and how can I persuade Ophelia to talk, assuming that's who it is, unless I have some way to threaten her? He had left his sword at the inn. It was clumsy to wear in town, and you never knew when you might run into an officious watchman or self-appointed good citizen, only too happy to point out that it was illegal for ordinary civilians to bear arms within the city limits. Nonetheless, he thought, as he retraced his steps to the inn, he was now going to have to take that risk. He would go back and fetch it, and then he would have her at his mercy.

Drusus buckled his sword belt and slipped an extra dagger into his boot. Then he wrapped himself in his travelling cloak. It would take an eagle eye to spot the weapons. Otherwise, he looked like any other travelling functionary, though even that might not be without risk, he thought ruefully. Roman imperial officers might not be very welcome here, even though the Goths were supposed to be allies under the terms of the treaty.

There were more people about when he slipped out of the inn and climbed the street once again, making their way to the church or perhaps the local dignitary's residence on the hill at the top of the town. Further up, the stream of walkers parted as a small cart drawn by a donkey made its way through the hustle and vanished round a corner. Drusus turned into the street leading to the gate through which the women had entered the house. An increasing feeling of anxiety took hold of him as he neared the entrance. How was he going to explain his errand to the inhabitants? What was he going to do when he confronted the woman? He had never liked physical violence and it looked like that would be unavoidable. His sleepless night had led him to two options, neither of which was particularly attractive. If the woman did turn out to be Ophelia, then Fortuna had handed him a wonderful bargaining counter in the conflict with Marcus Silvanus. Wouldn't Silvanus be willing to concede his demands in exchange for his wife's sister sound and healthy? That, of course, would require him transporting Ophelia from Agininum all the way to Britannia. The other option was simpler: to kill her as an inconvenient witness to what he and Vito had done.

He pushed at the gate leading into the yard and stepped inside. An old woman was sitting milking a goat. There was no sign of Ophelia or the two women he had seen in the town. His hand automatically felt for his sword, but he decided to try charm first.

"Good morning, mistress," he said.

The old woman looked up at him, letting go of the goat.

"What can I do for you, young man?" she asked.

"I'm looking for my sister. I heard she might have found shelter with you. One of our family's enemies has been causing trouble, but thankfully I've dealt with him." He patted the sword.

"I see," said the old woman, looking around as if for help. "Mmm… I'm sorry," she mumbled.

"Has something happened?"

"Mm… no, young man, but, what a pity that you have just missed your sister. My daughter's husband left with the donkey, and the mistress in his cart, well… it can't be long ago, before I started milking this goat, after Aija, that's my daughter, and the servant went down to the hostel to pick up their belongings." She patted the animal on the flank. "He's taking them to the monastery… do you know it?"

God's bollocks, thought Drusus, but he steadied himself. He made a slight bow and took a step back.

"I'm afraid I'm a stranger to these parts… Can you tell me the way?"

"Oh," said the old woman. "It's easy to find… just up the road across the hills. It used to be a villa, Claudius and Larissa's house when I was young… that was years ago, of course, but they were well known in the area. They often visited this house, you know, for the holy days when Christianity first arrived."

Drusus bowed again and retreated slowly. He had a sense that the old woman would not shut up now she had an audience, and every moment he stood listening to her prattle was a moment when someone he did not want to meet might appear and the people he wanted to meet were an ever greater distance away.

"Thank you, thank you, grandma," he said, then bowed again and made a dash for the street.

The cart was long gone, of course. He was unsure of the distance to this monastery, and even though a donkey cart might not be the fastest mode of transport, by the time he got back to the inn, gathered his goods and made his horse ready, how far could they have travelled? He could try to catch up with them on the road, but then he would have to take on the man driving the cart as well as two hysterical and frantic harpies. On the other hand, if they reached the monastery, then bluff and guile would be needed, and that was definitely more in his line. Let this putative Ophelia arrive, be lulled into thinking she was safe, and then he would take care of her.

❧ Chapter 34 ❧
Agininum

Their first impression of the monastery was one of honey-coloured buildings, radiating warmth after basking in the sun all day; of servants, hurrying into the yard to greet the carter and unload the provisions he had brought them. Of a friendly sister greeting them with a smile without even asking who they were, crouching down to reassure the anxious children.

"You must be thirsty after the ride," she said and then stood up. "My name is Sister Agatha."

"Mistress Anna can cook, Aggie," shouted Tygon from across the yard. "Her father was a baker."

They had been chatting on the journey.

"Anna?" said the sister, looking back and forth between them.

"Anna," said Ophelia, indicating Anna, "and I'm Ophelia. We so need your help."

"Mistress," said Sister Agatha, "we all need help in our own ways. Come with me and we'll find you some water, a cake for the children, and in the meanwhile, I'll run and speak to Sister Claudia. She always likes to meet our visitors."

They made their way through gardens and passageways towards the refectory. Ophelia could see that the monastery was built in an old villa that tumbled down the hillside in a series of courtyards and gardens. It reminded her of her childhood home. To Anna it looked like a palace from a fairy tale. She held hard to the children to stop them running off to explore, and the touch of their little hands in hers helped her feel that this was not just a dream.

The refectory had been created out of the main dining room of the old villa and was dim and empty and silent in the middle of the day. Anna and Ophelia took their places at the foot of a long table. The children sat beside them quietly with big eyes. After the noisy and crowded hostels and taverns they had lodged in on the road, there was a mysterious air about the place that held them silent.

A woman appeared, carrying a jug of water and four beakers and a plate of small cakes. She placed them on the table, gave Anna a careful examination and departed, saying nothing.

"May we take one, Mum?" asked Fredagunda, eyeing the cakes.

That was the meaning, thought Ophelia, uncannily reminded of the way that visitors had been received in her childhood home. No one was turned away, but then neither were they allowed to disturb the ways of the house.

As they finished the little meal, two sisters came hurrying over to them.

"If you could leave the children with us, the abbess would like to speak to you. We'll take them to the kitchen."

While one of the sisters took the children by the hand, the other led Anna and Ophelia through a shaded arcade towards the abbess's rooms. As she walked behind the sister, Ophelia gave up a silent prayer. They so desperately needed somewhere safe to stay. After the years living in a damp and wretched camp in the forest, this monastery seemed like they had come to heaven. And with Drusus apparently on their heels, the walls and gates added an extra comfort.

The abbess greeted them with a smile and asked them to kneel with her for a moment of prayer. Ophelia could see she was a woman of quality, carefully groomed and dressed, and with a look in her eye that revealed she was used to giving orders and being obeyed. When they rose, she invited them to sit on two stools, arranged in front of a carved and upholstered chair where she herself sat down.

She introduced herself as Sister Claudia and asked them to tell their stories. Ophelia took the lead. She worked hard to sound humble and modest but made sure to use her most cultivated tone. She was in need, but she still had her pride. She provided Sister Claudia with a brief and censored version of her capture, their life in the bandit camp, and their flight to safety. The abbess listened carefully, her eyes first on one and then the other, a look of sympathy on her face.

When Ophelia had finished, she spoke.

"These are troubled times, sisters, and sometimes it's hard to see the workings of the Lord amongst this conflict and pain. I… we would be happy to provide you shelter here for as long as you need it. But I have to let you know, we are a community where every member, lay or religious, has to make their contribution." She turned to Anna. "Our friend, carter Tygon, tells me that you can cook, Sister Anna."

Anna bowed her head and hoped, hoped that the monastery just needed someone who could bake.

"Sister Albina, our cook, has a great deal to do, and only this week she told me she had been praying for an assistant. Perhaps Our Lord, in his wisdom, has answered her prayer. I think I know of a place for you," said Claudia, "if you don't mind hard work."

Anna could not even manage a smile but simply nodded.

The abbess turned to Ophelia. She gave her such a look that Ophelia felt she had seen right inside her, but she said nothing to her, instead turning once again to Anna.

"Come, sisters, let's go and visit Sister Albina and find your children, and then, Sister Anna, you can decide if you would be willing to assist our work by helping to feed us."

Sister Albina could have been an incarnation of the devil himself, and that would not have led Anna to reject the abbess's offer. In fact, it was far from the truth, and Sister Albina turned out to be the woman who had served them in the refectory, hard at work while the children played with a cat by her feet. Her severe look vanished in the moment they entered the kitchen.

Anna knew at once that she could work here, and all that was needed was a sign from Sister Albina that she would be accepted.

"I had my doubts when Tygon said a young woman had just arrived who could help me. I didn't believe it at first, but… well, the Lord has his ways, I suppose, and I'm not one to question them."

Sister Albina let go of the wooden spoon and bowl she had in her hands and rushed over and enveloped Anna in her ample bosom.

"Now let's get to work, young lady," she said, "there's mouths to feed in this house."

It was enough, Anna thought. She was sure she would soon earn the respect of Sister Albina, but the abbess had said nothing about Ophelia – would there be a task for her?

"I think we can leave your friend safely here, Mistress Ophelia," said Claudia, and the two women left the kitchen and returned in the direction of the main building. As they walked, the abbess spoke.

"By your tone, I suspect that you are a woman of some education. From your narration, I formed the same opinion, although you never spoke of it directly." Her statement demanded an answer.

"My lady…"

"Sister," Claudia corrected her, "here we are all sisters."

Then why did you address me as Mistress a moment ago, wondered Ophelia.

"Sister, I received an education as a child as the daughter of a Roman citizen. That part of my life seems an age ago. As I have told you, I have lost my family, my husband and my other children. I can't bring them back. I didn't want to seem arrogant to you. I've no expectations. I need to reconcile myself with the life I have to lead now."

The abbess stopped and turned to Ophelia.

"An education, once given, cannot be taken away. An upbringing leaves indelible traces, Mistress Ophelia. I know how hard it can be. I had such a childhood myself. I had to work long and hard to earn the right to be considered Sister. Come with me and I'll show you my treasure, and then we'll see how long your modesty lasts." Her words sounded a little judgemental to Ophelia's ears, though the tone remained kindly.

Sister Claudia led her back among the buildings, but instead of turning towards her own sanctuary, she took another passageway and then opened a door into a high room, filled with light. Two women rose as she came in and stood with their heads bowed.

"Dear sisters," said the abbess, "please continue, as I show Mistress Ophelia our library."

Ophelia's eyes roamed around the room, taking in the wooden shelves with books placed carefully on them, and at one end a rack stacked with scrolls. She thought of her father's library at Verdaris. It had contained many scrolls and books, the Latin authors and even some Greek works, but not as many as she could see here. One book stood open on a stand. She hesitated a moment and then stepped forward. It had been years since she had seen a book. She examined the text. For a moment she had to make an effort, but then it came back to her. The book was written in Greek. She had not read a Greek text since she had been a schoolgirl, and even then, the boys had been privileged with more time from the tutor. Still, she could make out the words. It was the Gospel of St Mark, but written in Greek, not Latin, as she had learned the story.

"Behold, there was a sower who went out to sow," she read aloud from the manuscript, and then she began to translate. "And it came to pass, as he sowed, some fell by the wayside, and the fowls of the air came and ate it up."

"Very good," said the abbess, with a new warmth in her voice.

"It's been many years," said Ophelia, lowering her eyes.

"Can you form the letters, too?" she asked. "I mean Greek as well as Latin. Could you copy that gospel?"

Ophelia turned to her. "I think so, but I would need to practise. Writing in Greek is not a skill much in demand among outlaws."

"I can imagine there are Greek-speaking bandits somewhere in the world," remarked the abbess, "who need to hear the word of the Lord in their tongue. Ours, however, need the words in Latin, and, I fear, in other tongues, too, if any of them can read. If we're going to sow our seed upon the ground, we need gospels in Latin. You know the words of the Lord in that language?"

"Yes, Sister. My mother was a Christian, and we were all baptised into the faith. We learned at her knee."

"May she rest in peace, in the presence of Our Lord," added the abbess, suddenly recalling Ophelia's story and the tragic end that Ophelia's mother had most likely suffered. "Ophelia," she continued, "Sister Albina has not been the only one calling on Our Lord for assistance in her daily tasks. I, too, have been praying that I could find someone to help me copying these books. It seems that Our Saviour may have chosen you for that role. Will you take it on? Will you become our sister by tilling this particular corner of the Lord's vineyard?"

At the end of the day, Anna and Ophelia were shown their room. It was situated in what had been the living quarters of the old villa and, rather incongruously for a Christian house, it was still decorated with nymphs and centaurs from its previous incarnation as the bedroom of a heathen Roman. There were two beds and a place for their clothes. The children were exhausted and climbed onto the cots, Fredagunda ready to sleep next to her mother, and Lanius with his. Almost as soon as they lay down their heads, they fell asleep.

Anna was exhausted after spending the evening cooking, but Ophelia could not sleep. She lay still, staring up at the dim outlines of the paintings on the wall with an eerie feeling of familiarity. It was just such a room she had shared with her sister in her childhood, until it had been time to leave home for her marriage. Could it really be true they could stay, she thought, in this beautiful house, where the women seemed so friendly and welcoming? She felt as if a horrible weight had been lifted from her shoulders. A warm feeling of relief began to spread through her body, tingling but pleasant, a feeling she wished she could share, and as she did so, she remembered the strange half-dream she had had a few days ago, lying beside the trader. Could it be true that all her life she had harboured feelings which she had hidden, from herself more than anyone else? Could it be true that her feelings for Anna went beyond friendship? She remembered the gestures, the hesitant touches, the little looks that Anna had given her.

It had been no dream, she thought, but a memory. She had felt a desire for Livia, a desire that had only surfaced that one time, when her senses had been overwhelmed, and Livia had returned her caresses, and they had kissed, if only for a moment. And then Livia had gone, and she had pushed her feelings to the back of her mind again. And then with Anna she had looked away, turned away, all this time.

But then I was never quite so innocent, was I, she thought, even long before Livia? Lissa, the daughter of her father's friend, had been older than her and led the way. The secrecy of the woods, the warm sun, the soft grass, and the temptation had been too great. She had only been a girl, she had told herself, and girls do silly things, and then her father had told her she was to be married, and that drove away all other thoughts.

Ophelia glanced across to the other bed where Anna lay. Probably she had fallen asleep. Ophelia had to speak to her, tell her, but how? An impulse came over her. She had to confront her fears and do what she should have done long ago. She stepped from her bed and crossed the room. She gently picked up Fredagunda and placed her carefully down in the spot she had just left, next to Lanius. The little girl stirred but did not wake. Then she softly lowered herself down beside Anna. Tonight, it felt different. Tonight, it felt safe.

"Anna," she whispered, "are you awake?"

Anna turned towards her, half asleep. "Ophi, is that you?"

In the dark of the room, their faces were only inches apart.

"Anna, my darling, darling Anna," she said quietly. "I think we've found our new home. I hope we won't have to travel any further, and we can be here together, for each other."

Ophelia reached out and placed her arm across the shoulders of her friend. She pulled Anna towards her, and kissed her on the mouth, at first gently, and then with a sudden passion. She felt Anna's arm around her, stroking her back, so the two of them lay tightly locked together. She drew back her head a little way until she could see into Anna's eyes. They were glistening, glistening with tears, and with hope and love. It had taken so long for her to see Anna's feelings for her, only now when the tension and fear had evaporated.

"Anna," she whispered. "I love you, love you dearly."

With all they had been through, this woman had comforted her, taken care of her, like no one else had ever done. Anna whispered in reply.

"Ophi, I love you, and always have done, since the first day you came to the camp. Please promise you'll never leave me."

"I do," she replied.

She lay silent, enjoying the moment, and then she spoke again.

"Anna, my darling, I've something to tell you."

"What's that, Ophi?"

"I think I'm expecting a child."

Anna stirred, more alert.

"You haven't said anything."

"I wasn't sure while we were on the road. It has been so unpleasant, the journey, the effort, the heat, I thought perhaps… but now I just know it."

"I wonder how Sister Claudia'll take it," said Anna in the morning. She had been up early already, to the bakehouse, and had returned to the room to rouse Ophelia and the children.

Ophelia was surprised by Claudia's laughter, her congratulations, her embrace.

"It's the work of the Lord, to keep you here," she said. "Despite…"

"Despite what?" echoed Ophelia.

"Despite the fact that you and Anna are more than just friends. I saw it at once. Her eyes sparkle when she looks at you, and you… you're a reserved woman, Ophelia, and perhaps with good reasons, but even you can't hide love. 'Faith, hope, love, these three; but the greatest of these is love.' Our Lord said that. Show your faith, live in hope, and who can stand in the way of your love?"

"And you won't send us away, because of the child, because…?"

"Good Lord, no! You can't live in a place like this and suppress people's feelings for one another entirely. And as for the child, Mary the Mother of Christ might have been able to travel the roads of Palestine in that state and give birth in a stable, but she had the Lord's protecting hand over her. We lesser mortals do well not to push our luck. I've no wish to see you leave. I had already decided you and Anna can stay as long as you want. I need your help in the library, and if the Lord has seen to bless you with a child as a means to compel you to remain, I'll accept his blessing. And besides, it's good for us to hear the voices of children within these walls. I would say," she added with a chuckle, "the more the merrier, but that might lead my sisters into temptation."

Ophelia made her way to the library, deep in thought. She had been intending to continue to search for her family at some point, but she was already apprehensive of how they would receive her, back from the dead, with two fatherless children and now another woman as her lover. But why search after people who would surely disapprove of her when they could all continue living in a place where they could be useful, where she and her darling Anna could be accepted for who they were? Perhaps, when all was said and done, it was for the best to let her old family go, accept that the past was gone and would not return.

⳩ Chapter 35 ⳨
Agininum

Drusus saddled his horse, strapped on his sword and set out on his way, up from the town and across the hills towards the monastery. He had a feeling of dread. When he reached his journey's end he would have to act, one way or another, and yet the practical details bothered him. He was alone, a man, perhaps, and an armed man, but alone. How was he going to bluff his way into the monastery? How was he going to find the woman once he got there? What was he going to do with her, and even if all things went well, how was he going to extract himself, with or without her? There was a voice inside him that said it would be better if everything was a mistake. If the woman he was following was not the one he had conjured up in his mind, but a complete stranger. Then he could simply exchange a word and be on his way, to return to Agininum to meet Sismond, even to weigh the possibility of a reconciliation with Xancha. It was all very well assuming that action was needed, but being the man of action was quite another matter.

He had not ridden far before circumstances forced his hand. His mind had been so occupied by the problems confronting him that he had not noticed a change in the weather. A thick bank of grey clouds filled the western sky, and where the undulations of the landscape permitted a longer view, the distance was obscured by rain. The downpour hit him just as he approached the summit. He pulled up the hood of his cloak, but it hardly helped. He could barely see ahead, and on an unknown road he began to be worried that he might lose his way. There was no shelter in sight until he detected a grey smudge to his right, which gradually took the form of a long wall beside the road, and eventually a gate. He dismounted and, crouching under the meagre shelter provided by the arch, knocked as loudly as he could on the postern. A panel slid back and a pair of eyes confronted him.

"In the name of God, let me in," he begged.

The panel closed, and after a moment the postern shifted, opened, and he and the horse could pass inside.

He was still unsure where he was. Could chance have brought him to the monastery or was he in some stranger's house? He had the immediate impression of entering a villa of the old type, rather like his own old home of Agridurnum. Stables and barns clustered round a courtyard, and cloistered walks led off among the buildings, only dimly visible in the rain.

"Let me take your cloak," said the porter who had admitted him, a rough-looking peasant, "and I'll call for a boy to take care of your horse. Please wait here, until I can find our housekeeper."

Drusus did as he was instructed. He could hardly do otherwise. The downpour was intense and he had no desire to leave the shelter. He was grateful when a boy appeared to take his horse, splashing through the puddles that had begun to cover the courtyard inside the main gate.

"Stranger, welcome," came the sound of a female voice. "This rain caught us all by surprise, but we should be grateful for God's bounty as it will fill our cisterns."

The woman was wearing a plain grey gown, a shawl over her head, much as the housekeeper of any such villa would.

"May I ask my host's name?"

The woman laughed, an open, friendly laugh.

"Your host, why, it's Our Lord Jesus Christ! This is the monastery of Mons Agininum. I'm Sister Agatha, and Sister Claudia is our leader."

Drusus felt his stomach clench and could do no more than force an "Ah-hah" from his mouth.

The sister guided him among the buildings to a room containing half a dozen beds, evidently the guest dormitory, though there were no other occupants. She indicated the place where he could leave his baggage, then took him by the arm.

"Come, master, follow me. I'll find a quiet place for you to wait until dinner, the library, the scriptorium, perhaps, while your clothes are drying. You look like a man who loves a book."

He would rather have had a good glass of wine or a jug of ale, but the woman was already hurrying away under the shelter of the colonnade and he was forced to follow.

He first noticed her, seated at a lectern, with her back to him. She was bent over, carefully applying ink to a manuscript.

"Sister Ophelia," said Sister Agatha, "we have a visitor. May I leave him here to sit for a while and keep dry?"

"One moment," she said, before turning and rising to her feet, but Sister Agatha had left, leaving her alone with the stranger.

She stood silent, her brows furrowed, as if she could not believe what she was seeing.

"Ophelia Ursina?" asked Drusus, faintly and uneasily. His ears had not deceived him? The other woman had called her Ophelia?

His voice was unmistakeable.

"Drusus… Astrebanus…" she said, slowly, gripping her writing desk to steady herself, feeling sick and faint, feeling waves of clammy cold and sticky heat pass up and down her body.

Now he recognised her well enough, when he had been forewarned by the carter, when he had had her in his view in Agininum.

"No, no," he stuttered, now unwilling to admit where fate had led him, taking a step backwards, his hand reaching for the door, "no."

Ophelia Ursina… being confronted by her… it now seemed impossible, he thought, despite what the trader had said. She should be dead. Vito had been told the ambush was successful. There were no witnesses remaining. The treasure… it was buried in the forest. Amalric had assured him. And yet, there was something about this woman that suggested she could be Ophelia Ursina. She had used his name, must have recognised him, but how?

"You still think I'm dead and buried? You still think I'm lying in an unmarked grave along the Autessiodurum road?"

But how could Ophelia Ursina have escaped the ambush? How had she come to be here, so far from the place where she, or rather her bones, should be? How could she have survived the intervening years?

His silence spurred her to speak again.

"Do I have to remind you that my father was Publius Julius Ursinus, governor of Britannia Prima? Do I have to remind you that you arranged to have me murdered, by common thieves and bandits, along with my family and my children, my husband?"

There was a hard tone to her voice.

"No… I mean, no… yes?"

She had not been prepared to see him in this place, on this day, but she had feared this meeting long enough to have played the scene many times in her imagination.

"I don't have to remind you of what you did, what you arranged, what you bribed and threatened someone else to do because you were too contemptible and cowardly to do the deed yourself?"

"I don't know… I didn't do it. It was nothing to do with me. It was Vito who arranged it."

He stepped forward, reaching out, as if to touch her, as if he had to reassure himself he was not imagining her.

"Don't," she said, "don't touch me."

"I… didn't mean to," he said, withdrawing, again defensive.

"How did you find me?" she asked. She was puzzled, annoyed, angry even, that he had appeared just when she had begun to feel safe. He had obviously followed her from Agininum, but had he been pursuing her before then?

"I've been in Italia," he said, now on firmer ground, "and I'm returning home to Remis."

Now she remembered. Anna had picked up snatches of the conversation during the feast, snatches that had meant nothing to Anna, but which had added fresh pieces to her mosaic.

"Then you are far from your route here, Master Drusus."

"It was only a chance that brought me here. I… I had business to attend to…" He was gabbling, he knew it, still trying to grapple with the problem confronting him.

Her smile unnerved him further.

"An ill-chance then, for both of us," she said.

He took a breath, trying to think of different words, another approach, as if she were a witness, a suspect of a crime in a law court, needing to be lulled and lured into a trap.

"I met your brother, if you are who you say you are, in Ravenna."

She felt her stomach clutch. In Ravenna… then he was far beyond her reach. Then it was hopeless. Even if they could leave, they could never travel so far.

Drusus noticed the change in her expression. That had been a surprise to her, he mused. Perhaps he could drive home his advantage further. He managed to suppress a smirk.

"And after I had confronted him, he thought it best to flee, with the help of his friends, flee to Constantinople."

He saw her breathing, slowly. He expected her to react with distress to his revelation, but instead a look of relief crossed her face.

"Then he's safe from you, unlike the rest of us?" she said.

"The rest of you," he repeated. "Who are you thinking of? Your husband, your brother, your sister, Hypatia, perhaps?"

He was again waiting for a reaction, but none came, just the slow rise and fall of her chest.

"My brother Vito was killed," he countered, "executed as a traitor, by your sister and her husband. Perhaps you knew that already?"

She did not know what he was talking about. What could she have learned about his brother during the years living in Amalric's camp?

"What are you implying, Drusus Astrebanus? I've heard nothing, know nothing, and care nothing for your brother. If the man is dead, then all the better, given the misery he has sown."

She could see his face redden and become tense, a sign of anger at her words.

"How dare you?" he said. "How dare you gloat over my brother's death? You, whose father was a crook, and whose sister's a murderer."

"How dare *you* insult my family?" she replied. "You tried to kill us all, and you've failed, Drusus, you and your brother. Hypatia's in Britannia and Gaius has escaped to Constantinople. You've admitted your failure in your own words. And me?" She laughed bitterly. "Look at me, Drusus! I'm alive when you thought I was dead. The man you paid to kill us spared me, gave me his love, gave me his child."

She placed her hands across her belly with a smile.

Drusus frowned, confused for a moment. Had Amalric really betrayed his promise, or was she bluffing? He had seen no sign of her in the bandit's camp, but then Amalric was no fool. If he could lie about killing her then he could lie about anything.

"You can spare me the sordid details," he said, his anger rising. "You're coming with me, away from here, back to Britannia."

His hand shifted towards his belt, reaching for the handle of his sword to reinforce his threat, but there was nothing there. He had dumped it with his baggage in the dormitory.

"No," she said.

"Don't you want that? Back to your own country, to be with your sister, in your home."

"No," she said, "I have no sister. I have no home, not any longer, not after what you and your brother did to me. I'm not going with you, Drusus Astrebanus. I'm not going anywhere."

His frustration boiling, he took a step towards her, reaching out to grab at her. He had no coherent thought of what he would do, but he would wipe that look off her face.

"I'm taking you with me, Ophelia. I'll tell them you're my sister, that you have wandered away, delusional and mad. You know the law."

He took another step, clamping his hand on her wrist.

Ophelia could hardly comprehend what he was doing. They had been conversing, coldly, it was true, but with restraint. She was surprised by the sudden rage distorting Drusus' face, his lurch in her direction.

"Let me go!"

She drew back her arm sharply, catching him by surprise and freeing herself from his grip. She stepped back to put distance between herself and the angry man. She reached out for the lectern behind her, fearful of stumbling, and her hand closed around a cylinder of wood, the handle of the knife she'd used to sharpen her quills.

She never understood what took hold of her in that moment. It was impossible to explain to Anna when she asked, to Claudia, to herself, even. A combination, she supposed, of the knowledge she was not helpless, her own emotion mirroring his angry expression, the overwhelming feeling that he had no right to be angry with her, but that she had every right to feel wronged by him, to defend herself.

She seized the blade and raised her arm. He reached out for her again, for the arm she held out in front of him. She tried to fend him off, waving the knife in his direction. She felt a sudden tug at her hand as the blade dug into his flesh. He stepped towards her, reaching once more to seize her.

"Leave me alone," she hissed. "Leave me alone in peace."

She swung at him again, and the blade slashed across his arm. Blood oozed from the cuts, dripping onto the floor. Drusus stopped, raised his arms again, but now only to look down at the wounds. For a moment he looked helpless. She felt an instinct take over her, the instinct of a beast of prey confronted by a wounded animal, by the smell of blood.

"Don't think of it, Drusus" – she raised her voice, shouting now in British – "of trying to harm me. I've learned a lot of things living in the forest. I've had to kill animals, and one more wouldn't make much difference."

She slashed with the knife again, and another thin red furrow appeared across his arm.

He looked up at her, the emotion of anger replaced by one of paralysing fear. His expression drew her on. Memories of the past pushed her forward. Suddenly she seemed to hear the horsemen on the road, and see their glinting swords, the scream of her mother, her own scream as the wagon lurched, toppled off the road, and the feeling of tumbling, over and over down the bank towards the river.

She heard laughter, her own laughter.

"Mad, am I, Drusus? You want me mad? Your own sister, am I? Well, try and take me if you can!"

She lunged towards him.

"Soon they'll come and find me mad, howling and bathing in your blood. They'll have to drag me away and place me in a darkened room and bar the door. Then I'll be truly mad, as mad as I have every right to be."

She stopped abruptly, took a couple of deep breaths, her eyes fixated on him, staring. Drusus glanced from side to side, as if searching for a way to escape. Pray to God she did not take it into her mind to slash at his head. She could rip open his face, cut his throat, blind him with one blow. She took a step towards him, her foot skidding on the blood already on the floor, and he cringed, but instead of gouging at him, the hand with the knife dropped to her side, her mouth stretching into an unnerving smile.

"Leave me alone, Drusus," she said quietly, "to live my own life. Can't you see you've got what you wanted? My father is dead. My family is dead. I want nothing with you. It won't bring my old life back. That Ophelia died with her loved ones on the road to Lugdunum."

He stood panting, clutching at his arm to stem the blood that seeped between his fingers.

"And silver and gold, if that's what you desire – I know where my father's treasure's hidden… in the forest by Amalric's camp… but what do I want with that cursed metal, when I've found love, when I've found you don't need riches and treasure to be content, to be cared for, to have others to care for. Go on your way, Drusus, dig up my father's bowls and plates, his coins and jewels, and may they bring you more fortune than they ever brought him."

She took a step towards him, raising the knife once again.

Drusus' fear had frozen him, but deeper panic suddenly plucked at him. He managed to pick up his feet and, clutching his bloody arm, he turned and ran, out of the room and into the corridor, out into the rain, his steps splashing on the stones outside.

Ophelia was breathing heavily, dizzy and shocked at herself. The knife dropped from her grasp, clattering and skittering across the floor. She put her hands to her head and sank down, down among the traces of Drusus' blood.

The door to the library flew open, and Anna and Sister Agatha ran into the room.

Anna rushed towards her, crouching down, wrapping her arms around the sobbing Ophelia.

"What happened, what happened? Are you all right? Are you hurt? What's this blood? They told me that you were shouting, but nobody understood what you were saying."

Ophelia simply nodded her head, huddled in Anna's embrace. Sister Claudia appeared in the doorway, her eyes taking in the scene, the crouching women, the blood on the floor.

Ophelia met her gaze.

"Don't send us away, please, please don't send us away."

Claudia stepped carefully around the patches of gore and crouched down to her, raised her hand and placed it against Ophelia's cheek.

"Calm, my dear, calm yourself."

"I didn't mean to harm him," Ophelia was sobbing. "He wanted to take me away!"

"No one will take you away, my dear, no one. And no one will send you away."

Sister Claudia knew well that many of the women in the monastery had troubles in their past, often, horribly enough, with their own families, parents, brothers, sisters. It was best to try to leave those lives behind, difficult though that might be at times. The knife and the blood told their own story. She would not speculate on what had brought about the conflict.

She glanced at Sister Agatha.

"Find the man," she said, "and see that he's treated."

Sister Agatha hurried away. Drips of blood on the pavement led the way through the cloisters. She could guess where the stranger was heading. Better to collect the materials she would need from the kitchen: some strips of cloth, warm water and vinegar. She found him sitting on his pallet in the guest room, dabbing at his arm with the corner of his cloak. She crouched down in front of him and lifted away his hand. Slash marks from the pen knife scored his arm.

"This is going to hurt," she said, dampening a cloth in the water, "but it's best for you."

The man flinched as she wiped vinegar over the wounds.

"There," she said, as calmly as she could, "they're only scratches." They were not, she knew. The sharp little knife had carved furrows into the flesh.

Drusus watched her as she took a strip of fabric and wrapped it around his arm. Her patience, her calm voice and gentle touch brought back memories of his mother, before she died. He felt tears coming to his eyes. The sister pinned the bandage in place and stood up. He glanced up at her, not with desire but with desperation for comfort. His eyes were brimming over. His shoulders began to heave. He could not prevent himself. He clutched his hands to his face in a vain attempt to hide his weeping. She dropped to her knees and twisted round so she was sitting beside him, placed her arms softly around his shoulders and pulled him towards her, so that he was enfolded in her warm embrace.

How, how had everything gone so terribly wrong?

☙ Chapter 36 ❧
Gaul, again

Drusus had fled from the monastery, there was no other word for it. He had not seen Ophelia again. He had remained in the guest room in hiding. The kindly sister, Agatha, had found him, brought him a bowl of gruel. She had asked no questions but unwrapped the bandages, cleaned the wounds again, assured him how well they were healing and instructed him how to manage them over the coming days. He had taken his horse and ridden away, over the hills, down into the valley, across the bridge, and day after long day to the north. How was it, he thought, that the Ursini always seemed to survive? Gaius, smug in Constantinople, Hypatia, lording it over his lands alongside her husband, and now, now even Ophelia, who should have been a mere corpse, living in ease with her books. While he, who worked so hard, who struggled incessantly, was alone and injured and wretched.

The appearance of Senones did nothing to improve his mood. The city was swarming with military. The taverns and the hostels were ringing with the praise of Magister Constantius. Nonetheless, when Drusus attempted to travel south towards Autessiodurum, he was stopped at the city gate by a soldier.

"No one leaves unless in an escorted convoy."

"But I thought that the roads have been secured?"

"So they have, master, but for every bandit removed, there's a man who has depended on him for his own living and is now going hungry."

"You mean hanging all the bandits didn't serve as sufficient warning?"

"Does it ever?" answered the soldier. "It simply advertises the fact that there are vacancies to be filled. If you're in a hurry, come back tomorrow and join the caravan. If not, then the next will be on the Sun's Day."

Drusus and his horse joined the group the following morning, escorted by soldiers at the front and behind, as well as positioned at intervals up and down the column. There was no point in even riding the horse. The caravan travelled at the pace of the slowest. It was hardly a vote of confidence in the success of the anti-bandit campaign. Drusus' hopes began to rise. All might not be completely lost. They marched steadily on until they reached Autessiodurum. There he realised a problem remained. No one was allowed to leave the caravan. The next major town they would reach would be Augustodunum and then it would be too late. They would have passed the location of Amalric's camp. He had seen how stragglers were herded along and, if they were not capable of walking further, hoisted onto the wagons and compelled to continue on their way. How was he going to slip away from the convoy to find the hidden hoard while he was under surveillance of the escort?

Autessiodurum resembled a fort on a larger scale. The entrances to the town were sealed. No one passed in and out without permission. The pass he had been given by Tacitarius was dismissed with contempt. There was no alternative but to assemble with the company once again and march on.

It was only when they reached the hostel in the scruffy village which bordered Amalric's usual haunts that Drusus' increasingly frantic ruminating threw up a potential escape.

"I'm not feeling well," he muttered to the convoy leader, a short while before departure time. "It must be something I ate in Autessiodurum." In his desperate state of mind, pale and agitated, it was not hard to mimic illness.

"Aren't you well enough to ride on the wagon? One of the other men could lead your horse."

Drusus responded by clutching at his stomach dramatically, taking a stumbling step backwards, and then running for the latrines. The convoy left without him. At midday, when the village lay in a torpor, he cautiously entered the stables, unhitched his horse, and in a moment was on the road.

When he reached the point where he should turn off, he slackened his pace and began to scour the road margin for a sign of the track he needed to take to the camp. He was beginning to feel hungry and was looking forward to a hot meal when he arrived. He would never complain about rustic food again after his misadventures of the last few months. A little way ahead he spotted his target and, making sure the road was clear in front and behind, tugged at the reins and steered his horse into the woods.

The track was soft underneath, the woods almost silent. The camp was not far from the road, a couple of miles at most. It was darker amongst the trees, and lonely. Drusus began to feel worried once again. Supposing he ran into more soldiers. How would he explain himself? Could he bluff that Tacitarius had sent him out to report on the success of the anti-bandit campaign? Would that be sufficient to account for him riding alone through the forest? Supposing Amalric's men were on alert for strangers, shooting first and asking questions afterwards?

Ahead he saw a glimpse of sky through the trees. He was approaching a clearing, the clearing he was aiming for, he hoped. The trees began to thin, the gloom of the woods was scattered, and in a few more paces he was at the edge of the open space. The horse came to a stop, either of its own accord or by some unconscious action of its rider. Drusus slid off his mount and staggered forward a couple of steps, staring. The clearing was empty, abandoned. Here and there he could make out a few charred timbers which showed where huts once stood. Only those, and the burned circles in the open area in front of him, proved he had made no mistake. This had been a camp, the camp where he had feasted with Amalric on his journey south.

He took a few more hesitant steps, nearly tripping over a half-rotten log that must have served once as a seat. Only the scurrying of wild animals and the insects broke the silence. A single bird suddenly looped through the open space, a black whirr against the sky, and vanished over his shoulder. He made his way slowly round the clearing, looking this way and that, trying to recall how it had appeared that night, that morning, two years ago. He had sat over to the right, his back to the forest. The men and women had clustered around the fires here in the centre. At the end of the feast, Amalric had offered him a girl, a busty young woman with dark hair and brown eyes, he recalled. He had declined and slept alone, in one of the shelters, on a rough mattress stuffed with bracken.

In the morning he had risen early and rousted out his companions, both badly hung over. The same busty girl had found them some food, barley porridge, if he remembered right. How he could do with a bowl of barley porridge, served by a complaisant young woman, just now, but there was no one, nothing left. Where had he gone with Amalric when he had demanded to know where the hoard was hidden? Round, round the clearing to the far end. Here was a path, yes, leading down to a pond. This must be it. Thank God he hadn't trusted the bandit. Thank God he had demanded to be shown the place. Down this track… here he had stood, and Amalric had pointed… to a rock and a tree. The rock he spotted, the tree a little further away. He cautiously made his way down the path, until he was roughly halfway between the two, and then began to pace out into the woods.

He did not have to look very carefully. He had hardly deviated from the path when he spotted a hollow, dug in the earth. He ran forward, dropped the bags he was carrying and fell to his knees. Someone else had found the treasure. Someone must have taken it. He began to dig at the loose earth, sending it flying around him until felt a hard object, undulations, waves of metal. Amalric had not been lying, not entirely, and Ophelia had told him the truth. The Ursini were dead and gone and their treasure was his.

A sudden sense of relaxation came over him as he delved down into the earth and pulled up a silver beaker. A few more scrapes and it lay exposed, Publius Julius Ursinus' treasure, or at least the part that had been left behind by whoever had got there before him. How much was left, he wondered? Never mind that, he thought, I have to take what I can and get away from here.

Several of the beakers and small items fitted inside one another. He grabbed some vegetation and stuffed it around the sides so they would not rattle in the bags. He took up a bowl, rotated it in his hands, not admiring the ornamentation, but wondering how he was going to conceal it, given its awkward size and shape. A feeling of frustration and annoyance welled up in him. Damn the bowl, he didn't care about its artistic value, only about its value as bullion. He threw it onto the ground and then stamped on it until it was flattened. It gave him a certain savage satisfaction to pulverise Publius Julius Ursinus' precious silver bowl.

"The better stuff is always so flimsy," he said to himself as he slid the flattened oval of silver into the bag. The rest of the hoard received the same treatment.

He bent down again, his fingers closing on a small leather pouch. He lifted it out, peered in and then stuffed it inside his cloak with a satisfied grunt. He felt around in the earth at the bottom of the hole for a final time. There was nothing left to take out. The hole had done its duty. There was no need to fill it in.

When he returned to the clearing he slung the bags over the horse and looked around once again at the charred remains of the huts, the overgrown fireplaces. Even a man like Amalric had been unable to protect his own, he mused. Is this where force and violence lead, he wondered? Is that the lesson in this for me? That however ruthless and vicious you are, there's always someone more brutal, more cunning who will catch up with you and destroy you? Vito thought he was cunning, that he was cold-blooded, and he ended up with his head on a block. And now Amalric, an old soldier, a man who had survived countless battles, countless wars, and all that was left of his life were cinders and ashes. And yet, someone had dug at the hole, someone who had enough honour to leave him his share. Maybe Amalric had kept his word after all. Who knew who was lying and who was telling the truth, and who cared? His bags were filled with silver.

☙ Chapter 37 ❧
Remis, 420 CE

D rusus was in a quandary, sitting at a table in a small hired room, in one of the side streets of Remis. He had only taken on the case to keep himself busy. His client was a widow, a lady who was paying well for his assistance. She had been swindled out of a piece of land by a rich neighbour. Drusus was convinced she was in the right and, with a certain amount of self-satisfaction, had prepared a watertight case and an elegant speech for presentation to the court. His dilemma was that the neighbour, a man with a nasty reputation, had promised a bribe if he would muddle his argument in front of the magistrate, leave open certain obscure loopholes, which the neighbour's lawyers could ride through with a quadriga. Should he take the bribe and lose the case? He would risk the possibility that his reputation would plunge, but he would be able to live comfortably for another few months without having to lift a finger for anyone.

The discovery of Amalric's camp, burned and pillaged, had shocked him, but he had received a greater shock when he arrived in Treviri. He had travelled to challenge Apollinarius, to renew his claim to his daughter's hand. He might not be governor of Britannia. He might not be master of Agridurnum, but the treasure he had dug from the ground would be sufficient to meet the lawyer's conditions, to establish himself, to give Bryna a home.

Treviri was itself… capital of the frontier would be going too far, but among the gently decaying remnants of the Empire, Romans, Gauls, Germans, Franks and a host of other nuances of humanity jostled and pushed, each trying to get an edge over the others. To his surprise, Apollinarius' house stood silent, the gate closed, the yard deserted. The rooms gaped, emptied of their contents, those that did not lie in splinters and shards. There was no sign of the lawyer, his ailing wife, servants or slaves. Drusus enquired of the neighbours, in the taverns, but he was met only with evasions. The lawyer had been set on in the street. No one knew who was responsible. He had never recovered. His servants and slaves had slipped away, not quite in the proverbial night, but one by one, over time, taking with them his possessions in lieu of salary or manumission. His daughter had not been seen since.

Drusus had cried that night. He had cried for himself. He had cried for his frustration over a wife he would never have. He cried at the thought of Xancha whom he had left behind and the son he had never known. He had cried at the thought of the useless treasure that could not buy him the life he had dreamed of. On the ride from Treviri back to Remis he even toyed with the idea of throwing everything up and riding south once again. A sack of silver might persuade Xancha to take him back. Then he met his old friends, the brothers Cassius and Flavius, and as he recounted what he had found, a seed began to sprout within him, a seed of hate, feeding on the memory of his brother, feeding on the humiliations he had received, last but not least at the hands of Ophelia.

That hate had stayed with him, but he was not such a fool to become obsessed. He had to admit, applying his intelligence to practising law was a help in redirecting his emotions. In a few months he had built up quite a list of clients. His hardness had given him a certain reputation as a sharp opponent in front of the magistrates. Let's hope it's trickled back to Britannia, he thought, for the time when I need to take on so-called Governor Silvanus face to face, though I'm not going to count on the law alone.

He read through his case material once more with the pride of a man who had done a good job, with the resolve of a man who was sick of being on the end of others' slights. He had just decided he would put the rich man in his place, when a voice from the stairs outside distracted him, one of the clerks who ran errands for the lawyers of Remis.

"Master Drusus, I have a message for you. There's a man, I don't know his name, who wishes to speak to you. He said you could find him at Comenius' tavern at the second hour."

"What sort of a man?" Drusus' first thought was that he must be an agent of the rich neighbour, come to exert additional pressure in the lawsuit. His second was that it was some person of ill will, perhaps also connected to this suit, or to one of the other contentious cases he had become involved in, someone inclined to direct action, and that precautions would need to be taken. He would not be the first lawyer to find himself on the pointed end of a knife. If it could happen to Apollinarius it could happen to anyone.

"An ex-military man, I would say," said the clerk, "of the Alemanni, or a Frank, perhaps." That sounded potentially dangerous. He would pay a visit home before the meeting.

"Thank you," he said, passing the clerk a small silver coin, before rolling up the document and tucking it into his belt.

He took two side streets until he reached the house where he hired rooms on an upper floor, away from the noise and the smell of the street, but not directly under the stifling heat of the roof. He had been angry and sorry for himself when he first hired the rooms, shortly after returning from Ravenna. He, who had grown up on the largest estate in southern Britannia, living in two stinking rooms in a lodging house in the backstreets of Remis and paying for them by taking on lawsuits. But he did not want to waste the silver he had retrieved from the forest or the other treasure he and his brother had so carefully accumulated. A time would come when those would be needed.

From a chest in the rear of the two rooms, he extracted a leather jacket, studded with small iron plates. It was uncomfortable to wear for long, but there had been a few times when it had come in handy, dealing with cheating husbands or angry tenants requiring eviction. It promised protection against the use of what lawyers liked to call "edged weapons". It was handy against pointed ones, too. He also slipped a dagger into his boot before leaving for the rendezvous.

From across the tavern yard, a man waved him over, a man scarcely recognisable in the setting.

Drusus was barely able to control himself. He squinted at his old acquaintance. "What are you doing here, and dressed like that?"

Amalric had exchanged the dirty leather jerkin and rough trousers he had been wearing last time they met for a woollen cloak, over a well-cut tunic and leggings. A band (could it be gold?) was draped around his neck and several more jangled around his wrists.

"Waiting for you to show up," said Amalric with a faint smile. Drusus began to wince before the bandit started to laugh, standing up with a welcome embrace. "Joke, Drusus, joke! I was finishing off some business before I return up country… to my farm."

"I thought we had concluded our business," said Drusus. Amalric was clearly more pleased to see him than he was to see the bandit.

"Yes," continued Amalric, nonchalantly, "I've finished with robbing. It doesn't pay anymore, as I'm sure you saw if you came up the Lugdunum road. It's no way of life for an old man. Can I offer you some wine?"

Drusus would have liked to decline, to escape, but as Amalric still had him in a firm grip, he felt it would be unwise.

"I hardly expected to see you… again," he stuttered, with a weak smile. "Are you in need of a lawyer? Has your neighbour stolen your cow, or impregnated one of your maids?"

"Not me," said the former bandit. "I settle my disputes myself, in my own way."

Drusus did not need to ask how, but he followed meekly as Amalric guided him over to a table in the far, secluded corner of the yard.

Comenius appeared, followed by a servant.

"Your best wine, and a choice plate or two to accompany it," said Amalric, waving the tavern keeper away.

"Why then do you need me?" asked Drusus.

"I'll come to that," said the ex-bandit, "in a moment."

The wine was served.

"I could have sworn you were dead," said Drusus, "after I saw your camp."

"Ah, so you visited the camp, did you? I hope you found what you were looking for. I left your share, more than your share if I'm to be honest, but then I had had the chance to invest mine, and you did not. You know the fable, I suppose, of the man who buried his treasure hoping it would grow? One of the Christians' stories, I think."

He took a taste of his wine, swirled it around in his mouth and nodded with satisfaction.

"I always planned to move to the country when I retired," he said, replacing his glass on the table. "I mean the civilised, comfortable country, a nice little villa, surrounded by fields and orchards. That was always my dream growing up. And now I have found the place. There's only one thing missing…" He stopped talking and took another mouthful of wine.

"And what is that?" asked Drusus, understanding it was his duty to pose the question.

"A suitable woman… I had always dreamed of a little villa and a nice Roman wife. You know, the tall, slim, elegant, refined type of woman that we old soldiers never seem to get our hands on."

"Your woman… but I thought you had a woman in the camp?"

The ex-bandit glanced at him, thinking for a moment, trying to recall the time that Drusus had visited the camp.

"Ah, Anna, you mean. Yes, she was a cute little thing, you have to admit, but she would never have done as the mistress of a villa."

A nasty thought suddenly crossed Drusus' mind. He remembered Ophelia's words. The man who had given her his love. He gave his companion a sharp glance.

"You kept her, didn't you, you kept her alive."

Amalric's face froze in a blank expression.

"Ophelia Ursina," continued Drusus, his voice rising. "After Vito told you to kill them all, you kept Ophelia Ursina for yourself!"

Amalric's face shifted shape from blank to regretful.

"She was so beautiful, not so young anymore, perhaps, but just suitable for someone my age," said the ex-bandit, dreamily. "She would've been so perfect, so cultivated, so refined. I would've given her anything."

He suddenly turned and looked Drusus straight in the face.

"How do you know?"

For a moment Drusus hesitated. Was Amalric the only man who could walk around with secrets, who could choose silence over talk? Should he tell him the truth, that he had met her? Should he tell him she was as mad as a harpy?

"Did you go searching for her?" he asked.

"Regretfully, no. It was much too risky. I suppose she must be dead."

"No," said Drusus, "those fucking Ursini, you can't kill them. They always find some bloody way of escaping." It was on his lips to reveal the truth, but no, the deceitful bastard didn't deserve it.

"I had a son with her," Amalric said. "Little Alanaric, my son."

Drusus swallowed hard. "A son, too!" he cried, his hand white as he gripped his beaker. Of course the little brat he had seen her carrying must be Amalric's son.

"Your son," said Drusus, forcing himself to sound contemptuous. "How many bloody sons do you think you have? You've screwed your way from Gaul to Dacia and back again."

"That's not the point," said Amalric. "He was my son with her, with a real, civilised woman, not some way-station whore. Perhaps she did escape," he mused. "Well, her spirit must have, at least, since she still comes to me in my dreams."

Drusus shook his head to disguise a wince.

A servant appeared with the food. Amalric took another drink and shrugged.

"I failed, Drusus. I tried but I failed, I failed to win her over. I failed to protect her. I failed as a man and a father, but you know, my friend, I don't dwell on my failures. I move on, put them behind me, however painful, because carrying the pain is worse."

"Amalric, I'm so glad to see that you're prospering, but…" said Drusus, beginning to rise in the hope of avoiding having to share the meal.

"I know, Drusus," Amalric continued, ignoring his movement, "that you never give up, keep on trying however many times you fail. I suppose it's something I almost admire about you, never giving up on your dream, no matter how many catastrophes you leave in your wake."

Fuck you, thought Drusus, his anger rising, but it would not do to quarrel openly with Amalric. He knew only too well how many corpses the ex-bandit had on his hands.

"That's my personal business, friend," he said, shaking his head. "I wish you well with your farm. I hope you find another willing woman and may your yard overflow with little Teutons. I must leave you. I have other business to attend to."

"Not so fast, my friend," said Amalric, a harder note in his voice, gesturing for Drusus to sit. "Take a seat, enjoy some of Commenius' excellent food and listen to me." He spooned a portion of food into a dish and pushed it in Drusus' direction. "You haven't given me a chance to tell you why I asked you to come here. I have a proposal that might assist your business, since you are so determined to remain the implacable enemy of one Marcus Lucullus Ursinus."

"Silvanus," Drusus attempted to correct him, while re-taking his seat.

"It's better that you start to consider him as Ursinus and accept that he has been sitting securely as governor of Britannia Prima for a good while now."

"Too long," said Drusus.

"My thoughts exactly," said Amalric.

"What has this got to do with you?" asked Drusus. "You've never shown any interest in Britannia previously, except perhaps in the form of Ophelia."

"No, I'm not interested in Britannia," said Amalric hastily, "but I don't like to be idle. Once banditry no longer paid, the life of a country gentleman appeared enticing."

"About as enticing as lawyering," muttered Drusus.

"Probably," said Amalric, "though less dangerous, judging by your attire. But there you are correct. The frontier is altogether a little too placid just now, and, shall we say, I don't have the chance to use all the talents the gods gave me."

He smiled and took another mouthful of food before continuing.

"Your friend Ursinus doesn't make many mistakes, but now he may have made one, one that a clever and determined person could exploit to their own advantage."

He gave Drusus a knowing look.

"He's been strengthening his military forces, recruiting new men, casting his net wide for talent. My cousin's boy, Deric, he's thinking of taking up his offer, along with some of the other young men from the neighbourhood. The boys are expecting fighting, plunder, booty, sufficient glamour that women will throw themselves at them, and if they won't do so voluntarily, then as a result of a little compulsion now and then."

"Following the example of his uncle," said Drusus.

Amalric chose to ignore the interruption.

"I doubt it'll turn out how they hope. I've heard how Ursinus is ruling his province. They'll be living in forts, far from the comforts of town, patrolling day after day, and worse, drill and polish, and guard duty at various wretched toll stations. Not at all the life for an adventurous young man."

"It's what the army always did, so I've heard."

"You're right, and I've polished plenty enough boots in my time. It never did me any harm," said Amalric, "but you are beginning to catch my drift, Drusus. These boys'll soon be dissatisfied, and what do dissatisfied soldiers do? What have they always done, even under the Empire?"

"Revolt," said Drusus, "overthrow the leaders, put them to death… when they don't die themselves, of course."

"Precisely, boys will be boys, but they'll need leadership… if they are not going to end up dead in a ditch… in a foreign country, barely knowing the language. They don't understand the people. Now, with the right leadership…"

"And sufficient money," Drusus pointed out.

Amalric laughed and reached down below the table. "Now you're talking." When he drew up his hand, he quickly flicked his thumb, and Drusus' eyes were drawn upwards as a spinning, glinting object flew high into the air. When it hit the table, before it had a chance to bounce away, Amalric slammed his hand over it.

"What do you think that is?"

"Tell me," said Drusus, not liking the game.

Amalric withdrew his hand and revealed a shining silver coin. "Take a look."

Drusus picked it up and examined it.

"Isn't this one of the Franks' coins, or very like it? I thought they were only giving them out sparingly… to allies as tokens of friendship, to create the impression that they were worthy successors to the Romans."

Amalric chuckled.

"People run into hard times," he said, "and besides, I have contacts. I'm not the only one drumming up business, so to speak. There are more where this came from."

"Enough to fund a revolt?" Drusus glanced at Amalric, an image of his cousin's boy in his mind, an image of the bandit thirty years younger, and a whole gang of similar men. He had become resigned to the idea he would never be able to confront Silvanus directly, but perhaps, backed up by a gang of ferocious cut-throats, eager for plunder, he could.

"Enough to stir up trouble," said Amalric, "to build up young Deric's reputation, until the right opportunity comes along for a serious push."

"And where do I come in?" Drusus asked.

"You don't suppose I'm going to march over to Britannia, to some God-forsaken provincial hole, with a bag of silver coins in my fist, asking if anyone would be interested in starting a rebellion, do you, not at my age?"

"No, I did not think that."

"I – we, I should say – need a man with local knowledge, a man who can slip into the background without arousing suspicion," said Amalric. "Above all we need a man with the right motivation."

"I understand," replied Drusus, doubtfully. Thormond's words came back to him. The Goths had had to burn down Rome to get the Romans' attention. Is that what it would take? Would he have to burn down Silvanus' home to force him to cooperate?

"Are you satisfied with being a small-town lawyer?" asked Amalric.

"It helps pass the time," said Drusus.

"But you admit, it can be dangerous," said Amalric, gesturing to Drusus' leather jacket. "And just look what happened to Apollinarius."

"That was a pity. He was a good lawyer, though I had my differences with him on some personal matters."

"He had a cute daughter, I understand, though she has remained in Britannia," said Amalric, draining his goblet.

Drusus gave him a hard look.

"Apollinarius had it coming to him," the ex-bandit said, placing his goblet softly on the table. "He was an inquisitive bastard, and in the end he found out too much."

"Was it you?"

"I didn't say that, but you take my point. Lawyering can be a dangerous business for people who are smartarses, too nosy, who offend the wrong people."

Drusus thought for a moment of his client's rich neighbour. Supposing the man held a grudge? That could make life very uncomfortable.

"I have a case," he said, "a case I want to win. It's a matter of pride, and then… then I'll consider your offer."

"Very well," said Amalric. "Delicious," he observed, wiping round his platter with a piece of bread, "quite unlike the food in Britannia, I understand. They might need a little continental culture, don't you think?"

"I'll do what I can," said Drusus. "Just find me a whole bag of those silver coins and not just one."

Amalric stood, patted his companion on the shoulder and called over Comenius to settle the bill.

❦ Historical Note ❧

In 410 CE, the Roman Empire was in a mess. The rebellious general, Flavius Claudius Constantinus, unwillingly recognised as co-Emperor Constantine III, was harrying in Gaul. The Goths were marching through Italia, demanding unimaginable treasure, and when they did not receive it, occupying Rome. The extent to which the city was destroyed in the infamous "Sack of Rome" is debated by historians, but the event was seen as a turning point, signalling that the Empire no longer had the power and resources to defend its own capital. Even when Constantine III had been defeated and executed, and the Goths paid off with an offer of land and food, Britannia had been abandoned, barbarians swarmed the western lands, and the old system never fully returned.

The majority of this narration takes place in what is now France, and Ophelia and Drusus are travelling through a landscape and a political system scarred by these events. The history of France in late antiquity is significantly different from that of Britain, in that there was a great deal more continuity with the past, exemplified, not least, by the fact that the French speak a Romance language. Gaul had been one of the most important areas in the Roman Empire. For a while, the imperial court was even located in Trier (Treviri) in the north, now across the modern border in Germany, and some of the impressive buildings from that time can still be seen today. Southern France was a separate region with its capital at Arles (Arelate). Even if they were in something of a decline, the cities remained the chief seats of the Roman administration and of the church. This was also a time of transformation where the organisation of the Christian church become more formalised and the bishops began to take over some of the civic responsibilities hitherto wielded by the lay power.

There were times and places where anarchy predominated, where rival claimants to power clashed or where groups, the Vandals, Alans and Suebians, crossed the frontiers, but these outsiders were not just there to loot and pillage. Modern historians regard these groups, rather than ethnically homogenous "peoples", as a mix of opportunists, sometimes confronting, but often collaborating with the Romans. They knew the Empire, they traded with it, they took subsidies, and many of them had served in the Roman army or in frontier militias acting as a buffer between the Empire and the world beyond. Now, often pushed by intruders from further east, they wanted a share of the cake, not to destroy it. Indeed, in the year 414 CE, the Visigoths settled in the south of France and established their own kingdom, modelled in many ways on that of Rome. Even so, the leftovers of the invaders, disgruntled laid-off soldiers from the losing sides in the various civil wars, and, no doubt, run-of-the-mill criminals, took their opportunities to exploit the confusion, banding in groups known as the Bagaudes, who had a particularly strong presence in the Loire valley. A succession of military leaders, many of them drawn from the outsiders themselves, including Arbogast, Stilicho, Constantius and Aetius, struggled to restore order to Gaul and Italia, but the more success they had, the more they appeared as threats to the emperor and the men around him. The result was usually little thanks and an early death.

What we know about the past is shaped by the people who wrote history. Today it is well established among historians that every one of them has a point of view, typical of their times, that guides which facts and which events they select and the way in which they describe them. Until recently one interpretation dominated all others, that of the "dominant group", that is healthy, adult and usually high-status men. Such men may be shown doing "agricultural work, feasting, building, reading, ruling, fighting and carrying out judicial functions" (as discussed by Sally Crawford in her chapter in the *Oxford Handbook of Anglo-Saxon Archaeology*), while women are reduced to passive roles, and children are omitted altogether. This is despite the fact that women have been acknowledged to have had power and property rights in Anglo-Saxon society. The first book in this series, *Memories of a Fading Empire*, was written from this "dominant group" perspective – perhaps not surprising, since I am a man. The hero was a man, most of the other main characters were men, and they did manly things. The women played a relatively minor role. In this work, I decided to return to the start of the same story and take a different perspective. I am not sure how well I have succeeded, but I think it is important, even in 2021, for writers of fiction and non-fiction, especially those of us who are men, to remember that societies in the past did not only consist of kings and warriors, bishops and priests, simply because those men had a monopoly over the messaging in their times.

♥ Bibliography ♥

Here are the titles of a few books I have read while working on this manuscript which provide the basic history and different perspectives on the period.

Boin, Douglas (2020). *Alaric the Goth: An Outsider's History of the Fall of Rome*. Norton, New York. (I read this almost at the end of writing the present book, and I think this is a fun alternative view of history and captures the essence of the times in a readable manner.)

Bührer-Thierry, Genenviève and Mériaux, Charles (2014). *La France avant La France, 481–888*. Belin, Paris. (The first chapter, "La Gaule au Vᵉ siècle", was particularly useful and the city names used in this book were taken from the maps provided in this chapter.)

Crawford, Sally (2007). Overview: The Body and Life Course. In: *The Oxford Handbook of Anglo-Saxon Archaeology*, Hamerow, Hinton and Crawford, eds., Oxford, pp. 625–640.

Collins, Roger (2010). *Early Medieval Europe*, 3rd Edition. Palgrave Macmillan, London.

Oleson, John Peter (2008). *The Oxford Handbook of Engineering and Technology in the Classical World*. Oxford University Press, New York. (This is a very useful summary of a wide range of technologies used by the Greeks and Romans in chapters written by experts in their fields. It does not go into great detail, but rather explains what the capabilities were in the classical world, and the advances made by the Greeks and then Romans in each area.)

Roymans N, Heeren S, De Clerq W (2017). *Social Dynamics in the Northwest Frontiers of the Late Roman Empire: Beyond Decline or Transformation*. Amsterdam University Press, Amsterdam. (This is a book composed of a collection of papers and full of fascinating information which I have sampled from many of them.)

Wickham, Chris (2010) *The Inheritance of Rome: Illuminating the Dark Ages*. Penguin, London.

❧ Acknowledgements ☙

I would particularly like to thank my editor at The History Quill, Kahina Necaise. Her guidance and suggestions have been wonderful and whatever you might think of the present work, with her help, it is much improved over the original draft. I would also like to thank Cecily Blench for her excellent copy editing, and Naomi Munts for proofreading. Thank you, too, to the various people who have given positive feedback on my first volume, *Memories of a Fading Empire*, especially my mother, Leila, who was prompt to point out that book would have benefitted from a map… even more necessary in the present volume; to my children, Emily and Robert, who have mercifully kept their opinions on my writing to themselves, and to my wife, Marja. Lastly, I would like to thank my colleagues and the customers at Starbucks in Newtown Square, Pennsylvania, for the social support that has been so necessary during the COVID-19 pandemic.